CRAZY LITTLE THING CALLED LOVE

CHARLOTTE BUTTERFIELD

THORNDIKE PRESS

A part of Gale, a Cengage Company

SCC County Bookmobile Library
429 Hollywood Avenue
Carneys Point, NJ 08069
(856) 769-1082

 GALE
A Cengage Company

Farmington Hills, Mich • San Francisco • New York • Waterville, Maine
Meriden, Conn • Mason, Ohio • Chicago

Copyright © 2017 by Charlotte Butterfield.
Thorndike Press, a part of Gale, a Cengage Company.

ALL RIGHTS RESERVED
This novel is a work of fiction. The names, characters and incidents portrayed in it are the work of the author's imagination. Any resemblance to actual persons, living or dead, events or localities is entirely coincidental.
Charlotte Butterfield asserts the moral right to be identified as the author of this work.
Thorndike Press® Large Print Clean Reads.
The text of this Large Print edition is unabridged.
Other aspects of the book may vary from the original edition.
Set in 16 pt. Plantin.

LIBRARY OF CONGRESS CIP DATA ON FILE.
CATALOGUING IN PUBLICATION FOR THIS BOOK
IS AVAILABLE FROM THE LIBRARY OF CONGRESS

ISBN-13: 978-1-4328-5050-0 (hardcover)

Published in 2018 by arrangement with HarperCollins Publishers Limited

35097
5/18
$ 36.99

Printed in the United States of America
1 2 3 4 5 6 7 22 21 20 19 18

To Team P: Ed, Amélie, Rafe and Theo

PROLOGUE

Leila heard Jaipur before she saw it. The melodic whirs and clunks of the ceiling fan above her blended with loud shouts, incessant horns and revving engines from the market traders below.

This wasn't part of The Plan. Nothing about The Plan led to her waking up on Christmas Eve in a strange bedroom in Jaipur. This was actually as far away from The Plan as it was possible to be. She might also have lost the ability to open her eyes; she wasn't sure yet and wasn't ready to test it.

The irony was, yesterday had started so well. Or maybe it was the day before, she had no concept of days or time anymore. Using her air miles to upgrade herself at the check-in counter at Heathrow had been a spur of the moment inspired decision. She blamed the festive spirit that blanketed the airport's departures hall. Surrounded by rosy-cheeked loved ones jetting off on their magical Christmas mini breaks, who wouldn't have agreed to a little upgrade? After all, it wasn't every day you crossed the world to be reunited with your soul mate, so if you couldn't treat yourself then, when could you? Leila had never turned left at the plane's doors before. She had graciously accepted two, maybe five, glasses of champagne on the flight, enjoyed a three-course meal on a real plate with real cutlery and arrived in Mumbai ready for the surprise romantic reunion with her boyfriend Freddie, who was working there for three months.

Except he wasn't there.

Leila felt a bit sorry for the woman behind the reception desk at Freddie's Mumbai office who told her with undisguised pity that Freddie had moved to the Jaipur office a few weeks before. She could feel the receptionist taking in her carefully-put-together reunion outfit, noticing the plastic piece of mistletoe that Leila clutched in her hand thinking it would be such a romantic way to greet him, then looking down at her suitcase.

'Jaipur?' Leila had replied, with an enthusiasm that was fast evaporating into the smoggy city air. 'Wow, looks like I'm going to see more of your wonderful country then,' and after giving the woman a bright fake smile and a cheery wave, she had wheeled her suitcase out of the building and onto the bustling street. Her gusto faltered a smidgen more when she headed back to the airport only to be told that there were no flights to Jaipur, just a 15-hour train ride.

'It's an adventure, think of Freddie,' she'd chanted in her head, while giving over some hastily changed rupees in exchange for a bowl of biryani on the station platform.

Her stomach started making the rumbles of discontent about an hour into the journey, and after stepping over legs, bags, bodies and even more legs, bags and bodies, she found the toilet. In her previous life of just a day ago she wouldn't have even considered stepping into this cubicle, common sense and bowel control being two of her former major assets. Yet thanks to her delicate constitution, the urine-soaked box quickly became her spiritual home for the next three hours or so.

Somehow she'd finally found her way back to her seat, curled up into a ball and fallen asleep. She'd stumbled out of the station in Jaipur. Her eyes felt heavy, her stomach was in cramping knots and her appearance in complete juxtaposition with the business

9

class luggage label adorning her suitcase, which had now lost a wheel, because evidently fate had decreed that this day wasn't bad enough. A flashing neon hotel sign adjoining the station had beckoned her. She couldn't remember getting to the room, but had vague recollections of handing over her credit card to a bloke behind a desk.

And now she was here. On the 24th December. Lying underneath the world's noisiest ceiling fan. Hearing sounds of the city below that quite frankly terrified her. With no idea where in the heaving metropolis her boyfriend might be. Or why, thinking about it, he hadn't told her he'd moved. His last email, sent a week ago, was shorter than the others, granted, but could still be classed as very positive and upbeat. She remembered feeling a slight pang that he'd ended the email with *Cheers, Freddie,* rather than his previous sign offs that were variations of Yours, Hugs, Big Kiss, XOXO, which she was sure were edging ever closer to the L word.

They'd been dating for four months, which, ok, wasn't a huge amount of time for deep feelings to form, but when you knew, you knew. She'd met him at the horse races, which sounded a lot posher than it actually was. When she'd accepted her client's invitation to join them at Cheltenham for the day, she'd envisaged a box, a silver tray with unending rounds of canapés being passed around and fancy hats. In reality she was shoehorned into a minibus with fourteen men who started drinking even before the bus pulled out of Victoria coach station at 9am.

Freddie was sat directly behind her and kept pulling bits of her hair out of her bun somewhere around Oxford. She'd swung around in anger ready to launch into a spit-laden tirade only to see the most piercing blue eyes smile back at her. As much as she tried to act stern, her remonstration was laced with flirty overtones. 'Please don't do that, I don't like it,' she'd said.

'Please don't wear your hair like that then,' he'd fired back. 'You're far too cute to have a hairstyle like a granny.'

Cute. He'd said she was cute. She'd have preferred beautiful, stunning, even hot, but cute was ok. Cute was better than sweet. At five foot three, she'd even had a man pat her on the head before as he passed by in a pub, which admittedly ended in her throwing her wine over his retreating back. But when Freddie had called her cute, she didn't mind. In fact, as she swivelled around in her seat to face him, the rest of the journey was a lot more enjoyable. They'd spent the whole day together drinking, laughing, placing bets, shouting for the winners, and when his hand rested on her thigh on the journey home, she didn't move it. And when he escorted her home that night and she invited him in, and they sat on her sofa, she didn't move it either. And by then it was even higher up.

Two busy months of dating followed: pubs, parties, back to her flatshare, pubs, parties, back to hers, they'd settled into a sociable pattern that was rudely interrupted by his boss asking him to decamp to Mumbai, Jaipur, wherever the heck she was, for three months. It was a huge deal, this secondment. What a responsibility, of course she could excuse him a certain amount of brevity in his email correspondence, what type of girlfriend would she be if she didn't?

Her neck gave off an audible crack when she moved her head, and she knew she couldn't put off opening her eyes for much longer. As soon as she did, she looked up and shot out of bed faster than she'd ever moved before. The fan was attached to the ceiling by a threadbare wire that was making the four sharp blades sway in a large circle right above where her face had just been.

While she waited for her heart rate to return to normal, she ran her toothbrush under some bottled water and thought that at some point in the future, this was going to make great dinner party conversation. 'So how did you two know you were destined to be together?' one of their new friends, probably someone from the Montessori nursery their kids would inevitably go to, would ask, and Freddie would ruffle her hair and say, 'when this beautiful, crazy woman risked her life chasing me across India,' and they'd kiss over the marinated scallops presented in their shell and everyone would go 'ahhh'.

Yes, she thought decisively, this is a pivotal moment in our relationship, now I just need to find him.

The near-death experience with the fan meant checking out of the hotel was a necessity so she had no choice but to drag her suitcase behind her, over the pot-holed pavement, spilt food and animal excrement in between the hordes of people pouring into and out of the station next door. The noise of the traffic was deafening, and yet above it Leila heard the strains of Mariah Carey's *All I Want For Christmas Is You* belting out of a nearby shop and it gave her the steely determination to see her mission

13

through.

Leila looked down at the piece of paper that the receptionist in Mumbai had scribbled the address of the Jaipur office on. 'Excuse me', she said, touching the sleeve of a man standing chewing something by a faded orange rickshaw, 'Do you know this place?' She offered him the scrap of paper. He stared at her. Then looked down at the writing, his head moved, and he motioned for her to get in the cab and swung her suitcase into the tuk tuk after her with practised ease.

He perched on the saddle in front of her and started peddling into the oncoming traffic. 'Jesus! Oh my God! Careful, what the —' Leila's expletives were drowned out by the chorus of angry horns surrounding them. They slowed to let a couple of goats weave between the traffic prodded by a child with a big stick and no shoes. The rickshaw finally stopped outside a large, modern building and the man pointed. She gave him a fistful of rupees, the denominations of which she hadn't got the hang of yet. He started dancing on the spot, making her realise that she might have just given him enough to feed his family for a year.

After a brief exchange with yet another commiserative receptionist, Leila found herself back on the street clutching yet another piece of paper with yet another hastily scribbled address on it. Apparently Freddie had called in sick today.

Of course he had.

Because nothing on this god-awful trip could be that easy. Of course he couldn't have been at his desk and come down to see her in that fancy lobby and twirled her around so her feet left the floor.

Her long black hair was stuck to the back of her neck, but she didn't want to put it up as Freddie loved it down. The humidity had also made her make-up quite literally slide off her face in the last three hours, but none of that mattered, she was ten minutes away from seeing her future husband.

Room 114 was at the end of the corridor. There was a Do Not Disturb sign on the door, but Leila knew Freddie wouldn't mind being woken up by her, even if he was sick. Her heart pounded. This was the moment. This is when he would realise how serious she was, and that he loved her. Her fingers brushed the mistletoe in her pocket as she knocked on the door a couple of times, then heard his voice angrily shout, 'It says do not disturb!'

'Freddie, it's me!'

She could hear commotion inside the

room, a table perhaps being knocked over — probably in his hurry to get to the door — voices suddenly coming to an abrupt hush — the TV no doubt being muted. Then the door opened a fraction and Freddie peered around it, wearing a dressing gown.

'Layles!' She hated him calling her that, always had done, but never found the right time to tell him. Now wasn't the time either.

'Freddie!' She paused, waiting for the door to open more, or for him to invite her in, or for him to come out, or anything other than the two of them looking at each other through a two-inch gap. 'I'm in India!' She added completely unnecessarily.

'So you are! Wow! Um, how did you find me here Layles?' Still the door remained barely ajar.

She sighed and gave a self-deprecating laugh, 'I'll save that story for later, it's a cracker. Now open the door, let me come in!'

Freddie looked very quickly over his shoulder and shifted a little, 'Um, you know what, now's not really a good time . . .'

'Your office told me you were sick, don't worry, I won't pounce on you, I promise, I'll just keep you company until you feel better. It's Christmas tomorrow, maybe you could then call the office and take a couple more days off and we can make up for lost time, I've missed you so —' Her words tailed off as she saw a movement in the slither of room she could see behind him. 'Is there someone in the room?' she asked, pushing the door tentatively against his weight behind it.

'No, of course not! Why don't you wait downstairs and I'll just get dressed and come down?'

Then a cough came from behind him. A woman's cough. Leila pushed open the door with a force she hadn't known she possessed and saw a topless blonde sat on the bed pointing the remote at the TV. Leila's suitcase came crashing to the floor as her hand let go of the handle to fly to her mouth.

'Layles, I can explain.'

'I really don't think you can Freddie.'

'But I —'

Leila put her hand up to stop him talking. 'You know what Freddie?' She took a deep breath. 'I may be naïve and gullible and a romantic, and yes, an eternal optimist, but even I, in my sleep-deprived, stomach-cramping, starving state, fail to see how you can charm your way out of this one. Now excuse me, I have a train and then a plane

17

to catch.'

She shouted over his shoulder to the woman, who had thankfully covered up her bare breasts with a cushion, 'Good luck love, you're going to need it.' And she picked up the wobbling suitcase and strode off down the corridor.

'Layles, wait!' Freddie shouted from the doorway.

Leila kept walking, her head held high and shouted back without turning around, 'Bye Freddie. And for the record. I fucking hate the name Layles.'

CHAPTER 1

A month later . . .

Expensive does not necessarily mean best. Leila knew that. She was a landscape gardener, and would pick an everyday peony over a rare orchid any day and twice on Sundays, but when it came to chopping off over a foot and a half of her hair, opting for a hairdresser with an eye-watering price list seemed sensible.

The scissors hovered menacingly over her head. 'You're absolutely sure?'

'Absolutely.' Leila nodded. 'Never been surer.' A pause. 'No! Wait! Yes, I'm sure. Go ahead. No, stop!'

'Too late.' The stylist held up a long black ponytail. 'Oops.'

Between the shaping and feathering and smoothing, Leila was placated to hear the stylist make encouraging sighs and clucks. When she'd finally finished the dramatic elfin cut, and spun her round to face the mirror, Leila took a sharp intake of breath. This small act of defiance had instantly elevated her from sweet to striking in less than an hour.

'Why in God's name haven't I done this sooner?' Leila said out loud, more to herself than the stylist who had gathered a few of her colleagues over to witness the transformation. She couldn't stop touching her neck, and her ears felt weird, sort of breezy. But she couldn't get over how big her eyes were, and her cheekbones, which had previously been hidden under two curtains drawn either side of her face were sharp and sexy.

'Whoever he is you're doing this for, is a very lucky man,' said a voice under a head full of foils next to her.

'Oh no, there's no man. Or woman.' Leila quickly added after an attractive girl with a nose piercing placed her hand on the back of her chair. 'Just fancied a long overdue change.'

Being an empowered woman of the world, she ought to have been affronted at the wolf whistles that followed her down her street from the house on the corner that was having its attic converted. She did at least roll her eyes at a couple of women she passed as if to say, 'I know, neanderthals, right?' while allowing herself a little smile as she let herself in her front door. But then pretty much every time she stuck her key into the lock and pushed open the newly painted sage green door her mood was instantly lifted. She'd only moved in two months previously, and it was the first time she'd lived alone. And, thankfully, as she'd been given the key while Freddie was away, he had never set foot in it so it was completely free from toxic memories of any of her exes.

The flat was tiny, even by London standards, but at least it was all hers. It was in the basement of a tall Victorian townhouse. There was a steady stream of boots and shoes passing her living room window, which she oddly loved. She'd often choose feet-watching over TV at weekends, making up stories about the wearers of the footwear that ambled past, often in twos, or groups. You could always spot a first date by the nervous tottering and inappropriate height of heel. She loved the couples who walked in step with each other, placing right after left in perfect harmony.

When the estate agent showed her round, strategically placing himself over the largest of the damp patches in the hallway, he was understandably twitchy. It had been on their books for a while, and the vendor was getting desperate. He needn't have worried. Leila looked right past the discoloured walls, and due to her height, the low sloping ceiling in the galley kitchen didn't even make her duck. As soon as she'd glimpsed the private garden leading off the bedroom she was sold. It was a walled courtyard more than a garden, but in Leila's mind it already had trellises of trailing wisteria and honeysuckle. She imagined vibrant earthenware pots adorning every ledge and a small raised bed with a herb garden. And now, two months after she moved in, it had exactly that. The patches of damp had been gotten rid of too, and whitewashed walls made the formerly neglected cellar bright and welcoming. There was just about room for a double bed in the bedroom, but little else, so she'd designed a double bed on six foot stilts and one of the craftsmen at work had made it for her. So she ascended a ladder to bed every night, freeing up the whole of the floor space underneath for her desk that was placed in the middle of the room looking out onto the garden.

Her shopping bags made a loud clunk as Leila dumped them onto the kitchen work surface reminding her almost too late of the two bottles of wine that were in them. She then set about making the salad and marinating the chicken that she was going to serve her sister Tasha for lunch when she arrived.

It was the first time Tasha had seen the flat, despite only living two stops down the tube line. But when one of you owns a basement shoebox in Bayswater and the other a five-bedroom, three-storey townhouse on High Street Kensington, of course you'd choose to dine at the latter. But Leila wouldn't take no for an answer this time. Apart from the disastrous two years she'd lived with her ex-boyfriend Luke, whose table habits were so vile she never invited anyone round, she'd always shared her kitchen with an endless stream of flatmates, who commandeered every available pan or plate come meal time. This was, and it made her feel ashamed to admit it, the first time she'd cooked for her sister in thirty-two years.

The knocker sounded. That was another purchase that made Leila feel very grown up. One of the first things she'd done after moving in was take a screwdriver to the shrill doorbell and ceremoniously bin it, replacing it with a smart brass knocker like the one the Banks family had in Mary Poppins.

'Welcome, welcome to my humble abode,'

Leila wrapped her sister in a big hug and stood to one side to give Tasha enough room to squeeze through the door.

'Ooooo, I am loving the hair! Amazing! You're actually really pretty! And this is so quaint! And the neighbourhood isn't as rough as I thought it would be.'

'I'm sure there's a compliment in there somewhere Tash!'

Her sister laughed, 'Sorry, that came out completely wrong, let me rephrase. I just mean, wow, you look incredible, it's really nice around here, and from what I'm seeing of your flat while standing on the doormat, it looks really lovely.'

'I would say that it's bigger than it looks, but after the tour which will take all of, oh, seven seconds, you'll know that's not true.' Leila ushered her older sister into the living room, which was lined with books and pictures. Big vibrant canvases jostled for position next to black and white photographs, and vintage movie posters.

'It's very you.'

'Meaning?'

'Meaning, your personality shines through everywhere you look. I love it.' And Tasha meant it. She hadn't had much of an input at all into the decoration of her own home. As a well-meaning surprise, her husband

Alex had thrown an obscene amount of money at one of London's most well-connected interior designers who had transformed the once tired townhouse into a glittering show home. The end result was stunning, just if not exactly to her taste; but there was no way she could have acted anything other than over-awed and incredibly grateful at the big reveal, such were Alex's good intentions.

Tasha ran a finger along the spines of Leila's books — even having books on display would be wonderful, but Patricia-the-designer said they would look untidy and mess up her scheme. *Her* scheme. So, what books they had were hidden behind the 'concealed storage' doors. Apart from the massively heavy hardback book on Chanel that was gathering dust on the big glass coffee table. Glass. In a house with three kids in it. That was a clever purchase Patricia.

'Honestly Leila, this is perfect for you, it's just beautiful.' Tasha said as they stepped out into the garden. Leila had flicked the outdoor gas heater into life and despite it being early February, it was a beautifully crisp day. Tasha didn't need too much persuading to celebrate it being a Saturday without her kids by indulging in a glass or two of the champagne she'd brought with her. She reached over and touched her sister's wine glass with hers. 'I'm buying you champagne flutes as a housewarming present by the way.'

'But I don't drink champagne normally.'

'Well then, at least you'll have them ready for the next time I come over,' Tasha smiled. The sisters were sat at the little round white wrought iron table in the garden. What was left of the afternoon's sunlight was dappling the flagstones with specks of light. 'You seem very together, considering.'

'Considering, what?' asked Leila.

'Freddie. I know you liked him.'

'Not anymore.'

'Well no, obviously, but it's ok to be honest with yourself and grieve for a future you're not going to have.'

'Wow, a future I'm not going to have! Alright, Ms Doom and Gloom, I'm not terminally ill!'

'I know! I just mean, I know you, and in your head you'd have arrived in India thinking that he was going to twirl you around until your feet left the floor' — at this, Leila looked a little sheepish — 'before he booked the rest of the week off work and whisked you to the Taj Mahal where you'd get photographed on the same bench where

Princess Diana sat, and then he'd take you to a Maharaja's palace where he'd booked a candlelit meal on a roof terrace festooned with fairy lights, which is where he'd propose. Am I close?'

Leila stuck her nose in the air. 'Not remotely.'

'I had it spot on, didn't I?'

There was no point pretending otherwise to her sister, she could always see straight through her.

'But he wasn't right for you Leila,' Tasha continued earnestly. 'You do this, you hop from boyfriend to boyfriend, pinning unrealistic expectations onto each of them. Writing the script in your head of what you want them to say and how you want them to act, and if you keep doing that you'll always end up being disappointed.'

'Ok, oh wise one. How have you stayed married to Alex all these years then? What's the secret to finding and keeping the right one?' That stopped Tasha in her tracks. Running through Tasha's mind was the old predicament, to tell the truth or the heavily edited soft-focus version she usually wheeled out. The trouble was, Leila was the only one in the family who knew exactly how she and Alex got together seventeen years ago, and had kept the secret too, so fobbing her off with platitudes almost never worked. If their parents ever found out that their daughter had been Alex's mistress for a couple of years and was the reason for the breakdown of his marriage they'd be horrified. They didn't even know their son-in-law had been married before, let alone that he'd got Tasha pregnant which is why he had to divorce his first wife to marry her. But, that was fifteen years ago, so absolutely no point raking it all up now.

'Top me up before I answer that,' Tasha held out her empty glass, 'and can I just say how impressed I am that you have an ice bucket.'

'Thank you. Now stop changing the subject. You and Alex, what's your secret?'

Tasha sighed. 'Oh God Leila, I don't know. We don't expect too much from each other I guess.'

'That's romantic.'

Tasha laughed. 'I mean, we don't conjure up ideals that we know the other one can't live up to. We just get on with it, and have a lovely life, and don't think too much about the stuff we can't change.'

'Like what?'

But that was it. The shutters had come down and Tasha shook her head, 'Look at me, getting all deep and serious. But you

28

need to move on from Freddie Leila, you've been hibernating here since you got back from India and it's not right or healthy.'

'I have not been hibernating! You don't see me sat here in tracksuit bottoms and unwashed hair sipping super-strength cider through a straw do you?'

'Well, no, but you missed the last family Sunday roast, and that's unheard of.'

The once-a-month family roast dinner was sacrosanct. It had had a strict compulsory attendance order slapped on it for as long as Leila could remember. Making the trek from her university in Bristol down to Dartmouth every month for a slap-up free feed was a welcome respite from her usual daily diet of Super Noodles and breakfast cereals, but now she lived in London, the journey, and the time away from her friends, and boyfriend, when she had one, was a bit annoying sometimes. Not that she needed to worry about having a boyfriend now. Or ever again.

She knew that it was a cop-out, but heading down to her parents' hotel in Devon to be guest of honour at a pity-party just a couple of weeks after the Jaipur fiasco was not something Leila wanted to put herself through. Her mother Judy would no doubt have had her head on the side for her entire visit, while repeating the words 'plenty of fish' and her dad would simultaneously give her a smile and a wide berth should her emotions suddenly get the better of her. Her brother Marcus would have found it impossible not to make lots of barbed references to her disastrous love life, and while she normally would have batted these back quickly and effortlessly, this latest dating catastrophe had affected her more than any of the others. Not that she was able to say that out loud yet.

'So are you here as Mum's spy to report back on the state of my sanity then?' Leila asked.

'No! Not at all! Not really. No. Well, maybe a bit. But mainly I wanted to see my little sister and offer my shoulder, should you need it. It's ok to show your emotions you know Leila, you don't need to pretend everything's alright, when it's not.'

Later that afternoon, when the sun had disappeared for the day, two empty champagne bottles were upended in the ice bucket and Tasha had reluctantly left, Leila thought about what her sister had said. She was known amongst her friends as the Bounce Back Queen, never letting anything get her down, being ridiculously cheerful in the face of adversity, but she absolutely never wanted to feel as stupid as she did leaving that hotel in Jaipur again. It was midafternoon on Christmas Day in England when she had skyped her parents from India. Her mum, dad, sister, brother, nephew and nieces all squashed their faces onto the small screen, colourful cracker hats adorning each one of them. She should have been there. She should have been working her way through her dad's wine cellar with them, playing silly board games and listening to Radio Devon's festive party mix. But instead she spent the day alone, huddled on a grimy corner of the airport praying for a standby ticket to get her home.

She had stayed awake for every minute of the thirty-hour journey from Freddie's hotel room in India to her own bed in London, where she slept for almost two days straight. She didn't cry. She didn't even drink herself into oblivion with the free booze on board the flight. She just felt numb. And foolish. And she knew that she didn't want a man to make her feel like that ever again.

CHAPTER 2

A few weeks later . . .

'I reckon his photo was easily taken twenty years ago.'

'No!' Jayne cried. 'Who would do that?'

'What did he think?' Amanda asked, blowing the froth off her cappuccino. 'That you wouldn't notice that he looked nothing like his advert?'

'Profile,' Shelley sniffed, looking affronted. 'It's not an advert, I'm not advertising for dates, like you would a car, it's a profile. Anyway, thankfully he didn't see me as I'd chosen a table behind a pillar — thanks to Leila's suggestion — so I was able to leg it before having to spend an evening with him.'

Although this time it was her friend Shelley recounting this story of dating woe, it was a carbon copy of numerous blind date disasters Leila had suffered in her time. Brad Pitt morphing into Danny DeVito, Single Solvent Lawyer mutating into Married Bankrupt Loser.

'Do you remember me telling you about that guy who, when the bill came, put down a coupon he'd cut out of the paper for his half of the meal?' Leila added, to the shrieks of hilarity from her best friends. 'And he didn't even know why I didn't want to see him again!'

Shelley picked up the baton, 'What about those twins we met at that dating in the dark night, Leila, who said they were thirty-something bankers who lived in Canary Wharf and then at the end of the night we saw their mum picking them up?'

'Are you sure you two don't make some of these stories up to make me and Amanda a little bit envious of your exciting single lives?' Jayne asked smiling. 'I mean it puts my normal night of watching box sets in my pyjamas with Will a little in the shade.'

'And me and Paul. The most excited we've been in months is when a new series of 24 was announced.'

'Exciting single lives?' Leila yelped. 'Have you not been listening? Nothing about being a thirty-something, single woman in London is remotely exciting. Soul-destroying yes, exciting, no.'

'Oh I don't know, it has its moments.' As Shelley was a statuesque redhead with measurements Marilyn would weep for, her experiences tended to sometimes be a tad different to Leila's.

'Honestly, you two don't know how good you have it,' Leila said, pointing the end of her croissant at Jayne and Amanda. What she wouldn't give to spend evenings in her pyjamas with the love of her life rather than trundling down to a personality-less wine bar to speed date, or spending hours swiping left and right on Tinder. Trying to locate her future husband was more or less a full-time job, and she was sick of it.

'You know what?' Leila said, slamming her croissant down on the table. 'I'm done. Finito. Caput. No more, I'm taking some time out from dating.'

'You always say that. Every time you have a bad date, or your boyfriend turns out to be a dick, you say that that's the last time,' Amanda said. 'You're still in shock about careering halfway across the world for Freddie, you'll be fine in a few weeks.'

To be fair, her friends had tried to warn her not to follow Freddie to India. 'Men don't like to be surprised,' Amanda had said, ignorant of the irony in her statement seeing as she had proposed to Paul, and not the other way round. And Jayne didn't understand either, with her perfect marriage to Will, Richmond's very own Mr Darcy. It was only a matter of time before Shelley joined their cosy married club and Leila would have to fly the spinster flag alone.

As Leila walked the few streets back to her flat after their breakfast her phone vibrated in her bag.

Layles, flying back to London in a couple of weeks, let's hook up and I can explain. Miss you XOXO

Her stomach lurched and she didn't know whether to hurl the phone into the nearest wall or hug it close to her body in relief. In the first few weeks after coming back from India she'd replayed the hotel room scene over and over in her mind constantly, even sometimes concluding that maybe, just maybe, she might have been too quick to flounce off in a huff. Perhaps the girl wasn't completely naked, she could have been wearing one of those nude catsuits, so she was actually fully dressed, and possibly she worked at the hotel and had just delivered his room service and then was trying to fix his TV for him, which is why she was sat on his bed with the remote. Put like that, she occasionally felt a bit sorry for the short shrift she'd given him. She had even gone as far as to punch out a text to him that remained unsent, wondering if maybe she did owe him the opportunity to explain. But for him to suddenly get in touch now, a couple of weeks before his arrival in London, with his fancy bit thousands of miles away, just made her mad and not in the slightest bit sentimental.

No thanks. She pressed Send.

Don't be like that babe, doesn't suit you. See you in a couple of weeks XOXO

Her fingers hovered over the keypad. If she was angry before, it was nothing compared to the white-hot rage that coursed through her veins now. How dare he? What planet was he on that he thought it was ok to treat her like that, then have complete radio silence for two months and then resurface like nothing had happened? She wouldn't rise to it and send him a message back. Shaking, Leila slammed her front door behind her and threw her coat and keys down on the floor in the hallway. She was worth so much more than him. More than this ridiculous, fruitless man-search that made a little bit of her die inside with every unhappy ending. She'd had enough.

'Celibacy?' Thomas heaped two more roast potatoes onto her outstretched plate. 'As in, become a nun?'

Leila rolled her eyes, 'No, Dad, as in a man ban. I have taken a vow of chastity to sort my life out.' She ignored her older brother Marcus's immature guffawing next to her and passed the gravy boat on to her mum, Judy, who was sat on the other side, remaining uncharacteristically silent.

'Well I think it's a great idea. You've been like a beacon for complete prats for the last two decades, and it's time you concentrated on understanding your own energy field and what you're putting out to the universe.' Ever since her sister Tasha had decided to study Mindfulness and Visualisation to fill the void left by her youngest child reaching school age, she'd been peppering all her sentences with words like 'emotional intelligence' and 'cognitive defusion'.

'Thanks Tash. I feel very positive about it actually, it's going well.'

'So, when did you start this *man-ban*?' Judy finally ventured, rolling the last two words around her mouth as though they were part of a foreign language.

'Last Tuesday.' Leila replied.

They all erupted in the type of laughter that makes furniture shake. Even Tasha's three children joined in, the younger two, being only four and seven, had no idea what the hell they were howling about, but that didn't stop them. Marcus's annoying new girlfriend Lucy was chuckling away with the rest of them too, her perfect flicky-out hair bobbing along in time with her giggles.

'I'm glad that I amuse you all so much.' Leila huffed. 'Next time one of you makes an important life choice remind me to be equally as supportive.'

'Sorry darling,' Judy rested her hand on her daughter's arm. 'We are supportive, it's just that you haven't got a great track record with seeing things through.'

Leila put her hand on her chest in mock disgust. 'I am offended by that, Mother.'

'Violin. Ice skating. Veganism. Boot camp. Spanish. Watercolour painting. Salsa. Am I missing anything Thomas?' Judy had seven fingers outstretched in front of her as she counted off all the pursuits Leila had let trail off after getting bored.

'Ryan. Carlos. Simon. Steve. Robbie. Luke. Oliver. Liam. Freddie.' Marcus added. He always took sides with Judy. Such a mummy's boy. 'And those are the only ones you introduced us to. There must be more that never got to the meet-the-family stage.'

'That's not the same! At all! I have been very unlucky in love, and I haven't found the right hobby yet. Two completely different things.'

'You are a bit fickle sweetheart,' Thomas topped up her wine glass.

'Adding the word "sweetheart" at the end of that damning insult does not lessen it Dad. And I am not fickle. I am merely seeking perfection in everything I do.'

'And everyone,' Alex, Tasha's husband chimed in.

'Alex!' Tasha and Judy exclaimed at the same time.

'Let's not lower the tone, Alex, it is Sunday after all.' Leila thought Tasha's remonstration based on it being the Sabbath was a tad hypocritical — the last time her sister had attended church was her own wedding fifteen years ago.

'Right, let's change the subject. Yummy roast Mum, new chef?' It was a running joke in the family that because Leila's mum and dad ran a hotel, they got all their meals cooked for them, whereas in fact, apart from the occasional Ploughman's that Thomas would surreptitiously steal from the kitchen downstairs, Judy made all their meals.

It wasn't a spur of the moment decision, becoming celibate, despite what her family thought. Leila had always been interested in reading about women embarking on periods of self-discovery and contemplation, but had always measured her own sense of self-worth by leaping from one relationship straight into another rather than taking some time out. Admittedly, when she'd called for silence by pinging her mobile against her wine glass and giving her impassioned declaration to Jayne, Amanda and Shelley last Tuesday, she was fuelled by a few gin and tonics, but that was coincidental.

They too had followed a stunned silence with stomach-grabbing laughter. Then they'd laid bets on the table about how long she'd last. It was perhaps testament to her track record of inconsistency that there was currently £4000 in the pot. 'This is a bet I have to take!' her former flatmate Amanda had squealed. 'So if by some miracle and personality transplant, you pull it off, we give you a grand each, and if you don't then you have to pay each of us a grand.'

'Which basically means you'll have to sell a kidney,' Jayne warned. 'Don't take the bet Leila, you're just reeling because of what twatty Freddie did, in a couple of weeks, you'll think differently.'

'I will not,' Leila replied haughtily. 'My mind is set, and ladies, I take your bets. Start saving your pennies.' Leila had told them what she found herself trying to articulate to her family now. This man-ban was not a whim. And although she usually thought most of what her sister spouted about 'sending messages to the universe' was a bit far-fetched, Leila completely recognised that something needed to change, and this seemed a good place to start.

As much as Leila would like to think that it was her cooking and fantastic hosting skills that prompted Tasha to pop around unannounced later that week after work, she knew that her sister had an ulterior motive, which she wasted no time in spelling out.

'Now look, I want to talk to you about this celibacy thing.'

Leila leant her head back on the sofa and moaned. 'Oh no, not you as well, I've already had Mum's take on how ridiculous I'm being, I don't need you joining in the chorus too.'

'Far from it! I'm completely supportive of you, I actually think you should step it up a gear.'

'In what way?'

'Well if you're serious about remaining single, and are genuinely doing it for reasons of empowerment and regaining control of your life, and getting to know yourself better, and all the other reasons you got on your soapbox about at the last Sunday lunch, then take it more seriously. Do something that's going to change your life, rather than sitting at home being celibate listening to sad songs and lamenting your crap choice in boyfriends.'

'I am not listening to sad songs! I have a very upbeat music collection.'

'But put an end date on it, so that you have a period of time for self-discovery. You and I both know that you're not intending to be single forever, but why not do it for six months, or a year even. Twelve months of finding yourself. Make it formal. Write a blog about it, start a group. Make this year count.'

'You know what? I really like that idea. A year of me. Starting tomorrow. April 1st. April Fool's day. How ironic.'

'Maybe there's a group nearby you can join?'

'I'll have a look this week.'

'Have a look now.'

'I'll have a look later.'

'Now.'

Leila threw a cushion at her sister's head. 'If we're going to do this, can we do it in the garden? That's my happy place.'

'It's still March. Do we have to?'

'It's the last day of March, which is Spring time, and if you're making me do this, then yes, we do.'

Leila pulled on a sweater, lit a couple of candles in lanterns that were dotted around the courtyard and sat down next to her sister. She opened the computer and started typing. *Celibacy London. Chastity. Sisterhood. Female solidarity.* The sisters navigated their way through a bottle of red wine and sites selling promise rings written by the Christian far right and web pages for spurned women vehemently (and often violently) advocating a life of no-sex after vicious break ups. But they couldn't find a site, or group, or club for women like Leila who wanted the happy ever after, but just wanted to dedicate a chapter of the fairy tale to themselves first.

'So what now?' Leila asked.

'You make your own.'

'Just like that?'

'Just like that. It's very easy. I made a blog recently for my Mindfulness group. It's amazing how like-minded people find you if you put yourself out there.'

Leila drained her glass, and rested her chin on her hand. 'But I don't know that I want to be a beacon for every single woman out there.'

'It's not about everyone else, it's about your own journey and documenting it, and learning from it, and sharing it with other women who are in the same position. Do it. I think it would be really good for you.'

'You're so bossy.'

'I know. Now do it.'

Hello. My name is Leila, I am 32 years old and this is my first blog post.

'You shouldn't really give out personal information like your name and your age. And it's obvious that it's your first blog post as it's the first post on the blog.'

Leila slammed the laptop shut and glared at her sister. 'See? I knew I'd be rubbish at this.'

Tasha leaned across and prised open the screen again. 'As you were.'

'I used to think that it was you that was the saint, but now I realise it's Alex.'

'Leila,' Tasha said gently, 'Carry on.'

Leila gingerly started typing. Somewhere around the fourth line Tasha started stroking her sister's hair and by the time the last full stop was added, both sisters had tears pricking their eyes.

In the last fifteen years I've dated two cheaters, one closet homosexual, a man that spat out watermelon pips across a restaurant, another that referred to his man parts as Peter Pecker. One that cried like a baby during love-making, another that had four tattoos of different women's names on his arm (he wasn't related to any of them), one that tried it on with my friends, one that tried it on with my sister, and one that used to follow me home from work 'to keep me safe'. There was one that broke my toe (very bad dancer), another that broke my nose (very bad temper), and two that broke my heart. There was one that proposed to me every day for 87 days then married someone else two weeks after my final no, one that wanted me to wee on him, and in the process of chasing the last one across India I contracted amoebic dysentery and lost my luggage. I think it's fair to say me and dating aren't natural companions. Which is why I'm opting out for a year. Celibate. Chaste. Call it what you will, I'm staying single for 365 days to give my sanity a rest. I don't know what this year of self-discovery is going to be like, but I know one thing — it's going to be a whole lot more fulfilling and fun than being with, and getting over, all the men listed above. The journey begins here . . .

CHAPTER 3

'Jesus Layles, what have you done with your hair?'

It was almost seven thirty at night, the shutters were down on the shops flanking her smart Notting Hill office and the after-work crowd that normally hung about at the pub opposite had already dispersed. If it hadn't persistently drizzled all day perhaps the faded benches outside the pub would still have a few stragglers on them. Leila had stayed late to help a colleague on a community project they were working on, and the last thing she wanted was the now-cold latte that was being offered by Freddie's outstretched hand.

'Where have you been? Thought you clocked off at six, been waiting here ages for you.'

Leila sighed, 'Why are you here Freddie?' It surprised her that the only emotion to course through her was irritation.

'I came back.'

'Evidently. But why?' Leila shook her head again as Freddie motioned for her to take the paper cup, which he then balanced on a bus stop bench.

'You can't just leave it there, find a bin.'

'It's a gift for the next person to wait for a bus.'

'It's cold coffee Freddie, find a bin.' Leila stopped walking. 'Don't be a prat.'

'Is this about what happened in Jaipur?'

'It's about you littering up the streets of London for no reason other than not being bothered to find a bin.'

'You're still angry with me.'

Leila reflected on this for a moment, 'You know what, Freddie, I'm really not. I'm just grateful for finding out when I did that you are a monumental waste of my time and energy. Now, if you don't mind I've had a really long day and I want to go home. Pick up the cup, put it in the bin and go away.'

'I only came back from India to explain. You owe me that at least.'

If Leila had been a violent sort of person she would have slapped him at that moment. She did toy with the idea of rescuing the cold coffee from the bus stop purely to fling it in his gormless grinning face, but she resisted. 'Freddie. There is nothing to explain. You screwed up. I've moved on. Good night.' She stuck out her hand and hailed a passing cab. She slammed the car door leaving Freddie standing open-mouthed in the street. It was a dramatic statement more than anything else — she wasn't even sure she had any cash on her to pay for the cab. A quick rummage through her purse discovered that nope, she didn't. 'Um, sorry mate, can you just drop me here?' The cab had just rounded the corner, less than 50 metres from where she'd got in. In the driver's eyes, she must seem either deranged or extremely lazy. She looked in the rear view mirror and gave the cabbie a winning smile. 'And will you accept a three quid Pret a Manger voucher for the fare?'

My ex surprised me outside work today with a cold coffee and a bucketful of hard-done-by-ness. The old me may have relented a little. May have agreed to go for a drink. At the very least the old me may have listened to his attempts to explain why he felt the need to entertain a naked buxom blonde in my absence. But the new me didn't. The new me felt no stirring of emotion at all, no flicker of remorse or wistfulness. The new me is currently toasting myself with a well-deserved glass of cheap wine. Go new me.

There was never normally enough room in Alex's car for Leila to get a lift with them down to Dartmouth for the monthly family roast. Despite it being a Range Rover, once you'd piled in two adults, three kids — two of them in bulky car seats — and bags full of the necessary detritus to keep three kids amused for a long car journey and a weekend with the grandparents, the car was full. Which Leila thanked the Lord for every time she stretched out on the train, ordered a cheese croissant and cappuccino from the buffet car and read half a book. But fifteen-year old Mia had special dispensation to stay at a friend's this weekend, leaving a ten-inch gap between the two car seats that, according to her sister, had Leila's name on it.

'Remind me how Mia managed to get out of this, when I've been trying for the last fifteen years?' Alex said, at the same time as craning his neck around trying to go across three lanes of traffic to his exit.

'It's Imogen's birthday.' Tasha replied, flicking through the Saturday supplements that were weighing on her knees. 'And if we didn't let Mia go to the sleepover she was going to die. And I didn't want that on my conscience.'

'Aunty LaLa?'

'Yes Oscar?' Leila turned her head to answer her little nephew, who was staring back at her keenly.

'Play I-Spy wiv me pease.'

Leila loved her sister's kids, she did. But they were less than eight minutes into a four-hour car journey. On a Saturday morning when all her friends were having lie-ins with their husbands or drinking coffee out of impossibly small cups at a pavement cafe, she was feeding a constant stream of cheesy wotsits to two little monkeys. One of whom had a trickle of green slime oozing from his left nostril.

Just as the M25 turned into the M4 Leila put a Peppa Pig DVD in the player on the back of the passenger seat which seemed to distract Oscar from a never-ending round of I-Spy. 'Is Lucy coming as well?' Leila asked her sister. She obviously didn't do a good enough job at cloaking the disdain in her question because Tasha span around and asked her why.

'No reason, I just find her a bit, um, cold,' Leila shrugged.

'She's perfect for Marcus.'

'He's not cold!'

51

'No, but he is a bit nice but dim. She's the perfect trophy girlfriend, isn't she? With her perfect nails and perfect blow-dried hair.'

'She's wonderful. What's not to like?' Alex interrupted. 'Ow!' he said, rubbing his arm where Tasha had punched him. 'There's no need for that, I just mean, she's a bit of a looker, isn't she? Way above Marcus's league.'

'I'm not even going to respond to that. Ignore me, I shouldn't have mentioned anything,' shrugged Leila.

'I thought you were all about female solidarity and sisters doing it for themselves these days Leila?' Alex looked in the rear view mirror at his sister-in-law.

He was annoyingly right. 'I am, you're completely correct. I shouldn't speak ill of one of my own. Consider myself castigated.'

'Speaking of your man-ban —'

'We weren't.'

Alex ignored her and carried on, 'Speaking of your man-ban, I think I've found the perfect bloke for you. Name's Andy, new guy in the office, a real laugh, rugby player, single, loves a good time, likes his booze, he's not looking for anything serious, just a bit of fun —'

He wasn't the first to assume that her

celibacy vow was down to not meeting the right man, that she was just treading water until the next bloke came along. Shelley wasn't getting it either, and still expected Leila to accompany her to those horrific blind date nights where desperate men made rubbish jokes and you were expected to laugh. She'd got really shirty with her last week when Leila had turned down yet another offer of warm wine and stilted speed-dating chat in a Mexican restaurant.

'Andy sounds charming.' Leila replied from the back seat. 'But the whole point of a man-ban is to ban men, not sleep with them.'

'Who mentioned anything about sleeping with them? But you're only doing this because you're lonely, and I'm just pointing out someone to stop you being lonely, that's all.'

'Is that what you think? That I'm just try-ing to fill my time before the next man comes into my life? Oh my God Alex, you're so annoying.' After fifteen years of having Alex as her brother-in-law, Leila felt justi-fied in speaking to him the same way she would her own brother. 'That just shows your complete lack of depth and under-standing of women. I am doing this year — a whole year — to prove to myself and everyone else that I do not need to be attached to someone else to be happy.'

'There's no way you're going to last a year. How long has it been so far?'

'Forty-one days.'

'So on day forty-one of three hundred and sixty-five you're still going strong. By day one hundred you'll be doing the walk of shame from someone like Andy's house. Five grand says so.'

'I haven't got five grand.'

'According to you, you're not going to need it. So take the bet.'

'Fine.' Leila said, ignoring her sister's clucks of disapproval from the passenger seat. 'I'll take your bet, and raise you five.'

Alex accelerated down the motorway. 'Game on. Leila, Game on.'

The next day, Judy had just cleared away the remains of the sticky toffee pudding and placed the tray with coffee, and Lucy's peppermint tea, in the middle of the table when Marcus gave a little cough. 'Um, everyone,' he placed his hand on top of Lucy's. 'We have some news.'

Everyone jumped up from the table and loud declarations of 'Congratulations!' 'Fantastic news!' were exclaimed amid a flurry of hugs and kisses. Leila caught

Tasha's warning eyes over Marcus's shoulder, as if she was going to drop in the middle of her congratulations mention of his fiancée's frostiness.

'Where's the ring?' Judy asked excitedly.

Marcus looked a little uncomfortable, but Lucy didn't flinch, 'It wasn't exactly to my taste, so Marcus took it back and we're going ring shopping together this week to get something more suitable.'

'Bigger.' Leila mouthed to Tasha across the table.

'Oh, well, that's nice.' Judy said. It was very obvious to Leila and Tasha that their mother did not in fact think that was nice. In fact, her words of platitude were so fake, she may well have said, 'you made my son return the ring he painstakingly chose for you, you selfish, greedy mare.'

Tasha hurriedly butted in. 'So, any ideas for the wedding?'

Again, Marcus shifted uneasily in his seat, 'Um, well actually, Mum, Dad, we wondered if we could have it here?' Since the refurbishment three years previously, the hotel had been featured in all the wedding magazines as a must-visit location, and they had a booming bookings book filled with brides and grooms-to-be eager to celebrate their nuptials in the oak-beamed dining hall.

The outdoor terrace, built into the hillside, enjoyed panoramic vistas over the harbour and River Dart below and was the perfect spot for pre-dinner Pimms and a jazz band.

'That would be wonderful!' Thomas said, 'We'd be delighted to have it here!' We've got a lot of weekends left after October, or a couple in June next year if you want better weather, so let us know soon what dates you were thinking of.'

'July 1st this year,' Lucy said.

Judy laughed, 'Oh, this summer is completely chocka, I'm afraid, and that's only six weeks away! But I think we do have a weekend in September and then, like Thomas said, most after October?'

'No, we definitely want July 1st this year.'

'But that's a Saturday! We can certainly do a midweek wedding in July if you fancy it though? But I don't see what the rush is? It would be nice to take your time over planning it, rather than doing it all in a rush? Oh! Unless you're pregnant?'

Leila and Tasha cringed at their mother's lack of subtlety, but Lucy didn't flinch, 'No, I'm not pregnant Judy, but neither of us are getting any younger, particularly Marcus, so we don't see the point in dragging it out unnecessarily.'

'And we definitely want a Saturday Mum,

there'll be people travelling all over for it, and midweek wouldn't work,' Marcus added.

'I'm sure you can shuffle some things around for us Judy? It is your son's wedding day after all.' Lucy's smile made Leila itchy. The table had lost its joviality of a few minutes before and everyone's eyes were darting between Lucy and Judy and Thomas to see who would talk first.

'Let me look in the book, and we'll see what can be done.' Judy replied with a pinched smile.

This was absurd. 'You can't cancel someone's wedding just because Marcus has decided to get married then!' Leila heard herself exclaim. 'Those people had booked it last year, or the one before!'

Judy flashed warning eyes at her youngest daughter, while maintaining her slightly twitchy composure and smile. 'I didn't say I was going to cancel someone's wedding, just to see what could be done. Maybe we could ask a couple to move to the Sheldrake, or the Winbourne, but let's look in the book first shall we?'

Lucy clapped her hands together, 'Oh this is so exciting, how it's all coming together! We'll need to talk about menus Judy as soon as possible so that you can order in the ingredients, I want organic Welsh lamb for mains, and then for dessert . . .'

Leila excused herself and carried the empty coffee cups into the kitchen. Thomas followed her carrying the milk jug and cafetiere. She rounded on him before he'd even put them down on the countertop. 'Dad, you can't just cancel someone's wedding because Lucy has decided that's the date she wants! It's completely unethical and will damage your business! And you're talking about a prime date in July — you'd be getting ten grand at least for that date, are you just going to give it to them for free?'

'Calm down Leila, this all needs to be thought through before we make any decisions.' Thomas started loading the dishwasher. 'It's all just been sprung on us and we don't know any of the answers yet. No point getting all worked up. Pass me those plates there.'

'Well don't take too long, because I guarantee she'll have the invites sent out by next weekend, that's if she hasn't done so already.'

Her dad straightened up, 'Why do you care so much Leila, you've never bothered about our bookings or business much before, why now?'

'I just don't want you and Mum to be

completely walked over, that's all!'

'Feeling jealous is completely natural love, you're what, thirty-four now?'

'Thirty-two, and I don't know what that has to —'

'Thirty-two, and your sister is happily settled, and now your brother is getting married, and you're doing your nun thing, it's completely understandable you're going to feel put out and a bit green-eyed. Come here.' He held out his arms for a hug, and as much as she didn't want to, she found herself reluctantly falling into them, a little defeated.

It's odd making a declaration of how you want to live your life in complete contrast to those around you. Society is completely geared up for a man and woman to meet, fall in love, marry and have kids. Yet there are thousands, millions of us that don't fit that mould or expectation. I have gay friends, religious friends of different faiths, friends that have married inter-culturally, and each of them in their own way has come up against barriers to their happiness, for no other reason than people not understanding or being judgmental.

My decision to be single for a year is a personal decision based on my own unique circumstances. I haven't made a placard, or protested outside the registry office trying to convince couples about to marry to embrace my way of life. Instead, I'm just quietly minding my own business, trying to navigate through a pretty tricky time. I don't hate men, in fact I like them possibly a bit too much, which made me lose a bit of myself along the way. I'm only forty-two days into the three-hundred and sixty-five, and have been laughed at, mocked, accused of being sad and lonely, and there's currently a pot with fourteen grand of my family and friends' money who are fully expecting me to fail. But I'm not going to, and, just for the record, I'm allergic to cats.

Leila re-read her post from the night before while she was still in her pyjamas eating her rice krispies. She should have matured into more grown-up breakfast cereals by now, but the snap, crackle and pop still made her smile. She was in two minds whether to delete the post or not. Up until then, all her other entries had been so upbeat, extolling the virtues of single life. There were three hundred and three followers now, which was amazing, and the number was growing by a few every day. She got such a pulse of excitement every time she saw the number increase. When it went over the three-hundred mark she did a little celebratory dance in her tiny kitchen. But surely the whole point of writing this blog was to tell her story, describe her journey and the bumps in the road — or was it to paint a picture of a rosier version of her life that wasn't real? What did the followers want to read, and what did she want to write?

Leila got dressed and went to work and the post stayed live.

CHAPTER 4

'I don't think your sisters like me very much.'

Marcus knew that a long pause between his new fiancée uttering this statement and his effusive denial of said statement was not a good thing, but neither could he hand-on-heart disagree with her. He'd be lying if he said he hadn't glimpsed the side-eye glances that batted back and forth between Tasha and Leila when Lucy was around, not to mention the almost imperceptible eyebrow raising and whispered asides. He'd wanted so desperately for them all to get on, but for some reason his sisters, who were normally so warm and welcoming, were being a bit, well, off, with Lucy.

'I wouldn't necessarily say that I don't think they don't like you,' he finally offered.

'There are far too many negatives in that sentence for me to even begin to decipher it,' Lucy replied crossly. She slammed the fridge door shut and handed him a cold bottle of white wine. 'Can you open that? I know they might be protective of you, but I don't think they're giving me much of a chance.'

Marcus unhooked a corkscrew from the wall-mounted metal utensil rod and started turning it in the top of the bottle, pleased to have something to focus on other than forming a response.

'I mean, I think I've been perfectly pleasant, haven't I Marcus? I bring flowers to your mum every time we go down, I'm nice to Tasha's kids, even though they're always a bit mucousy, I even told Leila that her haircut suited her.'

'You said that she looked androgynous.'

'I said that the androgynous look suited her. Suited her, Marcus. It was a compliment.'

'I'm just not sure she interpreted it like that darling. They're different to you, that's all. They're not as . . .' Again, Marcus paused, and a dictionary of nouns ran like a ticker tape in front of his eyes until he rested on 'composed.'

'Composed?' Lucy put down the colander of lettuce leaves that she was swilling water through and rested it on the draining board. 'What the heck is composed supposed to mean?'

'Composed, calm, ladylike, call it what you will, they're a bit mouthy and emotional, act first, think later, that sort of thing. They all are, Mum and the girls, you're much more focused and poised.'

Focused and poised. Lucy liked that description of herself. It was exactly how she'd like to be thought of. Especially by her future husband.

'Here, get this down you. Cheers!' Marcus clinked his wine glass to hers.

'God,' Lucy groaned, 'I can't wait until we get the wine glasses on our wedding list, these stems are so clunky.'

Marcus hovered his hand over the pan that had been warming on the hob to check it was hot enough, before dropping a lump of butter into it, which immediately started sizzling and fizzing around the griddle. He picked up a large wooden spoon out of the china pot in front of him and held it a few centimetres away from his mouth, 'And today on *Marcus and Lucy Cooks,* it's steak au poivre. Lucy, can you tell me how you're making the sauce?' He moved the spoon in front of Lucy's face. She resisted for a couple of seconds then broke into a giggle as they acted out the now familiar cooking routine.

'Well, Marcus,' she said into the wooden spoon, 'while you're searing the steaks with a peppercorn crust, I'm mixing cognac and cream together, then we'll add this to the lovely pan juices. Back to you.'

'Thank you Lucy, that sounds delicious. Now as you can see, the steaks are browning wonderfully, and I'm just going to flip them over, and ta da!'

Lucy leaned over to speak into the spoon again, 'That really does look marvellous Marcus, and so easy to do at home.'

'Absolutely Lucy, even though we are indeed pros, even the amateur cook can master this dish.'

'Yes, spot on Marcus. Thank you for joining us today on *Marcus and Lucy Cooks,* until next time.'

Lucy had set the table in the dining room earlier that evening, as she did every evening. Even though the kitchen had a small circular table, which suited the purpose for breakfast just fine, a proper dinner always tasted better in the more formal surroundings of the dining room surrounded by candles. A couple of mouthfuls in, Lucy started talking again. 'I've found the dress I want to wear for our wedding, so I'm going to make some appointments this week.'

Marcus had his mouth full so just gave an

encouraging noise.

'I don't want to go by myself though, and Aimee and Emily are at work. All the magazines say that a bride should go with their mother, but the idea exhausts me.'

Marcus felt uneasy again. The relaxed frivolity of their pretend studio skit moments before had evaporated and he knew that he had to navigate this conversation carefully. He'd only met his future mother-in-law once, and she seemed nice, so was always a bit perplexed whenever Lucy mentioned her in a negative way. 'How so?' he asked.

'Just the expectation levels I guess, it's meant to be this seminal bonding moment isn't it, and Mum might cry or something, which would just be awful.'

'You could make a day of it, take the credit card, treat yourselves to lunch somewhere.'

Lucy grimaced. 'I know I should, I'm her only daughter after all, but I'm just a bit uncomfortable with it, what would we talk about all day?'

'Dresses? Shoes? I don't know Lucy, you're asking the wrong person. Why don't you ask Leila or Tasha to come along as well? You were saying earlier that you don't think they like you, this would be the perfect chance for them to get to know you better.'

It wasn't a bad idea, Lucy thought. Having another person there would certainly lower the risk of gushes of sentimentality from her mum, and it would be a nice gesture on her part to include his side of the family. She really wanted his sisters to like her, but she just didn't know how to make that happen. She wrinkled her nose. 'But what if they don't want to?'

'You haven't asked them yet. Ask. I'm sure they'd love it. All girls love dress shopping don't they?'

'Leila's a gardener, she lives in wellies.'

'She has dresses, I'm sure of it. When were you thinking of going?'

'This week. I'll book a day off work. Honestly Marcus, I have no idea how I'm juggling it all, it's exhausting trying to plan the wedding, while rushing about at work, doing everything for everyone. I literally feel as though I'm being pulled in a thousand directions all the time. I swear this wedding is going to be a complete disaster because of it. Either that or I'll give myself an ulcer with the stress.'

Marcus congratulated himself on another well-timed mouthful, he knew that Lucy couldn't abide bad table manners, so as long as he made sure to do dramatic chewing motions with his jaw, he'd be forgiven for not responding.

Lucy carried on talking, 'I don't even have time to concentrate on the flowers and centrepieces, it really needs my full attention to get it exactly right, and I just can't focus on that with work being so full on. I'm so anxious that the wedding is going to be ruined, and you deserve so much more.'

'Mmmm, you do have a lot on.' Marcus agreed. Which was always best.

'I do, don't I? And I really do want to be the perfect wife to you Marky, and make sure that our new house, when we eventually find one we like, is exactly right, and that we always have nice food in, and I'm just so concerned how I'm going to fit it all in, it's a little overwhelming.'

Marcus swallowed his last forkful and took a sip of wine. 'You know what I think? I earn more than enough for you not to work at all, there's no reason to get stressed about it all. Just resign and concentrate on the things that you want to. Simple. Right, shall I get dessert?'

As Marcus left the room with the dirty plates and busied himself loading them into the dishwasher, Lucy sat twirling the thick-stemmed wine glass in her fingers and smiled. Well, that conversation couldn't have gone better.

CHAPTER 5

Leila was so bored, she actually wished she was back sandwiched between two car seats trying to guess that 'I' belonged to 'I-brow'.

This was the fifth wedding dress shop of the day and she'd lost the will to live somewhere around dress three of the first shop. Except they weren't called shops, they were boutiques or salons. She'd learned that after getting the stare of death from one of the 'bridal liaisons' (shop assistants). Marcus had called her to prewarn her of Lucy's impending invitation, and he'd been so earnest, so heartfelt in imploring her to accompany Lucy and Lucy's mum shopping she couldn't say no. Well, no that was a lie, she'd tried, but he just batted her remonstrations away and guilted her into submission. 'She's hardly got any friends, and those she does have are stuck at work,' he'd said, completely oblivious to the massive neon warning sign that accompanied this statement. Who didn't have many friends?

Lucy's mum, Stephanie, was lovely though, which was a complete surprise. If pushed Leila would have admitted to have been expecting a buttoned-up platinum blonde with manicured talons and a designer handbag. She absolutely wasn't anticipating this wonderfully bohemian middle-aged woman bounding off the train, wearing a full-length paisley coat, with long curly greying hair. If Stephanie noticed Lucy's lacklustre greeting and stiff embrace she didn't say, just gave her daughter and Leila a wide smile as she took their arms and proclaimed excitedly that they were going to have so much fun.

The fact that each salon offered them a glass of champagne had lessened the pain but heightened the boredom. Leila was left sat by herself most of the time as Lucy was in the dressing room, and Stephanie was busy taking pictures of wedding dresses to send them to her son's girlfriend who was also getting married soon. Every boutique was a carbon copy of the one before. Each had a plush cream carpet, shag, Leila thought it was called, giving an immature snigger inside. Big armchairs or sofas were flanked with side tables, usually circular glass ones, with a box of tissues perched upon them, for teary mothers no doubt.

As the hours ticked by, Lucy was getting increasingly annoyed with each assistant, who kept giving sharp intakes of horror when she mentioned that her wedding date was in five weeks' time. 'I'm sure you're not trying to be deliberately difficult,' Lucy told the last one. 'So let's try and make this work, shall we?'

'Off-the-peg' was a term Lucy appeared to find offensive, wrinkling her nose and shrinking back a few inches every time it was mentioned. Her binder was full of princess-type dresses, all carefully cut out of magazines and placed in the relevant colour-coded section of the folder, after Flowers but before Poems and Readings. It's not that each boutique didn't have the exact eye-wateringly expensive gown she wanted, it's just it would take six–eight months to order and make. You'd have thought by the fifth time she heard this, Lucy would start to understand.

'I could always run it up for you my love,' Stephanie offered later that afternoon, holding out a tissue to her sobbing daughter. Lucy wasn't an attractive crier, Leila thought, and felt immediately very bad for having that thought.

'Run it up for me? Run it up for me? I

don't want a pair of bloody curtains Mother!'

That was a bit harsh, the poor woman was clearly trying to help. 'Lucy, I think at this stage you have two options, buy something —' Leila stopped herself just in time uttering a phrase that contained the word peg — 'already made.' Good save. 'Or maybe think about having one of the designs you love made, either by your mum, who I'm sure is a very accomplished seamstress' — Stephanie shot Leila a look of gratitude — 'or someone else, but I think you need to call it a day at trying different shops. Salons. Whatever.'

'I knew you'd try to sabotage today, I just knew it.'

Leila knew Lucy would be mortified if she realised that a little bit of snot was stuck to the outside of her nose and that her eyeliner had smudged on the left side. While this was immensely gratifying to see, and more than a little amusing, Leila knew that staying silent went against everything the new Leila stood for. So she passed Lucy a tissue and said, 'Wipe your nose and your eyes and how about we both pretend you didn't say that and I ring ahead to the next two appointments to see if they can do this dress any quicker?'

As luck would have it, there was a cancelled order at the next boutique in very similar measurements to Lucy's. It was Lucy that cited this as 'very lucky,' Leila couldn't help viewing it from the other side, thinking of the poor woman that drank the free champagne, paraded in her dream dress in front of her emotional mum and friends and then tearfully phoned to cancel a few months later. But for the purposes of familial harmony, Leila kept mute. Now was most certainly not the time to introduce the concept of perspective.

She must admit though, Lucy did seem to be extraordinarily fortunate. In the end Judy and Thomas hadn't had to cancel the couple on the 1st July, they did that themselves. And Marcus had also bartered a great price for the original couple's photographer who had already accepted a non-refundable deposit, which he knocked off Lucy and Marcus's price. It crossed Leila's mind fleetingly that this could possibly be that poor girl's dress too, but that would be slightly too weird. If she was indulging her darker thoughts, Leila wouldn't have put it past Lucy to try to break the other couple up just so she could glide into their day, but it was beyond spiteful of her to even think that. And in no way compatible with her new role of Champion of All Women.

'So what's next on the list then?' They'd just dropped Stephanie off at the train station and decamped to a nearby wine bar to take stock of the day and plan the next few weeks. In the absence of a sister, female cousin or any of her friends at all, Leila and Tasha had been drafted in as bridesmaids. Not willingly. And Tasha was away at a yoga retreat in the Peak District, which was very conveniently timed to coincide with this shopping trip.

Her sister was still reeling from being told that her kids were not allowed at the wedding. 'But they are your nieces and nephew!' she'd railed at Marcus. But he was adamant that Lucy had vetoed all children, regardless of blood ties. So Tasha had booked her weekend away to deliberately coincide with dress shopping. Meaning that now it was all falling squarely to Leila. 'It all' being every damn detail of the wedding it seemed.

'Ok, so table plans,' Lucy said studiously, peering at the long list in front of her. 'We have most of the RSVPs back now — Mum's going to chase the rest — I can't do that myself, it would be vulgar. And then we can start assigning table places. Leila, I've pinned some ideas onto Pinterest of what designs I want, so you can knock one up as you're a designer.'

'I design gardens Lucy, I'm not a graphic designer.'

Lucy looked at Leila blankly. 'It's all creative though, isn't it? It's literally just cutting out bits of card and mounting it on other bits of card, it's not rocket science.'

If it's not rocket science, Leila wanted to say, why aren't you doing it yourself, now that you've given up your job purely to organise the wedding. She couldn't believe it when Marcus told her that Lucy had resigned from her job as an event planner as she couldn't manage the wedding and full-time work. 'Poor lamb,' he'd said, 'the stress was really getting to her.' But Leila knew that Judy was bearing the brunt of all the planning, ironic considering the nature of Lucy's former career.

Judy had uncharacteristically let slip on the phone to her a few nights before that she was finding Lucy 'rather difficult' to deal with, and that in all her years of working with brides, 'Lucy has taken it to another level.' She even persuaded Judy to change the curtains in the dining room as they didn't match her flowers. Judy was incredulous when she told Leila this, yet still did it anyway, which Leila thought was the most incredulous thing. Since then, she had little sympathy for her mother's tales of wedding woe. Yet here she was, nodding along like a mechanical dog, saying, 'Table plans, ok. Anything else?'

'Yes, I don't know whether Marcus has mentioned this, but you need to bring a date. All the tables are for eight, and we can't have one of seven, it would look unbalanced and just wrong.'

'Um, ok, I'll ask Shelley. She loves weddings, always up for a bit of usher action.'

'No, no, it has to be a man, it's boy girl boy girl seating, we can't have two people of the same sex together, that would screw everything up.'

'You're sounding remarkably Republican there Lucy.'

The jibe was lost on her. Leila carried on, 'But I don't have any single male friends to bring, and you know I'm not dating anyone for another ten months.'

'Sorry, but I'm not having your silly vow of celibacy ruin my special day.'

Again Leila found herself biting her lip. 'Fine. I'll find someone.'

'No dreadlocks.'

'Got it.'

'He has to wear top hat and tails.'

'Done.'

'If he has tattoos he has to cover them up.'

'This advert is sounding stranger by the minute.'

Lucy's eyes widened, 'You're not really going to advertise to bring someone to my wedding?'

Leila considered carrying on the joke just for her own amusement, but GSOH didn't seem to be one of Lucy's qualities. 'Of course not. I have just the chap. He's a colleague, Jamie. Nice guy, been pestering me to go out for ages, I'll ask him, but I'll have to lay down some ground rules first.'

The conversation with Jamie the next day went exactly the way Leila anticipated. There had been a moment, a fleeting blink-and-you-miss-it-moment at last year's staff party when their eyes locked onto each other's and Leila was tempted to accept Jamie's ever so eager advances, but as she stood there deliberating whether to or not a leggy intern grabbed Jamie to dance and the moment passed. She waited until the office had thinned out at lunchtime and followed him into the small pantry where he was meticulously measuring out his protein shake powder into milk. 'Hey Jamie.'

'Lovely Leila, how are you?'

'Look, I have a favour to ask you. You can

absolutely say no, although I hope you don't.'

'Intriguing. Go on.' He leant back against the countertop. His sleeves were rolled up to his elbows, which made his biceps bulge a little. But then, he knew that. Leila was also heartened to see a tattoo-free forearm, which was another tick in a box.

'My brother is getting married, which in itself is a miracle, and I have to take a date and —'

'Yes.'

'I haven't finished my sentence.'

'Yes I'll come with you.'

'But you need to know, I'm two months into a year of celibacy, and so we'll be going to this as colleagues, friends even. But absolutely not as dates. It's in Dartmouth, at my parents' place, so I'll book you a room, but a different one to mine. I'm just lowering your expectations now, so you're not expecting a bit of wedding night fun and frolics.'

'Message received and understood.'

'Really?'

'Really. Would love to come. And you know, if the romance of the occasion, and the free-flowing champagne, means that your mind changes as the night wears on, then that's fine with me too.'

'It won't.'

'But if it does.'

'It won't.'

'But if it does.'

'It's on the 1st July, I'll email you the details. I'm getting there a couple of days before so you'll have to make your own way down, but I'll pay half your petrol. Is that ok?'

'Sure thing.'

As Leila left the pantry she heard him shout, 'But if it does!' She smiled as the door slammed behind her.

That evening she checked her blog statistics, she'd got another two-hundred and fifty followers over the last week, which took her total number to just shy of fifteen-hundred. And some had even started commenting too. At first they were just one or two words, like 'Yes!', 'Me too!' 'I feel the same', but then women started writing longer posts about their own lives and loves. Leila created another page on the site for women to share their stories, and it was garnering more and more clicks every day. The beauty of the internet meant it wasn't just local London women logging on; she'd had women from Scotland, Switzerland, all the way to Bermuda and California joining in the discussions. Leila couldn't help feeling a little proud that she'd created this forum for a community of women to come together, united in their tales of embracing single life.

It was the story of one woman, Namisha, that inspired Leila to set up a closed Facebook group in addition to the blog. Namisha had had an arranged marriage planned. She hadn't been too happy with the idea beforehand, but her family had told her that she could be pro-active in finding the groom, so she relented. After months of chaperoned meetings with different prospective men, she finally found someone she clicked with. The wedding date was set, over eight-hundred invitations were sent out, she sat still for four hours having her hands painstakingly decorated with henna at her Mehndi party, and had a red silk sari specially made in India and flown over. On the morning of the ceremony, just as the ballroom of one of Manchester's top hotels filled with guests, Namisha learned that the groom had run off with an American girl he'd been secretly dating for five years.

Although she kept her story brief and free from an outpouring of emotion, unlike some of the other recently-scorned singletons, the subtlety of Namisha's pain was imbedded in every word. Every one of Leila's break-ups had been a private experience, one where she alone suffered the pain and humiliation. She couldn't imagine what that poor woman went through in such a public way. Within a couple of hours, twenty different women had offered Namisha support, soothing words and a couple of women local to where Namisha lived even offered tea and cake to accompany their sympathy.

This website was becoming more than just Leila typing a few lines as she had her dinner each night. This was a virtual club that was making a difference.

That wasn't part of The Plan either.

There were only a certain number of ways you could organise twenty chairs in a small room, and Leila had tried all of them. Twice.

Rows were too formal. A circle too Alcoholics Anonymous. Around the edge of the room too pre-teen disco. She'd finally settled on having clusters of five seats around four tables, after all, Tasha did say that part of the workshop was going to involve writing. She put the three kettles on to boil, again. Everyone would be arriving in about ten minutes, and it would be good to be able to offer them a drink straight away rather than make small talk over the ever-increasing sound of bubbling water. And then remembered a warning she'd read once that you shouldn't reboil water or it could cause cancer. She wasn't sure of the validity of this, but now was not the time to worry about it. She had toyed with the idea of serving wine too — it was 7pm — but thought for this first meeting it would be good to start off sober. God, she wished she wasn't so sensible, she could murder a glass of pinot grigio.

Iris from Ealing was the first to arrive, nervously peering around the door. She clutched her bag in front of her as though she was expecting Leila to mug her.

'Hi,' Leila walked towards her with her hand outstretched. 'I'm Leila. You found us then? Thanks so much for coming, it's really exciting doing this, we've got lots of great things planned, we've got two speakers at this workshop, and, oh, great one of them's here now, why don't you help yourself to tea or coffee Iris, there's lots of different types — just all on that table over there, great.'

'Where have you been?' Leila hissed through her teeth at Tasha.

Tasha looked about the empty room, until her eyes stopped pointedly at Iris deliberating over peppermint or jasmine tea and said, 'You're right, I'm sorry, leaving you to riot control on your own was very thoughtless of me.' She leaned over to kiss her sister's cheek and whispered in her ear, 'Calm down sweetheart, it's all going to go brilliantly.'

Thirty minutes later, when every chair was filled, and twenty heads were studiously bowed, writing down their thoughts in twenty different types of handwriting, Leila allowed herself to breathe. Tasha and her friend Eva had put together a two-hour introductory session on mindfulness for the first twenty London-based women who replied. And the crazy thing was, she could have filled a room three times the size with the amount of people that wanted to come. She couldn't believe she'd been so disparaging in the past about Tasha's passion without really knowing too much about it, and it was incredible all the stuff she was saying. The whole premise of living in this exact moment and not letting your past or your future shape or affect your present, was something every woman in that room needed to hear and learn, and Leila placed herself firmly in that camp too. She'd spent so many years hankering after an ex, or impatiently awaiting the arrival of Mr Perfect, that she'd squandered the last decade looking back or forward and never stopping for a minute to just be.

'Another key thing,' Tasha intoned, 'is acceptance. Welcome in your thoughts, the negative ones and the positive ones, but don't see one as right, or one as wrong, give them space to exist, and don't judge yourself. Tune into everything you're feeling — the way the shower spray hits your body, the way a certain fabric feels, the smell of your perfume, the taste of your food — think and reflect on every sensation as you think or feel it.'

Leila was concerned beforehand that two hours sounded like an awfully long time to sit and contemplate your life, but the time just sped by, and it wasn't until the office cleaners came in, that she realised that they'd even gone over time.

'Ok everyone, we're going to have to wrap it up now, but thank you so much Tasha and Eva for coming and imparting your wise words, and honestly, I am so humbled to be surrounded by so many inspiring women. Hopefully this is the first of many events and workshops that we do, and please, any ideas you have, or topics you'd like to focus on, just drop me a line, I'd love to hear from you.' It was perhaps testament to how soul-revealing the evening had been,

but every woman had entered the room giving Leila a handshake, and left it giving her
a hug. That was pretty awesome.

'You've got an amazing thing going here,'
Eva said as she gathered up all the pencils
left on the desks. 'To get all these different
women in one space is marketing gold.' Eva
had left the world of corporate life coaching
a few months previously to set up her own
business. 'I gave my card to at least half the
women here tonight. By all rights, I should
have been paying you for the exposure, not
the other way round!' Each of the women
had paid a tenner to attend, and as Leila's
boss had let her have the training room for
free and even thrown in the refreshments,
Leila just split the two hundred between
Tasha and Eva.

'Eva's right Leila, you could have run this
evening at a profit tonight, and everyone
would have still gone away feeling happy
and fulfilled.'

Leila grimaced. 'I know what you're saying, but there's something a bit distasteful
at me making money from other people's
misfortunes. I mean everyone was here
because they'd been unlucky in love, I don't
want to start monetising their healing.'

'Think about it Leila,' Tasha said, getting
her car keys out of her bag. 'You're provid-

ing a service for these women — it's like a member's club — and if you started seeing it more like a business than a hobby, you could be making a pretty tidy side-line from it.'

Her sister's words were going around her head on a loop all the way home. It was so far removed from the reasons she started the blog in the first place. Just three months ago, it was an online diary, a place for her to vent and explore her feelings, and now here she was, an event planner, party host, mentor and head girl of a sorority that was growing larger every day.

As she'd been spending so much time on her website, Leila was woefully behind in her work, so when the weekend rolled around instead of pottering around markets with her friends or having lazy lunches she was hibernating at home trying to meet her deadlines. Her phone was ringing for the fourth time in as many minutes and Leila couldn't ignore it again. She hated being interrupted when creative brilliance was in full flow. Her company had pitched recently for a lucrative but immensely soul-destroying project doing the car parks and outside cafe areas of a chain of well-known supermarkets. It was the first time she had been chosen to lead a project in seven years of working there, and she needed to pull this off. Her dining table was piled high with blueprints and open books and markers, and huge unfolded plans had slipped off the table onto the floor, and somewhere under all this was her incessantly ringing phone.

'Leila. Marcus.'

She couldn't help but smile; her brother had such a knack for sounding so pompous. 'Marcus, what do I owe this pleasure to?' She was thankful it was him and not Judy who had phoned because she knew it wouldn't be a long call. Marcus was known for his brevity, unlike her mother.

'We had dinner with Tasha and Alex last night.'

'Thanks for the invite.'

Marcus either didn't hear her sarcastic retort, or more likely, just chose to ignore her, 'And Tasha was talking about your blog and Facebook page. I had no idea it was doing so well.'

'Too well at the moment! Work is so busy and then this is massively taking off, and I can't justify spending all the time I do on something that doesn't pay the bills.'

'That's why I'm phoning.' He then reeled off a list of five or six clients of his legal firm, big companies that Leila had heard

87

of, that were offering services that targeted professional single women. A bank that had special mortgage rates for single borrowers, a financial services firm that offered women better premiums on car and life insurance, a brand of wine whose latest advertising campaign focused on friendship and sharing, a sportswear brand that wanted to align itself with empowering women, and so on. 'Don't you see Leila,' he continued, 'your blog would be the perfect place for these brands to reach out to your women, and these people have cash to spend. Now I can't be seen to be involved in this in any way, obviously, but if you were to send them a short presentation about you and your site, I promise you they'd be interested.'

'Really?'

'Really. They'd pay for ad banners on the site, sponsorship of any more events you have, they may well offer your followers discounts, freebies, incentives, you could run competitions for singles holidays, God Leila, you could do amazing things with it. Why don't you talk to Dad about it? He does all the marketing for the hotel, and his strategy is sound. He's set up barters with different companies and now they have advertising logos on their brochures. Or, and here's an idea,' his voice had changed from purely business to something verging on excitement, 'You could run weekend retreats at Mum and Dad's hotel during the off-peak season — it would help them out in the quieter months, and you could pitch it as a . . . what do you call it . . . "finding yourself" short break or something like that. Get the sponsors to pay to have their branding there, every woman pays two or three hundred quid as well, give half to the folks and you're raking it in.'

'And then there's your cut too of course,' Leila couldn't help saying. It was so unlike Marcus to phone completely out of the blue just to offer some brotherly advice. Particularly now Lucy was firmly entrenched on the scene.

'This first session is free. But I will charge to look over any contracts you sign.'

And there was the brother she knew and loved.

CHAPTER 6

Leila stabbed the last phallic-shaped straw into a lurid cocktail in Lucy's kitchen, hearing the high-pitched shrieks of hilarity through the paper-thin walls. She paused to plaster her smile back on her face before re-entering the dining room.

'What's your favourite part of Marcus's body?' one of Lucy's friends from her book club read out to a chorus of girlish giggles.

'His forearms,' Lucy replied. 'He has amazingly strong forearms.'

Leila tried not to blink, and just focused on dividing out the drinks between the eight women, who were in various stages of inebriation, including, much to her complete embarrassment, her own mother, who was swaying glassy-eyed at the end of the table.

Lucy hiccupped after taking a small sip, 'What's in this one? It's lethal!'

'Um, lots of clear stuff and some blue

stuff,' Leila took a gulp of her own concoction without wincing. She'd passed the point that alcohol had any effect whatsoever. They'd spent the day gluing sequins onto stilettos as one of their hen party activities. Lucy had put Leila in charge of the day and evening, and then proceeded to forward Leila pins or links to exactly what it was she wanted them to be doing. So, early afternoon was glitzing up footwear, and then they had a mixologist come to the house and throw bottles about. Which Leila had to admit was pretty fun — hence her new-found talent for cocktail-making. Lucy had firmly rebuffed the butler in the buff idea, which was just as well as Leila had no intention of seeing a naked man for at least another two-hundred and forty-eight days anyway.

Looking around the table, it was the oddest mix of women she'd ever seen. Apart from her, Tasha and Judy, there were two women from Lucy's book club, an ex-colleague of Lucy's who was heavily pregnant so not drinking, another former colleague who was so drunk her eyes were crossed, and a tall, long blonde-haired, very athletic-looking woman who hadn't spoken to anyone apart from Lucy all afternoon. She also hadn't joined in any of the activities, instead she'd sat for most of the afternoon and evening with Lucy's wedding binder on her lap writing down numbers of florists, reception venues and photographers into her diary.

'Are you getting married soon too?' Leila turned to her, trying to kick-start conversation.

The woman looked up from the folder, 'Yes, I'm marrying Lucy's brother, Nick.'

'Oh, that's great. Congratulations.'

'Thank you.'

The woman put her head down and was scribbling again.

'I was with Lucy when we went wedding dress shopping and Stephanie was sending you pictures of some, wasn't she? See any that you liked?'

'I actually already have my dress, I was engaged before you see, but it didn't work out. But I love the dress, so have kept it ready for the next one.'

'Oh.' Leila thought frantically of what she was meant to say to that. 'That's, um, handy.'

'Same with the bridesmaid dresses. Although one of my cousins has put on loads of weight recently, so she won't be able to be a bridesmaid any more. Which is a shame because we were close.'

'Righto. Um, excuse me.' Leila reached across the table to an upturned sunhat and fished a rolled up piece of paper out. 'Shall I read the next one?' She paused before saying, 'What is Marcus's favourite position?' Oh God, why did she have to pick that one out?

'You have to be diplomatic here don't you!' The pregnant ex-colleague laughed.

'Not on our account, you don't, pretend your fiancé's sisters and mother aren't even here,' Tasha said with a lot more good humour than she was feeling. 'There's nothing we'd like more than to hear about our brother's exploits in bed.'

'We can cover our ears if it makes it easier for you to say,' Leila added.

Lucy's eyes casted to the left as she screwed up her forehead, looking like she was thinking way too hard about this question for Leila's liking. 'Um,' she said, biting her lower lip, 'to be honest, we've decided to save ourselves for our wedding night.'

Despite ten minutes of solid scrubbing, the wall still had a faint blue tinge to it where Leila had spluttered her cocktail all over it. 'Sorry about that,' she said sheepishly after the last of the party, Judy and Tasha, had been dispatched in a taxi, waving merrily and unsteadily, shouting 'See you in church!' noisily across the darkened cul de sac.

'It's fine,' Lucy replied in a tone that suggested that it wasn't. She turned on the main light and started sweeping the table's detritus into a bin bag.

'Here, let me, you go on up, you're the one that needs her beauty sleep ready for the wedding.'

Lucy's lips pursed into an unattractive pout. 'Thanks very much!'

'I didn't mean like that! You're getting married! It's late, I'll do the rest, honestly, it's fine, go.' Leila gave her soon to be sister-in-law a stiff hug and started the impossible task of picking the thousands of penis-shaped confetti out from between the floorboards.

Leila thought that she might as well wait until the dishwasher had finished to put another load in before she left, it's not as though there was anyone awake at home waiting for her. There was a small bit of wine left in two of the bottles, so Leila splashed them both into a glass and gave it a swirl. Marcus would be horrified. When they were teenagers they used to work in their parents' hotel in Dartmouth, and she and Tasha used to stow away the dregs from all the bottles they'd served to customers throughout the evening for them and their friends to share later. She'd decant all the whites into one bottle, all the reds into another, completely ignorant of blending grape varieties or vintages, and trudge to the sheltered safety of the local park to drink the stash and voice ill-conceived musings on the universe. She remembered with a smile that Marcus had been appalled that she had mixed a £200 bottle of 1982 Chateau Haut Brion Pessac-Lognan with a rough house Beaujolais, but she had just tipped her plastic cup at him in a mocking toast and downed the lot.

Jamie had saved a seat for her in church by putting his top hat on the pew next to him. At six foot five, wearing the top hat was never really an option, but Lucy had insisted on him at least carrying it.

'Emergency averted?' he asked as Leila hurriedly sat down and pinned the hat on her head. She hated hats.

'Yes, the roses were the wrong shade of pink.'

'Oh no, is your sister-in-law ok?'

'She'll live.'

They turned in time with the rest of the congregation as Lucy made her entrance to a loud fanfare of Handel's Wedding March, a predictable choice that had the rest of the church beaming. Her tight corset flowed down to a sharp A-line, with delicate crystal beading catching the sunlight that danced through the stained glass. Her long strawberry blonde hair had been tightly pinned into elaborate swags under a flowing veil. The hysterics over the roses a few minutes earlier were forgotten.

Back at the hotel, Leila hurried past the easel holding the seating plan straight into the dining room. She didn't need to look at it, she'd had three blasted attempts at making the damn thing, so knew its contents off by heart. The first two efforts didn't entirely 'encapsulate the theme' was how Lucy phrased it. The theme in Leila's mind now being 'sticking needles in my eye'. She'd also just had an earful from Marcus about the fact that Jamie had bailed straight after the ceremony to step in to replace an injured teammate at the last minute for an away rugby match at Exeter.

'His place at the wedding breakfast cost £65,' Marcus had fumed at her, as though she had gaily waved him off after tucking in his shin pads and hadn't been livid about it herself. Now she was dateless for a massive family wedding and incredulously £65 out of pocket as her brother accepted her offer to pay for Jamie's food. And Leila knew their parents were footing the bill anyway but didn't have the heart to have a screaming match with her brother on his wedding day.

Her table was already filled — now the only table with odd numbers in the whole room. 'Hi, Leila, hello, Leila, hi there, Leila, hello, Leila, nice to meet you, Leila, hello, Leila.' Introductions and obligatory reaching across the table handshakes done, Leila broke with the convention of waiting for the bride and groom to arrive and poured herself a massive glass of wine, broke a bread bun in half and slumped noisily sighing into her seat.

'That bad?'

Leila looked to her right. 'Worse.'

'Nice dress.'

Leila looked down. The coral bridesmaid's dress that dwarfed her tiny frame in a blanket of offensive, and probably highly flammable, chiffon could not in any way be described as a nice dress. In that instant every tiny atom of frustration that had been building up for the entire three-month engagement was ignited by the gently mocking tone of this stranger. She threw her head back and laughed a laugh so loud, so bordering on hysterical, that nearby tables turned to look. 'You have no idea,' she finally uttered. 'You literally have no idea.'

'Try me.'

Leila needed no encouragement. For the next ten minutes, even during the jubilant, albeit vastly rehearsed, entrance of Marcus and Lucy, she barely paused for breath. 'And another thing,' she added, 'Lucy even wanted me to wear a blonde wig to cover my dark hair because I would ruin the photos, can you believe that? And another thing —' Throughout this impassioned monologue the stranger had kept her glass topped up and was offering silent nods of sympathy. 'These god-awful shoes weren't available in my size so Ms Hitler ordered me ones a size and a half too small, so as well as looking like a festival tent, I now have four blisters and my blood has dyed the fabric a sort of putrid puce colour.' She paused. 'I'm sorry, you must be Rob, you work with my dad, is that right?' Leila remembered the name that she'd written on three table plans next to her own.

'No, I'm Ms Hitler's brother, Nick.'

Leila buried her face in her hands. 'Bollocks. Bollocks. I'm sorry. For the tantrum, not that she's your sister. I'm sure she's delightful. Deep down. Shit. I'm sorry.' She suddenly froze. 'Why did you move places? Nobody's supposed to move!' Her voice was now loud and shrill. 'This arrangement took away almost a week of my life that I will never get back, and I'll never hear the end of it if Lucy finds out. You're supposed to be on the other side of the table between Rob's pregnant wife Laura and a woman called Olga, who quite frankly sounds like a Russian lap-dancer.'

'Who is also my girlfriend. And is sitting to my right, but thankfully the hours she's spent in noisy strip clubs has completely ruined her hearing, so I think you got away with it.'

'Oh God.' Leila took a big gulp of her wine. She had no idea how much she'd drunk, but her verbal diarrhoea was in full flow, so a sizeable amount she reckoned. 'I'll just stop talking shall I?'

Nick grinned. 'Apparently some arsehole, my sister's words, not mine, dropped out just before the meal and so she needed to shuffle things around, so here I am, being captivated by the eloquence of my new sister-in-law. Lucky me. And if it's any consolation, I'm under strict instructions not to roll my sleeves up, regardless of how hot it gets because she doesn't want your family to know I have tattoos, and until last week I had long hair as well, that I had to cut off or my invitation was going to be revoked. Which I'm realising now may not have been a bad thing.'

'I had waist length hair until about four months ago, but then went for a bit of a drastic change. Which your sister says makes me look like a boy.'

'Oh Jeez. I'm sorry. And for the record, you don't.'

'I'm really sorry too. About everything, My no-show date, Lucy, and Olga. Who I'm sure is really lovely, or you wouldn't be marrying her.'

'I wouldn't be what now?' As if on cue, the blonde woman with long poker-straight hair from the hen party swivelled round in her seat and extended her beautifully manicured hand over Nick's lamb shank. 'Hi, I'm Olga,' she said. 'How are you?'

'Um, fine thanks, much better than I was. Nick has been cheering me up, sorry for taking up all his time. We met at Lucy's hen do?'

'Did we?' Olga started stroking Nick's arm with her fingernail.

'Yes, we were talking about your wedding and you were making notes on Lucy's bridal folder. And telling me about the bridesmaid dresses you've already got?'

Leila had never seen the physical manifestation of the phrase 'blood draining from face' before, but before her eyes it happened to both Nick and Olga at the same time. Nick retrieved his arm from Olga's tight grip, coughed and pushed his chair back. 'I need a smoke, back soon.'

Leila pushed open the door to the terrace and walked over to where Nick was lighting a new cigarette from the dying embers of the last one. 'I told the waitress to keep your lamb warm, they're clearing the table now.'

Nick shrugged, 'Cheers, but I've lost my appetite anyway.'

'So . . . I take it the engagement was very much in Olga's head,' Leila ventured.

'It's our fifth date. So yes, very much so, although now you mention it, she did insist on meeting Mum after the first one. To tell the truth I didn't even want to bring her today, but Lucy insisted as otherwise it would cock up the numbers or something. But it's a massive thing isn't it, bringing someone you barely know to your sibling's wedding?' He wasn't to know that this made Leila cringe a little. 'And I didn't want to give the wrong signals this was more serious than it was, and all the time she's been planning our wedding.' He took a deep inhalation from his cigarette and blew the smoke out. 'Jesus, women!'

'Can I take this opportunity to point out your audience?' Leila joked.

'Sorry. I'm just fed up of every woman I date trying to fast track from the getting to know you stage straight to the altar.'

'At least yours made the dinner, my date didn't even have a Pimms before he legged it to a better offer.'

'That makes me feel better. At least I'm not the biggest loser here.'

'You're welcome.'

'But at least you're now free to enjoy the party. I have to go back in there, break up with a fiancée I didn't know I had, and then I am going to have to call her a taxi.'

'But her name is Olga.'

'Oh, that's a bad, bad joke.'

They stood opposite each other both looking fittingly solemn. And annoyed. Leila's mouth began to twitch, and then Nick smiled the start of a bigger smile. Before long they were both convulsed in laughter that didn't stop until Lucy angrily shouted from the window that the desserts were being served.

Somewhere between the coffee and the first dance, in that lull that always happened at weddings when the bride and groom often disappeared to 'freshen up' while the dining tables were moved to make way for a dance floor, Nick put a tearful Olga in a taxi. He'd spent nearly an hour on a sofa in the reception with her begging him not to ruin her life.

'Double whisky please,' he asked the barman weakly on his return back to the bar. He perched on a stool alongside Leila, who too had made the transition to hard liquor. 'What a day.'

'Thank God it's almost over and we can all get back to our lives.' Leila lifted up her tumbler and clinked it against Nick's. 'Cheers to never hearing the phrase "but it's *my* wedding" ever again. I swear I have it on repeat in my head.'

'Why let yourself get so involved though? She's not your sister. I managed to not get roped in.'

'I know, I'm weak and impressionable. But I'm working on changing that. Spending a whole evening stuffing sugared almonds into tiny pieces of netting only for 200 people to pick them up and proclaim, "I don't like almonds," has made me realise I need to be more assertive.'

'It would have been cool being on that table with the woman with the nut allergy.

They all had Haribo sweets instead. They lucked out.'

'Indeed they did.'

They both sat in silence, staring ahead into the mirror behind the optics. As the background lounge music turned into a very loud One Direction hit, Nick leant forward and banged his head hard on the bar three times. 'Leila, I swear to God, if we don't find a way to escape this hellhole in the next fifteen seconds, then this is officially the worst day of my life.'

'Come on then.'

She led him through the maze of corridors through a door marked Staff Only, past a couple of waitresses staring at their phones, and through the spotless lino-clad kitchens. Leila ducked into her parents' office to retrieve a key from the desk drawer and then pushed open a disabled fire exit door.

The hit of cool evening air with the lingering scent of salt water was a welcome respite from the stuffy bar and they both took long breaths in. 'I love the sea.' Nick's eyes were closed, his face slightly upturned to the sky.

'Me too. As much as I love living in London I do feel my shoulders dropping a few notches whenever I get back here.' Leila pulled Nick to the very edge of the driveway and parted some of the thick branches of an oak tree. 'Come and stand here, in this exact spot.' Leila moved a foot to the left so Nick could take her place. The whole town was laid out in front of them. The panorama took in the whole of the harbour below, across to the Castle and Naval College on the other side of the town. Down on the water you could see the lights from the passenger ferry's last journey across the river, taking tourists back to the waiting steam train. 'Isn't that view incredible? I've tried taking photos of it so many times but it never captures just how amazing it is. I've tried painting it too, but nothing does it justice.'

Nick smiled at Leila's unexpected burst of sentimentality. 'Where are you taking me now?'

'You'll see.'

CHAPTER 7

The harbour master waved Leila and Nick through onto the main jetty that led to the smaller pontoons gently bobbing above the water. It was only eight in the evening, and the start of dusk was in the air. On the back of every boat people were having dinner, or sharing a bottle of wine, stretched out on the ubiquitous striped benches that adorned every stern.

'Careful, it gets narrow here,' Leila said, as they reached Thomas and Judy's pride and joy, a ten-year old motor yacht called Hendricks. Thomas had lobbied Judy relentlessly throughout Leila's entire childhood for a boat, and as soon as she had left home Judy finally relented. There was something very special about being a boat owner, Judy had confided after the purchase, like a magical membership to an exclusive club. Judy had thrown herself into the role, replacing the small round buttons on her navy blazers with some that sported anchors, and developing a wardrobe mainly made up of navy and white stripes. If the new hobby had been golf, not boating, Leila was sure diamond sweaters and plus fours would have been the sartorial staple. One always needed to look the part, didn't one. But it did mean that this evening on the marina, the two of them stood out somewhat, with Leila in her bright coral bridesmaid dress, and Nick in his tails — he'd misplaced the hat, which would have cost him the deposit from the hire place.

Using the key she'd taken from her father's desk drawer, Leila unlocked the canopy and climbed on deck.

'Permission to climb aboard,' Nick said saluting.

'Permission granted,' Leila laughed, grabbing his hand and helping him step over the side.

'Nice digs.' He said looking around.

'It's only marginally smaller than my flat, and a tenth of the price. Come down here, I'll give you a tour.'

They descended the five steps into the cabin, and Leila opened a cupboard that concealed a fridge fully stocked with a variety of alcohol. 'Beer, wine, champagne, or shall we stick with the hard spirits?'

'Do you know what, a beer would be amazing.' Nick started opening some of the other cupboards. 'This place is like a tardis, it's brilliant!'

Leila nodded her head along the galley kitchen, as she clicked the top off the two bottles of beer, 'Look down there, there's the cabin.'

Nick opened the small door, and just beyond it was a big double bed in the bow of the boat, the mattress tapering to a point at the end. 'I love it! Do you know what?' He turned around and accepted the beer. 'I've never even been on a boat that wasn't a ferry or a canoe. This is awesome. I would totally live on this.'

'It gets well stinky in winter with the damp, but it's lovely in the summer. You would have to start wearing a sailor's hat and slip on deck shoes and swap your cigarettes for a pipe though, or you wouldn't be allowed in the marine club.'

'I don't want to be ostracised for being a landlubber.'

'See! You already know the lingo, you're halfway there!' Leila led Nick back outside, picking up two more bottles of beer and a packet of peanuts out of the fridge on the way. She lifted the top of the bench that ran along the back of the boat and pulled some cushions out, putting them on two of the chairs around the table. 'Have a seat.'

A couple of minutes passed. They were both happy to sit and drink their cold beer enjoying the last of the sunshine away from the oppressive humidity of the wedding's dance floor.

Nick finally broke the silence, which Leila was glad of. She'd started to feel uncharacteristically shy. 'So Lei, can I call you Lei?'

Leila nodded. No-one had called her Lei before. It was quite nice.

'What's your brother like? I've only met him twice before.'

'He's quite nice. A bit earnest and serious at times, but a decent bloke. He's quite focused.'

'On what?'

'Mainly work, and now your sister.'

Nick leaned back in his chair, 'Ah. My sister.'

'You both seem very . . .' Leila tried searching for a word that wouldn't offend him.

'Different? Polar opposites?' He chuckled. 'We are as different as it is possible to be. I'm not really sure why, it sort of gradually happened. Dad left when we were teenagers, he was much more like Lucy. Very serious. Mum has always been this creative free spirit type — she's a poet.'

'A poet? That's amazing.'

'It is quite cool. Well, it is when she's writing what it is she wants to write, the other times she's selling her soul and writing the verses in greetings cards, you know the ones that rhyme cherish with marriage and christening with glistening.'

Leila sighed. 'I think there's a certain amount of soul selling whatever job you're in, although hers does sound particularly horrific.'

'How did a girl from a Dartmouth hotel end up in London if you don't mind me asking? What's your story?'

Leila took another swig of her beer. 'It's not very exciting really. I'm the youngest of three. There's Tasha, the eldest one — I don't know if you met her, she was the other one in this hideous get up — then Marcus, your new brother-in-law, and then me. Mum and Dad really wanted one of us to stay and help run the hotel. They were desperate for one of us to go to college to do hotel management and then take over and let them basically drink gin on this boat for the rest of their lives. But Tasha went off to London, got herself married and pregnant, not necessarily in that order, and then Marcus left, and all their hopes were pinned on me, so it was a pretty rough time when I told them I wanted to study landscape architecture instead.'

'You're an architect? Me too. Although I do buildings. Wow, ok, carry on.'

'That's so funny, where do you work?'

'Hills and Faulkner? Just by Tower Bridge?'

Leila started laughing. 'That's hilarious, one of my friends that I studied with works there, Amanda Stratham?'

'I know Amanda, married to Paul in Engineering?'

'That's the one. Small world.'

'So where do you work?'

'Halliday and Associates. Up in Notting Hill?'

'I applied for their graduate scheme, but got turned down.'

'What year was this?'

'2004, straight after graduation, why?'

Leila smiled. 'Would you still keep drinking beer with me if I told you I got it instead of you?'

'You're kidding me! This is insane. Wow. Ok, as we're almost related now and I am on your parents' boat drinking their beer, I guess I'll have to be nice to you, but I'm not pleased.'

'That's very generous of you.' Leila leant

her beer bottle across the table, 'A toast. To winners and losers.'

He clinked his bottle against hers laughing. 'I like you Leila. You're funny.'

'I like you too Nick.'

She didn't imagine it. A look passed between them that said exactly the same as what they'd just voiced out loud but the look was weighted with a lot more than friendly banter. This wasn't supposed to happen. She was three months into the year, she wasn't allowed to give and receive these kind of looks with nine months still to go.

'I'm a bit hungry,' she said, breaking the pause. 'I'm sure Mum and Dad have some kind of pasta sauce in the cupboard, or you could nip across the road to pick up some chips?'

Nick raised one eyebrow. '*I* could nip across the road?'

She nodded. 'It would be the most gentlemanly thing to do in the circumstances. I am, after all, dressed like a prostitute fairy.'

Nick stood up and took his wallet from the inside pocket of the jacket that he'd slung on the back of his chair. 'Salt and vinegar?'

'Lots of both please. And as many ketchup sachets as you can carry.'

'Girl after my own heart. Back in a min.'

Leila watched him getting smaller down the jetty and then ran inside to the toilet. She'd been bursting for a wee but didn't want to go when he was here because the flush made the most god-awful sound and it would ruin whatever moment was happening. But then, she thought as she frantically pulled her fingers through her short crop and pinched her cheeks to give them some colour, she shouldn't care anyway. She was off men. Completely chaste. Not interested in the slightest. If only he wasn't absolutely gorgeous in a rugged musician sort of way. With his dark messy hair that flicked over his collar, tattooed forearms and stubble, Nick was absolutely her ideal type, which was ironically the opposite of all the public school rugby players she seemed to attract. And an architect as well, it was just too perfect. Rather, it would have been had she not set herself up as a feminist icon for single women everywhere.

She'd just managed to get two more beers and arrange herself in her chair — relaxed but not lounging; contemplative but not aloof — when he came into sight down the floating walkway.

'Your chips m'lady,' he said, passing the warm wrapped parcel to her before vaulting over the side of the boat.

'You are a legend, thank you.'

The faint strains of country music could be heard from the boat on one side of them, and some Beatles from the other. Leila caught Nick's eye and smiled as he said, 'It's a step up from the wedding DJ's playlist at least.'

'I like it,' she replied. 'It's like Dolly Parton is doing a duet with John Lennon.'

As the songs changed and the chips were eaten, more bottles were fetched and the light completely faded, they shared stories and laughed into the night. At some point in the evening Nick had given Leila his jacket, and she inhaled a heady combination of aftershave and tobacco every time she breathed in. She'd moved the other two chairs closer to them, so they both had their feet up on the seats opposite them. Most of their neighbours on the marina had either pulled down the canvas roofs and walked back to their waiting cars and houses, or some had retreated into the downstairs cabins and a warm glow emitted from behind the curtains on the small portholes.

'There's something very romantic about the sea isn't there?' Nick said, looking wistfully across the water.

'Is that a line? Because it sounded like a line.'

He smiled. 'Would you want it to be a line? If it was a line?'

This was it, this was the crossroads where she could continue the evening down the wonderful path it had been going down, or she could stop it and they could go back to the wedding and pretend that they hadn't just met their soulmate. And she could bang her head against the wall for the rest of the night.

'I think I'd like it to be a line.'

Nick slowly leant over the table and tilted her chin up so her lips met his. He parted her lips with his tongue and his hand moved up to the back of her head. Leila leant in and rested her hand on his leg. When they finally broke away they were both smiling.

'We might be more comfortable in the cabin,' she heard herself say. Three months Leila. You've done so well for three months.

But for the next hour and a half she managed to keep any sort of feelings of guilt or self-loathing at bay. In fact, it was remarkably easy to not think of very much at all.

Despite how well acquainted they were with each other, considering the positions they'd managed to contort themselves into in the tiny cabin just moments before, there was now an uncomfortable silence walking back up the hill to the hotel. Nick had tried to take Leila's hand, but she'd put it firmly in her pocket. He'd then casually shoulder-barged her after making a joke, but she remained passive and distant.

'Look,' she offered finally, as the hotel came into view. 'There's something you should know.'

They kept walking, but their pace had slowed. 'You're married.'

'No.'

'But you are with someone?'

'Absolutely not.'

'You have a weird disease that you should have told me about before and now it's very probable that I have it too.'

'Oh my goodness, just listen to me!' Leila snapped. 'I am on a man ban.'

'You're on a what now?'

'A man ban. I'm celibate.'

'No you're not.'

'Well, no, technically for the last ninety minutes I have very much not been celibate, but for three months before that and for nine months from now on, I will be.'

'Oh.'

'Yes. Oh.'

'And is this a legally-binding arrangement, or can it be broken again?'

'It is ethically binding, which is worse.

Look, you're lovely, and I've had a brilliant evening, which is remarkable as I was fully expecting today to rank as one of the worst days of my life, but you turned it around.'

'As did you for me,' Nick added.

'But, the fact remains that I am monumentally rubbish at dating, like beyond rubbish. And after my last disaster that saw me with chronic diarrhoea on a train in India chasing my boyfriend halfway across the world only to find him holed up in a hotel room with a naked blonde —'

'Ouch.'

'Yes, ouch. So I decided that I need to have a year off men. And it was going so well until you turned up looking so stubbly and gorgeous and now I feel like a huge failure, and no-one thought I would stick it out. I have so much riding on me doing this, my reputation, the community I've set up, all the bets, which I know shouldn't be a factor but to pay out on them would absolutely cripple me, but all my family and friends are expecting me to fail, and I'm not even halfway through and look at me. I know I'm babbling but I can't help it.'

'Look Lei. No-one but us knows about what just happened. I can't pretend I'm not disappointed to not see you again, as I think you're pretty awesome, but if doing this single thing is so important to you, then let's chalk tonight up to drunkenness and heightened emotions, and shake hands and walk back into the hotel separately.'

Leila pouted, and not intentionally. She was genuinely gutted. 'I'm sorry.'

'Don't be. I'm sorry my stubble made you fall off the wagon.'

She smiled. 'Can we exchange the handshake for a hug?'

Nick wrapped his arms around her, and they stayed like that for what seemed like ages.

'Ok then, I'll go in first. Bye Nick.' Leila gave him a rueful look and started to walk away.

'Um, Leila.'

She turned back eagerly.

'You'll want to give me my jacket back or it might give the game away.'

The hotel was renowned for its breakfasts, and the spread didn't disappoint. Keen cruising enthusiasts, Thomas and Judy had brought the Royal Caribbean approach to the first meal of the day, with a pancake and waffle station set up next to a cooked-to-order omelette table, and heaving bowls of fruit salad sat alongside platters of cheese and ham. Dispensers of four different juices added colour to the bread and pastries display, as the wedding guests ambled along, exclaiming variations of 'this is amazing,' as they swapped their usual cornflakes for something more exciting.

'Darling! Over here!' Judy was half standing out of her seat waving at Leila, who had just entered the dining room. Judy was sat with Stephanie, at a window table overlooking the windswept terrace. The weather had turned during the night and drizzle relentlessly splattered the glass.

'Hi Mum, Stephanie, good sleep?' Leila said as she picked up her napkin and sat down opposite them.

'I slept like a baby,' Judy replied, as Stephanie nodded in agreement. 'You?'

'Yes, really good. Must have been all the dancing.' After Leila had snuck back into the hotel, she had slipped in amongst the throng on the dance floor jumping up and down to *Come on Eileen* and immediately joined in. Marcus had put his arm around her and they bounced through the rest of the song together, Leila making sure that everyone that should see her there had. She assumed that Nick played a different tactic and went straight to bed as she didn't see him again that evening. But she could see him now, heading straight for their table, and irritatingly he was every bit as gorgeous as he had been last night.

'Morning Mum,' he said, giving Stephanie a kiss on her cheek and sitting down opposite her, on the chair next to Leila. 'Morning. Leila isn't it?' he said, offering his hand for her to shake.

'Yes, that's right. Mum, this is Lucy's brother, Nick, he was on my table yesterday.' And on your boat, and on your bed. 'Nick, this is my mum, Judy.'

They shook hands over the table. 'Lovely wedding wasn't it?' Judy asked rhetorically. As if anyone would tell the mother of the groom otherwise.

'Lovely,' the rest of them all nodded.

'We're going to have a barbecue later, if the weather clears up, and you're very welcome to stay for it Nick. I've convinced your mum to stay for another night and go back in the morning instead, can I tempt you?'

'That's very kind of you Judy, but I have to be at work in London in the morning, so I'm going to leave soon after breakfast I'm afraid.'

'Leila's going back on the train then too, aren't you love — why don't you get on the same one? That'll be nice company for you both. Dad will drop you to the station at the same time then.' Judy was so transparent. She was enraptured by Nick the second his six foot two frame cast a shadow over the table, and hearing him talk so politely to her had elevated him into potential son-in-law territory. 'Stephanie was just telling me you're an architect as well, I'm sure you two will have lots to talk about. Don't you think so Stephanie?'

'Oh, yes Judy, so much in common.' Stephanie was eagerly nodding. Nick had spoken last night of his frustration that his mum and sister kept trying to marry him off at least twice a month to different girls, giving poor women like Olga such a strong sense of false hope. As Leila had seen first-hand his mum Whatsapping wedding dresses to a girl he'd had three dates with, she thought he definitely had a valid reason for his exasperation.

Leila shrugged. 'I'm booked on the 10.54 from Newton Abbott, if you want to join?'

Nick's head gave a slight movement, but it was difficult to see if it was a nod or a shake. She desperately wanted him to say yes, while fervently hoping he said no.

'Could do.'

Judy clapped her hands together. 'Wonderful, I'll go and tell Thomas.'

■ ■ ■ ■

They'd managed to spend the first half hour of the three-hour journey not talking, mainly because they were both engrossed in the track-suited couple directly opposite them kissing each other with such ferocious force it made their seats shake. When the couple disembarked at Exeter they both looked at each other in shocked horror.

'Well that makes my performance last night look a bit lacklustre. I apologise.' Nick ventured.

Leila started laughing into her hands. 'Oh my God!'

They were still shaking with giggles when the buffet trolley came round and Nick bought them both a couple of coffees. The train was quiet and they'd managed to score themselves a table, so they both took out their laptops and started tapping at their keyboards.

Leila imagined he was finalising the details for an orphanage in Cambodia or some other worthy community project she'd created for him in her head.

'Whatcha doing?' he said, catching her staring at him over her screen.

'Updating my blog.'

'Can I see it?'

'Sure.' She turned her screen around to face him. He scrolled through the site and clicked onto the Facebook page, and gave a low whistle. 'Wow, you weren't kidding when you said you were taking this seriously. You're a one-woman celibacy guru!'

'Hardly. To be honest, it's sort of spiralling a bit too fast. I got two sponsors last week —' she motioned to the two banners that ran vertically and horizontally along the edge of the webpage, one from the financial planning firm and one from an alcohol company, 'and they're paying me quite a nice amount to post things, and they are sponsoring a few events and workshops we've got planned. And more people are becoming members every day — it's becoming a full-time job to sift through the normal women from the weirdo trolls looking to infiltrate a site full of single women. And you wouldn't believe the amount of money I've been offered from dating agencies for my database, as if I would sell out like that! I take this really seriously.' She suddenly realised the irony of what she'd just said and to whom she'd said it to, and blushed.

Nick raised one eyebrow, 'Evidently. No-one takes celibacy more seriously than you do.'

'Shut up.'

He pursed his lips together in a smile and swung the laptop back round to face her. 'I'm really impressed. You've put a lot of effort into that, it's cool.'

'Thank you. Now ignore me while I write a two-faced post filled with lies about how great I'm feeling about choosing this life path.'

CHAPTER 8

Lucy

It was so bizarre that you could set your watch by the afternoon rainstorm. One minute you'd be lying next to the pool topping up your factor 30, the next the lifeguards would be wandering around the sunloungers that were still bathed in glorious sunlight warning everyone to start packing up their things and to head inside within ten minutes. Lucy had never heard rain like it either, it quite literally pelted down, big drops that relentlessly lashed the ground for a good two hours before vanishing and the sun reappearing over the Balinese paddy fields next to their hotel.

Marcus had remarked on their first day that it was perfect weather for honeymooners like them, meaning that they had an excuse to duck back to their room for a couple of hours in the afternoon and no-one would bat an eyelid. She told him not to be so vulgar, but secretly agreed with him. These afternoons holed up in their rustic Indonesian bedroom had become her favourite part of the day. After they would take turns in the walk-in shower, meticulously washing off the pool's chlorine and sun lotion, they'd spend twenty minutes or so making love. Marcus was extraordinarily gentle in that department. Then, still wearing the matching batik dressing gowns provided by the hotel, they would make a weak white wine spritzer for her, and a shandy using the local Bintang beer for him and set up the scrabble board.

'I have six vowels,' Marcus announced. 'Six.'

'What's your consonant?'

'Z.'

'Oh, that is very bad luck.'

They both stared at the board glumly. Lucy then pointed to the board, 'Look, if you use the r in quixotry, you can put zoaria down. And z will be on a triple letter.'

'Zoaria! Of course, that's the organism cluster thing isn't it?'

'Yes! Exactly!'

'Thanks darling.'

'You're welcome. Fancy a top up?'

And so the afternoons went on, a blissful lull in a blissful honeymoon. They ate meals served on banana leaves, wandered hand in hand through temples, counted geckos on their balcony ceiling, they even did a tandem parasail, all the while luxuriating in the fact that for both of them the hunt for a partner was over. The relief was palpable. Finding a suitable spouse had been all-consuming for Lucy and loitering somewhere near the top of a to-do list for Marcus, and now they could start the rest of their lives.

The afternoon rain was still making its monotonous drumming sound as the sun set on their last day, necessitating a rain-soaked dash to the bar for their evening sun-downers. Lucy giggled as she scrunched the water out of her hair. 'Well, I'm pleased I spent all that time blow-drying my hair tonight!'

'Me too,' Marcus replied running his fingers through his thinning hair. Lucy laughed and put her arm through his, which made his smile even bigger. He thought that Lucy looked beautiful whether she spent half an hour standing in front of a mirror with a blow dryer, or with soaking wet hair dripping onto her creased clothes like now. The fact that she hadn't insisted on a head-scarf or an immediate return to the proxim-ity of her hair products and a plug point suggested that this holiday had done wonders for her relaxation levels.

This morning was also the first time in their entire relationship that she hadn't slipped out of bed when she thought he was still sleeping to put her make-up on. Despite growing up with two sisters, the intricacies of cosmetics had passed Marcus by, and so it didn't occur to him that Lucy was even doing that until he heard the rustling of her make-up bag before she gently eased herself back under the covers and pretended to sleep. He didn't know how to tell her that she didn't need to do that. That she was his wife now, and he would love her for the rest of his life, regardless of whether she had that black stuff that goes over eyelashes and that beige cream thing that goes over faces.

'I don't really want to go home,' Lucy said softly later that evening as they sat opposite each other at the poolside restaurant. The air was fresh and clean after the rain and the dark sky was pinpricked with hundreds of stars.

'All good things come to an end,' replied Marcus.

'I know that. It's not like we can live here forever is it?'

Marcus popped an olive in his mouth. 'I bet there's a pile of papers on my desk so high that it resembles the Leaning Tower of

Pisa. Hopefully David will realise quite how indispensable I am after doing without me for a fortnight.'

'Of course you're indispensable, you're practically running that company Marky.' Lucy sighed. 'I'm a bit envious of you, now that the wedding's over I'm worried I'll feel a bit lost and purposeless.'

'If you really feel like that you could ask for your old job back, although there's no reason to money-wise.'

Lucy crinkled her nose, 'Oh God no, I don't want to put on corporate events any more. I just feel it's time for a new project or something.' *Like a baby,* she thought but didn't say. It's not really the type of thing you could blurt out over a nice dinner.

It hadn't been her idea not to consummate their relationship before their wedding; Marcus had suggested it and she was more than happy to go along with it. She'd never been particularly active in that department, finding the whole process just a bit too messy and sweaty, and because she'd written off most men before getting to that stage in a relationship, she'd never attributed much importance to it before. Marcus's reasoning for their abstinence was that it would make their wedding night so much more special. And it did. But as the physical side had not been fully operational, they'd also never had the chat about how they were going to navigate the issue of contraception. Even the word was ugly. She was so pleased they'd never said it out loud, she'd be mortified and Marcus would probably spontaneously combust with embarrassment. So Lucy had no choice but to assume that Marcus was entirely on the same page as her as far as that was concerned. They were married now. It was natural that a mini-Marcus-and-Lucy would follow. Completely natural. She might even be pregnant now. That's why the wedding date was so important, it was exactly three days before her ovulation, so the chances were, at that very moment, as she breathed in the Balinese night air, a tiny life was starting inside her.

CHAPTER 9

Tasha

It was almost a carbon copy of the last time. You would have thought Alex would have known his wife could spot the signs a mile off by now. If he was a little bit brighter he'd have changed the pattern, tried to throw her off course, or at least made a cursory attempt to conceal it.

The untrained eye might put his jauntier walk, increased affection and unprompted gifts down to an attentive husband merely being in a good mood and in love with his wife. To Tasha, these things meant something very different.

The first couple of times she couldn't bring herself to even break the seal on the new perfume, or to wear the diamond pendant he guiltily gave her. She instinctively knew that each spritz of the scent would smell of nothing but betrayal and that she'd feel strangled by the gold chain

131

around her neck. Was it so awful, she wondered, that this morning she'd put the bracelet he'd given her straight on, and that her first thought was that the milky opals really highlighted her tan?

Fifteen years of this meant that resignation had replaced resentment, which she knew didn't *sound* healthy, but it was fine. Tasha felt embarrassed when she thought back to the histrionics that had followed her finding out about his first affair shortly after they'd had Mia. She'd sat sobbing on the stairs while he concocted a web of lies and a chain of excuses.

He hated it when she used to cry, so she didn't any more. That's what his ex-wife did when she found out about Tasha and she wouldn't want to be like her. Alex left *her.* Anyway, apparently Tasha was funnier than Annie, his first wife, and prettier, and more emotionally stable, whatever that meant. She was also incredible in bed, the best he'd ever had. She was perfect. And then he met Janine. And then she was. Until he met Anais and she took up the ideal woman baton. Tasha didn't even know the name of this one. Once upon a time she would have asked. She would have wanted to know. Now, she knew it didn't make a jot of difference, it was just consonants and vowels.

Of course she experienced the familiar jolt of sour recognition when the phone went dead for the third time this week. She wasn't completely numb to it. But she also didn't see what there was to be gained from being hysterical about it. She sprayed the new perfume on her pulse point and raised her wrist to her nose. This one's actually really nice, she thought, turning the bottle to read the label: *Gucci's Guilty.* She couldn't help but smile. You couldn't make this shit up.

'We need a dog.'

'We do not need a dog. Found it!' Tasha crawled out from under the breakfast table, crumbs sticking to her knees, jubilantly holding up a small wellington boot. 'Oscar, I've got it here, come now, we're late.'

'A Labrador. A brown one.'

'They're called chocolate, and it's massively clichéd. Oscar! Now! Mia, did you pack the library book in your bag, it's library day. Oscar! I am not going to tell you again!'

'Surely that's what he wants?' Alex chortled behind the paper. 'How about a spaniel? Or is that clichéd as well?'

133

'It's a moot point is what it is because we're not getting a dog. And I could really do with a bit of help here please. OSCAR! Oh, there you are, here's your boot. Can you put your cereal bowl in the sink please, it's not going to take itself there, is it? Where's Talia? She was just here. Jesus people, it's quarter to nine already.'

'The ones with the big eyes and floppy ears, what are they called?'

'It's called put your paper down and help your wife goddammit.'

'Cocker.'

'What?' Tasha swivelled quickly round, one arm already in her coat, the other reaching round the back for the other sleeve.

'It's called a cocker spaniel. The kids would love it. We should get one of them.' Alex got up from the kitchen chair, where he'd been merrily sat savouring his breakfast, and began humming as he swilled out his coffee cup and placed it on the drying rack before kissing the top of her head. 'I'll take the kids to school, love, you take a load off. I'm going in late today anyway. Mmm, is that the new perfume I got you? Smells delicious.'

And just like that, the house was at peace.

Tasha made herself another cup of green tea and took it into her study. Patricia-the-

134

designer had vetoed her desire for burgundy walls, calling the idea uncouth. So on the day of the big reveal last year she opened the door to her sanctuary to be faced with green grey walls called *Borrowed Light*. She could have changed it, of course she could, but Alex would have looked so despondent about his surprise being rebuked. So instead she'd tried to cover as much of the insipid noncolour as possible with big prints of forests and ocean scenes. Hardly the character-filled art that adorned the walls of her sister's cosy basement flat, or the achingly expensive reproductions of old masters that Marcus would gladly swap his credit card details for, but it did the job.

Tasha took a sip of her tea and quickly flicked through her diary. It was filled with clients and workshops. Most of her friends complained relentlessly about not having enough downtime. They were always rushing about meeting friends for coffee, picking up something for the house at a little-known antiques place or the right ballet shoes for little Araminta or going to the gym.

A couple of years ago Alex had suggested that she find herself a little part-time job or something, she was sure he didn't mean to sound so condescending, but it's not as if they needed the money. But she also knew she needed to fill her time with something other than errands for the house or the kids or she'd go mad. So she'd signed up for her first kinesiology course and she was hooked. There was something very liberating about taking control of your own energy field. Of switching your body and mind on and accepting yourself completely. Maybe that's why this latest affair had just made her sigh, rather than reach for the nearest thing to hurl at his head like she would have done in the early days.

She didn't have anyone to confide in about this latest indiscretion, she couldn't. At the start she'd candidly spoken to a friend or two, who she then saw completely alter their behaviour towards Alex at dinners or events — giving him the cold-shoulder and frosty stares. She didn't need other people's judgement on the state of her marriage. There's no way she could have ever told Leila either, she was vocal enough about Tasha being his mistress back then, there's no way that her little sister would be able to be objective about this latest affair. No-one would understand why she was sitting there calmly organising her diary and not packing his belongings into a holdall and changing the locks.

If she was being completely honest, in the times of his faithfulness she found keeping up with him in the bedroom really tiring. If her friends were to be believed, once a week was considered good going for a couple married as long as they had been, but Alex was insatiable. At least when he had a girlfriend she was relieved from the nightly acrobatics. Oh God, she groaned, that did sound as awful as she thought it did.

Tasha was interrupted from her guilt at not feeling what she was supposed to be feeling by the phone ringing in the hallway.

'I've had a bit of a brainwave,' said her sister at the other end of the line. 'Well, actually, it was Marcus's brainwave, but I need your help.'

'That sounds intriguing . . .'

'Ok, you know the last couple of events have been really successful? Well I wanted to take it up a notch and organise a retreat for single women — a weekend away at Mum and Dad's hotel — and I want to have lots of different speakers and workshops and experts and I don't really have a clue how to put it all together, and work is really busy, and so I wondered if I can hire you as the event manager to organise it?'

'That's a great idea Leila, but I wouldn't have a clue about how to put on an event.

But I can certainly take one or two of the workshops, and I've recently met a couple of amazing women doing colour therapy and a brilliant life coach that completely sorted by friend Bev out — do you remember Bev?'

Leila answered in the affirmative, and then said, 'And the best news is I can pay you the going rate this time. Ok, do you have any suggestions who I can tap up to help me with the logistics of this?'

'You're not going to like it, but I have the perfect person.'

'Who?' Leila answered excitedly.

'Our new sister-in-law.' Tasha started speaking louder to drown out Leila's indignant shouts. 'Think about it Leila, she was in events, they're back from their honeymoon, she's got literally nothing going on with her life at the moment and she's a perfectionist, every i would be dotted and every t crossed.'

'And every hair on my head would turn grey and every modicum of sanity I still own would be instantly dissolved.'

'Every bride gets a little crazy in the run up to their wedding, organising your event would be entirely different. Give her a call next week when she's back, or meet up with them for dinner, and ask her then? If it was

Marcus's idea in the first place you should ask her in front of him and then she can't say no.'

'Oh God, dinner with Marcus and Lucy? Can't you and Alex come along too?'

Tasha hesitated. Even though she was accepting of Alex's current situation, she didn't know if there might be nuances of their behaviour together that Leila would pick up on. Her sister knew her better than anybody, which was ironic as she didn't know this side of her at all. 'Ok, cool, how about two weeks on Saturday? I'll tell Alex to keep it free.' Then Tasha added a sentence that made Leila freeze. 'Why don't we make it a proper sibling dinner to welcome them back, and invite Lucy's brother along too — what was his name? Mick?'

'Nick,' Leila said far too quickly. 'I mean, I think it was Nick. We were sat together at the dinner.'

'Yes, I saw you two huddled together early on in the evening before you disappeared for a while.'

'We weren't huddled, and I didn't disappear, I was dancing most of the night! And, for your information,' Leila's voice had taken on a haughty tone, 'We were talking shop, he's an architect too, so we were sharing resources. That is all.' Sharing resources,

Leila thought, that's a good one. 'And I don't think he's around, he works away a lot. And even if he was here I wouldn't know how to get in touch with him. So I think it's a no-go.'

'I think he gave his card to Alex actually because he was talking to him at the church and he was interested in investing in some stocks. I'll ask him when he gets in.'

'But like I say, there's probably no point, he'll be away,' Leila said.

'But we can check.'

Leila knew if she remonstrated any more her sister would start to get suspicious, so remained silent. 'Ok, let me know and I'll book somewhere.' Then she added disingenuously, 'More the merrier.'

I've been feeling a little wistful recently. I have been searching for the right word and wistful does the job. I'm not sad, or down or lonely, but I do find myself a bit more reflective than usual. But the stupid thing is, I'm not wistful for the past, for a relationship I had or a version of myself that I was, because I want to leave all that behind. But I'm feeling wistful for a parallel life that I'm starting to hanker for. A parallel life where the soup I make feeds two people at one sitting, not me for dinner and me again for lunch the next day. A parallel life where I don't have to press the half-full button on the washing machine because there's not enough dirty clothes to fill it. I don't need someone to accompany me to the cinema or theatre because I have amazing friends who are very able and willing plus ones, but it's these little small everyday tasks, like soup-making and laundry that reinforce the fact that I'm alone. So, yes, today I am wistful.

Leila closed her laptop screen and sat back against her sofa. Ever since Nick and her had exchanged a stiff hug and a rueful farewell smile at Paddington when they went their separate ways she couldn't stop thinking about him. Her boss even commented on it today as he said she seemed distracted. That's another good word. *Distracted.*

Maybe her mum was right, perhaps she just didn't have the willpower or strength of character to see something through. Maybe celibacy was just like the violin, ice skating, veganism, boot camp, Spanish, watercolour painting and salsa. But this time there was more at stake. She hadn't created a community of fiddlers or vegans or artists that depended on her to fly the flag for them.

There wasn't a group of ardent salsa dancers standing by in their ruffled skirts that would be disappointed and feel let down by her change of mind.

Leila opened her laptop again and deleted the post she'd just written. She wasn't supposed to be feeling like this.

The restaurant Leila had booked was a new gastronomic molecular place where a roast dinner was condensed into jelly form and every dish had a wisp of foam dancing on top of it. Resembling a science laboratory more than a conventional restaurant, the double height room had stainless steel tables and all around them diners were being served up three-Michelin starred fare in test tubes and petri dishes. Looking at the menu was proving to be a traumatic experience for Marcus, whose normal idea of experimental was Dijon mustard instead of Colman's with his steak.

'What the heck is parmesan air?' he asked the very patient waiter who had already been grilled on the intricacies of liquid lamb and foie gras frost.

'We can go to TGI's next door if you prefer Marcus?' Nick said as soon as the waiter had bid a hasty retreat. 'Our drinks haven't arrived yet. Seriously, if it's all a bit too weird for you, we can leg it before they even notice.'

'No we can't!' Lucy hissed to her brother. 'What would they think? Anyway, there's a waiting list as long as your arm to get in here, God knows how you managed to get us in Leila, I think it's all rather exciting! I'm going to have the invisible ravioli.'

'I'm going to stop at McDonald's on the way home,' replied Marcus sardonically.

Lucy kicked him under the table. 'Lighten up. Look, they've got wagyu, you love that.'

'I love it when it's a ten ounce lump of bloody meat, not when it comes in foam form,' Marcus grumpily retorted.

When Tasha had called Nick a few days before and invited him to this dinner he said yes straightaway. He hadn't been able to get Leila out of his mind and was desperate to see her again. It was bizarre, she was the complete opposite to his normal type, but then maybe that was a good thing. His friends always teased him for dating a conveyor belt of tall willowy blondes, and Leila with her short dark hair, and standing at least a foot shorter than him, was the absolute opposite of every woman he'd ever dated and yet there was something about her that was just compelling. She was spiky and neurotic and made him laugh. When he

143

walked into the restaurant and saw her he felt his heart hammer in his chest, something that never happened with Olga or indeed any of his ex-girlfriends. He looked up again and caught her eye over their menus. Leila looked down, embarrassed.

Lucy had moved her chair closer to Marcus and was running her finger down the main dishes on his menu, pointing out options she knew he'd like.

'Sea-bass?' Lucy prompted.

'It's proceeded by the word "powdered", so no.'

She tried again, 'Lamb shank?'

'Emulsion. Lamb shank emulsion. As in stuff you paint the walls with. Next!'

Leila could tell Marcus was putting a little bit of his affront on for effect, his eyes had taken on his familiar twinkle and he gave his sister a little wink as he continued to wind up his new wife who sighed smiling. 'You, Marcus, are infuriating.' His inability to embrace spontaneity had become a standing joke in their family, and he often played on this for comedic effect, which it seemed Lucy was beginning to learn. She was determined to successfully complete the order though. 'Pork Confit?'

'It says that it's served in a martini glass.'

'Yes, yes it does.' Notes of exasperation

144

were beginning to seep into Lucy's voice. 'And that's a problem why?'

'Because it's pig meat. Served in a cocktail glass. That's weird.' Marcus scrunched up his nose for added emphasis. Leila bit her lip trying not to laugh.

Tasha broke off from whispering to Alex and said, 'You have to choose the food Marcus, not the way it's presented. Come on, we're all starving here, just pick one for goodness sake.'

'And you think eating flavoured air is going to fill you up? How much is this costing anyway?' The menu didn't have any prices on it, a red flag to Marcus if ever there was one.

'It's a set price, and anyway, it's on me, I've just got a fabulous new client that got confirmed when you guys were away, so we're celebrating,' Leila said.

Nick leaned forward in his seat. 'That's amazing Lei, was it the museum or the children's centre?'

'Museum.' Leila looked round the table to explain more, while trying to ignore the effect that him calling her Lei was having on her insides. 'We pitched my designs to the Honeywell Museum — they're doing a massive renovation on all their grounds, and they've accepted my proposal! So we're turning fifteen acres into interactive gardens, with lots of hidden activity areas and sculptural gardens with sensory activities for children and adults with learning difficulties. It's going to be lovely, I'm really excited about it.'

'Wasn't it the Honeywell Museum you did a proposal for too Nick?' Lucy asked, vaguely remembering the blueprints that were cluttering up his dining table when she visited his flat before the wedding. It was annoying, his table would have been perfect for her to practise her table settings on, but he had refused point blank to clear the plans for her to lay out her napkin samples.

'Yeah, they wanted to make some structural changes inside too, but that's on hold at the moment while they get the outside done first, that's why I suggested that Leila go for it when we met at the wedding. That's brilliant news Leila, well done.' He raised his glass and they all clinked theirs together.

The Honeywell Museum would be Leila's biggest job yet. When Nick had tipped her off about the museum also needing landscaping, she'd tried to keep her excitement in check, but failed spectacularly, spending far longer than she should have done on the speculative proposal. Her company had been up against six other landscape architects and couldn't believe it when she'd got the call to say they'd won it. Leila thought it was a shame that Nick wouldn't be working on the same project at the same time, but then maybe that was very much for the best. It had been four weeks since the wedding and in that time she'd managed to concoct an image of him in her head that was as far removed from the reality in front of her as it was possible to be. In her head he'd become portly, acne-ridden, spat when he talked, had visible nose and ear hair — it was so annoying that he was as gorgeous as she remembered; it would make forgetting him again so much more difficult.

'Leila, don't you have something to ask Lucy?' Tasha said, nudging her as the waiter cleared their tiny amuse bouche starters away.

Leila inwardly groaned, she was hoping she wouldn't need to bring this up in front of Nick. Talking about her celibacy just highlighted her lack of willpower and dramatic lapse of focus on board the boat. She gave him a quick look before talking. Damn it, he was being very attentive. As were four other pairs of eyes around the table, apart from Alex who kept checking his phone, which was the height of rudeness.

'Um, well, it was Marcus really that gave me the idea, but I have a couple of new sponsors for the site who are keen on me doing an event of some kind, with workshops and speakers and bill it as some kind of wellness retreat for single women.' At this Leila paused and snuck a quick glance at Nick to see if he was going to contradict her or laugh or roll his eyes, or do something else horrific and embarrassing that would let everyone else know that she was a fraud. But he was just staring at her with a supportive smile on his face. 'And I spoke to Mum and Dad and their Autumn bookings are very slow, so I thought I'd kill two birds with one stone, which is a horrible phrase because I like animals and certainly don't want to kill them, even birds, which aren't actually animals anyway.' *Shut up, you're babbling.* 'So I want to do this weekend away at the hotel and organise different events within the event, and I've got no bloody clue how to do it. And I thought that you, Lucy, might be able to help me?'

Her monologue was exhausting, and no-one was talking. Why was no-one talking?

'Lucy sweetheart, you were just saying in Bali that you needed another project, this would be perfect,' Marcus said, before turning back to Leila. 'How much are you going to pay her?'

'Um, I haven't really thought about it, I don't know how much to charge for the tickets, or how much to give Mum and Dad, and the speakers. This is what I need help with, this isn't my forte at all.'

'So, if I did this I could choose my own fee?' Lucy said, her interest piqued.

'That's not what Leila said though, is it?' Nick said, voicing Leila's own thoughts out loud. 'She just wants your help and advice, not to fund your entire Christmas shopping.' Leila could have kissed him right there.

'I'd have to work out my daily rate.'

'Good God woman, what else would you be doing with your day? Leila's your sister-in-law now, and she's asking you for a bit of advice because this is what you've spent years doing, surely you can give her some pointers without giving her a bill at the end of it?'

'Nick, this is none of your business,' Lucy said, physically turning her back to him and facing Leila square on. 'It sounds really interesting Leila, let's make a date this week where you come over to mine and we talk it through.'

Or you could come over to mine, Leila thought. It wasn't as though Lucy couldn't afford the time or the money schlepping

149

across London on public transport, but of course she said none of this, gushing instead, 'Thanks so much Lucy, that would be brilliant.'

The rest of the evening passed in a whirl of flavoured air, copious bottles of wine and fun, noisy chat. At one point Leila's foot brushed Nick's under the table and an electric current passed between them making them both lock eyes in surprise. A smile played on Nick's lips and Leila could feel herself blush. This was very inconvenient.

CHAPTER 10

Although the summer terrace was the hotel's major draw for guests, it was the colder months when Leila really loved being back in Dartmouth. The oak-panelled drawing room with its deep inglenook fireplace crackling with flames was both cosy and grand at the same time and everyone that came for the Well Woman weekend in the first week of November said variations of the same. Most of them were from cities and Judy and Thomas had nailed the 'country retreat' feel, even down to studded leather sofas, thick plaid curtains and wooden stag heads on the wall.

The weekend itself couldn't have gone better. Lucy had excelled herself, thinking of everything from an afternoon tea welcome on the Friday afternoon right down to little gift sets in each of the bedrooms containing upmarket cosmetics and the latest books by each of the speakers. The best bit was, pretty much everything was bartered off with the sponsors so it hadn't cost a penny. Leila and Lucy had spent many evenings and countless email conversations batting ideas back and forth for the weekend's agenda. It was important, Leila said, that the women didn't feel as though they were being preached to, or in any way belittled or seen as lonely spinsters. Whereas Lucy wanted to do as much as possible for as little as possible.

Leila wanted to devise a fun and varied weekend where workshops were blended with socialising, while Lucy wanted some pampering and relaxation thrown in for good measure, and the combination worked brilliantly. A nail business in Exeter had set up a mini salon in the hotel's sun lounge, with big copper bowls placed on the floor in front of the armchairs for express pedicures, and a few more therapists were on hand for neck and shoulder massages. Next door in the library, a roll call of eminent local and London-based speakers were giving talks throughout the day. That was where Tasha's little black book had proved invaluable. Most of the experts were friends of hers, from her numerous courses; a colour-therapist, a sound energy consultant, and a positive life-affirming life coach. Interspersed with these were women specialising in kinesiology, Reiki and meditation.

One of the larger meeting rooms had been completely taken over by a scene Blue Peter presenters would have salivated over. Sticky-back plastic, swathes of ribbons, beads, paint and magazine cuttings littered every table and most of the floor as women set about creating their visualisation boards. The idea was to think about the life you wanted, and to fill the board with the inspiration you'd need to achieve it. Tasha insisted that this was one activity the three of them were not sitting out. 'Surely we need all the help we can get in finding the path we're meant to be on?' she'd said to them convincingly at lunch. So they'd spent a couple of hours indulging their inner child and cut and glued and stuck until three blank canvases were crammed with pictures, messages and life-affirming quotes.

It was quite telling to see how different the finished boards were. In the centre of Leila's she'd scrawled in gold pen, 'Throw kindness like confetti' and in smaller looped writing she'd printed 'Life is better when you're laughing'. Beautiful photos of wild flowers like lavender and cherry blossom added vibrant blues and pinks to the mix. She'd cut tiny triangles out of a gingham

153

fabric and fastened this mini bunting along the top of the canvas, giving the whole board an enticing country festival feel. Lucy's on the other hand, was the polar opposite. Never a fan of freehand Lucy had been surgically attached to the ruler and mini spirit level all afternoon, carefully measuring out equidistant boxes in which she had stuck images of jewellery, a Prada handbag, a white Range Rover Sport, a red Aga, a golden retriever and two blonde little girls. After Tasha told her that 'It needs to be inspirational, not aspirational,' Lucy begrudgingly scrolled through her beloved Pinterest and copied down the quotes 'Life is short, buy the shoes' and then, sensing she was being judged, 'The best is yet to come.' She also added in a couple of pictures of an ivy-clad manor house and a deserted beach, because, well, everyone liked beaches. It was Tasha's that was the biggest surprise though. The queen of taupe had created a cornucopia of riotous colour, reds and oranges fizzed alongside turquoise and teal. Giant starbursts surrounded the words 'You've got this' and 'Be Bold, Be Brave, Be You'.

Leila didn't want it all to be what Judy would (and did) call 'new age nonsense' so she persuaded a literary agent friend of hers to persuade one of her rising comedy authors to come and hold a book club dinner on the Saturday night. Sian had worked the comedy circuit for ten years before turning her hand to novels, so knew how to work a room, and a few one-liners in, each of the fifty women there were in stitches. Fifty women. Thankfully they had each been responsible for getting themselves to the hotel, as that would have been a logistical nightmare. One woman had flown down from Edinburgh that morning, while others had made journeys up from Cornwall, down from Birmingham and across from London.

Leila knew it sounded corny, even saying it just in her head, but it felt as though real friendships were being made that weekend. She saw several women swap cards or type in numbers into their phones as they were leaving. And all the sponsors were incredibly happy as the women lined up to take leaflets, book repeat appointments or have their books signed.

'Penny for them.'

Leila didn't know how long Lucy had been standing next to her, witnessing her smug grin, but then Lucy's expression was similar. 'I can't believe it went so well,' Leila said.

'I can. We'd planned it all to perfection.'

Typical Lucy, Leila thought. It was unlikely that she'd ever had to resort to Plan B, C or D. 'I just mean, I'm not used to something going exactly to plan, I guess.'

'That's why you asked me to help.'

'That's very true. Speaking of which, I need to give you a cheque for your fee.' Leila turned to go and fetch her bag when Lucy put out her arm and stopped her.

'Actually Leila, I was thinking about this. You've created a real niche in the market, and I think this could be the start of something pretty incredible. So I wondered if you would consider making this event a regular thing, and maybe even making our partnership a bit more formal?'

'More formal?' The words conjured up for Leila a different dress code and more old-fashioned language.

'As in we think about running this as an actual business.' Her sister-in-law was biting her bottom lip and her hands were fidgeting in her pockets. Leila thought it was the first time she'd seen a vulnerable side to Lucy.

'But I'm a landscape architect Lucy, planning this weekend has eaten into so much of my work time as well as my evenings. If my boss knew that for the last month I've had seven windows open on my computer and only one of them was work-related he'd be livid, and I can't afford to lose this job now I have a mortgage.'

'But that's where I come in Leila. I have loved being involved in this weekend, it's given my life a bit of purpose again and I can see the potential of this as a proper money-making business. And you don't need to do anything apart from write about it online and be the front of house host on the day. You created this amazing community of women. They look up to you. And anyway,' Lucy said, flexing her huge diamond, 'I'm a married woman now, so I could hardly be the face of the operation could I? It needs a strong single woman. It needs you.' Lucy put her head slightly on the side and pouted. 'Just think about it Leila. It's the start of November now, we could organise the mother of all Christmas parties in a few weeks. A "new year, new you" weekend in the first couple of weeks of January, an anti-Valentine's Day do the month after that — it would be like printing money.'

It sounded feasible. In fact, it sounded like a lot of hard work. But Lucy would be shouldering most of that. Her 'printing money' comment both repelled and attracted Leila at the same time. She had stretched herself beyond what was sensible buying the flat so the idea of some extra cash was very welcome, but Lucy sounded so mercenary about the events. She hoped she wasn't making a huge mistake by nodding her agreement. Only time would tell.

So, how'd it go? Nx

Leila smiled. Nick and her were now messaging on a daily basis. It started off with him thanking her for the roast duck frosting and rhubarb gazpacho. Being thoroughly British about the whole thing, she then had to bat his thanks away and instead thank him for coming. And then he had to firmly insist she accept his thanks and this volley of politeness then turned into friendly banter. Unromantic, unsensual, nonerotic, friendly banter.

Surprisingly perfect. Lx

Just like you, she thought as she pressed send.

So pleased. I know you think she's a nightmare, but I think you make a good team. Nx

Funny you should say that. Your sister has convinced me to do more events. Please

158

tell me I'm not going to regret this. Lx

You're not going to regret this. Anyway, don't you have your fancy project to concentrate on? Nx

Speaking of which, I need a good contact for granite, my usual guy let me down — can you ping me a number asap — having a marble crisis. Lx

There's nothing worse than a marble crisis. Here you go — 0897 546 9003, his name's Paul McCartney. Yes, I know. Nx

Wow. I know the Wings stuff wasn't as good, but really? Granite? Lx

Too easy. Expected better from you. How's it going? Marble crisis apart? Nx

Really great, loving it, onto final stretch now. Handover in 4 weeks, eek! Come down to the site and I'll show you — I'm there on Tuesday and Wednesday next week — you free? Lx

Sounds great. Tuesday? About 1.30? I'll take you for a late lunch after if you fancy? Nx

'Mind your head!' Leila ducked Nick's helmet down under a swinging chain from a crane. 'So this is where the sensory wall is going to go, that's arriving tomorrow, and over there —' Leila pointed to a mound of frost-topped rubble, covered by a green sheet, 'is the neoclassical garden.'

'Looks lovely.'

Leila shoulder-barged Nick and laughed, 'Well it will, just not until my hedges are planted, and this stupid ground frost is making that impossible. I swear I'm going to have to bring industrial heaters in to thaw it out if this keeps up. I checked the weather and it's meant to get warmer by the week-end, so that still gives us a bit of time.'

'I haven't got much on at the minute, so happy to come down with a hairdryer if that helps?'

'You jest, but I may need that!' Leila swung her leg over a metal bar and clambered up some scaffolding, looking behind her she yelled, 'Come on slowcoach, up here!' She started tearing off some plastic sheeting. 'This beauty is an original reproduction of Antonio Canova's *Psyche Revived by Love's Kiss.* Isn't it amazing?'

'An original reproduction you say?'

'I knew you'd say something like that. Yes Nick, it's an original reproduction, and I'm well aware of the paradox in that. But look, isn't it beautiful? Surprisingly the Louvre said no to us having the original, which is odd. I mean, who do they think they are? But doesn't it scream enlightenment and romance and power?'

'It is amazing. And school groups are going to love the fact that you can see her boob and both their bums.'

'You are such a boy,' Lucy grimaced. 'Now aren't you treating me to lunch?'

Nick returned from the bar carrying two large glasses of red wine and holding a bag of crisps between his teeth that he then dropped on the table. 'I ordered the baguettes but this will keep us going. Seriously though Lei,' he said as he sat down on the small stool, 'I'm really impressed with what you've done. When you told me the deadline for this I couldn't believe you'd get it all done in time, most people would have taken twice as long to get it all in place. You've done an incredible job, you should be really proud.'

His words made her feel a bit warm and fuzzy. 'Thank you, that means a lot coming from you. It's been really difficult staying on track with this while trying to pull off the event too, but I'm really pleased, and I know it looks as though there's a lot still to do, but it's all superficial stuff. It'll be fine. But anyway, what about you — how's the villa in Dubai going?'

In one of his emails he'd told her that he'd pitched for a lot of work in the UAE, designing buildings that defied gravity with 180-degree rotations, lifts for Lamborghinis, and triple height expanses of curved glass. He'd flown out to the Emirates five times in the last month alone, presenting his designs to clients who believed that their big wads of cash should be able to overcome basic laws of engineering. Meetings that made him slink into bed back in England, exhausted but invigorated.

'It's good, it's challenging, but aside from the different protocols for planning permission and building regulations to contend with, it's an architect's dream. This one has an underground grotto that's a whole entertainment space, it's got a nightclub, a cinema, a bowling alley, it's amazing. And you would love what they've done with the pool, half of it is outside the building, and half flows through the house in channels under a glass floor, it's incredible.'

'Budget?'

Nick laughed. 'What's that?' He finished his wine and saw that she had an empty glass too. 'Another one? Shall I get a bottle?'

It was now completely dark outside, and they had just started on their third bottle. They had wavered before ordering it — the leap from two bottles to three always commands a moment to consider the implications — but they'd managed to move to a table in front of the fire and, together with the blackness of the afternoon outside the steamed-up windows, the pub seemed so cosy and warm that they were both reluctant to leave it.

There were six more weeks until Christmas, but the pub landlord had evidently got into the festive spirit early with paper chains hung from corner to corner, and a slightly misshapen fir tree decorated with clashing baubles in every colour. Regulars had scribbled messages on scraps of paper that hung from pegs along the bar, displaying their wishes for the coming year, everything from world peace to asking for a better variety of sandwiches on the menu. The music had been turned up as the afternoon progressed into early evening and festive tunes had made the mood merry and bright, or maybe that was the wine.

'I think about you quite a lot.'

'Nick, don't.'

'But I do. Every day. A few times every day.'

'This isn't right.'

'Don't you feel the same?'

'Nick, stop it, we said we wouldn't do this. You know I can't do this.'

'But it's Christmas, can't you make an exception for Christmas?'

'It's not Christmas, it's November, and absolutely not. You wouldn't say that to an alcoholic would you? Oh it's Christmas, have that bottle of Baileys. Why is celibacy any different? I've made a vow.'

'With yourself.'

'I have thousands of women following my celibacy journey Nick.'

'And I really don't think they're here now.' They both looked around at the mainly male regulars. Those who weren't propping up the bar were propping up each other.

'Nick, stop, we need to talk about something else.'

'Ok, so what are we going to do next? We've pretty much finished this,' Nick tilted the bottle to one side, to see about two inches left in the bottom, which he drained between their two glasses.

'We could go back to the museum and

walk about? Everyone will have left by now, and I didn't show you my mausoleum.'

'As chat up lines go, "I would like to show you my mausoleum" is a pretty scary one.'

'It's not a chat up line! I genuinely want to show you my mausoleum.'

'I can honestly say, in all of my thirty-four years I have never heard those words used together in a sentence. Come on then,' he heaved her to her feet and held out her coat for her, 'show me your mausoleum.'

Their boots crunched on the hard ground, their steps made even more unsteady due to the bottle and a half they'd each consumed. Holding on to each other, laughing and joking, they made their way through the dark undergrowth and weaved around piles of earth and cordoned off holes in the ground until they reached a dark grey stone structure that loomed in front of them. 'Original reproduction of a tomb?' Nick asked cheekily.

'An original original I'll have you know. This is the tomb of the 5th Earl of Blahblahhum, who died in the 16th century.'

'Oh, the Earl of Blahblahhum. I've always loved him. And his wife, the Earless of Blibahhoohoo.'

'The very same,' laughed Leila.

They both stood in the blackness staring

up at the engraved block of stone. Nick slowly turned, reaching out a finger into the coldness to tilt her chin slightly upwards before brushing his lips to hers.

And she gently kissed him back.

Surprisingly Nick was the first to break away. His breath was warm on her face as he asked, 'Is this ok?'

'Yes and no, but don't stop,' Leila murmured. He wrapped his arms around her padded jacket and pulled her in closer. His nose was cold against hers, she couldn't feel her feet anymore and his stubble was a little itchy, but none of it mattered. She didn't know how long they were kissing for, it could have been ten seconds or ten minutes. When their mouths finally came apart they both broke into matching, natural, spontaneous smiles.

'Hello you,' said Nick.

'Hello.'

'I think the wine got the better of us.'

Leila wasn't sure the wine had anything to do with it. It may have weakened her resolve, but then she was starting to realise that perhaps being strong-willed was not one of her personality traits. Nick still had his hands clasped around her back as he looked up at the looming stone in front of

166

them and said, 'Nice mausoleum.'

'I told you it was something special.'

'Indeed you did. I'm very glad you brought me here, to see it close up. Thank you.'

Leila smiled. 'Me too. And you're welcome.'

'I'm sorry for compromising your man ban,' joked Nick.

His words snapped Leila back to the present and out of her romantic fog. She wiggled free of his grasp and said, 'We should be getting back. They have security cameras on site, I could get in a lot of trouble for doing this.' She started walking back towards the exit, her hands thrust deep into her pockets, and Nick ran behind her to keep up.

'Lei, wait.'

She kept on walking and didn't turn around. Eleven months ago she'd been stamping down an Indian corridor with a man she thought she loved shouting after her. This time was remarkably similar and yet so different.

'Lei, look, I know it's important to you, this being single thing, I'm sorry, I really am. I didn't mean for this to happen. We can just go back to being friends. The moment just came and I wanted to kiss you, and I'm so sorry if I've misjudged it and put you in an awkward position, Lei, slow down.'

But Leila kept gathering pace until they had nearly reached the gate.

'Lei!' Nick swung Leila round to face him, but she refused to meet his eye, instead staring resolutely over his shoulder. 'Please, listen. I know this year of celibacy is really important to you, and I'm assuming that this reaction you're having now is because you feel angry that you think you've failed in some way. I'm sorry, it's all my fault. I shouldn't have said anything, or done anything. It's my fault, not yours. Lei, look at me.'

Begrudgingly she met his gaze, and immediately wished she hadn't. His dark brown eyes were kind and concerned and she felt her resolve, which had seemed so strong and ardent a few seconds before, start to thaw. 'Meeting you was never part of the plan Nick. Well it was part of The Plan but not part of this year. And I can't just give up now, so many people are counting on me to see it through.'

'But they don't need to know.'

Leila looked at him, suddenly realising that he just didn't get it. 'Goodbye Nick.'

In the first few days after that night Leila

became erratic. She alternated between melancholy and jubilation, one minute silent and withdrawn, the next frantically bashing out missive after missive on the blog and going into overdrive with the Christmas party planning.

She dodged Nick's messages, emails and texts, reading some and deleting others.

As the week before Christmas dawned, it was the night of the forum's Christmas party. A hundred and fifty women had all paid sixty quid for a three-course meal, guest speakers and a band. And Lucy was insisting on Leila making a welcome speech; 'Something inspirational, aspirational and heartfelt,' she said.

Oh-kay then. No pressure.

Her page remained stubbornly blank. She had less than two hours before women started filing into the private room above one of London's swankiest bars — Lucy had managed to coerce a few of the sponsors to pay for the venue — and Leila hadn't got past the word 'welcome'. She hadn't even had her hair or nails done yet, and was fast running out of time to make it to the salon. Her dress needed ironing, or at the very least should be hung in a steamy shower room, but Leila had no inclination to get it out of the carrier bag under her desk.

She was a complete fraud.

One hundred and fifty women, assuming their host was a kindred spirit, had paid good money to spend an evening in her company, bonding over shared experiences and similar outlooks, and she was deceiving all of them. She actually felt a bit sick about standing up in front of all of them pretending to be something she wasn't. Harping on about the joys of celibacy and being alone when just a month ago she was locking lips with the tall, dark and handsome brother of her sister-in-law slash new business partner.

But like Nick said, no-one else knew. Which in itself was excruciating. If the boat, the bar and the tomb had happened before the ban, she'd have spent hours regaling her friends, her family, anyone who asked her how she was, with every tiny detail. But instead, not a single person, apart from the two of them, knew. That provided a little solace later that evening as she stood up in her creased black evening dress and tapped a wine glass asking for silence.

She told the eager crowd a little of her own journey that had led to her making the celibacy vow. For a few of the guests, who had been followers of the blog from the start, none of this was news, but most of the women there had jumped on the wagon later. Her tales of dating woe struck chords with every woman there. She spoke about how she used to truly believe that somewhere in the world was a man wishing he was with someone just like her. 'It used to give me comfort on lonely nights thinking that everyone has one person that they're meant to be with, but I now know that's crap. There's not one person that's going to make me happy and a couple of billion that won't. The maths just doesn't add up. It's not logistically possible. What is possible though is learning that your self-esteem and confidence shouldn't come from another person. You are the only person like you in the world. You're unique. You're pretty freaking awesome.'

Buoyed by their applause and laughter she somehow found the words she wanted to say, despite her cue card only having the words Welcome, Thanks, Enjoy, on it.

Lucy, Tasha and Shelley were giving her big thumbs up from the back, so it must be going well. Jayne and Amanda had turned down Leila's invite based on their marital status. Their exact words were, 'But as we're not single we'd feel a bit deceitful about taking up two places for women that are genuine.' They weren't to know that their words stabbed Leila like an ice pick in the

171

stomach. By that reasoning, she should be excluded too.

'To us!' Lucy raised her champagne glass and Leila and Tasha touched their flutes to hers. The three of them were the only ones left in the room. It was just after 1am and they'd all collapsed on one of the sofas and kicked off their stilettos. 'Lucy, once again, you've excelled yourself,' Tasha said. 'You think of everything.'

'It was a team effort,' Lucy replied, with uncharacteristic modesty. Leila thought that she'd definitely softened since the wedding. Maybe it was just the emotional intensity that had made her so blinkered and single-minded before. Perhaps the real Lucy was actually alright. It would explain why Marcus had picked her out of all the other pony-club graduates that he'd brought home over the years. And she couldn't be as bad as Leila had first thought if Nick was so damn near perfect. Him and Lucy shared the same genes after all.

Leila had tried so hard to keep Nick out of her thoughts tonight, which wasn't helped by the good luck message he sent just as the first guests arrived. At least she assumed it was a good luck message, she hadn't opened it fully and so she'd only

172

seen the first line *'Hey you, have a . . .'* come up as an alert on her home screen.

Their kiss was thirty-four days ago; surely he should have got bored and moved on by now? Past boyfriends that Leila had dated for months, even years, had found a replacement for her affections in under a fortnight before, so why was he being so persistent? She didn't dare hope it was because he felt the same as she did.

Leila suddenly became aware of both her sister and sister-in-law looking at her. And she had no idea why, she'd tuned out of their conversation but was vaguely aware it was about Christmas next week.

'So Leila, does 4pm suit?' Lucy asked.

'Um, sure . . . ?'

'I can't believe Mum and Dad have surrendered the turkey so easily,' said Tasha, with more than a hint of barely disguised bitterness. 'I've been trying to get them up to ours for Christmas pretty much every year since Alex and I married, but they've never said yes.'

Leila suddenly had a sinking feeling. 'What, we're not going to Devon this year?'

'Oh my goodness, have you been asleep all this time?' accused Tasha. 'We've just been talking about this. Lucy and Marcus are hosting us all this year.'

The familiar expression of smugness was back on Lucy's face. 'Judy didn't even protest. I think she was quite relieved that there is now a viable option to having it at theirs.'

Leila looked at her sister to see how the words 'viable option' were sitting with her. Not good it seemed. She opened her mouth to speak before Tasha could. 'Ok, a change is sometimes good. Great, so four o'clock on Christmas Day then. Isn't that a bit late?'

'No, Christmas Eve, silly! I've got the menu sorted for the full three days, and it builds up a bit of festive spirit if we're all together for the night before as well. The local church does a lovely Midnight Mass and I've bought lots of games, and mapped out the walk we'll do on Boxing Day afternoon. And you have to wear festive nightwear too. It's going to be great.'

Leila had a sudden pang for the heavily scripted Christmases she'd experienced every one of her thirty-two years, right down to the same jokes and brand of crackers. But of course Lucy would want to host it; she would too if she had just got married, moved to a ridiculously large house on the edge of the commuter belt and had enough free time to spend days poring over festive cook books.

'And while I've got you both here, you need to choose your person for Secret Santa. As there's so many of us, I thought it would be better to just spend £100 on one person instead of £50 on everyone.'

It wasn't that it was a bad suggestion. In fact Leila had been worrying for weeks about how she was going to compete with her much more financially-able family on the gift front. But she also loved pottering around Portobello Market for something suitably bohemian for Tasha, and visiting Jayne's husband's deli in Richmond for a bespoke hamper for her parents, and finding something obscure and exotic for Marcus. Tasha had already emailed her the wishlist for Mia, Talia and Oscar — it went on for three pages. Thankfully she hadn't bought anything from it yet, but a trip to Hamleys was an annual pilgrimage she loved. But saving near enough £500 on presents made diluting her sentimental side pretty easy.

'Ok, so how do we do this?'

'I've inputted everyone's name into a spreadsheet and you need to give me a number between one and twelve and I'll tell you who your person is.'

'Why twelve?' asked Tasha, mentally counting up all the family members and only getting ten.

'My brother and mum are coming too. Ok, Leila, you first.'

Leila felt like she'd been winded. How the heck could she avoid Nick for seventy-two hours straight, especially over what should be a period of goodwill to all men? All men except the one you accidentally slept with, ignored, then kissed, then pretended didn't exist. Except he did, and now, to add insult to injury, he was going to be seeing her in Christmas pyjamas. Bugger.

CHAPTER 11

Did you know? L

About what? And what happened to the Lx? Nx

Christmas. And the x was not an accidental omission. L

Didn't you get my message earlier on? Nx

Leila looked back at her inbox and clicked on Nick's earlier text that she'd assumed was a message of good luck salutations. *Hey you, have a sit down and take a deep breath. Lucy's invited us both for Christmas. Don't worry, I'm going to get out of it. I don't want you feeling awkward. Nx*

Ok. Just seen it now. Just because I'm very grateful I'm temporarily reinstating the x. Don't get too excited. Lx

Excitement in check. Hope you have a good Christmas. Speak in the new year? Nx

Leila allowed herself to breathe a sigh of relief. She'd felt physically sick at the idea of sitting across from Nick with just a turkey carcass between them. Just by being around him her heart rate was permanently raised, her stomach knotted and she completely doubted her ability to appear normal in his company in front of her whole family. Yet she also felt bad that he was going to miss out on a family Christmas with his mum and sister just because of what had happened between them. Leila knew that Stephanie would be really upset not to be with both her children, and Lucy would hold a grudge against Nick for ages, regardless of what alibi he managed to concoct.

If anyone should bow out, it should be her. Except what possible reason could she invent that would placate her parents? And she wouldn't want to anyway — as much as her family irritated her at times, spending Christmas alone in her flat sounded incredibly depressing. Even if Jayne and Will or Amanda and Paul made room at their table for her, which she knew they would, she'd still be feeling pangs of family-sickness all day. This wasn't just a case of missing a Dartmouth Sunday Roast, this was Christmas. And if *she* felt like this, it was completely unreasonable for her to ask Nick not to come.

Hey Nick, it's ok, no need to make other plans. Pretty sure I can resist you for three days, you're not that handsome. L(x)

Glad to see the x wasn't temporary after all. And only if you're sure? Must admit, I wasn't looking forward to telling Mum or Sis! Nx

I'm sure. However you may well wish you hadn't bothered turning up when you open my Secret Santa gift . . . L(x)

Isn't the whole point of Secret Santa that you don't know who gives it to you? Nx

Is it? Oops. L(x)

The clue's in the name . . . Nx

Leila leaned back against her kitchen counter and smiled.

Much like most things in life, the excited

anticipation was the best bit of Christmas. Sharing knowing smiles with everyone else carrying a suitcase and bag of wrapped presents on the train was a once-in-a-year event, solely saved for Christmas Eve. Looking around her crowded carriage at all the different people, young and old, travelling solo or in groups, smart and groomed or ruffled and rugged, Leila felt the special bond they all shared. The cross-country rail service that linked central London to its one-horse station in Bedfordshire fifty-five minutes away had also embraced the festive spirit. Free mince pies and mulled wine were being pushed through the four carriages by a cheery middle-aged woman who had a flashing reindeer badge stuck to her name tag introducing herself as Valerie.

Leila had tried, and for the most part succeeded, in quashing any feelings of concern about how the next three days would pan out. Instead, she'd followed some of Tasha's teaching and whenever the first swells of anxiety started to surface, she simply imagined her fingers being hollow tubes that she inhaled through, envisaging the air entering her body and tracing its path through her limbs.

She would have considered this all to be mumbo jumbo a few months ago, but it worked, and she felt quite calm and positive about the next three days. After all, she really enjoyed Nick's company, and there was no reason for there to be any awkwardness. No-one knew that she knew the location of a very intimate mole he had, and she knew he would never let on over the Boxing Day cold cuts that she had a collection of freckles on her behind that resembled a hexagon.

It was just going to be a lovely, fun seventy-two hours. And if she kept repeating that to herself, it might well come true.

Marcus was standing on the platform waiting for her. How he managed to appear both irritated at the train's eight-minute delay and relieved at its eventual arrival was a look he'd cultivated as his own. He'd always been the more serious one growing up. He put this down to being the only boy, but Leila's friends had brothers who threw themselves fully into princess dress-up time, or tea party fun, but Marcus never did. You would have thought having two sisters would have helped him relate to women, but he always seemed so awkward with girlfriends, a cross between stand-offish and clumsy in his affections. Leila supposed that's why someone as focused and headstrong as Lucy suited him so well. A gentler sort of girl might have confused his bumbling with disinterest, but Lucy saw in him another project.

'You're late.'

'Happy Christmas Marcus!' Leila reached up and kissed her brother's cheek. 'I've had a lovely journey, two mince pies and two cups of mulled wine. Not sure it's possible to feel more festive.'

'Well I hope you're not drunk or full, Lucy's been cooking all day.'

'Ho Ho Ho. Come on Marcus, it's Christmas!' Screeching the last two words in the voice of Noddy Holder made the other people on the platform turn to stare smiling, but Marcus was oblivious to this, marching on ahead carrying his sister's case.

She was the last to arrive, at forty-five minutes past her scheduled arrival time of 4pm. Any feelings of ill will on Lucy's part were immediately smothered by an incredibly effusive welcome from Leila's two nieces and one nephew who flung themselves at her as soon as the front door — adorned with mandatory wreath — was opened. 'Hello, hello, oh you look smart! Talia, is that a new dress? Wow, Oscar, you're already in your pyjamas! Anyone would think you're excited about going to bed tonight! Hey Mia, I swear you get a foot taller every time I see you.' It wasn't an act, Leila genuinely thought her sister's children were her favourite people on earth, and the feeling was completely mutual.

Judy and Thomas had also entered the hallway, but were hanging back letting their grandchildren have the first hugs. It had been a long drive up and Thomas was looking a little tired, but his face broke into a huge grin when his youngest daughter stepped forward to kiss him. Judy instinctively reached out her hand to stroke down a patch of Leila's hair that was sticking up at the back.

'You're looking suitably festive Mum, new jumper?' Judy had dispensed with her usual white and navy attire, after all, they were nowhere near the sea now, and was instead sporting a red and white Nordic knitted sweater.

'It is,' her mum replied proudly. 'Kitsch jumpers are all the rage apparently.'

'Well, you are rocking it.' Leila dumped her bag near the door and wrapped her mum in a big bear hug. 'Sorry I'm late, the train was delayed a bit.'

'Oh we don't mind. Lucy might though,' Judy added in a conspiratorial whisper.

'How fraught has it been on a scale of one to ten?' Leila whispered back.

'About a six, with potential of a nine.'

'Wonderful. I'll just pop in the kitchen and say hello, then bid a hasty retreat.'

The smell from the oven and stovetop were marvellous. If you could bottle the scent of Christmas and then waft it about, it would be the exact aroma emanating from that kitchen. Lucy was crouched down in front of the newly-purchased red Aga watching the clove-studded roast ham brown, while a massive pot of mulled wine with orange peel, cinnamon sticks and nutmeg was being slowly stirred by Nick.

Neither had seen her enter, and there was a split-second moment of indecision when Leila wavered by the door, biting her lip. She had to do it. She couldn't avoid speaking to him for the entirety of Christmas. 'Happy Christmas Eve!' she sang out.

Lucy stood up, her hair slightly coming out of her fancy up do, and her face faintly flushed. Leila wondered if she'd perhaps been a little too ambitious with the menu and her hosting arrangements. 'Oh good, you're here now, ten more minutes and the ham would be burned.'

'I think what my sister means is, great to see you Leila, happy Christmas Eve, how was your journey?' Nick smiled and ducked his head to hers so his lips brushed her cheek. A charge of electricity passed between them and Leila knew he felt it too as he locked eyes with hers and then took a step back for his sister to greet her.

'Um, it smells wonderful in here,' Leila said, giving an exaggerated sniff to emphasise her observation.

'Can I interest you in a glass of mulled wine?' Nick said, picking up the ladle that was resting on the work surface next to the hob.

'That would be fabulous, thanks. Is there anything I can help with?'

'Well you can take your suitcase upstairs for a start as it's cluttering up the hallway and we're going to sing carols around the tree straight after dinner,' Lucy reproached.

Nick gave Leila a smile over Lucy's head and rolled his eyes in a silent apology for his sister's lack of tact.

'Right-o. Which room am I in?'

'Second on the left, you're sharing with Mia.'

'Wonderful. At least I'm not with Talia and Oscar jumping on the bed with their stockings! Since Mia's turned fifteen she sleeps for England,' Leila joked.

Lucy looked horrified. 'Well not tomorrow she won't. We'll be opening presents at eight, breakfast at nine, church at ten, and

185

lunch at one.'

Leila nodded, swallowing down a smile. 'Well, that sounds very . . . organised. I do like a plan.'

Nick made a funny noise from the hob, and she could see his shoulders shake in an appreciative giggle.

Tealights flickered on every shelf in the dining room, and the effect was magical. A gorgeous centrepiece of wild berries, holly and ivy all intricately woven together ran the length of the reclaimed oak dining table, with fruits spray-painted gold nestled in between the delicate twigs and leaves. Leila sat between Stephanie and Mia at dinner, and the conversations alternated between talking about the rise in popularity of 'Congratulations on your Divorce' greeting cards with one, and why teenage boys liked showing their pants above their jeans with the other. Across the table Nick was being introduced to the intricacies of Paw Patrol Top Trumps and doing quite well if the height of the pile of cards in front of him and the size of Oscar's bottom lip was anything to go by. Being childless and nephew-less meant that he obviously hadn't yet learnt the golden rule of throwing a game so the adult never won.

At the end of the table to her right, Judy, Tasha and Lucy were talking about her. Well, about the future events that they had planned, she kept hearing her name dropped into conversation and the future events that they had all planned. It felt a bit weird but nice that each of them had now profited from her celibacy site: Tasha had many repeat clients from the workshops, the hotel accounts were showing a healthy spike for a normally slow winter, and Lucy had embraced the event planning with gusto. Then Leila heard her mum say, 'She's surprised us all to be honest, I don't think any of us thought she'd see it through.' Murmurs of agreement came from both Tasha and Lucy. If only they knew.

To her left, Thomas and Alex had fallen into their natural default position of talking about sport. Safe son-in-law and father-in-law territory at dining tables up and down the land.

Lucy had evidently swallowed the manual on how to create the perfect family Christmas because no sooner had the baked ham been devoured, she started getting the ingredients ready for the hot chocolate they were going to enjoy on their return from Midnight Mass.

'I'll stay behind and babysit the kids,' said

Alex rather too quickly. 'We can't leave them here alone.'

'No, Alex, Leila's already offered to stay behind, you're coming with me,' Tasha replied. It was one thing knowing your husband had a mistress, it was entirely another to sanction him messaging or calling her on Christmas Eve as they prepared to play Santa to their children sleeping upstairs.

'No, it's fine,' Alex insisted. 'I'm not really a churchy person anyway.'

'Tough. You're coming.' Tasha's tone was non-negotiable. 'I think we both know you have some sins that need to be absolved.'

The penny suddenly dropped and Alex's eyes widened. 'I'll get my coat.'

'I'm happy to babysit,' Leila said. That would be one less hour in Nick's company.

'I'll stay too,' Nick suddenly said, running his hand through his hair. 'We'll get the hot chocolate ready for your return.'

Leila did a little dance in her head.

Coats, hats and scarves were pulled on and boots unearthed from the downstairs shoe cupboard, and then quiet suddenly descended on the house. Even Mia, who had only taken off her headphones for the duration of dinner, had shrugged her agreement, pulled down her beanie and set off

188

on the short walk through the village to the church. Talia and Oscar had been asleep upstairs for hours, both wearing new Christmas pyjamas and dreaming of nibbled carrots and half-eaten mince pies.

'It's going ok, isn't it?' Nick said, washing up the last few glasses from next to the sink and putting them on the drying rack. They'd tuned into the local radio station where festive tunes were merrily on high, giving the kitchen a wonderfully relaxed feel, for the first time that day.

Leila picked up a tea towel. 'Yes, of course. Lucy seems to be one step away from a nervous breakdown though.'

'I have a feeling it's going to get worse before it gets better. Tomorrow's menu would make even Jamie Oliver nervous.' He passed a wet soapy glass directly to her.

'It's quite fun having you here,' Leila ventured. 'When it's just my family it can get a bit argumentative, but everyone seems to be on their best behaviour.'

'What was your sister saying about Alex's sins earlier?'

'Oh God knows, he probably left the toilet seat up again, or played golf when he should have been at a ballet recital.'

'I like them though, you're lucky to be part of such a big family. Christmas is usually a very sedate affair, with just me, Mum and Lucy.'

'When did your dad leave?' There was a pause in which Leila thought that she'd misjudged the air of solidarity and she quickly apologised for asking. It was Christmas Eve, she shouldn't be bringing up bad memories.

'No, it's fine, it's been a long time, I can talk about it without needing a tissue or therapy.' He lifted the plug out of the sink and dried his hands on the towel Leila was still holding. 'I was about fourteen. He got a job in South Africa, he's still there. I go to Cape Town every so often to visit him and he's alright, living the life he wanted to live.'

'Was it tough when he left?'

'Harder on Mum. But she's great — she had to forget all about her artistic ambitions to become poet laureate and instead write radio jingles to support us, but I think she's happy. She's got a . . . what do you call it at that age? Companion? Male friend? He's been around for about twelve years. Tony. He's a decent bloke.'

Leila shut the last glass into the cupboard and leant back against the sink. 'So. What now? We could always open another bottle of wine and then hide the evidence at the bottom of the recycling bag?'

'I like your thinking,' Nick replied.

They sat amiably at the shabby chic kitchen table for three quarters of the bottle, chatting about work, and living in London, and their friends. Then Nick broke a short silence by saying, 'I would never tell them you know.'

'I know.'

'I just wanted you to know that you can trust me. It sounds like most of your ex-boyfriends haven't been very nice, and I wanted you to know that I am.'

'You're not an ex-boyfriend either.'

'No, and I hope I never will be.'

His statement hung in the air, and for a few seconds neither of them spoke to dispel it.

'I really like you Lei. And I'd really like us to give it a go and see what happens.'

'Nick, please, you know all the reasons I can't.' Leila stood up. 'Not for another three months.' She started gathering up their glasses and picked up the wine bottle to signal that their chat was over. He rested his hand on her arm.

'Put it down and look at me.'

She reluctantly put the glasses and bottle down on the table and sulkily raised her chin to meet his gaze.

'There are lots of reasons why no-one can

know that we're dating. But that doesn't mean we can't date.' Leila rolled her eyes, which Nick ignored as he continued. 'I don't want to jump straight into anything serious either, I spent years witnessing a toxic marriage play out, my mum and sister are desperate to marry me off and I just want the privacy and space to have a relationship with no external factors influencing it. I know that your reasons are just as, if not more, important, but we clearly enjoy each other's company. I think you're absolutely gorgeous, and I would very much like to kiss you again.'

She would have done. In fact she'd already started leaning in and closing her eyes when the front door slammed and they guiltily leapt apart.

CHAPTER 12

For the first time in many years, Leila didn't have a pile of tat by her slippered feet on Christmas morning. Before Lucy instigated the one gift per person rule, she'd have been the polite recipient of endless scented candles, bath smellies, some stationery and the odd book on seeing the world from above. But even though she was yet to receive hers, the calibre of gifts given this morning was remarkably good, which gave her a sense of hope. Thomas was enthralled with his new model speedboat, complete with leather-upholstered seats and real wood decking. Judy had put her new cropped leather jacket on over her pyjamas, and Tasha was stood in front of the over mantle Art Deco mirror admiring the way her new earrings caught the light.

'Leila's next!' Alex was crouched under the huge fir tree that Lucy had sourced from a local eco farm, passing the gifts to his youngest daughter, Talia, to divvy out to each of the grown ups. Leila's present wasn't under the tree; it was leant against the wall behind. It must have only been an inch or two thick, but almost half a metre long and wide. It was wrapped simply in brown paper with a sprig of holly stuck to one corner.

'Thanks Talia, oooo, how exciting!' Leila looked at Tasha, who she assumed was the Secret Santa for this gift, but she was busy uploading games onto Mia's new tablet. Everyone else was making cooing noises at the size of her gift. She carefully unstuck the holly and put it to one side, and then peeled off the sticky tape from the paper. It was an unframed canvas, but it was face down, with only the string on show. Leila carefully turned it round and gasped. It was an oil painting of the view from the exact spot she loved standing in at the front of the hotel at the edge of the driveway, looking between the branches. It had been painted at dusk and the setting sun cast long shadows over the hilltop path, while lights from the boats illuminated the dark water of the marina. Leila looked up and scanned the room, everyone seemed as enchanted by the picture as her.

Everyone except Nick, who was standing

in the doorway, his hands in his pyjama pockets.

She looked at him and instantly remembered telling him how she could never replicate the view in photos or her own paintings. He must have commissioned it. For far more than the allocated one hundred pounds.

'Nick? Was this from you?' Leila asked. Everyone turned to look at him. He suddenly realised how extravagant and thoughtful this present was. Far too much so for two people who were only supposed to have shared a table once at a wedding and once at a restaurant.

'I'm afraid I've got to come clean,' Nick started, and Leila's eyes widened at the thought of him spilling. 'I didn't spend anywhere near the budget,' he added. 'I picked it up at a car boot sale, it's of an estuary in Norfolk, but I thought it looked a bit like Dartmouth so bought it for whoever I got in the Santa draw. I can top up the remaining amount with vouchers if you like?'

A flurry of 'It's lovely!', 'What a find!', 'Luck of the draw,' and 'Got to know where to look' followed, and in the middle of the furore Leila caught Nick's eye and he winked at her.

As soon as the presents were all unwrapped, next on Lucy's agenda was breakfast. Organic scrambled eggs with home-marinated smoked salmon and bucks fizz were set out on the kitchen island for everyone to help themselves, and Leila took advantage of the hubbub to slip away and follow Nick upstairs. The door to the bathroom was ajar and he was standing at the basin brushing his teeth, still in his tartan pyjama bottoms and black T-shirt.

'Hey.'

'Hey.' Nick spat out the toothpaste and rinsed his mouth under the tap.

'I love my gift,' Leila said, still standing in the doorway.

'I'm glad.'

'And I know it didn't come from a car boot sale in Norfolk.'

He shrugged apologetically, 'I didn't really think through the giving part of the gift, and suddenly everyone was looking and it seemed quite an inappropriate gift for someone I hardly know.'

'I think you know me quite well.'

Nick straightened up and smiled. 'I think I do too, but none of them do.' He nodded his head in the direction of the hallway as he dried his hands on the hand towel next to the sink.

'Anyway, I just wanted to come up here and say thank you.' Leila took a step towards him and tenderly kissed his cheek. As she breathed in against his skin she reached out her hand to hold the back of his head and moved her mouth around to meet his. Without breaking away, her foot gently kicked the bathroom door until it closed behind them.

He hungrily kissed her back, taking a handful of her short hair in his grasp, his other arm around her waist, pulling her in even closer. His tongue searched hers out and he lifted her easily onto the edge of the sink. She wrapped her legs around his waist, and they kissed as though it was the only thing to do on a wintry Christmas morning as frost blanketed the ground outside.

'So, this is wonderfully unexpected,' whispered Nick. A floorboard creaked outside in the corridor and Nick silently slid the bolt across the inside of the door.

Leila giggled, and Nick put his finger to his lips smiling. 'Sshh. I don't know about you, but I think this looks pretty damning if we're discovered.'

She was still wearing the novelty pyjamas that she had painstakingly picked out at M&S once she knew that Nick was going to see them. Lucy's insistence on a Christmas nightwear theme had been tricky to navigate, sidestepping all the cute but deeply unsexy offerings for one that offered the balance between festive and flirty. This two-piece set had spaghetti straps, yet little reindeer motifs on the three-quarter length trousers. And judging by Nick's second kiss, which was even more intense than the first, her sleepwear was doing the job.

'We should go and get breakfast,' Leila reluctantly said, gently jumping down from the basin.

'Do we have to? Can't we stay in here all day?' Nick stuck his bottom lip out.

'To be honest I had higher hopes for the location of our first proper date.'

Encouraged, Nick replied, 'So this is a date is it?'

'In the loosest sense of the word,' Leila stood on tiptoe and gave him another kiss. 'Wait here for a couple of minutes.' She then very slowly pulled back the lock and opened the door a crack. Seeing the coast was clear, she gently eased herself through the open doorway and ran down the hallway.

Church that morning was non-negotiable. Even Alex, who seemed quieter than normal didn't suggest staying behind to be on turkey watch. They walked down to the church in pairs, as though they were on a school trip. Leila walked in time with Marcus, slipping her arm through his for support as they made their way down the icy path.

'You seem chirpy this morning sis,' Marcus said.

'It's Christmas morning, the sun is shining, the ground looks snowy, I've had two glasses of champagne and it's not even 11am — of course I'm chirpy.'

'I know it's a bit different to our normal Christmases, but it meant a lot to Lucy to have it here.'

'You don't need to explain Marcus, I'd be the same, and she's doing a great job. I just wish she'd relax a bit and enjoy it.'

Her brother sighed. 'I know, but she just throws herself into things and wants everything to be perfect. I've tried telling her, but it's no good. Apparently her dad was like that too — the opposite to her mum and Nick.'

At the sound of his name being spoken aloud Leila's heart leapt a little. And as Marcus had brought him up, she could legitimately carry on the conversation without it seeming odd. 'Um, they're really nice, aren't they? Lucy's family, I mean?'

'Yeah, they're ok. Her mum's a bit loopy and way out, but Nick seems a decent bloke. Bit of a ladies' man though. Lucy says he goes through women like water. But then, if I looked like him, I probably would too.' Marcus, it was true, was not a natural heartthrob, but he was distinguished in a country set type way. More tweed and slip-on brogues than tattoos and stubble, but he'd never been short of girls at the pub twirling their hair when he talked to them.

The mention of Nick's name in the same sentence as the phrase 'ladies' man' chastened Leila's good mood slightly. When they were on the boat in Dartmouth he'd said that he and dating didn't go well together, which she'd assumed meant that he hadn't met the right girl, but what if the problem was him instead?

'Mind you,' Marcus added, 'It's nice to have another bloke in the family after being outnumbered for so long.'

'You've had Alex,' Leila reminded him needlessly. Marcus and Alex had always had a strained relationship; Alex was a polished city boy, flash with cash, loud of mouth and he collected symbols of his success for a hobby. Her brother was much more down to earth and would rather have a pint of ale in the local pub than a bottle of Cristal champagne in a private members' club.

They'd reached the churchyard, and

Thomas proudly held the gate open for his family to traipse through. They were all wearing their best outfits, most adorned with a new gift. After shaking the vicar's hand and wishing the other smiling parishioners a Merry Christmas they slipped into the pews. It was a small church, only twenty or so rows, but every spare space was taken by the time the organ started up with the familiar strains of *O Little Town of Bethlehem*. At the last minute Nick had squeezed on the end of the pew next to Leila, so their shoulders squashed into each other. His hip pressed against her side, with an intensity that wasn't entirely necessary, but very much welcome. Her arm closest to him hung by her side and during the second hymn he clasped her hand in his, unseen amongst the folds of their coats. His large hand easily encased hers, their fingers entwined in the warmth of his pocket.

Leila made sure that on the walk back up to the house after the service she wasn't coupled with Nick. She was probably being too self-conscious about it, but after the painting, and their synchronised disappearance at breakfast, she didn't want to raise any suspicions. He must have felt the same as he was quick to stroll on ahead with Lucy, listening to her reel off a minute-by-minute account of what needed to be done to make the meal perfect when they got home.

Leila was sandwiched between her parents, who had embraced the new setting for Christmas with remarkable ease. 'It's quite a relief to have a Christmas morning where I'm not wearing an apron,' Judy confided. 'At first, I was a little concerned at whether it would feel as special, but I'm really enjoying myself. And it's nice not to have to keep popping downstairs to check on the guests.'

Thomas was a lot more adept at switching off from the hotel below their flat than Judy was. Once the door between the two zones was closed, Thomas didn't think about bookings, or menus, or Room 2's late checkout, or Room 14's dodgy TV that kept freezing on adult cable channels. Judy found it more difficult to compartmentalise her private life from her role as innkeeper and landlady. Leaving the hotel in the very capable hands of their team of managers over the busy Christmas week was a first, but Leila thought her parents were weathering the freedom very well.

'Oh, I meant to say Leila, five of the women that came for your weekend away have booked a week in the spring, isn't that good? And one of them recommended us to a friend who's getting married, and so we've got that in April as well, isn't that great?' Thomas said.

'We have to say Leila, that we are so very proud of what you've done with the website and the club,' Judy continued. Leila opened her mouth to correct the word club to community, but realised she was being pedantic. 'I think you know that we all had our doubts that you'd see it through, but we couldn't be prouder with what you're doing, and have no doubt that you're going to last the distance now.'

'Yes love,' her dad took up the baton. 'I know we all teased you at the beginning, but you've proved us all wrong, we're very proud.' With that, he put his arm around his youngest daughter's shoulder and Leila walked the rest of the way back to the house in a guilty silence.

Operation Christmas started even before hats and scarves were properly hung up on the hooks that Marcus had drilled into the wall that week. Lucy bounded into the kitchen to take the turkey out and parboil the potatoes, and Tasha and Mia were dispatched to the dining room to start laying the table, with a photoboard as a reference of how Lucy wanted it to look. Nick was ordered to go outside and cut some sprigs of holly and mistletoe from the front garden to tuck into the napkin holders that Lucy had found on Pinterest, Leila had been given a chopping board, knife and a bag of carrots, Stephanie was in charge of putting some festive tunes on the stereo while Judy and Thomas were on grandchildren duty in the living room.

'Oh no! You're cutting them the wrong way!' Lucy exclaimed over Leila's shoulder, 'I wanted them to be sticks, but you're doing them round!'

'Um, sorry, but won't they taste the same?' Leila replied.

'But they're going in the same serving dish as the beans and they're not going to be the same shape now!' Lucy whined.

'Worse things happen at sea,' said Marcus coming into the kitchen, his arms full with logs he'd retrieved from the shed. He paused behind Lucy to kiss his wife on her head.

'That's hardly helpful Marcus!' Lucy huffed, bending down to open the oven, which shot a puff of hot steam into her face.

'Can I help?' Alex said, putting his hands on Lucy's hips to steer her protruding bottom out of his path. 'I'm a champion cutter-upper.'

Lucy stood upright, a little flushed, probably from the steam, possibly from Alex's playful manoeuvre.

'Leila, can I borrow you a minute?' Nick said, peering his head around the back door.

Leila put down her peeler and steeped out into the cold garden in her socks, closing the back door behind her and blowing into her hands to warm them up. Nick sprang out from behind the corner, holding a sprig of mistletoe over their heads, pushed her gently backwards against the wall and pressed his lips onto hers.

'Nick!'

'Sorry, couldn't resist. In you go again,' and he pushed her back inside the kitchen. Leila tried to continue grating and chopping without grinning like a Cheshire cat, but it was impossible.

The rest of the afternoon passed by in a blur of convivial family time and snatched moments of intimacy. Nick's foot brushed hers intentionally under the table. Her hand momentarily rested on the small of his back as she reached around him in the kitchen. They gave each other secret signs, like an almost imperceptible eyebrow raise, a subtle wink, a half grin. Her tummy was constantly whirling with butterflies and she couldn't stop smiling.

Later that afternoon, with everyone else

asleep in front of the afternoon movie, heads lolling onto sofa backs and bodies slumped onto beanbags, Nick's head nodded towards the door. Leila followed him out to the corridor where he took her face in both his hands and gave her a long lingering kiss before they furtively slunk back into the lounge. They sat next to each other on the lounge floor, their hands entwined until Marcus started stirring from his sleep and they sprang apart.

Later that night Mia was still awake, tapping on her iPhone under the covers, so Leila couldn't sneak down to Marcus's study where Nick was waiting for her on a blow-up bed. She'd whispered her intent to try to come down and keep him warm, but she now knew that it was impossible and it was already after midnight. She retrieved her phone from her bag and started typing.

Mia still awake. No chance for escape. But what do you say about making a hasty retreat from here to mine tomorrow morning? Lx

I say that sounds splendid. Happy Christmas Lei. Nx

CHAPTER 13

Nick was going to be here soon. Despite living relatively near each other they'd decided to leave Marcus and Lucy's separately, and she'd had an hour's head start. Lucy had made no attempt to disguise how livid she was when Leila had claimed that her upstairs neighbour's leaking bath necessitated an immediate rush back to London.

'Well, can't it wait until tomorrow?' she'd hissed. 'It's Boxing Day, I have the whole day mapped out.'

'You can't ignore a leak,' Alex said. Leila was momentarily grateful for his interjection until he followed it up with, 'I'd better come back to London with you to help sort it out.' Thankfully Tasha was having none of it, so at least Leila didn't need to concoct a more complex web of lies as to why she needed to fix this plumbing problem alone. She had no idea what excuse Nick came up with as she'd already left by then. She just hoped he'd managed to get through the barricade that Lucy may have put in front of the door to stop any other guests making a run for it.

Leila ran around her flat like a whirling dervish, shoving her dirty laundry into the bottom of her wardrobe, disposing of whatever it was that was in the fridge that was making her kitchen smell, taking a speedy shower, and hiding her mug that a blog follower had sent her that read 'God must have been a woman with a sense of humour. I mean, she invented men didn't she?' She lit a row of cinnamon-scented tea-lights on the mantelpiece, built a pyramid of logs and rolled up paper in the grate that was now flickering with flames, switched on the fairy lights that she'd threaded through the branches of the dwarf pine Christmas tree that stood in a bright red pot, and the living room was suddenly transformed into a romantic winter wonderland.

A quick glance at the clock confirmed that he was now late. Leila opened up her laptop.

Hope everyone had a very happy Christmas! Mine was lovely but uneventful.

The lady doth protest too much, Leila thought, deleting the last two words she'd just written, just as the knocker sounded. Her nerves were making her fingers fumble with the lock. She could see Nick's outline through the mottled glass panes in her front door.

As she opened it, he handed her a plastic bag with the name of a well-known chain of petrol stations on it. 'I didn't know if you had any food in, so I bought us lunch.' Leila peered inside to find an assortment of sausage rolls, crisps, Cornish pasties and two bottles of wine.

'Wow, you know how to treat a girl. First date in a bathroom and a Boxing Day meal from a garage.'

'This may explain why I'm still single.'

'Well, according to my brother, you're something of a ladies' man.' Leila ushered him into her living room. She wasn't planning on repeating what Marcus had told her, but seemingly her mouth was able to move independently of her brain.

'Am I indeed? Lucky me.' He moved to dodge Leila's kittenish shove, and instead reached out to grab her and pull her down on top of him on the sofa. They play-wrestled for a couple of seconds before they started kissing, and pulling at each other's clothes.

'Shall we go into your bedroom?' Nick

murmured.

'I sleep on a bunk bed,' Leila whispered back, kissing his neck.

Nick raised himself up on his forearms, 'Um, you what now?'

Leila smiled. 'I sleep on a bunk bed. You'll bash your head on the ceiling.'

'Or you will.' Nick added cheekily.

They stayed in the living room. All afternoon.

'It's really cool how you can guess people's lives from their feet,' Nick said in the early evening as the street lamps illuminated the pavement outside and he and Leila were cuddled on the sofa naked under a blanket.

'I love doing that. You can tell a lot about someone from their gait.'

'From their what?' he teased.

'Their gait. Their walk. Some people take big long strides, others totter along, some amble slowly looking at the world around them, others shuffle. It's a fun game.'

'I can think of another fun game. Shall I close the blind first though?'

Nick stayed the night, which she hadn't planned for. But then The Plan seemed to have been torn up, burned and rewritten many times in the last year. It had been a long time since Leila had woken up in her own home with a man beside her. Even longer since it was someone she really, really liked. After mercilessly teasing her about her choice of bedroom furniture, while heaving himself up the ladder onto the bunk, they'd both fallen into a dreamless sleep, his leg casually crossed over hers.

The French doors out to the garden were deliberately free from curtains or drapes. Leila liked to be woken by the sunlight, and the sound of the birds talking to each other as they drank from the small fountain she'd installed along one of the borders.

'My eyes! My eyes!' Nick cried, pulling the cover up over his head. 'Why is it brighter than fire in here?' He mumbled from underneath the duvet.

Leila laughed. 'Because it's nearly 10am and the world wants us to wake up.'

'I need coffee.'

'I can't carry it up the ladder, so you're going to have to come down.'

'Oh yes, the ladder. I momentarily forgot that I was twelve again.'

Leila ignored this and started climbing down. 'We could have it outside. It's a lovely day.'

Nick stuck his head out from under the duvet. 'Leila, it's the 27th of December. It's about two degrees outside. I love that you love your garden, but there's no way I'm putting my coat, hat and scarf on to sit and have coffee outside.'

'Do you have plans today?' She would never normally have been so forward, but then she'd never experienced forty-eight hours quite like this before. And as she was standing on the ground and he was still lying on the bunk, she couldn't see his reaction, which helped.

'After I work up the courage to get down the ladder you mean?' he replied. 'Or after I convince you to climb back up and keep me company up here all day?'

'We've run out of snacks. We need supplies to keep our energy up.'

'I like your thinking. I just had an idea about how we can spend the day. I think I owe you a proper first date.'

Leila stepped a couple of rungs up and poked her head up at the foot of the bed. 'Interesting. What did you have in mind?'

'It's a secret. Now put the coffee on.'

Two hours later found them wandering hand-in-hand through the panelled library of Sir John Soane's Museum in Holborn. Nick couldn't have chosen a more perfect place.

'Do you know,' he said, 'this is the room where the body of his wife Eliza lay after she died? And he covered the coffin with ostrich feathers.'

'Really? Ostrich feathers? That's lovely,' Leila replied, trailing her hand along a row of leather-spined books.

'And there are over thirty thousand architectural drawings in this house, I wonder if when they open my house to the public after my death they'll find the same number.'

'Doubtful. Don't you save them all on your computer?'

'See, that's the trouble,' Nick said. 'The romance of our profession has completely gone — even if one day I design a building so incredible, so iconic, what is the National Trust going to do, sell tickets to see my laptop? Right, I've decided, from this moment on, I'm going to hand sketch my designs, and you have to make sure they fall into the right hands after my demise.'

'What if I die before you?'

'You can't. I won't allow it.' He pulled her hand, not giving her time for the gravity of his comment to properly sink in. 'Lei, look at this.' They stood in front of a grand portrait of Sir John in all his finery, his elbows resting on the arms of his chair, his eyes kind and smiling. Nick read the small discreet label next to the painting. 'He's seventy-six here. Looks good for it.'

'Must be the velvet waistcoat, velvet takes years off you.'

'I'm noting all this down for when my time comes.'

'Why wait 'til then? I say seize the day, wear that waistcoat now, live for the moment.'

She was silenced by Nick pressing his mouth on hers and murmuring, 'you're wonderful.'

The walls of each room were crowded with faded oil paintings, shelves of curios, stuffed animals and books, thousands of books. 'You know what these are, don't you?' Leila said, pointing at a series of similarly styled paintings hanging in a chronological row. 'It's the Rake's Progress. Eight paintings showing the life of that bloke, Tom Rakewell, look, it's described on this sheet here, we studied this in History of Art at school. In the first one he gets lots of money off his dad, in the second he has all these fancy suits made, then in the third he spends it all on prostitutes and orgies and booze, the fourth he's arrested, then he marries some old woman to save him from a life of misery and crime, then he starts gambling, goes to prison and ends up in the madhouse.'

'Very impressive. Remind me to invite you along to the next pub quiz night, we'd make a fortune.'

'Sadly I know a lot about very little, and very little about a lot,' Leila replied modestly, pleased with his compliment.

After trying and failing to dodge the rainstorm that accompanied their run back to her apartment from the tube station, they now sat cross-legged opposite each other on the sofa while their clothes drip-dried over the old iron radiator. A smattering of crumbs and drops of mayonnaise from the sandwiches and picnic bits they'd laid out dotted the upholstery. They shared a bottle of wine, which they both agreed was decadent, but necessary for this dark, wintry afternoon.

'Lucy and Marcus would hate this,' Leila stated.

Nick made a sound like a car alarm and then affected his sister's accent. 'Ee-oh-ee-oh-ee-oh, crumbs on the sofa, Marcus we have crumbs on the sofa.'

'Oh stop it!' Leila playfully shoved him. 'Ok, sorry, won't mention them again. You could always try and take my mind off them.'

'Don't need to ask me twice.' In two swoops of his arms, and to the noise of Leila shrieking in laughter, Nick swept everything, all the packaging, crusts, everything, onto the floor and they made noisy frantic love with the feet of strangers splashing in puddles outside the window.

Nick came back into the lounge a while later carrying two steaming mugs of tea. He'd put on a T-shirt and was wearing his boxers. 'If I ask you how you're feeling about this will it provoke a guilty hand-to-head reaction?'

'I was just thinking about that. And no, it won't. Although it should. Maybe that speaks volumes about my morals,' Leila gave a rueful grin as she gratefully accepted the cup and took a small sip. 'I do feel quite torn though. And a bit gutted I didn't meet you either nine months ago or in three months' time.'

'I could disappear out of your life and re-appear in April if you like?'

'That sounds very sensible. And very horrible,' replied Leila.

'So what's the plan then? Are we going to sneak about for the next four months and only come clean when you can legitimately couple up?' Nick sat down on the sofa next to Leila and pulled her feet onto his lap.

'I don't know. Does that even sound possible? We're practically related now.'

'That makes us sound like we qualify for a real life story in *The Globe*. We are not related Leila.'

'Not in *that* way, we're not, but our lives are entwined with each other's now that Marcus and Lucy are married. What if we start dating and then have a horrific break up and then at every family party we have to see each other and secretly spit in each other's drinks when they're not looking?'

'Wow. Psycho alert.'

'I just mean, it's not straightforward, is it? What happens when Lucy and Marcus have kids and at their Christening I'm there with my new boyfriend, Chesney.'

'Chesney Sounds like a catch.'

'It was the first name to come into my head — and you're there with a leggy blonde called —'

'Heidi'

'Veronica.' Leila glared at him. 'And there's a horrible atmosphere and you end up punching Chesney out of jealousy, and I step in to break it up, and Veronica gets involved and pulls my hair —'

'She wouldn't. She's a peacekeeper. A real gentle soul.'

'And the Christening is ruined, and our

family never speak to us again.'

Nick stifled a smile. 'Granted, the future is fraught with potential disaster, but maybe, just maybe, it might turn out to be rather wonderful as well.'

'With your track record and my track record?' Leila reminded him.

'I knew you were having second thoughts.'

'I'm not. It's just there's more at stake with us, if it does go wrong. And trying to make a relationship work when we're keeping it secret adds a whole load of different challenges doesn't it?'

'And excitement? It'll be like we're having an affair without having an affair.'

'Are you always this glass half full?'

'Only when I wake up in a room with curtains and after I have two cups of coffee.'

CHAPTER 14

Lucy

Apart from a dentist appointment on Wednesday and the oil being delivered for the boiler on Thursday, Lucy had nothing planned this week. The past seven months had been a whirlwind of organisation and logistics. First the wedding, then the Well Woman weekend, then the Christmas party, then Christmas. And now, here she was, on the first week of January with nothing to do at all except listen to the sound of the washing machine spinning round.

Lucy had wanted to try and talk to Leila over Christmas about the event in February, but she seemed in such a hurry to leave on Boxing Day morning that you could almost see steam coming off her Ugg boots. It was really inconsiderate of her. Lucy had printed off a timetable of events on neat little cards and left them in each of the guest rooms to ensure everyone knew what was happening when, so Leila couldn't have missed the fact that there was going to be a cold meat buffet at 1pm, followed by a three-mile walk to the lake and back. And Leila leaving early opened the floodgates for Nick to follow suit as well. The trouble with being single for so long, thought Lucy, is that it made people very self-absorbed.

Marcus was also guilty of being pre-occupied with his own agenda lately. Not that he'd ever actively wooed her, or gone out of his way to sweep her off her feet; it was, if anything, the other way round. Lucy smiled to herself as she recalled his rabbit-caught-in-headlights look as she told him that hers was a G&T. But men like Marcus need a bit of guidance as to what would make them happy. What she hadn't considered though was that marriage could be this lonely. It was all she'd ever wanted. It might perhaps be different if she was still working, at least then she'd have a schedule to stick to. But if she was still at the events company, she didn't know how she'd be able to maintain the house, keep on top of what Alina the Polish cleaner was up to and plan Marcus's dinners with visiting vice presidents from the American office. She knew he appreciated her, in his own undemonstrative way, but it would have been nice for him to buy her a nice piece of jewellery occasionally like Alex did for Tasha, or upgrade her car with his end-of-year bonus, without her telling him to.

She thought she'd be pregnant by now. After all, it's what couples in their thirties did after getting married. Someone had once said to her, or had she read it, she couldn't remember, but having children was what couples did when they ran out of things to say to each other. It wasn't exactly like that, in fact it wasn't like that at all. She and Marcus had settled into a really great way of life, having a baby was just the obvious next step. Everything was in place, so it would be perfect timing.

They'd finally bought their own house after years of making landlords richer. It certainly wasn't the forever home she'd wanted, but it was a step closer to it. And it would be a great place to bring up kids while they were young. She'd made sure that the local primary was rated Outstanding by Ofsted. She didn't look at the secondary schools, they'd have moved counties by then, Oxfordshire maybe — she'd always liked the idea of the Cotswolds. Her heart had sunk when she saw the house was pebble-dashed rather than red brick, but it was handy having a brother who was an architect, as Nick said it wouldn't be too hard to remove it, just costly. They needed to do that soon, she thought. It was a shame there wasn't time before they hosted Christmas but no tradesmen would work in the snow, which was annoying.

The kitchen also hadn't been updated since the seventies; Nick said that they should keep the orange splash back as it was 'on-trend retro' but it wasn't his kitchen, and she and Marcus had much more minimalist tastes. Actually, she didn't think Marcus had any tastes when it came to interior decor, which made things easier. She'd replaced the tiles with stainless steel, which was better, although it did show fingerprints up something chronic, she needed to find something for that. White vinegar maybe.

Marcus had flatly refused to call the small front bedroom 'the nursery' like she had when they first viewed it on that wet day in October, and referred to it instead as 'the cupboard' or 'the box'. She'd painted it yellow — 'the colour of sunshine,' she'd called it at the time, no need for him to know that she'd chosen it because it would work for a girl or a boy. Or both. Her granddad had been a twin.

Another thought struck her as she flicked

back through the calendar to check on her cycle dates — if she did push Leila to plan a whole calendar of events for single women over the coming year, might it be a little inconsiderate of her to be pregnant at them? Her bump might be construed as a 'look what you can't have' taunt. But then she doubted she'd be one of those women that completely doubled in size, she'd probably be very compact until the due date, so she might even fit in better with the women who were a little . . . rounder.

Leila answered her phone on the second ring, which put Lucy in a quandary. Did she keep up her affront at Leila's early exit on Boxing Day? Or did she try and be friendly seeing as she did want Leila to come round to her way of thinking and agree to more events? In the end Lucy opened the conversation with a couple of barbed references to Leila's 'emergency' and how wonderful the country walk was that she missed, unaware that Judy had already told Leila that the scenery wasn't a patch on South Devon's and the ground was so hard with frost it made your knees ache. Lucy then went on to talk around the topic of events in general, saying how post-Christmas was such a lull in people's social lives and wasn't it a shame that there weren't more things to do? 'Oh hang on,' she said seamlessly. 'Why don't we plan the next few months of workshops?'

Leila had seemed distracted during the phone call, Lucy thought afterwards. Which was fairly typical of her sister-in-law, never focusing on one thing at once, trying to multi-task to the detriment of whatever it was she was trying to do. But it did mean that she agreed, albeit a little half-heartedly, to Lucy planning an event every fortnight, from small book-club type get-togethers in coffee shops and wine bars to weekends in Dartmouth every month. This was an event planner's dream gig, a client who didn't really know what they wanted and a target audience that was growing in size every day.

She had to admit, when Leila first mentioned this idea of hers to be celibate for a year, back at Judy and Thomas's Sunday lunch, she thought it was a massive over-reaction to a bad break-up, not that she had any experience of a bad break-up herself. She had neatly and swiftly disposed of all her past boyfriends as soon as she realised they weren't marriage material. She had never met the long list of Leila's exes that Marcus reeled off that day, but she assumed that Leila stuck around with boyfriends for far longer than she should have done.

Before Lucy met Marcus, she had a finely tuned radar that could tell within the first minute or two of meeting a man whether he could possibly factor significantly in her life, and if not, well, it would be a waste of both their time and energy to carry on a conversation, let alone a romantic dalliance. Lucy gave an involuntary shiver at the thought of still being single now. It had been a time-consuming pastime researching the right circles and men to align herself with. Thank goodness that was all done and dusted.

Hearing some of the women's stories at the workshops did occasionally strike a chord with Lucy, of course they did. And not all the women were misguided, or not making the best of themselves. Some had genuinely had awfully bad luck with men stealing money, being serial cheaters, abusive, or in the case of Kim, an attractive thirty-something insurance broker from Wigan, her ex was an actual con-artist who ended up in prison. Lucy couldn't imagine ever being taken in by anyone like that herself, but to her surprise, she had felt tears pricking at her eyes when these women were confiding their secrets. Many of them had hidden the extent of their misery from their friends and families, wanting to shield themselves from their judgement or pity, yet they felt safe opening up to Leila's community of women. That was pretty amazing.

Before they'd even done a single workshop or event, back at the beginning when she and Leila were brainstorming what to do, Lucy had suggested hosting singles evenings where they would also invite men along and try to play matchmaker but Leila was horrified, saying that was the opposite of what she wanted to do with the site and the events. Lucy recalled her sister-in-law's voice going up an octave and her fist slamming down on the table as she implored Lucy to 'try to get it.' Apparently the community wasn't about lonely women looking for a happy-ever-after as a couple, it was for single women coming together and embracing who they were, and the workshops were meant to be designed to help them understand themselves better.

Lucy still wasn't completely sure she understood. How could you get to know yourself better? You *were* you. You didn't need to sit in a quiet room and think of a happy place to understand yourself. But then, if women were happy to part with upwards of three hundred quid to do exactly that, then who was she to contradict them?

Her eyes flitted around the kitchen again, stopping to rest on the visualisation board she'd made at the last event that was propped up on the dresser. What was it Tasha had said? Inspiration not aspiration. Looking at the pictures now, the Aga, the dog, the handbag, the shoes, she realised that Tasha was right. This wasn't a motivation tool, it was a shopping list. Aside from the picture of the two little blonde girls, which gave Lucy a sharp and painful pang, she could make everything else hers that very afternoon simply by getting her credit card out. There was no impetus, no incentive on this board like there was on Leila's and Tasha's. But how did they know what they wanted in life and she didn't? Even the word 'visualisation' made her feel a bit silly, what was she meant to do, close her eyes and suddenly her dream future would float before her eyes? That didn't seem very likely.

Just then the alarm sounded on her phone. 6.45pm. Marcus would be beginning his fifteen-minute walk from the train station now, which gave her a quarter of an hour to re-do her make-up, brush her hair and open a bottle of red to let it breathe. On her way out of the kitchen she stirred the cassoulet that Alina had made earlier on in the afternoon and left simmering in the oven. How on earth would she have been able to do all this if she was still employed?

CHAPTER 15

The hedonistic, passionate whirlwind that was the week between Christmas and New Year had given way to a very sedate start to January. Nick was working from his firm's Dubai office for a fortnight and he'd flown out on the 3rd. The project that had consumed most of his time for the previous year was nearing completion and he needed to be on site every day. He'd been gone for eleven days now and for Leila, a mist had descended on the time they'd shared together. She found it difficult to recall with any real clarity the feelings she thought she'd had. Looking back, the five days together seemed like a fantasy, not reality. She had never laughed so much, or felt so at ease with any man before. He had such a relaxed outlook on life that felt so calming, but maybe she was imagining that too?

They wanted to avoid bumping into any-one they knew, particularly as they found it difficult not to be extremely tactile with each other, so they'd spent most of their time in her flat. They'd ventured out to small cafes and bars that they knew were off the radar for anyone in their circle, even travelling a few more tube stops than necessary to ensure anonymity. They'd spent New Year's Eve wrapped up in numerous layers grilling steaks on a barbecue on her patio and drinking champagne from wine glasses as Tasha had never got around to buying the 'new home' flutes she'd promised.

They'd both been invited to fancy parties, one of Nick's colleagues had even booked a table at the Oxo Tower that Nick was invited to join, while Jayne and her husband Will were hosting a party in their new wine bar and seemed genuinely disappointed when Leila stuttered her excuses. In previous years, Leila would've snapped up the opportunity to get dressed up and work her way through the wine list with her best friends, but the low-key way she spent it with Nick, huddled up in their fleeces toasting marshmallows on the barbecue, ranked as her favourite dawning of a new year yet. She thought Nick had said the same, but now Leila couldn't remember if he had actually said that or just nodded in agreement when she had.

She had to give Nick credit though; he was great at staying in touch, sending emails and messages throughout the day, and often following up with a phone call when he was in his hotel at night, but the four-hour time difference meant that he'd sometimes fall asleep clutching the phone and slept through its vibration.

Another downside of the forced separation was that absence made the heart grow guiltier. Which wasn't helped by Lucy phoning and catching her at a particularly off moment, and Leila had suddenly found herself agreeing to a gruelling calendar of events over the coming months. The last few weeks, if Leila was being honest, had all felt a bit off. Work was hard, and not rewarding in any way. Her kind and acquiescent boss had been replaced with a tyrant who was enforcing a strict clocking in and clocking off routine, and some of the more interesting projects that had come in were being allocated to everyone else, which left her with the patio courtyard of a local library, and the front walkway and car park of a Travelodge to get her teeth stuck into. He'd also done away with the traditional meeting rooms, replacing them with 'breakout clusters' where you stood around high tables and workshopped your issues. As she'd been using the quietest meeting room at the far end of the corridor to take Nick's international calls in privacy, this had been a particularly galling change to accept.

She'd been seriously contemplating going it alone for a while now, but these changes made the need more pressing. She and Nick had spent a few hours talking over the pros and cons before he went away, and he was really supportive, even saying that he'd probably be able to pass some clients her way. It was such a leap of faith though. And with so much uncertainty in her life, was now the right time to add to it?

On top of this, to say that she was beating herself up about lying to her followers was an understatement of epic proportions. She was self-flagellating every time the thought of the blog flitted into her brain, and now with all these meetings planned, her mouth literally went dry when she thought of how deceitful she had been. And selfish. Not to mention weak-willed and self-centred. Fickle. Spineless. Impressionable. Disloyal.

Leila banged her head on her desk, which made her colleagues at nearby work stations all look up. 'Watch out!' one of them hissed, but it was too late.

A shadow fell over her desk. 'Leila. A word.'

It was the first verbal warning she'd ever received, and she felt like she was fifteen again and had been caught buying Diamond White in her blazer. The library client had complained about her lack of enthusiasm for such a high-profile challenge. The twenty-square metre space out the back of the library had previously only been used for recycling dog-eared books, and now it was to be a 'shaded reading area offering an al fresco pastoral experience for literature lovers'. Why wasn't she more excited by this? Why indeed? The press release made it sound amazing. In reality, it was a patio with a retractable awning. Yawn.

'You're worth more than that Lei,' said Nick later that evening when she'd re-counted her day for him. 'You need a new challenge. I wasn't going to say anything until I knew for certain, but I've got another project confirmed in Dubai — a new resi-dential compound of two hundred houses, and they need a landscape architect for the whole project.'

There was a pause, in which he was trying to guess her facial expression, which was hindered by the crackly line and three and a half thousand miles between them. 'I recom-mended you and they want to meet you. I'm coming back to London for a meeting next week and then flying straight back out — do you fancy joining me for five days so you can meet them, see the site and meet the team? They'll pay for everything.'

Leila's stomach lurched. She knew what this meant, five solid days of being together. No clandestine calls or stealthy, snatched minutes together for five whole days. 'But what do I tell my boss?'

'That he can stick his verbal warning up his clocking-in machine.'

'What about my family?'

'What about them?' Nick asked patiently.

'Well, Lucy and Stephanie must know you're in Dubai, and then if I suddenly go there too, Stephanie could tell my mum, or Lucy could, and then they'd put two and two together and —'

'Take a breath Lei,' Nick joked. 'You're over thinking this. Remember, no-one else knows that we're dating. If anyone cares enough to wonder why we're working on the same project, it's just a case of two people in the same industry, and family, helping each other out. You have to relax about this. No-one will find out about us. Please say yes Leila.'

'Because you want my landscaping expertise, or you want to whisk me away to Dubai, ply me with booze and spend five days lying next to me naked, apart from getting dressed for one quick meeting with a Sheikh squeezed into our schedule of debauchery?'

'Definitely landscaping.'

'That's ok then. I'll think about it.'

'We need to tell them soon.'

'Ok. I've thought about it, and yes.'

'Oh my.'

'Yes Nick. Oh my.'

They'd agreed that she should check in first and then text him her seat number, 9A, so he could request the one next to her when he checked in. He didn't understand why she was being so cautious, it's not as though Heathrow was teeming with people they knew, but she felt safer knowing that they couldn't be spotted together before they were through security.

She had been so excited about the trip she hadn't anticipated the crushing stabs that kept attacking her every time she spoke to her mum about preparations for the next weekend retreat, or fielded one of Lucy's hourly calls, or had Tasha on the phone extolling her newfound strength of character. Her sister had been so enthusiastic about her resigning from her job, in fact the whole family had. Tasha had even recommended the hotel that she should stay at in Dubai. Apparently Alex always stayed there when he went on business trips and he'd said it was lovely — not that he usually got enough time to enjoy the amenities of the hotel, by all accounts he was holed up in an indeterminate glass tower for days on end. Leila was hopeful that her own business trip might not be quite as full-on work-wise.

To her surprise, they'd all got behind her setting up on her own. 'Before the last eight months, I wouldn't have thought you had it in you,' Judy had said, 'but you've proved us all wrong Leila, and shown that you can put your mind to anything.' *If only you knew.*

Nick wasn't in the business class lounge, and didn't appear at the gate either. The plane had started boarding the families and being in business class she was invited to board 'at her leisure' but there was nothing leisurely about the way her eyes kept flitting to the gate desk. He must have had second thoughts. Perhaps Lucy had found out somehow and was about to blow the whistle on them. The thought made her shudder.

She was now one of the last passengers left, and had to make a quick decision what to do. No, she didn't. This trip was not about spending time with Nick, it was a business trip. Somewhere along the line she had forgotten the reason for the entire visit. She had responsibilities, she had a reputation to build, a potential client to impress, the Nick aspect was a mere bonus. In fact, it's better, she thought as she gave her boarding pass in and turned left at the door. Nick would have been a distraction, this way she could legitimately be absolved of all guilt and have a good, profitable meeting. Yes, this had totally worked out for the best.

'Hello you.'

Her heart flooded with relief and a big smile broke over her face as she saw a familiar face sat in seat 9B.

'I thought you weren't coming,' Leila said.

'I snuck past as you were doing that nervous twitching thing where you crane your neck and dart your eyes about.'

'I was not twitching, I was probably stretching.'

'Yes, absolutely. Nothing better than a pre-flight stretch. Are you going to sit down or are you still giving your muscles a flex?'

'Are you going to be this annoying for the full seven hours?'

'Probably.'

'Wonderful. I'd better have a glass of that then, thank you,' Leila took a glass of champagne off the tray the cabin crew was offering. Nick reached across her and took one for himself.

'Cheers. Here's to . . .'

'Deception and lies.' She clinked her glass against his.

'That's cheery. Was thinking more along the lines of adventure and amore.' He clinked her glass again.

'Guilt and duplicity.' Another clink.

'Devotion and passion.'

'Dishonesty and betrayal.'

'Soul mates and serendipity.'

In spite of herself she laughed, 'You're ridiculous. Are you not feeling an ounce of remorse?'

'Remorse? No. A smidgen of guilty excitement, yes. But I'm sure that will lift as soon as the wheels do.' Right on cue the engines whirred and the plane sped across the runway carrying them above the clouds. Nick was right. As the distance between them and their respective families lengthened, the feeling of tightness in Leila's chest became less noticeable, and when Nick reached across the armrest and wrapped his fingers in hers, she felt completely, and totally, at ease.

When they landed in Dubai it was as though a blanket of caution had been lifted. Every time they'd met in a café, a bar, a gallery, or

237

somewhere else they weren't meant to be, they'd subconsciously flicked their eyes around the room first, checking, always checking. But neither their friends nor family knew anyone in Dubai, so to everyone else at passport control they were just a couple. As they wandered around duty free picking out their eight-bottle allowance, they were the same as all the other husbands and wives. As they argued over who should pay, they were just like everyone else. Standing in the taxi queue to their hotel, sandwiched between Tony and Claire from Newport and Andy and Samantha from Exeter, they were Nick and Leila from London. Nick and Leila, Leila and Nick.

They'd had to pretend to be married when they booked in, so they were even Mr and Mrs Whitfield at the check-in desk too. 'No, thank *you,*' Leila told the concierge as her suitcase was delivered to the room with a 'thank you Mrs Whitfield' greeting. A handwritten note on a fruit basket from the manager welcoming them to the hotel, imploring Mr and Mrs Whitfield to have a nice stay, was a lovely touch, as was the message that appeared on the TV screen when they turned it on on their third day, having had no need for any external entertainment for the first seventy-two hours.

'I'm loving this,' Nick said languidly in the afternoon on the second day, stretching out his toe until it nudged hers on the next sun-lounger. 'Is it almost beer o'clock?'

Leila looked up from the laptop that was balanced on her bare stomach as she'd decided that work was more bearable in a bikini in the sun. 'Not until we've run through my pitch one more time.'

'Oh come on Lei, it was perfect the other three hundred and seventy-four times we've done it. Don't overthink it, it's going to be great. *You're* going to be great.'

'And we can't get drunk again tonight, the meeting's at nine am.'

'Oh rubbish, so we have to have an early night? That sounds awful,' Nick nudged her toe again.

'Nicholas. Stop it. Right, go from the bit where you talk about the colonnade linking the club house to the gym, and then I'll do my bit about the different textures sur-rounding the pagoda.'

'And you'll reward me how exactly?'

Leila raised one eyebrow and smiled. 'Exactly as you wish.'

'Oh my goodness, this is exciting! Ok, are you ready for the most thrilling speech containing the words "covered walkway" you've ever experienced?'

'Ready. Are you ready for the most electrifying couple of hours you'll ever spend horizontal after that?'

'Ready.'

They couldn't get back to their room quick enough after finishing their run-through, Nick chasing Leila giggling through the corridors of the hotel, careering around corners while making F1 noises and narrowly missing a housekeeping trolley. Laughing and breathless, Leila stuck the card into the lock and the door flung open to the unmistakable and rather overpowering scent of fresh lilies. A massive bouquet took up the whole of the desk, an explosion of white flowers wrapped extravagantly with pink tissue and tied with raffia.

'From the manager? A bit excessive,' said Nick ripping off his shorts and diving spread-eagled onto the bed. Leila took the small card out of the envelope that was tucked among the blooms.

Good luck my darling, you're going to be amazing. We are just so proud of you and all you are achieving in your life, Mum and Dad xxxx

The energy and raw passion of the minute before was extinguished. Leila put the card down and walked past the bed Nick was lounging on. She opened the balcony door and slumped onto a chair. The flowers were a simple, thoughtful gesture, and yet they made her feel sick.

The swish of the balcony door sliding back startled her and Leila swung round to see Nick standing in the doorway, a hastily grabbed towel covering his modesty.

'I read the card,' he said quietly.

'Oh.'

'That was nice of them.'

'Yes.'

'So . . . what now?'

'I don't know.'

'But the amazing sex is off?'

She swivelled round angrily.

'What? I'm kidding! Trying to lighten the mood, come on Lei, chill out and stop feeling so on edge all the time.' He knelt down beside her on the balcony, his hands enveloping hers on the arm of the chair. Leila didn't try and move hers away, so encouraged, Nick moved a chair next to hers and they both sat staring out over the pool and beach bar below.

'Hey, isn't that Alex?' Nick suddenly said, craning forward for a closer look.

Leila tried to follow his gaze to see where he was looking. There was a man who did bear a striking resemblance to her brother-in-law, currently engrossed in rubbing sun cream all over the back of a slim, young brunette. He lifted up the tiny string that ran across her back to slide his fingers underneath. Whoever he was, he was taking sun protection very seriously.

'No, it can't be. He's on a course in Cyprus, I think Tasha said.' Leila leaned back in her chair and picked up a magazine.

'No, Leila, look, it *is* him!'

Leila put the magazine down and stood squinting against the balcony railings. The man had stood up now, hastily covering his excitement at the exuberant sun cream-spreading with a towel. His face was raised to the sun, which was low in the sky over the block Nick and Leila's room was in so he was facing them square on. Leila immediately ducked down under the cover of the balcony balustrade.

'What are you doing?' Nick laughed.

'Ssshhh, it is him! I don't know if he saw me though. Stay down!' Leila hissed.

'But wasn't it Tasha that recommended you stay here? So you're meant to be here, it's him that's not.'

'Oh yes.' Leila stayed crouched down though. 'But I don't want him to see that I've seen him.'

'Why not? You should go down and confront him about why he's here doing what he's obviously doing with someone he shouldn't be doing it with.'

Leila looked horrified. 'It might not be like that! She could be a colleague,' she searched for the rest of the sentence that would make her brother-in-law's actions seem innocent. 'With a history of skin cancer, and he was being honourable, helping her reach the bits she couldn't.'

Nick raised one eyebrow. 'Your desire to find the best in people is commendable Leila, but while that might be a colleague, there's nothing honourable about what he's doing. You need to call him out on it.'

Leila hugged her knees. Tasha was going to be devastated if she found out. *When* she found out. Leila couldn't stand by doing nothing and be complicit in Alex's betrayal. But then by blowing the whistle on him, her own double life might be uncovered too. Oh God, why did things have to be so damn complicated all the time?

Nick got down on the floor next to Leila, their backs resting against the half-height railings. 'Ok, so what are our options? One, we ignore what we saw, as it might very well be innocent, although it's not. Two, we, by we, I mean you, find him and tell him what you saw, and see what he says. Three, you go straight to Tasha and see if at the last minute the location of his course changed from Cyprus to Dubai and in this conversation see if you can find out about any colleague with suspected melanomas.'

In spite of her gloom Leila smiled. 'Four, he saw me, and possibly even us, depending on how long he's been at this hotel, and blows the whistle on us.'

'No, we'd have seen him before, and anyway, if he knew that you were here, then he wouldn't be parading his mistress around would he?'

'She's not his mistress Nick! We didn't see them humping on the sun lounger or anything, I think we need to give him the benefit of the doubt.'

'Ok, so I propose a fifth option — we follow him and find out what's going on.'

'I think you've been watching too many Bond films.'

'Think about it Lei, that way, we'll know for sure what we're dealing with. There's no point at all causing a family rift if it's just a case of sun lotion.' Nick elbowed Leila, 'It'll be fun. He obviously doesn't know you're here, so isn't expecting to see you, which means you can sneak about a bit without him noticing. You could, of course, get totally into character and wear a black abaya and hijab so you're totally in disguise, but then getting into bars might be tricky.'

Leila admitted it did make more sense to get to the bottom of what Alex was playing at before furiously wading in. She was so annoyed. They were having such a lovely time, and she couldn't afford to have yet another distraction before the client pitch tomorrow. Now that she'd resigned from her job, winning this project was vital. If the flowers had never arrived, and if they hadn't seen Alex with the other woman, she and Nick would have spent the rest of the day in bed. They'd have ordered far more dishes than they needed from the room service menu, and asked for the mini bar to be restocked. They'd have lain on the dark beach at night counting the stars while smoking cigarettes and making sand angels. They'd have showered together, lathering the soap into each other's bodies and laughing, they would help each other walk over the slippery floor before making love on the carpet. They'd have slept curled tight into each other, his hips pressing into her, and they would have woken up smiling.

But instead, her bum was numb from sitting on a tiled balcony, her guilt had returned, and she was currently plotting how to break up her sister's marriage.

A couple of hours later Nick flung a carrier bag from the neighbouring party shop at Leila, who deftly caught it. 'I got you a choice of these.'

'Don't you think this is all a bit OTT?' Leila said, rummaging through the selection of wigs he'd just bought. 'I mean, surely wearing an Ariel the Mermaid wig would draw more attention rather than less?'

'But he's known you for what? Sixteen, seventeen years? He's going to spot you straight away if you walk around looking like you.'

'So why don't you do it then? He's only met you three times, I bet he wouldn't be able to place you if you wear your glasses and not your lenses, and put a cap on?'

'I'm happy to if you really don't want to take on this mission.'

'I really don't want to take on this mission.' Leila ran a hand through her short hair. 'And it is definitely him. While you were out I asked at reception. They wouldn't tell me his room number, but they confirmed it's him.'

'Right. We need a plan.'

Plans don't necessarily work out the way you want them to, Leila thought in her head before batting away her negativity and replacing it with pragmatism. 'Ok, so it's 7.30 now. If I know Alex, he's going to be hitting a bar for a pre-dinner beer pretty soon, then going to a fancy restaurant. If the lady in question, and I use the term "lady" loosely, is more than just a colleague, then he's not going to want to stray far from their room for dinner, so they can get back there quickly.'

'Oh, that's a good shout. Hang on, how do you know that?' Nick asked.

'Because it's exactly what I would do,' replied Leila cheekily. 'Which means, if you do a quick scout of the bars, and in the meantime, I'll ring round the restaurants asking if they've got a booking in his name. Of course, he could just be chancing it and turn up without a reservation, but if he wants to impress her, he'd have planned ahead.'

'You're good at this deception lark, should I be worried?'

'I'm the product of too many hours watching crap detective programmes and reading romance novels — the combination is now proving useful.' Leila grinned. 'Ok, go, go.' She shooed him out of the room and pulled the hotel directory out of the top drawer of the bedside cabinet. Her finger ran through the dining options and she picked up the phone. DoJos and Andiamo were a no, but she struck gold with China Garden.

'Yes, table for two at 9pm, Alex Banbury.'

She tapped out a message to Nick to tell him where to head to. She was desperate to go down there with him, but what would be the point of blowing their own cover just to catch Alex out? So she had no option but to turn on the TV and choose between BBC World or an over-acted Columbian soap opera. She opted for the latter. Now she just had to wait.

Nick didn't come back until almost ten, by which time Leila was pacing the room. His shoulders sagged dejectedly as he shut the door slowly and sank into the armchair in the corner of the room.

'Well?' Leila demanded. Looking at his posture and demeanour she could tell the news wasn't good but she didn't yet know quite how bad it was.

'So I saw him.'

'And?'

'And they are very obviously sleeping with each other.'

Leila exhaled noisily and leant her head back.

'But then he saw me watching them, and it was obvious that I'd seen them kissing, and walked over and tried to act as though I was his best friend. He was all, "Mate, you know what it's like, you would do the same wouldn't you?" I told him that no, I wouldn't, not if I had a lovely wife and kids, and then he started getting a bit fidgety and told me that I was mistaken and I hadn't seen anything at all.'

'So then what?'

'Then he went back to his table, threw me the guiltiest of looks over his shoulder as he was hurrying the poor woman out of the restaurant just as her food had arrived.'

'Poor woman? Hardly!' Leila angrily interrupted.

'To be honest, I don't even know if she knows he's married, so I'd reserve your irritation for him.'

Nick was right. Leila had heard enough sob stories from her website to know that all might not be what it seemed. Tales of married lovers whose wife, or in the case of one woman from Birmingham, wives plural, suddenly popped up in family homes were alarmingly commonplace. Alex, on the other hand, was more than familiar with his own marital status. What a dick.

'Right that's it, who does he think he is?' Leila started frantically pulling on her shoes.

'Lei, don't. There's nothing to be gained

249

at all from you barging in there all het up and shouting the odds. Think about it. He obviously doesn't know you're here, he doesn't even know that I know you outside of family gatherings, so you're not implicated at all at the moment.'

'I'm so sorry you're involved in this. Thank God he didn't get nasty with you.'

Nick laughed. 'Don't worry about that. I'm about half a foot taller than him, ten kilos heavier, and back in the day I dallied with tae kwon do. He's a jumped-up city boy who's been caught with his pants down.'

Leila flinched at Nick's description of events.

'Just leave him, and instead work out how you're going to tell Tasha that her husband is cheating on her.'

'How the heck does one do that?'

'I honestly have no idea. How old are the kids again?'

'Fifteen, seven and four.'

'Oh Jesus.'

'It's not the first time though,' Leila said quietly. 'No-one else knows this, but he was married before. And he had an affair with Tasha. She was an intern at his company and he got her pregnant, and she told him that he had to marry her or she was telling his wife. I'm the only one she told.'

'Karma strikes.'

'Nick! It's not Tasha's fault!'

'I'm not saying that, but what goes around comes around, leopards can't change their spots —'

'Any more clichés that you want to throw around to make your point?'

'If he'll do it *with* you, he'll do it *to* you.'

'Jesus Nick, I didn't actually want another one!'

'Don't take it out on me Lei, I'm just saying that —'

'I know what you're saying. And it's not very helpful. This is going to devastate Tasha, and it seems to be one big joke to you.'

'Hey, that's unfair. I was the one who went and followed him remember?'

'Yeah, but more so that you could prance around pretending to be a spy rather than because of any heartfelt urge to help.'

'You know what, the mood you're in, I can't really win with you can I?' Nick picked up his cigarettes that he'd thrown onto the desk and turned to walk out on the balcony. Not wanting to give him the satisfaction of being the one to walk away, Leila turned and stormed into the bathroom, noisily locking the door after her to emphasise her frustration. She splashed water on her face and tried to gain some perspective. She didn't mean to take out her rage on Nick, he'd been nothing but supportive all afternoon. He didn't have to get involved the way he did. She should be thanking him, not shouting at him. Not one of her ex-boyfriends would have helped the way he had, and none of them would have put up with so much drama so early on in their relationship. He must feel like she'd been continually testing him at every step. She couldn't blame him if he was in the bedroom now packing his suitcase and settling his half of the bill. The thought made her want to cry.

She breathed a sigh of relief as she came out of the bathroom and saw his mess still scattered around the room — his book on the bedside table, his sunglasses on the TV cabinet, and his suitcase still empty at the bottom of the wardrobe. Nick was sat on the balcony, a beer from the minibar in one hand, and the glowing nub of a cigarette in the other. Leila slid the glass door closed behind her and silently pulled up a chair to sit beside him. 'I'm sorry,' she offered finally. 'I really am very grateful for you helping today, and it's him I'm angry at, not you. You're wonderful.'

He gave her a sideways glance.

'And I think I might be falling in love with you.'

He smiled, picked up her hand, kissed it and simply said, 'Lucky old me.'

She won the pitch.

When they returned to their room after signing the contracts, the pungent smell of the lilies — long gifted to the appreciative housekeeping staff — still lingered. 'You should be over the moon Lei, this is going to launch your business and be a massive money spinner for you.' Nick stood behind her and massaged her shoulders. 'I'm really proud of you.'

Leila wished she could feel as happy and carefree as she should, seeing as the meeting couldn't have gone better. The two Emirati business owners were reassuringly invested in the landscaping and communal areas. For many clients, the outside spaces were afterthoughts that yielded no profit, so why bother doing anything more than the bare minimum? But not only did she have a healthy budget to spend on hard materials and planting, they were also keen on pushing the design envelope and seeing something truly innovative from her. She thought back to the plans she'd been half-heartedly putting together a few weeks before for the budget hotel and the library's patio, just so her company got richer while paying her a pittance. Working on this project was not only going to be so much more enjoyable and rewarding, but her fee was eye-watering compared to her old salary.

'I still can't believe it, to be honest. I owe all of it to you though,' Leila turned round and stood on tip toe to give Nick a lingering kiss.

'Do I take it from that lovely display of affection that you've calmed down about the other things that we're not talking about?'

'Yes. I'll talk with Tasha when we're back in London. There's nothing we can do from here, and actually, Alex has done us a favour, because we blatantly can't risk venturing out of the hotel and bumping into him, so we're stuck in this room until our flight tomorrow afternoon . . . sigh . . . what to do . . .' Leila was silenced by Nick pressing his lips against hers and backing her up until they reached the bed and he playfully pushed her back on it.

'By the way,' Nick said, pulling her close to him under the covers after a rather vigorous hour of lovemaking, 'I think I love you too.'

CHAPTER 16

Tasha's kitchen was once featured in *21 Beautiful Homes*. The white Shaker-style units were described by the salivating journalist as 'Hamptons-esque', while the pale Tiffany blue walls 'introduced a coastal chic feel into the culinary centre of the family home'. Everything from the tea towels to the crockery matched the blue and white colour scheme. Everything except the bright pink kettle that Tasha had bought in a petty act of rebellion against the flawless scheme. That, and the haphazard array of paintings that Oscar had done at nursery that were tacked up with fridge magnets that Alex kept moving onto the side of the big white Smeg fridge, and Tasha resolutely kept moving back to its front.

'So you must be really chuffed,' Tasha said to her sister, pouring boiling water into two mugs. 'I forgot to ask, is instant ok? I can't be bothered to fire up the bean grinder and wait for hours for a cuppa.'

'Sure, it's fine,' Leila replied. 'Yes, I'm really happy about it. I even started sketching some ideas for the project on the flight back.' She reached out to accept the proffered mug. 'Thank you. I can't believe that I stuck around in a rubbish situation for so long before breaking out on my own.' That was too blatant, Leila thought, she should have started softer. She tried to meet her sister's eye to gauge her response but she wasn't looking.

'I mean, sometimes, things seem ok, don't they? When you're in the middle of it, I mean,' Leila continued earnestly. 'But it's only afterwards, when you've got out, that you realise how amazing your life is now. And you wonder why you hadn't done it before.'

'But you did eventually, didn't you, that's what counts.'

Was Tasha talking in riddles too? Or was she still referring to Leila's job? 'I guess. But I think people are too quick to just put up with situations when they don't necessarily have to.' That should do it, Leila thought, she's bound to know what I mean now.

'But you liked your old boss didn't you? It's only since this new despot started that you started to hate it, so you weren't suffering for too long.'

Dammit, Leila thought, Tasha hadn't a clue what she was on about. Maybe subtlety wasn't called for. 'Everything ok with you?' she asked innocently, blowing the steam off her coffee.

'Fine thanks. Mia's mocks are going well, and Talia's just got her ten-metre swimming badge, so yes, couldn't be better.'

'Great, great. And Alex? He's well, is he?'

Leila wondered if she imagined a slight narrowing of Tasha's eyes at the mention of her husband, but there was no mistaking the intonation in Tasha's voice as she frostily replied, 'Very.'

But still Leila pushed on. 'He was away recently wasn't he? On a course or something? That go well?' She was pleased with the way that came out. Just a run-of-the-mill friendly enquiry. Nothing else.

'Yes. In Cyprus. I told you that.' Tasha's reply was curt.

'Oh lovely. Cyprus is one place I'd love to go to. Did he have much of a chance to look around when he was there?' Please say that at the last minute it changed to Dubai, please let Alex not be the monumental shit that I'm starting to realise he is, implored Leila silently.

'Unfortunately not,' Tasha replied, her voice relaxing as she realised that Leila's questioning was based on nothing but sisterly interest. 'The hotel they were staying in was a bit off the beaten track, so nothing much around it — there was hardly any mobile signal at all — I only heard from him twice the whole week! There was a conference centre on site, and I think he was holed up in there most of the time, but he seemed to get a lot out of it, said it was very informative. Another one?' Tasha gestured at Leila's empty cup.

Leila made her excuses and quickly gathered up her things. She didn't know what to say. She'd been hoping that Tasha would make her job easier and confide in her that things weren't going well, or that she had suspicions about Alex, or something, so that Leila's news wasn't so much of a shock. But as everything seemed rosy in her marriage, Leila just couldn't bring herself to shatter a family to pieces.

All the way home on the tube, Leila's thoughts flitted wildly. One minute she'd convinced herself to stay out of it, but the next moment she found herself trembling with anger when she thought of how Alex was treating her sister, and seemingly not caring about it. She couldn't just stand by and watch from the sidelines as Tasha was made a complete fool of. So she made a detour to Embankment and walked through the revolving glass doors into Alex's building.

When Leila asked for Alex it was clear from the receptionist's raised eyebrows — a tricky manoeuvre seeing as they seemed to be tattooed on — that she wasn't the first young woman to waltz in demanding an audience with the charming trader. And it was also evident that Alex was incredibly surprised to see her sat in reception.

'Leila, what a fantastic surprise.' He gave her a kiss on each cheek, and swivelled her around to face the receptionist, 'My sister,' he announced. Unnecessarily and inaccurately Leila thought, why would the receptionist care? But then she saw the smattering of freckles over the receptionist's nose, indicative of some winter sun, and as she turned her head slightly to greet someone, a long brown ponytail swished behind her and everything suddenly became clear.

'In-law. Sister-in-law,' Leila said loudly, loud enough for everyone in the large lobby to hear. 'As in, he's *married* to my sister.'

Alex quickly shuffled her out onto the street, past a few of his colleagues huddled over their cigarettes, and down a small side street. 'What are you doing here Leila?'

'How was Dubai?'

To Alex's credit, his face drained of colour. She hadn't known what reaction to expect. Based on Nick's experience, she was fully prepared for him to deny everything, but he didn't. He even stumbled back a bit and steadied himself against the wall behind him. 'He told you.'

'No-one told me anything Alex. I was there. I saw you.' She didn't elaborate, she didn't need to. His hands were covering his face and she could see he was shaking. 'What are you going to do now?' he asked weakly.

'Depends whether you're going to go back in there,' Leila nodded towards his building, 'and tell your girlfriend that you have a lovely wife and family and that you've made a massive lapse of judgement.'

'Thank you Leila, thank you.'

'I haven't said that I'm not going to tell Tasha, Alex, just that I'm going to give you a chance to do the right thing first.'

'I'm pretty sure Tasha knows, Leila, it's the kids that don't. I don't want to lose any of them, please, it's only a bit of fun, nothing serious, Tash knows that.' He looked pathetic, his face pale, his eyes suddenly looking tired and wan.

Now it was Leila's turn to look shocked. There was no way that her self-assured and zen-like sister knew about his affair and hadn't done anything about it. He must be lying. 'Just go and sort it all out Alex,' she said wearily and left him standing there totally shell-shocked.

As soon as Leila left the house Tasha angrily loaded the cups into the dishwasher. Leila knew. She must know. She'd been insistent on the phone yesterday that she *must* come round for a coffee this morning to tell her all about Dubai, but once she'd arrived she had barely mentioned her own week at all — just incessant questions about Alex. She didn't need her sister's ignorant judgements on the state of her marriage. What worked for them might not work for everyone, but surely she had the right to live her own life the way she wanted to. Tasha slammed the dishwasher door shut and absentmindedly turned it on with only two dirty mugs inside. And damn Alex as well. In the past he'd always been discreet, if he was now making mistakes and going public with whichever young girl he was hanging around with then that was just inconsiderate.

What number was this one? Ten? Fifteen maybe? She closed her eyes. *It's not you,*

Tasha told herself, *it's him. You are kind, and strong, and amazing. It's his own insecurities that make him do this.*

She stood barefoot in the middle of the kitchen, the beautiful, eye-wateringly expensive kitchen with its full-extension, self-closing drawers that Alex had picked out of a glossy catalogue and realised, not for the first time in her marriage, that her husband really was a prize idiot.

Tasha crossed her legs and arms in the hook-up position she'd been taught in Brain Gym. It was meant to coax the two sides of your brain to work in tandem, to boost self-esteem and clarity in moments of anxiety or confusion. She took ten deep breaths in and out through her nose and could feel her sanity slowly being restored.

CHAPTER 17

Nick stuck his head under the covers as a biting breeze swept into the bedroom. Leila was deftly opening the French doors leading to the garden with one hand, while the other one was balancing a breakfast tray carrying a cafetiere, two coffee cups and plate of pastries. She was still wearing her pyjamas, but had put her thick duffle coat on over the top. A bobble hat and mismatching scarf completed the look.

'Lei,' came his muffled voice from under the thick winter quilt. 'I love your sense of romance, I do, but it's sodding February.'

'It's Valentine's Day! And when I bought this flat, I looked at the garden and thought, one day, when I meet the man of my dreams I'm going to have breakfast on Valentine's Day out here. So get up.'

Still firmly ensconced in his duvet tent, Nick mumbled, 'Is it raining?'

Leila laughed. 'No, but it's pretty nippy. I

263

left your fleece at the end of the bed. And your thick ski socks.' Nick used to be a keen skier, even spending a couple of seasons helping out in a family friend's Canadian ski school before he headed off to university, and his knee-length, heavily darned ski socks had been faithful companions for almost two decades.

When she was scouting around for some warm clothes to put out for him while he was still sleeping, she was thrilled to see his threadbare familiar ski socks had taken up residence in the drawer she'd cleared for him. He'd started leaving some of his other things at Leila's too. It started with a spare toothbrush and every time he left the flat for his, she found more little things — a book he was halfway through still on the side table in the lounge, a much-loved hoodie and a couple of work shirts in her wardrobe, and now, the ski socks.

It made sense — after all, since they got back from Dubai, he was spending four nights out of seven at hers. It wasn't just a matter of logistics, but admittedly his flat was much further from her work, and he shared the trendy warehouse apartment with his cousin, who she'd met briefly at Lucy and Marcus's wedding. Although Nick swore he was a decent guy and wouldn't tell anyone if he saw her in her pants getting water in the night, she didn't want to risk it. Nick had also said a few times how relaxed he felt at hers. But that didn't mean that he could spoil this vision of romantic perfection she'd cultivated in her head by staying in bed.

'Nicholas.'

'Uh-oh. I got the full name.' Nick popped his head out of the top of the cover and leaned over the side of the bunk. 'Breathe out,' he demanded of Leila, who was sat just outside the door on one of the white wrought iron garden chairs.

She turned around, looking back into the bedroom. 'What?'

'Before I decide whether or not to join you in this ridiculous farce, I want to know if I can see your breath when you blow out. It's the deciding factor in me getting out from this lovely toasty bed.'

Leila's mouth formed an O and she slowly breathed out. 'Nope, no breath. Get up Romeo.'

Once he'd warmed up by having two coffees in quick succession, and using two more socks as mittens, Nick passed Leila an envelope that he took out of his tracksuit bottoms.

'What's this?' She smiled as she took it

from him.

'Open it,' he ordered, breathing into his hands to warm them up.

Unfolding the paper, her small smile became a big grin as she read further down the page. 'Are you serious?'

Nick nodded.

'This is by far the geekiest and most wonderful thing that anyone has ever done for me.' Leila stood up suddenly, all the pastry crumbs from her lap falling on to the patio as she jumped on Nick's lap and hugged him. In her hand the paper detailed a map that they were going to follow that day. The map was of the counties surrounding London with various crosses dotted all over the countryside. The day she'd taken him to the Museum's gardens, in November, he'd asked her in the pub what made her go into landscape design and she remembered animatedly talking about her inspiration, a woman called Gertrude Jekyll, who was born in the 1840s, and designed over four hundred gardens. She'd studied her as part of her degree but never seen any of her gardens for herself, and Leila recalled saying that doing a tour of the ones near London would be near the top of her bucket list. And Nick had obviously remembered.

He'd evidently researched all the gardens

open to the public, she realised, and even a couple that weren't. He admitted that a couple of sweet-talking phone calls later and even the closed ones had become part of the day's itinerary. 'So, by my reckoning,' he said, 'we have about forty-five minutes before we need to be on the road . . . We've had breakfast. A shower for each of us would take about ten minutes, which leaves thirty-five minutes . . . What to do . . . on Valentine's Day . . . Hmmm.'

They were a little late getting in the hire car that Nick had stashed around the corner from the flat the night before, but neither of them minded. He'd even forward-planned the snacks and entertainment for the journey, with some newly-down-loaded podcasts and a bag of salted caramel popcorn waiting on the passenger seat.

The first stop was Munstead Wood in Godalming, which had been Gertrude Jekyll's home. The ten-acre garden, set amongst wild woodland had been restored following her original plans by the current owners, and they opened the gardens to the public on only three or four days a year. February 14th was not one of them. It was testament to Nick's charm that they'd agreed to open the gates to them that morning. Despite spring not yet pushing winter into the past, there was a surprising amount of colour in the gardens. The bushy perennials no doubt painstakingly chosen for their year-round appeal over a century ago were blooming. And as Leila got back into the car, her camera filled with hundreds of photos, and her grin touching both ears, she realised she'd never been so happy.

'That was amazing,' she gushed. 'It's amazing isn't it, how one person can create such an amazing scene, it's like a painting.'

'Amazing,' Nick teased. 'Now, as I know how much you like tombstones, I'm taking you to a cemetery. I know, I know, romance is not dead — did you see what I did there — dead — graveyard — get it?'

'I get it,' Leila groaned.

They both stood in front of Gertrude's grave. On the stone were three words under each other: Artist, Gardener, Craftswoman. 'That's pretty cool isn't it,' Leila mused. 'I wonder if anyone would call what I did with the Travelodge's front hedge and walkway artistry?'

'Don't forget the dentist's car park you told me that you did last year. That was some pretty impressive craftsmanship right there.'

'Yep. All very honourable projects. Worthy

of a mention on a tombstone.' Leila smiled. 'In all seriousness though, I really appreciate you putting me forward for the Dubai gig. I know the work I did on the museum was a real step up from all the patios and car parks I normally had to do, but I was working as part of a team on that, the Dubai project is all mine, and while it's not quite on Gertie's scale, I do think it might be the start of something pretty exciting.'

'I wouldn't have recommended you though if I didn't think you'd be brilliant at it. It had very little to do with wanting to share a hotel room with you for five days.'

'Very little, or nothing?' Leila teased.

'Very little,' he smiled back.

They'd been lucky with the weather. The rain had held off, and the sky was clear, although it was bitingly cold. Nick took Leila's hand and put it inside his warm pocket, still clasping his. 'Have you read the poem *The Dash*?' he asked.

'No, I don't think so. I'm not a poem sort of person really,' replied Leila.

'Well nor am I, but I read it at my Gran's funeral a couple of years ago, and it's stayed with me. It's about how when you die, on your grave, or plaque or bench or whatever, is your name and two dates separated by a dash. And that dash denotes your life. In the case of Gertie here,' he motioned at the grave in front of him, 'eighty nine years condensed into a dash.'

'That's pretty deep.'

'I'm a deep sort of guy,' Nick smiled, tightening his grip on Leila's hand. 'But think about it Lei. Look around at all the dashes. These people might have saved lives, taken lives, made people laugh, stood shouting at the top of mountains, dived into the sea and swam with sharks, watched children being born, maybe watched loved ones die, they might have danced until dawn, got rip-roaringly drunk on home-made cider, and when they were buried, people were sad. Hopefully. Can't imagine there'd be too many hated sociopaths in Godalming.'

'You'd be surprised. I've seen *Midsomer Murders.* It's the sleepy villages you need to watch. They're hotbeds of sin and debauchery.'

'That's true.' Nick took his hand out of his pocket and swivelled Leila to face him. Tenderly he tilted her chin up and kissed her. 'You're freezing!'

'It is a bit cold,' Leila admitted, stamping her boots on the hard ground.

'Ok, back in the car, lunch is at a pub not far from here.'

■ ■ ■ ■

When they collapsed onto her sofa five hours later in front of the crackling fire, the afternoon had finally surrendered to darkness outside the window. Their noses were pink, their cheeks were flushed and their spirits completely energised, while their bodies were exhausted from a day of walking around the countryside.

'There's a bottle of red with our names on it in the cupboard if you can bear to move,' Leila said, gently nudging Nick with her toe. Just then the knocker sounded.

'Are you expecting anyone?' Nick asked as Leila begrudgingly got off the sofa to tell whoever it was knocking that they'd got the wrong address.

'Nope. Get the wine,' she shouted back.

Nick heard Judy's voice first and leapt up in alarm. His eyes darted frantically around the room trying to see where he could hide. Leila had chosen blinds for the windows instead of big bulky curtains so no opportunity for concealing himself there, and no big pieces of furniture to crouch down behind either. He rapidly hurled himself across the corridor into the bedroom. It was almost zero degrees and he was barefoot so he couldn't go outside, and as it was the first time Judy and Thomas had visited, Leila was bound to show them the courtyard. He could hear them advancing down the corridor. Leila's voice was unusually loud, as she asked them in more polite terms, what the hell they were doing here. He suddenly had a brainwave and climbed the ladder to the bed where he flattened himself under the duvet, concealed behind the high sides of the bunk.

'Dad treated me to afternoon tea at the Savoy for Valentine's Day as a surprise, and we were on our way back to Paddington, when I thought we'd pop in and say hello, as you're probably feeling pretty low today, with it being the day of love and everything.' Judy's head was tilted to the side, and she stroked her daughter's arm as she was talking. 'So here we are. In your lovely, cosy, flat. Give us a tour then.'

As Leila entered each room she quickly scanned it for clues of Nick. She'd managed to quickly fling his big boots into the hall cupboard as her parents had come in, but there was evidence of his presence everywhere, even if he himself had gone AWOL. Two toothbrushes in the mug next to the basin; his work bag hanging on the back of a dining room chair; a few of his sports magazines next to the toilet and an Arsenal mug on the draining board that her father was currently holding in his hand.

'Didn't have you down for a footie fan Leila?' Thomas said.

'It's a joke gift, from work. My leaving present,' she added hurriedly.

'Seven years you worked there, and all you got was a mug?' Judy asked incredulously. 'No wonder you wanted to leave. After all you did for them!'

'I know, right?' Leila rolled her eyes and bustled her parents out of the kitchen before they spotted the six empty wine bottles lined up by the recycling bin and jumped to the assumption that she was replacing men with booze.

'Interesting choice of book Leila,' said Judy, picking up part of her Valentine's present to Nick that was on the end of the kitchen worktop. It was a rude coffee table book on the nude dancing clubs of 1920s Paris.

'Yes, well, um, expanding horizons and all that. Let me show you the garden,' Leila trilled noisily, cautiously opening the bedroom door and breathing a sigh of relief that Nick wasn't in there. A pile of his dirty washing was, but Leila quickly draped her dressing gown over the top of his pants and socks on her way past. 'Let me turn on the lanterns, and you can see better.' A quick flick of a switch and the garden was delicately illuminated with lanterns strung on wires that nestled in between the bare branches.

Judy and Thomas were standing in the doorway in front of her, all with their backs to the open door leading back into the bedroom when Leila felt a gentle thump on her back. She looked down and a balled up pair of socks lay by her feet. She looked round and saw Nick's eyes looking over the side rail at the top of the bunk.

Judy turned to speak, and Nick's head bobbed back down. 'This is really super Leila, really great. And you've done it out so beautifully, hasn't she Thomas?' Her dad nodded his agreement.

'Oh thanks Mum, still, you'll want to be on your way now.' Leila put an arm round both her parents' shoulders and guided them back into the bedroom to quickly go through it back to the hall, but annoyingly Judy stopped in the middle of the room, about two foot away from Nick's head.

'Actually darling, there's no rush, we decided on the way here to stay overnight, so we called Tasha and she's making up the spare room for us and said to invite you along for dinner too. We're going to get a takeaway. She said Vietnamese, but your father's stomach isn't great with foreign food, so hopefully there's a curry house near hers that we can steer her towards.'

'Doesn't Indian count as foreign food?' Leila asked.

'Hardly darling, Tikka Masala is Britain's national dish, I saw a programme on the BBC about it.'

'I've got plans.'

Judy and Thomas both studied her for a moment. Finally her mum broke the silence. 'Is it one of those anti-Valentine's Day evenings where you burn pictures of your ex-boyfriends and stand around chanting? Or is the book in the kitchen a clue and you've become a lesbian?'

'None of those! No, I just have, um, a thing, that I need to do, that's a thing . . .' Annoyingly Leila's brain went completely blank and she couldn't finish her sentence.

'See Thomas, it was just as well we stopped by, she's in a right state.'

'Well why don't we stay with you here then darling?' her dad said, 'I haven't slept on a bunk bed in years, if you don't mind taking the sofa?'

'Ok, you know what? I will come to Tasha's, let's go now,' Leila hastily said, usher-

275

ing them both out and shutting the bedroom door behind her. She reached for her coat, realising at the last minute that it was hung over Nick's, so she hastily hung it back on the rack. 'Let me just grab another coat from the bedroom, this one has, um, ice cream on it.'

'Ice cream? In February? Give it to me and I'll try and get it out while you get yourself ready.' Judy's hand was outstretched ready to take it.

'No need! I'll sort it out later.' Leila bundled up both coats in her arms. 'You go outside, I'm just behind you.'

Leila shut the bedroom door behind her, flung the coats on the floor and hissed, 'Nick? Nick?'

Nick sat up as much as the low ceiling would allow, propping himself up on his elbows. 'Have they gone?'

'They're outside. I'm so sorry, I had no idea they were coming, they're not the greatest planners.'

'It's ok. You should go to Tasha's now.'

'But what about our Valentine's night?'

'What Valentine's night?' Nick replied sulkily.

'Don't be like that,' Leila whispered back. 'I didn't know they were coming.'

'It's cool, I'll head home. I've got an early

meeting anyway.'

'You don't have to. Stay here, chill out, have the marinated sea bass and oysters that was supposed to be our romantic meal tonight. Wash it down with the bubbly that's in the fridge door,' Leila added ruefully.

'Yeah, stuff myself full of aphrodisiacs and then go to bed alone, that sounds fun.'

'Will it keep 'till tomorrow? We could have a belated Valentine's? I'm really sorry.'

'You could always tell them the truth, you know. It's quite easy. Mum, Dad, lovely to see you but I really do have plans, see you in a couple of weeks in Dartmouth.'

'Nick, you know I can't. Look, I need to go, they'll come in looking for me in a sec. Please stay.'

'I'll see.' Nick lay back down on the bunk bed. 'You should go.'

'Ok.' Leila said sadly from the foot of the ladder. 'Bye then.'

'Bye then. Happy Valentine's Day.'

'Happy Valentine's Day.'

Leila thought that it was bloody typical that for the first time in the history of Valentine's Days she finally had a lovely boyfriend, but instead of sitting opposite him lovingly feeding him oysters, she was sat on the tube between both her parents.

'You needn't be sad Leila,' Judy said comfortingly.

'I'm not.'

'Or feel inadequate.'

'I don't.'

'It's to be expected, today of all days. I did say to Thomas, didn't I Thomas, that we should have invited you to the Savoy with us, instead of letting you fester in your flat by yourself, but you wouldn't have liked it, it was just lots of couples. It might have been a bit awkward for you.'

'Mum, I'm fine. Honestly.' On the one hand she wanted to shout about Nick from the rooftops, and on the other, she was irritated that everyone seemed to think that the path of happiness was only a route taken by couples. Had she been like that too? Before throwing herself into the celibacy club, had she looked at women like herself on the tube, on Valentine's Day, sandwiched between a set of parents and felt sorry for them? If so, she was appalled.

Would she rather be with Nick now? Yes, of course. But there were many things she'd rather be doing now, so that wasn't necessarily a reflection on being in a relationship. She tuned back in to her father holding his nose and reading out the names of stations on the tube map opposite him.

'Dad,' Leila said wearily. 'What are you doing?'

'Rehearsing for a job as a station announcer, in case the hotel packs up.'

'Sterling effort Dad, really good. Just try and keep it down.'

'Keep practising Thomas, we may well need some extra income soon,' said Judy.

'I thought everything was going well?' Leila said. At Christmas, they'd reported record bookings over the festive season, and were fully booked well into the new year.

'It's just slowed down a bit. We could do with another injection of good PR, like another couple of events. Lucy mentioned at Christmas that she was keen, but it was difficult pinning you down to a date.'

Leila shifted uncomfortably in her seat. She had been massively preoccupied, and didn't realise that her parents were depending on her so much. 'Well, you know, what with starting up my company, and the Dubai project, the event planning has all just fallen behind a bit. I'll call Lucy this week.'

'If you wouldn't mind my love, it was a real boost for the takings in November — we had to restock the wine cellar after you all left! It would be great to get something in the diary for early March, and then another in April. Wedding season is a bit slower this year, we've had a few cancellations.'

To her right, Thomas laughed. 'We should put the bride in touch with you when they call to cancel, shouldn't we Leila? Another single woman looking for enlightenment, eh?'

Thankfully the train was slowing to a halt at their station so Leila didn't have to answer.

There was no reason why Judy and Thomas would have picked up on Alex's guilty look as he opened the door to them. After all, in their eyes he'd been the model son-in-law for sixteen years. Good-looking, a success-ful financier, provider to their grand-children, and the remarkable gifts he regu-larly bestowed on their daughter never escaped Judy's notice.

Leila saw it though. Alex's quick glance to her, then to them, then back to her. A rapid assessment of whether they knew. Of whether she'd told them the truth on the Circle Line. He bellowed an overly enthusi-astic 'Hello! Hello! Welcome!' that was not only out of character, but also rather creepy.

'Hi Alex,' Leila said, breezing past him as he ducked his head to meet her cheek, leaving him puckered up in mid-air.

'Hey lovely,' Leila greeted her sister with a big hug. 'Why's it so quiet? Where is everyone?'

'The younger two are asleep, and Mia is on her first date!'

'Aww, no, really?'

'I know. He picked her up about half an hour ago, they've gone to the cinema.'

'Who picked who up?' Judy said, entering the kitchen and hearing the tail-end of the conversation.

'A boy called Stefan picked Mia up to take her to the cinema,' explained Tasha.

'In a car?' Judy asked.

'Yes.'

Judy didn't say anything, just raised her eyebrows and her face contorted into a 'well, you know what teenagers do in cars, don't you, and you're just going to stand by and let that happen are you? What kind of mother are you?' look that had Tasha reaching for the bottle to refill her glass.

Leila accepted a glass of wine from her sister. 'That's so sweet. And on Valentine's Day too.'

'Speaking of Valentine's Day, how are you doing?'

'Not you as well! I'm fine!'

'It must be hard.'

'Not really. It's liberating. Right, what takeaway are we having?'

Just then the doorbell went, signalling the arrival of the food. Leila went into the kitchen to take the plates out of the warmer. Who has a plate warmer she thought, what a monumental waste of worktop space. Not that that needed to be a consideration in Tasha's palatial kitchen, but in her own flat there was barely enough space to put a chopping board down between the draining board and the gas hob.

She suddenly became aware of someone directly behind her.

'I just wanted to say thank you,' Alex whispered.

'Don't. I didn't do it for you.' The plates were burning Leila's hands and she felt uncomfortable having this conversation with her sister in the next room.

'It's all sorted out. I just wanted to tell you that.'

Leila shrugged. 'Good. Don't bugger it all up again.'

'I won't. It was never serious though Leila, I just get . . . distracted. That's all.'

'I'm really not interested in your concentration problems Alex, just don't do it again.'

The door swung open and Tasha came

bounding into the kitchen. 'Oh good, you've got the plates. Alex, here's the cutlery and I'll just grab the salt and pepper.' As Tasha passed Alex he grabbed her and made a show of dipping her back to give her a theatrical kiss that had Tasha giggling like a teenager. Leila left them to it.

The rest of the evening was pleasant enough. Her parents were on top form, bubbling with excitement at being 'in town' and oblivious to any awkwardness or barely concealed animosity in the room. Why wouldn't they be though? Alex was putting on a show worthy of an Oscar, even kissing Tasha's hand at one point as she reached over him for another poppadom.

It got to about nine, and Leila suddenly felt a wave of tiredness surge over her body. She'd walked miles through country estates, bending down to sniff flower beds, reaching up into branches, and she now felt like she was on an emotional rollercoaster. There were too many secrets knocking about her normally very ordered family for her to feel anything other than exhausted. She made her excuses and left.

As she put her key in the lock she could hear voices from inside the flat.

She instinctively put her keys between her

283

fingers in the prime stabbing position — a move she'd been taught in the local village hall when she was sixteen. The self-defence teacher had also decreed that if attacked, you should just sing a nursery rhyme really loudly into the attacker's face, which would disarm them for a few seconds, long enough for a quick car-key jab to the throat, or a knee to the groin, and you'd be fine.

As she tiptoed into the hallway, she could hear two male voices, neither of which she recognised. They seemed to be coming from the bedroom. She should have retreated and called the police, that was what someone more sensible would have done, but instead, she edged closer to the ajar door and peered through it. She allowed herself a sizeable sigh of relief when she saw Nick sitting in his coat, scarf, gloves and thick woollen hat at her outside table. His feet were up on the seat opposite him and a bottle of red sat alongside the radio that was loudly piping out a debate on Talk Sport.

'I thought there were burglars here!' Leila said, bounding into the garden and wrapping her arms around his neck from behind.

'Burglars who were discussing the finer points of this week's friendly with Spain?' Nick teased.

'I couldn't hear what they were saying!'

Leila sat down in the chair that Nick's feet had just vacated. 'So. You're still here?'

'Is that ok? I could go if you want me to?' He made a move to get up and Leila pushed him back down.

'No! I want you to stay. I'm really glad you stayed.'

'I nearly didn't.'

There was a pause in which both of them weighed up whether this was going to turn into an argument, or whether they should just let it go. Nick was the first to speak. 'I don't want to end today fighting Lei, but you do have to stand up to them some time you know. All this sneaking about is getting a bit boring. I'd love you to meet my friends, and I'm gutted that next weekend you're going down to Dartmouth again for your family meal without me. I just feel a bit, invisible I guess.'

'I know.' Leila leaned forward in her seat and rubbed his leg. 'I was thinking that tonight with everyone having a takeaway together and I'd have loved you to be there too. But what's two more months? It's nothing.'

'So how was it?'

Leila shrugged. 'As expected. Alex was a monumental toolbox. The folks and Tasha were lovely. Mia was on her first date.' Leila stuck out her bottom lip as if to say 'how sweet is that?'

'Wow. I guess she is fifteen though.'

'Which is far too young for anything other than a friendly game of table tennis at the local sports centre,' Leila joked. When she was fifteen she remembered holding hands with Paul Taylor on the bus on the way back from a school trip and feeling as high as a kite when he invited her to the leisure centre that weekend to watch him in a ping pong tournament. It wasn't a euphemism. She really did sit for six hours and watch him ping and pong his way through four heats only to lose in the semi-finals. He didn't even try to kiss her after that, and it was going to be another eighteen months before anyone else did either.

'When I was fifteen —' Nick started, and Leila held her hand up to stop him talking.

'Do I want to know this?' she asked.

'When I was fifteen —' Nick continued, 'I had a very worldly older girlfriend called Theodora who showed me everything I know today. You should look her up and thank her.'

Leila caught the now-familiar glint in his eye and jabbed the car key that was still between her fingers into his knee. 'Why are you out here though, it's freezing!'

'I don't know, I wanted to see what all the fuss was all about I guess.'

Leila smiled. 'And have you?'

'A little bit. Although I can't feel my toes anymore.'

Laughing, they pulled each other up, until Leila was standing in line with his chest. 'It's still Valentine's Day you know.'

'Is it? How convenient.' Nick led her seductively back into the bedroom. 'Just one thing though, while I think of it. Do you think at some point in the near future I can convince you to chop up your bunk-bed and use it for firewood?'

CHAPTER 18

Lucy

It had been two hours since Lucy had done the last test. She'd read the books, devoured the forums, she knew that the hormones were strongest in the first wee of the day, but she couldn't wait until tomorrow to test again. There were three used sticks already carefully wrapped in tissue, put back inside the boxes that she'd placed inside carrier bags and buried deep inside the kitchen bin.

She'd been drinking lots of water at lunchtime so she'd have to go to the loo again, but thinking about it, that had probably diluted the hormones so that's why it wasn't showing up positive. That would be it. She wouldn't drink anything more today and then do one more before bed. Zipping up her jeans she quickly swilled her hands under the tap and answered her phone that had been incessantly ringing.

'How are you doing? I've been worried.'

Don't say anything nice, Lucy telepathically willed Leila, chewing her lip. Please don't say anything else or I might just dissolve into tears that may never stop.

'Lucy?'

'I'm here, sorry, just a bit flat out.'

'What with? Do you need help? I'm bored, I've been staring at the same set of plans for hours and I need external stimulation or I might combust. Why have you gone underground? I've been trying to reach you for days.'

Lucy stared at the floor. She knew that her voice would waver if she spoke, that she wouldn't be able to hide anything from Leila, but no one knew. No one had guessed that she'd been trying for a baby ever since their wedding day seven and a half months ago with nothing happening at all. That she'd charted her dates, taken her temperature, peed on ovulation kit after ovulation kit, meticulously timed sex down to the perfect minute, even pulling Marcus into a pub bathroom to try desperately to get pregnant. A pub toilet. He'd relished the new her, the wild abandonment of needing him right there, right then. He didn't know that after he left the cubicle she shuffled down on the closed lid and placed her legs high against the back of the door for ten minutes. He never needed to know that.

'Oh you know,' she croaked, 'crazy busy with . . . stuff.'

'Just wondered if you fancied meeting me in town and we could chat about the next event?'

Would walking around the high street dislodge any eggs trying to attach themselves to her womb? Lucy wondered. She'd tried to stay relatively still for the last week or so, even forgoing her daily Pilates classes as she wanted to stay upright or horizontal, and all those bends and stretches might cancel out all her hard work. And it was mid-morning. The shops would be crammed with mums and their buggies, taunting her. She couldn't put herself through that. Not today.

'I'm waiting for something to be delivered to be honest, so I have to stay in,' she replied.

'I'll come to yours then. I'm desperate for a break.'

Lucy calculated that if she said no, then she could spend the afternoon doing the mindfulness meditation that Linda from Wisconsin on the infertility forum had sent her; apparently, it worked for her in conceiving. It was all about eliminating the stress from your life, which was laughable, she'd never felt so wrung out emotionally. Then she could make herself the vitamin A and D shake for dinner and take another test after that. But then again, maybe organising another event was just the thing to take her mind off this.

'Sure,' Lucy said weakly. 'Come on over.'

It was the best thing that could have happened in the end. Leila wasn't the same Leila who had been at hers at Christmas, all twitchy and distracted. This Leila was calm, and making jokes and totally absorbed with planning the March retreat, to be held three weeks from now. And almost an hour went past without Lucy feeling the unused pregnancy stick burning a hole in her pocket. Maybe this was what she needed. A reason not to dwell on her inability to make another human.

'So, shall we say the 10th March? That's a weekend isn't it?' Leila picked up Lucy's phone to look at the calendar just as it buzzed with another app. A map appeared on the screen with a little blue dot moving slowly down a line on it. 'What's that?' Leila asked innocently as Lucy snatched the phone away.

'Lucy?'

She had nothing to be ashamed of. It was perfectly normal for a wife to want to make sure that her husband was safe.

'It's a GPS tracker. I use it to know when Marcus is on his way home so I can heat up our dinner.' Lucy could hear the stand-offishness in her own voice. But she could hardly tell Marcus's own sister that she was convinced that he was having an affair. Every other Tuesday he went to a building in Liverpool Street, he was there for an hour or so and then came home, always citing work as the reason for being late, not knowing that she watched the blue light leave his office and travel across London. The potential reasons had been consuming her. Could it be a mistress? Even a brothel? She was trying to build up her confidence to go there one Tuesday and catch him out but part of her was too nervous to know the truth.

'A GPS tracker?' Leila laughed, assuming her sister-in-law was joking. Seeing Lucy's expression of contriteness, Leila's tone changed. 'Does my brother know that you're stalking him?'

'A wife cannot *stalk* her husband Leila. I just worry about him working in central London every day, what with all the nutters out there, and this gives me peace of mind, that's all. And I do, for your information, use it to know when he's on his way home so I can get things ready for him.'

'But does he know?'

'It's an app on his phone, so it's hardly like I put a chip in his neck when he was sleeping.'

Leila could feel herself getting incensed on her brother's behalf. 'But does he know it's there?' she pressed.

Lucy started shuffling their notes together. 'Ok, so, I'm going to get in touch with the speakers and book the band and you're going to gather the sponsors together. Yes? I like the idea of hosting a week away abroad somewhere when the weather heats up, so make sure that you keep that travel company on side for that. And will you check the date with your mum, or shall I do that?' Lucy stood up. Both questions in her sentence had been rhetorical. The conversation was closed.

'Oh, and while I remember, you know it's Marcus's 40th at the end of March? We've booked a big house in the Cotswolds for the night, and I'm planning a Murder Mystery party, so keep the 24th free too. It works out about 150 quid a couple, but as you're on your own, you'll still need to pay that I'm afraid as you'll have your own room for the night, is that ok?' Again, the question wasn't posed as one that needed a reply.

Leila's stomach lurched as she realised something else. 'That sounds great, but who else is coming?'

'We haven't sent out the invites yet, I've been a bit preoccupied, but both sides of the family, plus a few of Marcus's friends from university.'

Both sides of the family. That had to mean Nick surely? Him and Leila were practically living together now, how on earth were they meant to pretend they barely knew each other for two days? Now there was a question that definitely did need answering.

'So hang on,' Nick said, muting the TV, 'not only are we not allowed to sleep in the same room at his birthday weekend, we're paying three hundred quid between us for the privilege of not doing so?'

'That's about the size of it, yes.'

'That sounds rubbish. We could go away ourselves for that, and be able to talk to each other, rather than just exchange pleasantries and stay out of each other's way. I'm not going to go.'

He'd been in a bit of a strange mood all evening, Leila thought. He'd been given two tickets to the theatre for the weekend by a client but it was the Dartmouth Roast this Sunday, so she'd told him she couldn't go, and since then he'd retreated into himself and been a bit snippy. He knew that once a month she went back home and it had never bothered him before.

'What's wrong?' Leila asked. 'You're being a bit off.'

'I'm just getting a bit fed up of the whole sneaking about business. We're getting on really well, we've been together properly now for two months, but in that time I've pretty much moved in, and yet not one other person knows that we're together. I want you to stay over at mine occasionally and sleep in a bed that I can actually sit up in.'

'I thought you were warming to the bunk? You said it was fun.'

'I'm six foot two Leila, it's not fun. But it's not about the bunk, I want to take you down to Mum's next time I go — she already really likes you and would be really happy about us — and I want to come down to the hotel for the next roast with your family and be a normal couple.'

'God, not this again. How hard is it to wait another month? You knew seeing out the year was important to me, and yet you're keeping on and on at me about changing my mind. It's not really fair.'

He took her hand, 'I'm sorry, I thought I could do this whole secrecy thing, but I can't. I'm not made for subterfuge.'

'I don't like it either Nick, but I've dug this massive hole and I can't see a way out of it at the moment. It's the end of February now, I've got an event in two weeks' time, then Marcus's birthday, and a couple of weeks after that the year is up and I don't need to be single anymore.'

'You're not single now,' he answered sulkily.

'Bad choice of words. I don't need to be *perceived* as being single then.'

'If this is about the bet money I can pay that. I have savings.'

'It's not, and that's weird, it'd be like you're buying me.'

Nick grimaced. 'That is a whole different kind of role play.'

'You know it's about more than the money. I know and you know that I've failed at keeping my celibacy oath, but no one else does, and I feel as though I'd be letting everyone down.'

'Your mum and family would be thrilled for you, to know that you're happy. They wouldn't give a toss about the vow.'

Leila knew he was right, but it wasn't just about them. She felt a massive duty to all the women that logged on every day, that opened up their hearts and told their stories; women who felt part of a community of like-minded people. For them to find out that the woman who'd started it all was living a lie would be a monumental let down.

'Five weeks Nick. That's all it is now. Come on, it'll be fun. And please come to Marcus's weekend away, we can pretend that we're having an illicit affair and sneak around the manor house hiding in the library or in the billiard room.'

'I think you're confusing this weekend with a game of Cluedo.' But his face broke into a weary smile. 'Six weeks Lei. April 1st comes and we go public.'

'Deal. Now give me a kiss.'

'I love it here. This is going to be my happy place.' Leila looked around her friend Jayne's bookshop wine bar. You could glimpse the deep claret walls through the floor to ceiling book shelves and a big oak counter with an old-fashioned brass hand-rail and footrest gave the room a gentlemen's club feel, but without the pompous old men. An archway led through to a deli, that Jayne's husband, Will, ran. As it was evening time the deli was closed. A little red rope hung across the opening, attached to the wall either side with brass hooks, like the kind you found in old-fashioned theatres.

It was the first time Leila had been here since it opened. It was shameful really, Richmond was on the same tube line as Bayswater, with only a quick change at Earl's Court and yet it always seemed too long a trek. Leila had studied at the same design school as Jayne's twin sister Rachel, and after graduation lost touch with them both. About five years ago Rachel had been designing the interiors for the same restaurant that Leila was doing the landscaping for and their friendship picked up where it left off.

'My book club comes here every Tuesday,' Amanda said. 'Although since we moved the club from a cafe to a wine bar, we talk less and less about the books!'

'Are there any single men at your book club?' Shelley asked, reaching into the ice bucket for the wine bottle.

'One,' Amanda replied, then laughed when she saw her friend's raised eyebrow and piqued interest. 'But his name's Norman and he's about a hundred and three.'

'Not that I need a man to feel complete and happy Leila, before you jump on me with your feminist opinions,' Shelley added good-naturedly.

'I wouldn't do that!' Leila replied.

'Why not? You have every other time I've

mentioned men.'

'I have not!' She had.

In an uncanny mimicking of Leila's voice, Shelley said, 'Oh Shelley, you need to look deep inside yourself to truly find happiness. Most women think men will save us from the worst thing that's being alone, but the worst thing is being in an unfulfilling partnership. Once you understand and embrace being by yourself, it's only then that you can find love that will last and the true meaning of intimacy.'

Leila banged her head on the table. 'Oh God, did I really say that?' Her friends laughed at her embarrassment.

Amanda ruffled Leila's hair affectionately. 'Do you know what though, you know what you were telling us about the five love languages? It's really helped me and Paul. He read the book you lent me, which in itself is a miracle as it doesn't have pictures or football league tables anywhere in it, and we took the online quiz about which is your love language.'

Amanda ignored Shelley snorting and carried on. 'And now I know that when he MOTs my car, that's him saying that he loves me, and I shouldn't expect him to write me a poem saying it because that's not who he is, and that I should receive his love in the way that he gives it.'

'Hang on,' Shelley said. 'He MOTs your car and that means he loves you?'

'Yes,' Amanda and Leila chorused.

'Doesn't it just mean that he got your car MOT-ed?'

'No, it's so much more than that! I know that my love language is Words of Affirmation, and that his is Acts of Service. So I know that when I do something for him — it could be anything, like picking up his dry cleaning, or writing the Christmas cards, or walking the dog, he sees that as me telling him that I love him. And he knows that if he tells me once a day that I'm amazing, or beautiful or he's really proud of how I've done something at work, then I'll know he loves me.'

Leila couldn't believe how much Amanda had listened when she'd told her about the love languages. They'd had a session on it at the last workshop and it really struck a chord with Leila. She'd always expected boyfriends to instinctively know her love language, and couldn't understand why bunches of flowers, or in the case of Freddie, cans of pre-mixed Pimms, left her completely cold. It was fascinating how everyone was so different.

'What's yours Jayne?'

'What are they again?'

'Words of Affirmation, Quality Time, Receiving Gifts, Acts of Service, or Physical Touch.'

'Physical Touch. Have you met my husband?'

They all burst out laughing. Jayne's husband Will was, Leila had to admit, almost as good looking as Nick. Nick, who immediately knew that her love language was a complex combination of all five. Nick, who was desperate to tell the world that he loved her. God, she was such a fraud.

Amanda and Shelley had just left, and Jayne flipped the open sign over to closed. 'Stay for one more?' she asked Leila, walking back towards the bar counter.

'Sure. Now I'm my own boss I can eat a McDonalds hangover cure at my desk and no one gives me dirty looks.'

Jayne poured them both a large Amaretto over ice and handed a tumbler to Leila. 'Everything ok? You seem a bit, I don't know, preoccupied.'

Leila took a big breath in. 'Can I tell you a secret and you literally cannot tell a living soul?'

'This sounds serious.'

'I've met someone. And he's really, *really* nice.'

Jayne shrieked and did a little dance on the spot.

'But I'm meant to be celibate and so it's been a really big secret, but he's perfect for me, and he thinks I am for him, but it's really complicated, he's sort of related to me, and it's all just getting too much leading this double life, and I'm lying to everyone all the damn time, and I feel like such an imposter.' Leila wasn't sure at which point during this monologue she'd started to cry but now big fat ugly tears dropped into her lap and when Jayne pulled her into a hug she willingly collapsed into her friend's embrace.

'It's ok, it's ok. Um, when you say you're sort of related, you're not dating your brother are you?' Jayne joked, making Leila smile.

'Not quite. You know Lucy, Marcus's wife? Well it's her brother, we met at their wedding.'

'Wasn't that last summer?'

Leila nodded. 'July. But I told him about the celibacy vow and he was fine about it and even said he'd wait for me, but then we kept bumping into each other at things, and then when we spent Christmas together that's when it all started properly, so it's been over two months now, and it's horrible pretending to be single, going to parties and everything alone, when you just want to climb to the top of the Shard with a megaphone.'

'So why don't you?'

'I can't. So much is riding on the blog and I need to see out the year.'

'No-one would hold you to the bets you know.'

'That's what Nick said too, but it's not about that.' Leila knew that her friends wouldn't make her pay, and she had so much dirt on Alex there was no way that he'd be able to insist on her honouring it. 'I never meant for my thing to become a thing, you know what I mean?'

'I think I do. Obviously your eloquent explanation of it is helping me understand,' Jayne teased. 'Look, you have what, a month left of the year? That's nothing, keep going the way you're going and then after that I'll buy you the megaphone myself.'

'Thank you,' Leila sniffed, wiping what was left of her mascara all over her sleeve.

'And just a word of advice, don't say out loud again the words "he's sort of related to me" again, because a) that's not true, and b) it's a thousand different shades of icky.'

CHAPTER 19

Lucy carefully folded her trousers over the hanger and put them back in the wardrobe. She could hear the low hum of Marcus's electric toothbrush through the bathroom door. Thank goodness he was the type to automatically close the door while performing his ablutions. One of the ladies at her book club said that she and her husband went to the toilet in front of each other, which was just disgusting, she'd never even burped in front of Marcus, let alone anything else. How on earth was a man meant to see you in an alluring light after seeing you do that?

She dropped her underwear into the laundry basket, spritzed a bit of her perfume on her pulse points and got into bed naked. She hadn't planned on sleeping with Marcus tonight, she wasn't ovulating, so there was no real point, but it was his birthday, and she was sure there was a rule in the good wife's handbook about that.

At the foot of the bed their suitcase was already packed and ready for the morning's drive to the manor house in Bishop's Norton. She'd scheduled the Waitrose delivery of all the food and drink for the weekend at 11am, so they'd need to be on the road by 8.30 at the latest to get there in time to suss out which cupboards would be best for what.

Everyone else was going to get there just after lunch. She'd made it clear in the invites that people should eat before arriving; they weren't made of money.

Leila slipped her hand under the covers and woke Nick up in his favourite way. 'Morning sleepyhead,' she purred. 'It's mini-break time!'

'Can you wake me up when it's Monday morning again,' he groaned. 'And can you wake me up like that again then too?' he added, pulling Leila on top of him, careful not to bump her head on the ceiling.

'Come on, it's going to be fun, two nights in the countryside, yomping through fields and drinking red wine in oak panelled drawing rooms.'

'I love a good yomp as much as the next man, but I think you need to lower your expectations Lei,' Nick yawned, 'this week-end is not going to be fun. It's organised by my sister, your parents are going to be there, your brother-in-law too, who is not really speaking to either of us, and a smattering of stuck up lawyer mates of Marcus's. It's hardly an 18–30s weekend in Lanzarote, yet it's costing more.'

'I never had you down as an 18–30s kind of guy?'

'Actually it's my idea of hell, worse than the weekend we've got planned. Ok, come on then. I'm assuming your mum will be wearing some kind of country casuals tweed outfit?'

'Almost certainly. Now hurry up.'

They were going to arrive together, under the premise that they lived reasonably near each other and could talk about the Dubai project on the train. If anyone asked. Which Nick thought was highly unlikely, but Leila thought it was good to be prepared with an answer.

Tasha had apologised to Leila that they couldn't offer her a lift, but they were driving to the Cotswolds via North London to drop the kids off at a friend of hers for the weekend, as once again Lucy had imposed a strict no-kids rule. Tasha was quite pleased about that this time though, as she felt that a weekend away in a country house with Alex was just the thing their marriage needed. She'd seen on the manor's website that there were two rooms with four posters in them, and was determined one of them had their names on it.

They were in a really good place in their relationship now, and she was so pleased she'd stuck it out. That was the thing, she thought, as Alex weaved their Range Rover towards the M25 — things were never as clear cut as they seemed from the outside looking in. If a friend of hers had told her that their husband had a string of lovers as long as the traffic jam they were just approaching, then she'd have unequivocally told her to pack his bags this instant. But her situation was different.

Alex gently nudged his wife's elbow off the armrest dividing their seats. 'Tell me more about this four poster bed then you gorgeous woman . . .'

Yes, her situation was very different.

Having experienced Christmas Lucy-style, they were all prepared for a military-operation, spreadsheet-tastic birthday week-end of meticulously planned hilarity, and Lucy didn't disappoint. Every bedroom door had an index card taped to it with the person's name who would be occupying it. Rather unnecessarily Leila thought, passing a couple of doors in the corridor before she got to hers, one had a 'v' in brackets and one had a 'n' — obviously standing for 'vegetarian' and 'nut allergy'. For the life of her Leila couldn't imagine a scenario where someone's dietary requirements would be relevant to where they were sleeping. She pointed it out to Nick who was following her at a respectable distance.

'Why, just why?' Leila asked.

'I think it's very thoughtful,' Nick replied. 'Imagine you'd like to introduce yourself and thought, I know, I'll bring a little gift as a hello, and you take a Peperami to the vegetarian and a sculpture made entirely of almonds to the nut allergy person. Awkward. This very careful and considerate planning means that now that won't happen.'

'I'm going to miss you Nicholas.'

'You won't miss me too much, look at this, we're right next door to each other. That's handy . . .' Nick had stopped outside two adjacent doors, their names clearly printed and devoid of brackets. He looked up and down the empty corridor. 'Go on then, let's have a look at yours first and see which one we'll sleep in.'

She turned the handle and the door opened into the tiniest little box room she'd ever seen. 'This can't be right, it's a cupboard.' She didn't see it at first as the curtains were drawn, so her eyes hadn't adjusted to the dark, but in the corner under the window was a very narrow single bed.

'It's the size of your flat, what are you talking about?'

'Seriously Nick, I've paid 150 quid for this. My sister is currently bouncing up and down on a king size four poster bed in a room you'd fit five of these ones into, and they're paying the same.'

'I'm joking, look, you can sleep in mine anyway, so don't worry about it. Come on, let's see mine.'

Nick's room was marginally bigger, with a fireplace, but he too had a very thin single bed. 'Lucy's having a laugh with these rooms. Even if you knocked them through to each other they'd be minuscule, what kind of architect designed these?'

'I bet they used to be dressing rooms for the big bedrooms, like little ante-rooms where the maids prepared the lady's clothes for the day.'

'And the footmen would sneak up on

them like this,' Nick pushed Leila against the wall and started snuffling into her neck.

Giggling she pushed him off, and just in time as Lucy poked her head around the door and said, 'There you are. We were wondering where you got to.'

'Um Lucy, are there any other rooms with slightly bigger beds?' Leila asked.

'Why? There's only one of you?'

'Well, it's just we're . . . I'm . . . paying the same as a couple, and I don't think it's fair that we . . . I . . . get a tiny box room and everyone else gets an enormous suite.' Her voice tailed off as she clocked that Lucy had pursed her lips and folded her arms. 'Of course, if not, then that's fine too. Just thought I'd ask.'

'I have put a lot of effort into this weekend Leila.'

Nick jumped in, 'Lei . . . la . . . isn't saying that you haven't Luce, it's just that these beds don't look as um, comfortable, perhaps, as some of the others, it's not the size that matters.'

'Don't you sleep on a bunk bed Leila?' Lucy asked curtly. 'I would have thought this would be luxury compared to that.'

'You sleep on a bunk bed?' Nick turned to Leila incredulously. 'What, like a proper bunk bed? With a ladder and everything?'

She tried hard not to laugh; he looked so dramatically disbelieving, despite the fact that he'd woken up in said bunk bed for most of the last ninety odd mornings. 'Yes, Nick, I sleep in a bunk bed. But I'm thinking of chopping it up and using it for firewood.'

An hour later everyone had arrived and so had the rain, meaning that Lucy's programme of 'lawn games' were hastily swapped for her Plan B activities of 'board games', which Alex and a couple of the lawyers quickly amended into 'drinking games'. Leila had never played Monopoly to the rules that were now in place, and the game that she'd previously found to be incredibly tedious was given a new lease of life. By five o'clock she was the proud owner of a full set of yellows, three out of the four stations, and was well on her way to being absolutely plastered.

'I think I need a power nap,' Leila slurred to Nick, who was sitting by her side. 'Take me up please. Pleeeease.'

'I'm very flattered, but I hardly know you,' Nick replied smiling, rolling his eyes at the other players for added effect.

'Oh yes. Sorry about that. Thought you were someone else,' Leila said, rising unsteadily to her feet.

That was a rookie error, thought Leila as she padded up the stairs to her room. She shouldn't have drunk so much that she let her guard down, and they were only four hours into the whole weekend. She'd have to stay much more in control from now on. And away from the spirits tray.

'Pssst. Pssst.'

Nick was already at the top of the stairs having taken the back staircase to the first floor. He was hiding behind a wide column, poking his head round. 'Lei. Pssst. Lei.'

She looked up and her face burst into a spontaneous grin. Leila realised that he must be as drunk as she was as he started doing the thing where half your body is hidden and you move one leg and one arm up and down like a snow angel. Her dad used to do that in her mirrored wardrobe to make it look like he was levitating when he had a few too many.

'What are you doing?' she whispered back as she reached the top step.

'Coming to keep you company for a bit.'

'Did anyone see you leave?'

'Most people are crashed out or gone for a walk now the rain's stopped. Lucy's Murder Mystery starts at eight in the drawing room. Word of advice — I called it a lounge earlier and she wasn't happy, so don't do that.'

'I need to sleep, I'm a little drunk,' Leila confided, proving her last sentence by standing on tiptoe, leaning in, putting her finger to her lips and giving a loud 'SHHHHHH' into Nick's face.

They fell asleep on her little bed, which not only was barely the width of one person, it also sagged deeply in the middle, meaning they were both essentially lying on top of each other on a tiny hammock. They woke up to the sound of a persistent gong echoing loudly on the floor below.

'Shit! Is it dinner time already?' Leila gasped, struggling to get out from under Nick. 'Nick, Nick, wake up, it's eight o' clock!'

'What? Shit!' He ran to the door, flung it open, then slammed it shut again, putting his back against it. 'Jesus, everyone's coming down the corridor.'

Leila was crouched down next to her open suitcase flinging items left and right, burrowing into it trying to find all the different elements that made up her costume. Completely as expected, Marcus had thought the idea for a 1920s themed Murder Mystery party was ridiculous, but despite it being his birthday he was swiftly and deftly overruled by his wife. When the invite came through the post, a neat little white card trimmed with gold, it had an Art Deco font announcing the pleasure of Virginia Lily-white's attendance at an evening soiree. Also in the envelope was a character description — Virginia was the eldest daughter of a wealthy sugar importer, and was engaged to be married to a dashing landowner called Charles Willingham.

'Are you Charles Willingham?' Leila had excitedly blurted out when she called Nick at work that morning.

'Are you on drugs?' he'd replied. It turned out that no, rather disappointingly, Nick was not her fictional fiancé. His name was Rob-ert Medlow, and his provenance was rather more dubious.

'I'm sure I packed gloves!' Leila whined, deciding that turning her case completely upside down and shaking the contents all over the floor would be much more efficient in finding what she needed. 'Aha!' She wriggled into the white lace flapper dress, which was adorned with hundreds of beaded tassels hanging down from the hem. Finishing the outfit with a matching se-quinned headband, elbow length gloves and a long cigarette holder, she was ready to go. Nick, however, was still loitering behind her door peering through the keyhole. 'Look, I'll go out and let you know when the coast's clear, but then you need to get ready really quickly — here's your tie and braces.'

After googling Gatsby outfits, he'd gone for what could best be described as 'mobster mash up' — pin striped suit, black shirt, white tie, and a pair of vintage black and white spats they'd picked up on eBay. But their get-ups were positively dull compared to the wonder that was Judy and Thomas who were waiting at the foot of the stairs for her.

'Mum, Dad, just wow!' Leila said, turning her mother around so she could get a better look. She wasn't sure quite how many peacocks must have died for Judy's head-dress, but it was definitely more than one.

'And Dad, that is quite the outfit!' He was Jimmy the chauffeur, and had embraced his new role with unbridled enthusiasm. Wide leg beige trousers were held up with scarlet braces, and a bow tie and flat cap completed his look. He'd even rolled up his white shirt sleeves to show a little smear of engine oil on his hairy forearm.

'When Lucy first told us about the theme, I must admit I was a little wary, but I think this is jolly fun,' Judy confided as they walked into the library arm in arm. Lucy had hired waiting staff for the evening, who were stood around in tuxedos with silver trays filled with wide-brimmed glasses of champagne and lemon drop cocktails — apparently the cocktail du jour in the 1920s. At the far end of the library a jazz trio were playing, and everyone was tapping their feet along to the jaunty music. Leila felt that it was only a matter of time before Lady Mary glided in and Carson announced dinner.

She spotted Nick wander into the room, take a drink and sip it while looking round the room. He would hate this, this forced joviality and small talk with strangers. It was ok for her, she knew most of Marcus's university friends and she had her whole family here, but Nick just knew her and Lucy, who was probably bossing the caterers around or measuring the distance between the table settings in the dining room. Stephanie was in Scotland at a friend's 70th so had sent her apologies. Not that hanging out with his mum would make things better, but at least he would have had someone else to talk to. Leila desperately wanted to go and squeeze his hand but Judy had a tight grip on her daughter's arm. Judging by the height of her heels, it was probably for practical support rather than because of any maternal affection.

'Good evening lovely family members,' said Tasha embracing her parents and then Leila. 'You all look amazing.'

'Loving the hair!' Leila gushed. Tasha's shoulder length brown hair had been set into 1920s waves, with a diamante chain looped over her forehead.

'I honestly think I was born in the wrong era, I'd love to wear this get-up every day.'

'Me too,' Judy agreed, 'but I'm not sure it's practical for the boat.'

'Where's Alex?' Thomas asked, obviously feeling a little outnumbered by the women in his family, as he so often did.

'Helping Lucy move something in the dining room. I was hoping we'd grab a power nap before dinner like you did Leila but Lucy kept him running round all afternoon doing loads of odd jobs, honestly that man just can't say no.'

It was a bad choice of words and Leila had to bite her lip until it almost bled to stop herself agreeing with her. She felt bad that she'd slept most of the afternoon, Lucy must be so mad at her for ducking out of helping her with the arrangements for tonight.

'I think I'll just go and find Lucy and see if she needs me to do anything,' Leila said, pulling her dad's flat cap over his face as she left them. Her shoes made a pleasing clip clop sound on the tile as she crossed the hallway. Lucy definitely had a knack for putting on show-stopping events. As Leila pushed open the heavy oak door of the dining room she heard Lucy's laugh. Her intricate headpiece and quite a lot of her hair had got caught in Alex's watchstrap and she was desperately trying to wriggle free.

'Oh Leila, thank goodness you're here, Alex, the numpty, has got his watch stuck and I can't get out, and dinner's almost ready to be served. Can you help us?'

Leila couldn't help smiling at the two of them contorted together, especially as Lucy's giggling was infectious. She couldn't believe Lucy was taking it with such uncharacteristic good grace, particularly as when she'd finally managed to release them both it looked like Lucy had been dragged through a hedge backwards.

'Erm, you might want to go and fix your hair a bit.'

'Do I look dreadful?'

'Not at all,' Leila lied, 'but a bit of a touch-up might be in order.'

'Can you stall the troops in the drawing room for a bit then, won't be a minute.'

As Leila rejoined her parents, a smiling

man in a garishly striped blazer chose that moment to walk towards her holding out his hand. 'Hello, I think I'm marrying you.'

'Well it's about time someone did!' Thomas boomed, laughing at his own joke.

'You must be Charles,' Leila said ignoring her dad and extending her own hand.

'Keith actually, but yes, Charles for to-night. I'm a banker.'

'Don't be too hard on yourself Keith,' Leila replied straight-faced. 'I'm sure you're alright when people get to know you.' Keith didn't get it but Leila heard Nick give an appreciative snort of laughter as he passed by behind her.

The dinner gong sounded and they started filing across the tiled hallway. A blackboard sat on an easel decorated with Art Deco style writing that read 'A little party never killed nobody' and little place cards denoted where everyone should sit. Leila thought it was too much to hope that she'd be near Nick, but as she reached her place her heart skipped when she saw that he was sitting directly opposite her. He raised his eyebrow at her in a flirty secret greeting before turning to politely introduce himself to the heavily rouged woman on his right.

Leila was flanked by two men she'd never met before, one was a monosyllabic man wearing a boater who looked as though he'd rather chew his own feet off than be where he was. The other — the speakeasy club owner who had a wonky sticker announcing his name as Four Fingered Fred — was absolutely hammered after spending the afternoon playing blackjack. By the time the starters were finished she'd already peeled his paws off her arm twice and Nick looked like he was going to lunge across the table and tighten his bow tie around his throat.

A shrill scream cut through the laughter and for a moment it seemed as though everyone had forgotten that at some point in the evening there was going to be a corpse. More than one, Leila thought grimly as she batted Fred's four fingers away from her behind while everyone left their seats to go and check out the grisly murder scene. Just by the back door in the kitchen Marcus was lying on the floor with ketchup oozing out of his head onto the flagstone floor. He didn't think that having it in his hair was entirely necessary but Lucy squeezed it on regardless before arranging his limbs in a suitably 'dead' way. A croquet mallet lay carefully discarded nearby with a squirt of sauce on too for good measure.

Despite initial misgivings, and there were lots of them, everyone apart from boater man who'd disappeared upstairs after dessert, agreed at the end of the night that it had been a fantastic success. Leila found it surprisingly hilarious, being a glamorous alter ego for the evening, and it was a massive ice-breaker, as Lucy no doubt knew it would be. It was gone 1am when Leila gave Nick the prearranged sign of two tugs on her ear denoting her exit from the party. He made a hasty retreat a few minutes later. He was looking forward to getting to know Virginia Lilywhite a little better.

'I take it all back,' Marcus said, throwing his trousers into the corner of the room that was evidently now the dirty washing pile. 'That was really good fun.' He climbed into bed and snuggled into Lucy's back, surprised to find her completely naked. 'Mmmm. What did I do to deserve this?'

Lucy turned around and kissed him, her mouth wide and inviting. He put her uncharacteristic wantonness down to the lemon drop cocktails, or maybe the sexiness of the prohibition theme. He certainly wasn't to know that seeing him lie on the floor playing dead had momentarily stopped her heart beating.

CHAPTER 20

'When I started this year, I had no idea that it was going to spiral into this wonderful, supportive, nurturing group of amazing women. It was a solitary journey I embarked on to give myself the strength to believe that I didn't need to be defined by having a partner. I'd said it before, pretty much after every break up, but it was always a bit tongue in cheek, I never really meant it. But this time was different. By not actively scanning a room for a potential boyfriend or having my ears prick up at the mention of someone's single friend I found myself relaxing. Once I took the pressure away to be part of a couple it was incredibly liberating. And God, I've learned so much about character types, my own personality and the traits in others. I've learned to relax, truly relax, not just veg out in front of the TV on a Friday night and think that's relaxing, but proper mind-going-gloriously-blank relaxing. I'm now a lot more mindful of every moment and of everyone. We can't possibly know the stories of everyone we come across in life and I was certainly guilty of making judgements without stopping to think about why people are the way they are. As this year went on it became less and less about celibacy and more about friendship and womanhood and, well, me. The year is coming to a close now, but I've decided not to shut down the site and blog like I was planning to, as I believe that men now have very little to do with what we talk about here and why we enjoy each other's company, either online or in person at our meet-ups. It's about being the best version of yourself, whether you're in a relationship or single. So I salute you. I salute your bravery, your spirit, and your uniqueness. Because, quite frankly, each and every one of us is nothing short of incredible.'

The room erupted in applause and whistles. Over half the room stood up, guilting the seated into standing too. Leila knew she was probably the shade of a beetroot standing up on the stage by herself, but it was overwhelming feeling the sisterly solidarity and love coming from the hundred or so women that were there. It was the final night of the four-day spa break and she knew it had been their best event yet. If she hadn't been one of the organisers, she knew that she would have really enjoyed being one of the guests, which was proof in itself.

The packed programme of massages and facials was broken up with workshops, small group sessions, whole-group talks and just the right amount of down time to have a swim, chat in the hot tub or escape to a quiet corner with a book. As they'd taken over the whole spa they'd even managed to coerce the catering team to relax their juice-only menu and include real food you had to chew, and they were even allowed to bring their own booze in for the evening meal. The stick-thin spa manager had failed to hide her disapproval as the corks were popped, rolling her eyes and pursing her lips, but even that didn't dampen Leila's high spirits.

It had actually been Nick that convinced her that the community didn't need to dissolve just because her year of celibacy (cough cough) was ending. 'But it's not about celibacy really is it?' He'd said, 'You don't all sit around and bash men and talk about how great it is not to shave your armpits do you?'

'No, we haven't done that for a long time. The man-bashing bit. The armpit thing is a matter of personal choice,' Leila had replied. But he was right, she'd been so caught up in feeling guilty about running a singles club while not being single she didn't even notice that its focus had changed, and women in relationships would get just as much out of these sessions as single women would. She had run the idea past Lucy and Tasha and both were really quick to agree. Too quick. They'd both been independently quite sad that Leila might insist on calling time on what they'd set up, and were hugely relieved when Leila said that the shop was still open for business.

'Cheers ladies, what a team,' Lucy said, raising her glass of sparkling water and touching it to Leila and Tasha's wine glasses. The last of the women had gone to bed, and the three of them were just having a quick nightcap before turning in.

'Cheers. You've both been brilliant. I couldn't have done any of this without you. Thank you,' Leila added.

'Are you not drinking Lucy?' Tasha asked.

Leila looked at the glass in Lucy's hand. 'Hang on. You weren't drinking last night either were you? Oh my God, are you *pregnant?*'

'Ahhhhhh! That's amazing!' Tasha made a move to hug Lucy, but Lucy batted her away.

'No, no I'm not. It's complicated.'

The sisters looked chastened. 'Sorry,' Leila said, 'I just thought . . .'

Lucy shook her head, and as she did she felt her eyes start to prickle. 'It's um, not as easy as I thought, getting pregnant.'

There was a pause. Leila didn't know what to say, she had no words of advice or even any experience she could draw on to make Lucy feel better.

'But you've only been married nine months,' Tasha said comfortingly. 'That's not long to be trying for. It'll happen.'

'But that's nine months of me charting my temperature every month, taking every supplement under the sun, doing just the right amount of exercise, not drinking coffee or coke, eating loads of raw vegetables, not eating anything tinned or bottled, or —'

'Nothing tinned or bottled?' asked Tasha.

'Yes, to avoid the high BPA exposure,' said Lucy as though Leila and Tasha were ignorant heathens for not knowing. 'And I love swordfish and tuna, but I can't have that either because of the mercury. And I've even, you'll laugh at this' — Leila thought that was highly unlikely — 'I even fibbed to Marcus about where I was a couple of days ago and said I was visiting Mum in Norfolk, but instead I went down to Cornwall on the night of a full moon to this massive stone that has a hole in it, Men-an-Tol I think it's called, and I walked through it seven times.'

Leila and Tasha just stared at her. She'd lost the plot. She'd always been wavering on the edge of looniness, but surely even Lucy should realise this level of intensity wasn't normal.

'Um, I'm not sure what to say,' Leila said just to stop the silence. 'Maybe just relax about it?'

'Relax?' Lucy shrieked. 'Nobody ever got pregnant from relaxing!'

Leila replied that she was sure that she'd read somewhere that stress was one of the biggest factors in having problems conceiving. 'I just mean maybe if you started to enjoy, um, life a bit more, and maybe had a glass of wine or a piece of tuna, you might not be so, um . . .' *Think Leila, think of a polite way to say bonkers.* 'Worried.'

Lucy turned to Tasha. 'You've got three kids, how did it happen for you?'

Tasha shrugged. 'I'm sorry I can't be any help with this, Alex has super sperm, we literally did it once at the right time each time and it happened.' Tasha added, 'I'm sorry,' as an afterthought, realising that she had probably been a little insensitive. 'What does Marcus think about it?'

'We haven't talked about it. I think he just assumes it will happen when it happens. He's so queasy about things like this though, we both are, there's no way that I could ever ask him to go to do his business into a pot or anything, I'd die of embarrassment.'

'So how do you know the problem's yours?' Leila asked.

'That's the thing, I know it's not, I've had every test going, I went to a private clinic a couple of months ago and had everything checked and scanned and I'm completely fine. So it must be him, but I'm hardly going to say that to him am I?'

'But you have to. You'll drive yourself crazy otherwise.' Leila felt pleased that she'd omitted the -er at the end of crazy, but in her head it was there.

'It's fine, I'm coping with it.'

'You're obviously not though, are you?' Leila said. 'It sounds like it's all you can think about.'

Lucy's knuckles whitened around her glass. It felt like a massive betrayal talking about Marcus like this, but also, it was such a relief to tell someone how she was feeling.

'You know your brother, he'd be devastated if he knew that he couldn't, you know . . . he's so manly, and proud, so I need to figure this out by myself. I didn't expect this to happen you know, I've never been in this type of situation before where I've wanted something so badly, and yet can't find a way to make it work.' Lucy shook her head as if to banish the negative thoughts, and she stood up. 'Thanks for listening girls, I feel better after talking about it. Right, I'd better get to bed, we've got an early start in the morning. The spa manager says we all need to leave by ten.' She drained the last of her water. 'Night night.'

'Night.' Leila and Tasha chorused.

'Jesus.' Tasha said as soon as she was sure Lucy was out of earshot. 'Poor Marcus, should we tell him?'

'How? How would that even come up in conversation? So Marcus, about your swimmers . . .'

'I think we could find a more tactful way than that Leila!'

Leila shrugged. 'No, just leave them be. It'll happen for them, like you said it's only been nine months. But I'm glad I'm not shutting down the website, I think it's probably become a bit of a lifeline for her to organise stuff other than her BPA, mercury and caffeine consumption.'

'That's not normal is it?'

'If this year has taught me anything is that there's fifty million definitions of normal out there.'

'I think one of us should chat to him. You know just generally, about life. See how he is. I would but I'm manic now with the kids for the next few weeks,' Tasha shrugged apologetically.

'So it's down to me. Again.'

'You don't have to lead in with a question about his private bits, but just fish around, see how he is, gauge how he's feeling. Check if he knows that his wife is one folic acid tablet away from spontaneously combusting.' If Tasha was right and Lucy was teetering on the edge of a nervous breakdown then maybe she should also raise it with Nick, he was her brother after all, and knew Lucy far better than she did.

'Fine. I'll do it. But you owe me.'

'How about I buy you those champagne flutes I've been promising to for a year?'

'I'll believe that when I see it.'

They paused in front of Diego Velazquez's *The Rokeby Venus*, voyeuristically looking at Venus's reflection in the mirror held by Cupid. Her sensuous curved body and unseeing stare rendered them both silent for a moment. They'd done this before, met for a quick sandwich and wandered around a gallery for the rest of his lunch hour. It was Marcus that suggested The National Gallery today. The noise of the school groups and Japanese tourists lessened the seriousness of the conversation they were knee deep in.

'Lucy's been a bit weird lately,' Marcus started.

'Weird how?'

He shrugged and put his hands in the pockets of his coat. 'Like one minute all over me and the next literally pushing me away and hiding in the bathroom.'

'Do you think there might be something bothering her that maybe she hasn't told you about?'

'What, like an affair?'

'No! I'm just saying that there must be a reason for her being like that. There's no way she's having an affair. Lucy? No way.'

'They say it's the ones you least expect.'

'There are the ones you least expect, and then there's Lucy. No, there must be another reason. Is she worried about anything? Something not going to plan, or not working out the way she hoped?' Leila was trying to spit it out, she was, but she and Marcus had never had deep confiding chats before and this was harder than she thought it would be.

'No more than usual. She does throw herself into projects, like your events and our parties. I think that maybe her perfectionist ideals are just taking their toll, that's all.'

They'd stopped again in front of Raphael's *Madonna of the Pinks* depicting Mary holding a plump and content baby Jesus. This gave her the perfect lead in. 'Babies are cute aren't they?' Leila said, waiting for him to either agree or make vomiting noises. He was quiet. 'So, do you think you and Lucy will start a family soon?'

'I hope not. We've only just got married. Plenty of time for that. I just want to enjoy my time with her. I know you think that she's a bit bossy and demanding, but she's pretty much perfect for me.' He smiled, walking on to the next painting, his hands in his pockets. 'I know that you and Tash think that I'm a bit of a buffoon, and I know I can be, but Lucy keeps me grounded, stops me getting all pompous and I really like her company. She's very sweet when you get to know her, and we have lots of laughs together. I think a baby might upset the balance.'

'It's what a lot of couples do though, isn't it, I mean you've just turned 40, she's 34, it must be around the right time?'

'Can I tell you a secret?'

Leila inwardly groaned. She didn't know how many more bloody secrets her brain was capable of housing.

'I'm taking part in a medical experiment.'

She was not expecting *that*.

'I knew that Lucy wasn't on the pill, and I didn't want us to get pregnant, but a vasectomy seemed too, I don't know, radical, and a mate of mine told me about this synthetic testosterone that they're trialling and they were looking for people to try it out on, so I volunteered. And so far it seems to be working. I go every two weeks and get my hormone levels checked, and the great thing is that as soon as we're ready for kids, I stop taking it and within a month or so everything's as it should be.' He seemed very pleased with himself and Leila suddenly felt desperately sorry for Lucy, putting herself through all sorts of invasive tests and hardcore diets and needless anxiety all for nothing.

'Would it not have been easier to, you know, just *talk* to Lucy?'

'Oh no, I wouldn't know what to say. It's all a bit . . . intimate . . . isn't it?'

'Isn't that the point? Of marriage I mean?'

Marcus grimaced. 'Not in my book.'

Leila felt much more hopeless than she did before. How could she intervene further without massively compromising either of their trust? Marcus paused, then added. 'Another thing that's quite odd, she sometimes knows things about where I've been when I know I haven't told her, and I wondered . . . no, it's silly, don't worry about it.'

'What?'

'You're going to think I'm really stupid.'

'You're my brother, so I already do. What is it?'

'I sometimes wonder if she's having me followed? See, doesn't it sound ridiculous?'

Leila suddenly remembered the GPS tracker app. Lucy's insecurities were obviously at fever pitch. 'You probably did tell her and forgot.'

'No, you know a few weeks ago when we met for a last-minute drink after work, in Notting Hill? Well when I got home she knew about it. How's that even possible?'

'I texted her when you were in the toilet to see if she wanted to join us,' Leila lied without missing a beat. She felt a strange sense of compassion for Lucy now, what a mess.

'Oh, that's ok then. God I feel really silly saying that now. Ignore me.'

On her way home to Nick, Leila couldn't help wondering how both her siblings had ended up in such dysfunctional marriages. And how much did she now tell Nick about Marcus and Lucy? If he knew that Marcus was duping Lucy, then he'd feel compelled to tell her, she was his little sister, but then she didn't want to hold back and have secrets from him either. Maybe she could give him a heavily watered down version, cherry-picking the least offensive bits from both sides to tell him, but then what would that solve?

'Hi Honey, I'm home!' Nick trilled, dumping his bag and coat in a heap in the corridor. 'Something smells . . . burned . . .'

'It was meant to be a chicken and salsa tray bake, but it's now a charcoal and soot tray bake. We may have to get a takeaway.' Leila kissed him. 'Good day?'

'Yeah, the clients loved the second phase drawings, so that's now going out to tender, and Mike's really pleased, as it basically pays the whole company's wages for another six months.'

'That's good news, I was reading in the paper —'

'The Globe?' Nick teased. It was a standing joke that she ought to expand her news sources to ones that didn't have stories on reality TV stars in their bikinis, but she wasn't yet ready to wave goodbye to her guilty morning routine.

'No, actually, some other very highbrow current affairs paper that you don't know about, it said that developments and new projects are picking up again, so hopefully that means things will be getting better.' Nick's company had been laying people off left, right and centre, and Nick was convinced that his would be the next name to be called into HR on a Friday afternoon. He really wanted to set up on his own too, but they knew that the two of them working from the same tiny flat would probably sound the death knell to their relationship before they'd even gone properly public with it. Which, according to the diary, was meant to be tomorrow.

'I saw Marcus today,' Leila said, carrying an open bottle of wine and two glasses through the bedroom to the garden as Nick followed with a bowl of cashews. There was something about being outside that made her more eloquent and she needed all the help she could get if she was going to broach the topic of his sister's questionable state of mind with him. 'We went to the National Gallery.'

'Ooo, nice. Did you see the Rokeby Venus?'

'She sends her love.'

'How's Marcus doing? Did he enjoy his birthday party?'

'A surprising amount actually. He couldn't believe how much effort Lucy had put into it all.' That was good Leila, she thought, great opening.

'It's what she does best though isn't it, stressing over every detail.'

That couldn't have gone any better, he'd even used the word stressing. 'He thinks that maybe that's the problem though, maybe she does get so involved in tiny details that she works herself up unnecessarily.'

Nick threw a handful of nuts in his mouth, 'Nah, she's always been like that. Her room at home was immaculate, she never had a hair out of place, all her stationery and pencil holders all lined up on her desk, she's always been Miss Perfect.'

'The trouble with that though is when something doesn't go perfectly, you can get yourself all worked up then, can't you?'

Nick raised his eyebrow at Leila. 'What's not gone perfectly?'

Dammit, she'd gone too far too early. 'Nothing in particular, Marcus was just saying that he worries that she gets so involved in whatever she's doing that it's maybe not great for her health.'

'Is she sick?'

'No, she's not sick, just a little, fraught.'

'The thing with Lucy,' Nick said, leaning back in his chair, 'is that she gives this impression of being one step away from needing sectioning, but she's fine. Tell him not to worry about it. Now look, do you know what the date is?'

Leila smiled, 'Yes I do, it's March 31st.'

'Which makes tomorrow . . . ?'

'The first day of us being able to have very obvious public displays of affection?'

'Exactly. So how are we going to do this then?'

'Well we've been having very obvious *private* displays of affection for the last three months, so I think we know what we're doing . . .'

'You know what I mean! Are you going to just drop it into conversation with your sister, or shall I come down to Dartmouth with you for the next Sunday lunch, or are we going to be all 21st century about it and just change our Facebook statuses?'

She'd be lying if she claimed that the different scenarios hadn't been constantly running through her brain. She'd rehearsed the big announcement in front of all her family, she knew they'd be so happy for them. They all seemed to like Nick and him being Lucy's brother just tied everything up really neatly. As long as they didn't give too much of an indication that they'd been dating in secret then no-one should feel too duped or annoyed they'd been kept in the dark.

'I think it would be really great for you to come down to Dartmouth for the next family lunch and we can tell everyone then. They all know that we've been working on the Dubai project together, and we can just say that we grew closer doing that and started to enjoy each other's company and then now that my year is up, we've decided to give it a go.'

'Give it a go?'

'You know what I mean, see what happens.' She knew Nick was fishing, but decided to play along. 'Why, what do you think will happen?'

'I think that by the end of the year I'll have put a ring on it,' he smiled.

Leila just about managed to stop herself from jumping onto his lap, mainly because she wanted to play it cool, but also because the chairs were wobbly enough as they were. 'Oh you do, do you?' she flirted back.

'Maybe.' He shrugged. 'See what happens.'

She threw a cashew nut at him and, pleasingly, it hit him on the nose.

Then the phone rang.

Chapter 21

Leila knew something was horribly wrong. It had nothing to do with the time, 9pm on a Thursday night was just within the limits of phone-call etiquette, but instinctively she knew it was bad news.

Tasha's voice was gasping. 'Leila, I need you, I need you to come here and look after Oscar and Talia, it's Alex, he's been knocked over. He's in a bad way, I need to get to the hospital. Can you come now, straightaway? He's in surgery. He hit his head. Leila, oh God, can you come now?'

Tasha was standing in the open doorway as Leila's taxi pulled up outside. She already had her coat on and was holding a small overnight bag. 'Can you keep the cab!' she shouted, rushing down the steps, jumping the last two. 'They're asleep. Mia will be back in a bit. Down play the accident, tell her not to worry, but it's bad, it's really bad. I'll call when I know more.'

She gave her sister a quick hug and climbed into the back seat. Leila saw her mouth directions to the driver and the car sped off down the dark street.

When Tasha's call had come an hour before, Leila's face turned ashen as she tightly gripped her mobile alerting Nick to silently go and get her bag and coat and lay it down on the arm of the sofa next to her. He'd gone out on to the street to try to hail a cab while Leila flew around the flat shoving chargers, a jumper and her cash card into her bag. As they stood together on the pavement, taxis hurtling past without their 'for hire' lights on, he'd cradled her into him, telling her it was going to be ok. That it was all going to work out alright. His soothing tones almost convinced her.

Then his phone rang. And everything was far from alright.

No-one was answering her messages, and Leila had nothing to do except pace the living room. She couldn't even have another glass of wine as she wanted to keep a clear head for whatever happened during the night. Oscar and Talia were fast asleep and Mia had come back an hour or so ago and was listening to music in her room, oblivious to the fact that her father was undergoing emergency surgery at that exact moment.

The television was muted. Leila needed to be able to hear the buzz of her phone and any murmurings from upstairs. Moving pictures of a travel programme flitted across the screen. Happy people enjoying colourful drinks and seafood platters sitting outside Greek tavernas. Outside the window, laughter from the wine bar on the corner flitted through the glass, revellers oblivious to the children sleeping a few doors down while their father lay unconscious and their mother rocked back and forth on a plastic chair in a hospital prayer room, speaking to God for the first time in her adult life.

I'm sorry that I've never done this before. I don't know why I'm here. I just felt I needed to be. I'm sorry, I shouldn't be here, if someone comes in here that needs you more than me, I'll go. I don't know what to say. Don't let him die. But also don't let him live if he's going to be a vegetable, he wouldn't want that. Let him be ok, not dying or a vegetable. Please Father, God, I don't even know what to call you. I tried praying when I was a teenager too, do you remember? I was bad at it then too. Oh God please, we

343

need him. We need him to live. I need him to grow old with. They need him to grow old with. I never thought this could happen. Is this to punish him? Or me? It's one of your commandments isn't it? I remember that, is that what this is God? Because he didn't listen? But he loves me Father, God, he does, I know it. And if you let him live I know he won't do it again, I know he's stopped because he's told me. After the last one, he's told me there will be no more, and I believe him Father, I do. So please, please, believe him too and let him live.

The door behind Tasha slowly pushed open. She turned around and then reverently reached for her bag so the woman could have some privacy in her pleading too. The lady was older, late sixties maybe. The age where you expect to be spending time in hospital, waiting for your husband to come out of surgery. She gave her a small smile as she passed her, a smile that said, *I know what you feel, because I feel it too.* A jolt of recognition surged through Tasha as their eyes connected. The woman's long grey hair was pulled tightly back in a bun, she was devoid of make-up, bohemian jewellery and colourful clothes, but it was definitely her.

'Stephanie?'

'Oh my, it's Tasha isn't it? Marcus's sister? Oh thank you so much for coming, he's in such a state, I didn't want to leave him in the room but I wanted to come in here for a moment.'

'Marcus is here?' Tasha didn't understand. Perhaps Leila had called him? It was sweet of him to be so emotional about Alex's accident, she knew that Alex and him had had their disagreements over the years. But of course he'd be here for her. To support her during this time, he was her brother.

It was only as she was walking away from the prayer room down the corridor that she realised that didn't explain why Stephanie was here as well.

The Relatives' Room was deliberately impersonal. Tasha tried not to think of all the different families that had passed through this room. Sitting on the same worn plastic seats, reading the same helpline numbers on the wall, taking tissues from the same cotton tissue holder, gazing at the same innocuous Monet print on the wall. The television was chained to the wall, which was strange; thinking of opportunistic theft at a time of bereavement or waiting for news of a loved one was disconcerting.

'Tasha, you came!' Marcus said entering the room and enveloping his sister in a big hug, and as soon as his arms were wrapped around her his tears started falling in large unmanly sobs. His body shook as he held onto her and she let herself finally cry too. She had no idea that he would be so affected by Alex's accident, but then they had been brothers-in-law for nearly two decades.

They were sat side by side, with their backs to the wall, facing the door. After their emotional embrace they were silent. Waiting for news.

'They said it wouldn't be too much longer,' Marcus ventured finally, stretching his legs out in front of him.

'How do you know? They told me it could be hours yet,' Tasha said, turning to look at Marcus.

'They told me it wasn't going to take more than an hour, two at most.'

'Who did you speak to? Why didn't they talk to me first?' Tasha's voice was rising.

Marcus raised an eyebrow. 'The orthopaedic surgeon just before they took her in. Why would they tell you first?'

'Marcus, you're not making any sense. Took who in? What are you talking about? Why is an orthopaedic surgeon doing brain surgery?'

At that moment the door rebounded off the little door spring mounted on the skirting board and Nick crashed into the room.

'Nick, thanks so much for coming mate,' Marcus stood up and shook his brother-in-law's hand. 'We don't know too much more yet, but she's stable and it seems to just be her leg that's broken.'

'That's good. God, it could have been so much worse.' Nick then turned to Tasha. 'And how's Alex, any news?'

Tasha opened her mouth to speak, but Marcus spoke first. 'Alex? Alex is here?'

'He was in a car accident, he's in surgery now.' She looked from one man to the other. 'What's going on, are you not here for him? Whose leg is broken?'

Nick spoke first. 'It's really bizarre, but it seems that both Alex and Lucy had accidents at the same time. Just as you called Leila about Alex, Marcus called me about Lucy.'

Tasha covered her mouth with her hand. 'Oh God Marcus, I'm so sorry, I didn't realise, I thought you were here because you'd heard about Alex! I had no idea that Lucy's hurt too.' She sank heavily back into her chair. 'Jesus, what a night!'

'I don't even know what Lucy's doing in London to be honest, she said she was visiting Stephanie in Norfolk for a couple of days, but Stephanie said that she hadn't heard from her since my party.' Marcus slumped back into his chair. 'I don't know what's going on any more.'

'There'll be a simple explanation for it I'm sure,' Tasha said, covering Marcus's hand with her own. 'Maybe she was visiting friends, or planning a surprise for you. Just be thankful that she's going to be ok. At this point I have no idea if my husband is still alive.' Marcus tightened his grip on his sister's hand. He couldn't find the right words to reply.

Nick sat the other side of Marcus. He was unusually quiet, reflective. Thankfully the other two didn't know him well enough to pick up on it, and they were too consumed with their own thoughts and anxieties to care anyway. But Nick had suddenly reached the horrible conclusion the other two were yet to. This was much worse than they could imagine.

Lucy's surgeon was the first to bring news. The operation had gone well. She was yet to come round, but it shouldn't be too long. Her leg was broken in three places, the side of the knee cap had been shattered, but rebuilt as best they could for now, but a future surgery was almost certain. A nurse was with him and as the surgeon left the room she stepped forward and gave Marcus Lucy's handbag and the small Louis Vuitton suitcase that he'd merrily put in the boot of her car earlier in the day before waving her off to Norfolk.

'These were with your wife when she had her accident, the police just dropped them off.' The nurse then turned to Tasha. 'You're Mr Banbury's wife, aren't you? I have some of his belongings too at the nurse's station in A&E, I'll just be a moment and I'll come back with them.'

The room regained its silence when she left. Tasha was just staring ahead, but her eyes were unseeing. Marcus sat clutching his wife's handbag to his chest; relief was flooding through his body and Nick was battling with the crazy thoughts that were going around and around his head. If his suspicions were right, it was just a matter of time before the lives of everyone around him were obliterated into tiny pieces.

Just then, Lucy's bag started to vibrate. Marcus unclasped it and retrieved her phone and turned off the calendar alert. Illuminated on the screen was the word *Ovulating*. It didn't mean anything to him; of course, he knew what it meant biologically but he didn't know why it would be on his wife's phone. They weren't trying for a baby or anything. Maybe that's just what women did, tracking their monthly, things.

He clumsily tried to jab the phone back in the bag and it slid off his lap onto the floor. Lipsticks, keys and pens scattered all over the floor. Nick bent down to help him pick things up and handed him Lucy's purse and a key card. 'Here you go.'

'Thanks.' Marcus shoved everything back into the bag, but stared at the key card. It was for an upmarket hotel not far from the hospital. Why would Lucy have a hotel key card in her bag?

'Here you go love.' The nurse came back with a transparent zip-lock bag with Alex's wallet, phone, keys and a few other bits in it. 'These were in his pockets, they're probably safer here with you than with us, you get all types in here in the middle of the night.'

Tasha gratefully reached for them, just seeing his worn brown leather wallet made her smile. She'd bought it in Switzerland for him when they were skiing a couple of years ago, picking it out of a beautiful little leather shop in a mountain village. She'd even met the tanner as well, who beamed with pride when she'd bought it. It was a daily occurrence for Alex to shout through the house asking if she'd seen it, and clutching it now, through an anonymous see-through plastic bag was surreal.

His phone was there too. How many secrets did that hold, she wondered. He'd never lost *that* around the house, no, he was too careful for that. He'd probably deleted all the messages that wives weren't supposed to see. Not that she'd go snooping through anyway, she'd prefer not to know. Especially now. None of the past mattered now, he just needed to get through the surgery alive and they'd work everything out.

There was half a pack of chewing gum as well, typical Alex, always trying to hide the sneaky lunchtime cigarette she knew he still had by frantically chewing gum on the way home. There was a credit card loose in the bag too, which was odd, she thought, tracing its rectangular shape through the plastic, why wasn't that in his wallet? She brought the bag closer to her eyes so she could see it and realised that it was the carbon copy of the one her brother was holding in his fingers.

Nick held his breath, looking between Tasha and Marcus, working out which one would be the first to realise. Marcus's brow was furrowed. He had no idea why Lucy would be staying in London when she should be in Norfolk, it was all very strange and mysterious. Tasha knew all too well what hotel key cards meant, but didn't understand where Lucy came into it. Why would her sister-in-law be staying at the same hotel as her husband?

Then her eyes widened.

Nick was watching her reaction as it happened and he could tell the exact moment the penny dropped. Tasha's mouth was slack and she leant her head back against the wall. Not even ten seconds passed before Marcus's thought processes caught up and he suddenly said, 'You don't think that — no, it couldn't be that . . . I mean, it's got to be a coincidence surely . . . they wouldn't have been . . .' He didn't finish his sentence.

Nick knew he was intruding. He shouldn't be there. If his sister had been having an affair with Alex, then he had no right to be encroaching on this moment of realisation. But he couldn't very well just stand up and leave either. The room started feeling uncomfortably hot, and he needed to get some air, to call Leila and tell her what was going on.

He started making the moves to stand up

and Tasha angrily rounded on him. 'And where are you going? Going to run to your little sister and tell her that we're on to her?' Her voice shook and her face had paled. 'How dare you sit here and pretend that you're all friendly and that you care about our family when your sister has been busy ripping our family to pieces. You probably even knew about it too!'

'I swear I didn't know,' Nick said, sitting back down, but turning to face her. 'Tasha you have to believe me, I don't have a clue what's going on, any more than you do. Let's not jump to any conclusions before we know for certain.'

'What other explanation could there be? My husband, the serial philanderer has really done it this time. And how stupid is your sister? To throw away everything for a quick fumble with her brother-in-law. It's sick. She's not right in the head.'

'That's hardly fair to say before you even know what's going on,' Nick said gently.

'Fair? Fair?' Tasha angrily spat. 'What's not fair is that I waved my husband off to work this morning, and now he's lying dying down the corridor after sleeping with my sister-in-law. So I think I know what's fair and not fair, don't you? Can you get out now, I don't want to hear your fake words of concern.'

Marcus had been silent all through Tasha's tirade, but now wearily looked up. 'I think it's best you leave now Nick. Thanks for coming.'

'Can I at least pop in and see Lucy before I go?' As soon as Nick spoke he knew he'd made a mistake saying her name out loud.

'Lucy?' Tasha spat. 'Lucy? Sure, go on, and while you're there pull a few tubes out will you?'

'There's no need to —'

'There's every need Marcus, she's lying there with a broken leg, poor little Lucy. Alex is in brain surgery and my whole life, and yours, has just been shattered. And I don't need Nick here telling me to calm down or wait to find out for certain, bollocks to that. Now can you go please Nick and leave our family the hell alone?'

As he took in his first deep drag of nicotine just outside the hospital entrance the implications of what his sister had done were becoming clearer. There was absolutely no way that Leila and him could come clean about their own relationship now, not when her whole family would be gunning for his.

Leila answered on the first ring. 'Any news?'

'Quite a lot.'

'Is Alex . . . did he make it?'

'He's still in theatre. Lucy's out, broken leg in three places, but she'll be ok.'

'Oh thank God.' Relief flooded Leila's voice. 'Have you seen her yet?'

A pause. Nick was trying to choose his words carefully to minimise the impact. 'Not yet . . . There's something else. Um, it looks as though it wasn't a freaky co-incidence. It seems as though, um, Lucy and Alex were together when the accident happened.'

'What? I don't understand?'

'We don't know anything for certain, Alex and Lucy are still out for the count, but they both had the same hotel room key in their belongings.'

'Nick you're not making any sense, they had the same room key? What does that even mean?'

'It means they lied about where they were — Lucy told Marcus she was in Norfolk visiting Mum, Alex was apparently meant to be away in Manchester for the night, and instead they were both in London staying at the same hotel.'

The silence that ensued told Nick that her brain was working overtime trying to compute all this. 'As in, they were *together*

together?'

'It looks like it, but as I said, no-one knows anything for certain. It could all be a big misunderstanding, but Marcus and Tasha are in a bad way about it.'

'Oh God. Oh God Nick, this is very bad. But it can't be surely, he wouldn't do that with Lucy, surely?' Leila suddenly stopped. She didn't know whether now was the right time to tell Nick about what she saw at the party, but there had been too many secrets flying about lately. 'You know at Marcus's 40th weekend? Well, just before the dinner I found them together, and he had his watch strap caught in her hair and they were laughing about it. I didn't find it strange at the time, but it was just the two of them and how the hell does someone's watch strap get stuck in your hair unless you're up to no good? I didn't tell you because I didn't actually see anything bad, it was just odd. It could've been completely innocent.'

'I think we both know that Alex and innocent are not two words that naturally go together,' Nick said.

'But how stupid is Lucy to be taken in by him? And when she has lovely Marcus too. Jeez, what a slut!'

'Leila! That's my sister, and until we know what's gone on, we can't make judgements

356

and call names. I only called you as I
thought you should know, not for you to
slag off my family.'

'Slag's the right word.'

The phone then went dead.

CHAPTER 22

Lucy

Most people find it tricky to pinpoint the exact moment their life veered off its familiar, well-worn channel and plunged them deep into misery. Many are quick to blame a combination of events, an escalating of circumstances that multiplied and ballooned beyond their control. Invariably, eyes look heavenward and shoulders resignedly droop, and words like 'fate', 'destiny' and 'God's will' are thrown about to make people feel better.

Shifting the culpability onto a higher being, an invisible force that interferes in lives makes tragedies easier to bear. Considering yourself a blameless pawn in a pre-destined game absolves you of the guilt; it stops the endless what-ifs from diseasing your days and plaguing your nights. Lucy didn't have that luxury though. She knew that her perfect life unravelling was entirely of her own making.

She had a choice, of course she had a choice. She'd started this. She had built the tiny snowball that had gathered pace and speed and momentum and was now nothing less than a sodding avalanche poised to smash her perfect little life into a thousand pieces.

When she opened her eyes after the surgery and Marcus wasn't there, she realised that he must know. If it had just been a normal car accident, if her leg had been crushed under a van in Norfolk for instance, where she was meant to be, he'd have held a vigil next to her bed, she knew he would. He'd have been sitting there in his crumpled suit, looking bereft and worried and his eyes would have softened with relief when she opened hers. He would have tightened his grip on her hand and stroked her palm, telling her that he was there, and it was all ok. Except this way, the events leading up to this accident meant that it wasn't. And knowing that made her eyes fill with tears that she couldn't blink away.

'Is it true?' said a deep voice at the end of the bed. 'Are you having an affair with Alex?'

'Nick,' Lucy smiled weakly and opened her eyes.

'I'm really sorry to ask you this Luce, when you're only hours out of surgery, but it's all kicking off and I just want to hear you say it.'

Lucy closed her eyes again and didn't open them even while she replied. 'No Nick, we're not having an affair . . . We nearly did . . . We'd planned to. Well not an affair, but, it's complicated.' She lay back on her pillow exhausted. It wasn't just the surgery, she was emotionally finished.

'You both had the same hotel key and were knocked down by the same van, what was going on?' This time her brother's voice was softer, he perched on the edge of her bed and reached for her hand. 'This isn't you Luce, what happened?'

Her tears slowly returned and pooled in the corner of her eyes. 'I've been trying to get pregnant ever since the wedding and nothing.' She looked at him. 'I know the problem isn't with me, I've had tests and it's not me. So it's Marcus, but I didn't know how to tell him, he's so proud, he's so private, and there's no way that he'd want people to know, or even talk about it, let alone go for tests. And I wanted a baby so much Nick, so much. It was all I could think about, I didn't think that I could live another day without being a mum. And Alex has been flirting with me for so long, and Tasha once joked about how he was incredibly fertile. And at Marcus's party when he was meant to be helping me set up he was all over me, pestering me to meet up with him, and I thought, that if I just met him once, at the right time, maybe, just maybe it would work, and then Marcus and I would have a baby and it would all be ok, and everyone would get what they wanted.'

'Oh Jesus Lucy.'

'But then we checked in to the hotel that he'd booked, and I couldn't do it Nick, I kept thinking of Marcus, of his brown eyes, and his smile, and big arms and I knew that I didn't want my baby to be anyone's but his, and I didn't want Alex anywhere near me and so I just ran out the door and straight into the street. He ran after me and we didn't see the van. Oh Nick, what the hell have I done?'

'It's ok, it'll be ok. At least you didn't go through with it. It's ok. Look, you shouldn't get upset. Just relax, and calm down, it'll be ok.'

On the other side of the curtain Marcus put his head down and turned to walk away. He'd heard everything and he completely disagreed with Nick. Everything was not going to be ok.

■ ■ ■ ■

Two floors up and three wards over in the intensive care unit, Tasha sat next to Alex's bed. They had managed to stop the bleed and the swelling was going down. What seemed like a bleak prognosis ten hours ago had taken on a more positive slant now. Nevertheless, his pale, lifeless body was still hooked up to tubes and wires. The harsh overhead lights made his skin almost translucent, his mouth hung open with exhaustion and sedatives, his eyelids closed, mute and unseeing. He didn't have any parents or siblings, and so it was just her. And however much she hated him at this moment, she wasn't going to leave him. Not tonight anyway.

Judy and Thomas were going to come up in the morning to look after the kids for a while and thankfully Leila seemed fine to stay the night. When she'd called her sister to update her, she seemed to know everything already. Tasha assumed that Marcus must have called her first.

She'd met him for a lukewarm coffee in a cardboard cup from the all-night canteen just before he went home. He was in a bad way. Which of course she was too, but she'd had sixteen years of rehearsals for this moment. Marcus told her what he'd heard Lucy tell Nick, and he was devastated. It was a lot for him to take in, but Tasha had never seen her brother so visibly shrunken in size and personality. Finding out that his wife was planning to sleep with her brother-in-law to get pregnant, and was plotting to pass the baby off as his was the stuff of soap operas, not his carefully ordered life.

She refrained from pointing out what Nick had, that nothing had actually happened and that was the important thing, because she didn't believe that was true. Whether they had followed through with the plan or not didn't matter to her, the intent was there. And as she knew Alex better than anyone, she would stake the house on the fact that he wasn't chasing Lucy across the road to check on her state of mind, he was chasing her across the road to try to get her to change it.

The ward was quiet. It was an hour or so before sunrise and the nurses were doing their final checks before the shift change. Tasha hadn't slept, despite being given a blanket and some pillows by one of the nurses. Alex was going to wake up again soon, they told her. They'd reduced his meds and he'd started to flex his fingers and stretch in his sleep. Part of her didn't want him to wake up just yet. Sat here, in the stillness of the dawn she was his wife. Present tense. As soon as he opened his eyes she'd have to say out loud what she'd been rehearsing in her head. No amount of begging or remorse or promises was going to alter the words of her speech that she knew she had to make.

She must have fallen asleep, her chin resting on her chest, when suddenly the nurse pushed past her chair to remove Alex's breathing tube. He coughed and winced with the pain. After the nurses had asked Alex to move different parts of his body on demand, count backwards, and name some capital cities, they left him alone with her.

'Darling,' he said weakly, reaching out his hand for her. Tasha took a step back so his hand merely brushed air. 'Tash?'

'Why weren't you in Manchester, Alex? Like you told me you were?'

'The meeting got moved to London at the last minute, I didn't see the point in telling you, what's the difference to you which city I'm in? Come on Tash, I'm properly sick.'

'We live in London Alex. We live less than thirty minutes' walk from the hotel you'd booked into.'

To give him his credit, he tried to arrange

his face into a confused expression, while answering in what he hoped was a surprised tone. 'Hotel?'

'Yes Alex. The hotel you'd booked to seduce my brother's wife in. Is it coming back to you now?'

'Lucy? Yes, it was really strange, bumping into her on the street like that,' he closed his eyes as he carried on talking, 'when I saw she was running in front of the van, I did my best to save her, but it was going too fast and we didn't stand a chance.'

'And was it just a coincidence that you both had the same hotel key?'

'Hotel key?' Again Alex made sure his intonation hit the balance between complete innocence with a little bit of curiosity thrown in for good measure.

'Yes Alex. The hotel key that was in your pocket and her handbag.'

'Well, I can only think that maybe Lucy had two keys and dropped one and the ambulance guys thought it was mine.' Casually he added, 'Speaking of Lucy, is she ok?'

'Yes she's ok. Broken leg but ok.'

'Oh that's good. So it's all worked out ok in the end.' He settled back on the pillow and sighed contentedly as though the last twelve hours were a horrible dream and now they could start planning their next holiday.

Tasha summoned up every ounce of self-restraint to not grab the pillow and put it over his face. Instead she leaned in closer and whispered, 'If you believe that Alex, you're an even bigger fool than I think you are.'

Most couples' first arguments were over messiness, or lateness, or remote-hogging, or some other triviality that seemed so incredibly important in the moment that it was worth having a fight over. Leila reckoned that possibly this was the first ever lover's tiff to be caused by the man's sister breaking up the two marriages of the girl's siblings. This was a story the bosses at daytime TV would salivate over.

Leila knew that she shouldn't have called Lucy a slut. Or a slag. At least not out loud. But Nick shouldn't have been so reasonable about it all, so measured and upbeat. There was nothing reasonable about what had happened. Even after she'd received his long text message that went on for four screens explaining all the reasons why Lucy agreed to meet Alex, Leila still couldn't summon up the level of sympathy for her that Nick had. It was a crazy idea, who went behind their husband's back to try and get pregnant with someone else anyway? It was utter madness. 'She must have been so desperate,' Nick wrote. She must have been delusional more like, Leila thought. 'Thank God she changed her mind in time,' he'd added at the end. As if that made it all ok and they could all pretend nothing happened. Maybe being delusional ran in their family.

Sending her a text instead of calling suggested that Nick was still monumentally annoyed at her, but wanted to keep her in the loop. Leila quickly finished her shower and closed the bathroom door quietly so she didn't wake the kids up; there was another hour before they needed to be up for school and Tasha would be back soon. She adored her nieces and nephew but didn't feel ready to single-handedly shoehorn them into uniforms and force-feed them cornflakes.

Tasha had sounded very tired on the phone, which was understandable as she'd just spent the night wondering if her husband was going to live, while facing all of these extra revelations alone. Leila remembered what Alex had said to her the morning that she had turned up at his work, about Tasha knowing about his affair and being ok with it. Was she going to do the same now? Leila wondered as she put some fresh coffee beans into the grinder and set the timer on the oven for some M&S croissants she'd found in the freezer.

'Mmmm, it smells like a deli in here,' Tasha put her bag down next to the breakfast bar and hoisted herself up on to one of the stools. 'Ooo, they're still hot,' she said dropping one of the pastries onto her plate and licking her fingers clean of the crumbs. 'Kids still asleep?'

Leila thought the question was unnecessary, had they been awake they wouldn't have been enjoying hot croissants in amiable silence, there'd be a tornado of activity and noise circling them, along with indiscriminate flying objects and strange smells.

'Yes, I looked in on them a couple of minutes ago and all still snoozing.'

'I might keep them off today. I just want to keep them near me, you know?'

Leila nodded. She did know. When it wasn't clear whether Alex was going to make it or not she'd sat by Oscar's bed watching his little rosebud lips quiver with deep breathing and watching the slow rise and fall of his tiny chest under the duvet. He wasn't even her child, but there was something about watching children sleep that was deeply soothing and hugely unsettling all at once, as though all the troubles of the world just disappeared and yet seemed so much bigger at the same time.

'How is he?' Leila said finally. She couldn't not ask, but equally knew that her voice couldn't betray any feeling of any kind. She had to sound neutral, breezy, non-judgemental. That was a tall order for just three words.

'He's fine. He's awake. Talking shit.' Tasha brought her mug up to her lips and took a sip of her cappuccino. 'He denied every-thing, of course.'

Leila stayed quiet. She felt that Tasha didn't need any prompting this time.

'He tried to make it sound as though he was this maverick hero who spotted a poor damsel in distress and tried to save her by pushing her out of the way of the van. He even denied having the key card in his pocket and said that both keys must have fallen out of Lucy's. But do you know what I did?' Tasha laughed, high on adrenaline from having stood up to her husband for the first time in sixteen years. 'I called his bluff and I rang the hotel there and then and asked to be put through to Mr Ban-bury's room and they tried to connect me to it. It rang out of course, but it proves he'd booked it. He didn't have anything to say then. And I left. I don't think he was expecting that.' She gently put the cup back on the worktop. 'I'm not going back either. Not this time.'

Leila let Tasha's words hang suspended in the air for a bit, knowing that her sister was going to keep talking.

'It's not the first time you know. Or the second. Or the third. It's probably the twelfth, maybe fifteenth. And you know the most ironic thing? This one, this straw that broke the camel's back wasn't even an affair! This is the only time that Alex hasn't actually slept with someone else, and this is the one that I'm going to leave him over.'

There she'd said it. It was out there and she couldn't take it back. And she didn't want to, which was the most liberating thing. She'd turned a blind eye for so many years, pretending that she was alright with the conveyor belt of mistresses passing through their lives, even convincing herself that it didn't matter, but it did. And she wasn't going to sit back and let it happen anymore.

'So what now?' Leila asked, running her finger round the milk foam inside her cup and licking it off.

'Now, I call a really good solicitor, put six bottles of Prosecco in the fridge, invite some girlfriends over and start packing his things.' She raised her coffee cup to Leila. 'Cheers.'

CHAPTER 23

If it was possible to get bruises from mentally beating yourself up then Leila would be black and blue. What was she thinking, calling Lucy those names to Nick, or anyone for that matter? She'd obviously learned nothing from the last year at all. All that crap that she'd spouted at the end of year event, about not judging other women, understanding their stories before casting aspersions on their life choices. Lucy was quite clearly not in her right mind, and she didn't need Leila getting all feisty and throwing insults about. She had just broken up the marriages of both her siblings — but on the other hand, she was the sister of the man she loved, and somehow, in the course of the last year she'd become a friend. Jesus, could this get any more complicated?

Nick had agreed to meet her for breakfast in a local cafe. She didn't want the first time that they saw each other to be in the flat.

That was their haven, their romantic sanctuary, that wasn't the place for arguments and recriminations. Not that she thought there would be, she was planning to go in softly, try and repair the damage she'd done by suggesting his sister was a lady of negotiable affection.

He was already sat at one of the greying Formica tables. It was probably the fact that he looked like a man on the edge that had persuaded the manager to open the doors fifteen minutes early. She could see through the glass that his shoulders were drooped and he was nursing a massive cup of coffee. He was still wearing the same clothes as yesterday, as was she, and his stubble had taken on a life of its own.

'Hey,' Leila said, slipping into the seat opposite him.

'Hey.' He raised his eyes to meet hers and gave her a small smile that betrayed his tiredness.

'I'm sorry I said what I said about Lucy,' Leila said straight away. 'I shouldn't have called her those things, it's just been such a whirlwind of emotions, and they came out of my mouth before I could stop them.'

'It's ok. At that point we didn't know why they were meeting. It could have been an affair, rather than just a poor woman longing for a baby.'

Leila knew she had to tread carefully. Obviously Nick was taking the line of thought that Lucy was being desperate rather than deceitful. Which he would, of course, it was his sister. But that didn't change the fact that she'd left a trail of destruction in her wake.

'Can I have a strong black coffee please?' Leila said to the hovering manager. 'And a bacon sandwich?'

'Can you make that two please?' Nick added. He fiddled with the sugar sachets that were in a small metal pot on the table. 'How's Tasha?'

'Packing up Alex's things.'

'Oh God, he didn't — ?'

Leila suddenly realised the horrifically wrong conclusion Nick had jumped to. 'No, he didn't die. He's going to be fine. But Tasha's leaving him.'

'I see.' He didn't look up from lining the long thin sugars end to end.

'How's Lucy?' Leila asked gingerly.

Nick didn't look up as he replied, 'I'm going back in there in a bit, Mum's back at her hotel having a shower and I'm picking her up at ten. She should be out tomorrow.'

'That's good.' She didn't know how to ask where Lucy was going to stay. When she spoke to Marcus on her way to the cafe to meet Nick he'd been in the process of changing the locks.

It was as if Nick knew what she was thinking without her saying anything. 'She's going to stay at mine for a while as it's on the ground floor and she can't manage stairs yet. My cousin's going to live with his girlfriend until Lucy's a bit better. Mum and I are going to take turns looking after her for the first week or so until she can get about a bit more.'

'Right.'

'She never meant for all this to happen Lei. She's in a really bad way.'

'I'm sure that's true Nick, I know she wouldn't have intentionally plotted to split up two marriages, but she did. And we're stuck in the middle of it.'

Just then their breakfasts arrived and they both looked up gratefully for the distraction. Leila had been so hungry, and yet now couldn't find the appetite or energy to eat.

'Have you spoken to your mum and dad?'

'Yes, they arrived at Tasha's just as I left. Mum's distraught as you can imagine, Dad's being all silent and stoic. He's going up to Marcus's tomorrow, Mum thought it better he went by himself.' Judy had surprised everyone by suggesting it this morning, but she knew that Marcus would respond much better to her husband's quiet empathy rather than her own outpouring of tears and sympathy.

'This doesn't need to change anything Leila you know. I mean, between us.'

She was glad he'd said it. She needed him to say it. But that didn't mean it was true.

'Of course it won't. It's just going to be a bit tricky at the moment. I think we probably need to keep us a secret for a while longer. It's not the right time.'

Nick nodded sadly. 'Yep.'

'I need to go now, I promised Tasha I'd take Mia to the hospital this morning to see Alex and I need to nip back to the flat first.'

'Can I come back to your flat with you to get a few things as I'll need them at mine?'

His words cut through her. It was the first time in months he'd referred to the flat as 'hers'. Apart from the odd night here or there when he was away visiting clients, they hadn't slept apart since the middle of January. It seemed impossible that it was only last night that they were joking around in the garden talking about getting married. Now he was coming to collect his 'things'.

The walk back to the flat was mainly done in silence. Unlike the loved-up couples that strolled amiably past Leila's living room window, Leila now found herself scurrying two paces to Nick's one. Despite her being more than a foot shorter than him, they'd always walked in time before. Perhaps he'd deliberately slowed down, or taken smaller steps in order for her to keep up, but this morning they were not in sync at all. It was a tiny thing, not worth mentioning, but it made Leila want to cry.

Back in the flat she handed him his Arsenal mug. 'Here you go.'

'I've got mugs at home Lei, why do I need to take that?'

'I just thought you were getting your stuff?'

'Not all of it, just a few bits to tide me over.' He stopped packing his wash bag and straightened up. 'Why, do you *want* me to take everything?'

'Of course not! I don't want you to take *anything*! I just didn't know what you meant, that's all.'

'If you want some space, I can take everything?'

'No, that's not what I want at all, God Nick, please just take a toothbrush and leave everything else here. Please.'

She didn't mean to sound so begging, but she couldn't help it. Seeing his open bag being filled by all the little detritus she'd come to love seeing scattered about her flat was heartbreaking. She knew it was only supposed to be temporary, but a nagging sensation deep inside her stomach told her that it might not be. Nick walked over to the chest of drawers and took out a couple of T-shirts, some boxers and his ski socks. Leila's stomach lurched.

'Why do you need those?'

'What?' Nick said, looking down at the pile in his hands.

'The socks. It's April, you don't need those.'

'I have tiled floors Lei, they're cold, and these are so comfy.'

'Please leave them.'

'They're just socks.'

How could she tell him that they weren't just socks, that they represented so much more than that? She'd sound crazy. So she just said quietly, 'Fine. Take the socks.'

The couple sat opposite them on the tube were staring wide-eyed and open-mouthed. It was understandable, the question had taken Leila completely by surprise too. She hadn't yet had a chance to ask Tasha what information had been shared, or what the party line was, and was totally not prepared for Mia to ask on a crowded train whether

Leila knew that her dad had had lots of affairs. A man to Mia's right was doing a better job of keeping his curiosity concealed, allowing himself only a subtle peek over his paper at them.

'Um, what did your mum say about it?' Leila replied in a quiet voice.

'She said that Dad was going to live somewhere else as even though she loved him very much, she didn't trust him, and didn't want to be married to him anymore.'

Leila guessed correctly that Mia had caught Tasha off guard and her sister was so emotionally battered from the night before that it just wasn't possible to roll the words in sugar before saying them out loud. And Mia was sixteen now, and not a naive sixteen-year-old either, she was perfectly able to understand that relationships can go sour. But judging from Mia's shell-shocked expression and pale face, she wasn't as mature and capable as Tasha had perhaps thought.

'These things happen Mia, and the important thing is, is that your dad's going to be ok. It doesn't really matter if your mum and dad live in the same house anymore does it, they won't love you any less.'

'You don't need to feed me clichés Aunty Leila. I'm sixteen, I know how these things work. I am, or I was, the only one of my friends to have both parents still together.'

Well that's a damning indictment on modern society, Leila thought.

'This is our stop, come on.'

Alex was decidedly chirpy for someone who had been through brain surgery and a marriage break-up on the same day. He motioned for them both to sit on the side of his bed, but neither of them did.

'The doctors said that I should be able to come home in a couple of days.'

He didn't even stumble over the words 'come home'.

'That's good news,' Leila replied. A large part of her wanted to pick up his lunch tray and batter him in the face with it, but the other part also wanted to try to understand why he continually risked everything. He'd essentially been her brother for nearly seventeen years and she couldn't just shrug and not care about what happened to him.

'Mum's packing all your stuff,' Mia said bluntly.

Alex chortled. 'She'll come round.'

Leila had to physically jam her hands into her pockets to stop her from reaching for the half-eaten yoghurt pot and smearing it all over his smug grin. 'Not this time Alex.'

Alex rolled his eyes at her. 'Of course she will. She always does.'

Leila didn't have to do anything in the end to wipe the self-satisfied smirk off his face because Mia did it for her, shouting 'You really are a prize shit Dad!' at the top of her voice, kicking the catheter bag that was hanging over the side of his bed and running off past the nurse's station to the sound of Alex's anguished howls. Mia wasn't to know that she'd quite literally kicked him in the very place that had caused all the trouble, but it seemed quite appropriate in the circumstances.

'Mia, wait!' Leila raced down the corridor after her niece, whose bravado had dissolved into heaving sobs just outside the ward's double doors. 'Darling, it's ok, it's going to be ok.' Mia's body felt weak and tiny in Leila's arms.

It was astonishing how the bottom could fall out of your life in a single moment. Just yesterday Mia had come second in a geography test, moaned about the school lunch choices, chattered all the way home on the bus with her friends, argued with Tasha over the volume of her music, and now, less than eighteen hours later, her childhood seemed like a very far away memory.

On the floor below, Nick was putting his

supermarket-bought flowers into a vase on Lucy's bedside table. He knew that carnations were not normally to her taste but she'd smiled such a grateful smile that he felt bad for not spending more than a fiver on them. The magazines he'd bought her the night before in the small hospital shop on the ground floor lay unread underneath her make-up bag, which was also unopened. Nick thought it was probably the first time since Lucy had hit puberty that he'd seen her without lashings of mascara and her shiny lip gloss, and without them, she looked really young and fragile. He wanted to give her a big hug but her leg was suspended in a weird contraption hanging from the ceiling and she now had a cast on her arm too.

'What happened to your arm?'

'It started swelling in the night and they took an x-ray this morning and it's fractured too.'

'Oh Luce, that's rubbish, that's your right one as well.'

'I know, I was just coming to terms with the fact that I can't walk for eight weeks and now I can't write or get dressed properly either.'

'Don't worry, Mum and I have sorted it all out, you're coming to stay with me for a bit. Wait, before you argue, you need someone to help you, at least for the first couple of weeks until you get used to it, and Mum's going to stay too.'

'I would have you at mine, darling but it's only a tiny place on the third floor, and there's no way you'd make the stairs,' Stephanie said, stroking her daughter's hair, noting happily that she hadn't yanked herself away from her mother's touch for probably the first time in nearly thirty years.

'Can I not go back to my own house?' Lucy asked quietly.

'I don't think that's really an option at the moment Luce, Marcus was a bit cut up about everything. I'm sure he'll come round, but it's probably better you give him a bit of space.'

It was a lie. Nick didn't think he'd come round. He'd been questioning himself over the last few hours about what he would be doing in Marcus's position and he didn't think he'd suddenly get over it either, and he was nowhere near as stubborn and bombastic as Marcus seemed. But he couldn't tell his sister that. His little sister whose face was as pale as the pillow she lay on, whose limbs were uncomfortably bound in tight plaster and who needed any ounce of hope she could get that she hadn't

382

screwed things up as royally as she thought she might have done.

The minute hands had moved nine little dots forward and neither father nor son had spoken after the words 'Coffee', and 'Yes please' had been uttered.

They were incredibly similar, Thomas and Marcus, to the point that Thomas had built a small outbuilding in the garden when Marcus was around twelve for the two of them to escape to in times of female over-load. There were no 'girls keep out' signs or anything like that hanging on the door, but Tasha, Leila and Judy knew that this was a sacred testosterone-only space. Thomas had rigged up a small portable TV where they watched big football and rugby games, and there was a small under-counter fridge with low-alcohol beer in it for Marcus to feel manly without Thomas feeling guilty that he was encouraging underage drinking. There was a certain amount of irony in be-ing twenty metres away from a big hotel with lots of empty rooms while the two of them were huddled in a little shed watching a six-inch square TV, but it was their little hideaway.

Back then, sometimes whole afternoons would pass when nothing at all was said out loud, the two of them completely comfortable with the silence. This silence was different though.

Thomas was the first to speak, uncomfortably running his hand along the worktop as he did. 'Um, so, any news?'

'Nick just texted, her arm's broken too.'

'That's a bit of bad luck.'

'I don't think luck had anything to do with it.'

'I just mean that's a bit more difficult to cope with, isn't it?'

'Than what? Than learning that your wife was planning to get pregnant with another man and was going to trick me into believing for the rest of my life that the baby was mine? That she thought I might be infertile and she wasn't going to tell me? That she was quite happy going behind my sister's back to sleep with her husband? Her own brother-in-law? Than essentially learning that the woman you married is completely certifiable?'

Thomas didn't know where to start with his son's outburst. He naively thought he'd come here, have a coffee, tell him to look on the bright side, possibly give him a manly sort of back pat handshake and then report back to Judy that everything was fine. He didn't expect Marcus to be so angry, but then why would he? He didn't know all the intricacies of what had gone on. It was just so confusing.

'But she didn't —'

'She didn't! She didn't! Oh that's ok then, let's all go back to normal then shall we?' Marcus picked up his cup, one of a set of eight they'd got as a wedding present. They had hand-painted multi-coloured polka dots on it and Lucy loved them. When they'd moved in together she'd boxed up all his chunky Ikea mugs and left them on the doorstep of the charity shop on the High Street and filled their crockery cupboards with dainty delicate artisan pottery instead. She always tutted at the way he loaded them into the dishwasher. 'They're hand painted Marcus,' she used to remonstrate at least twice a week. He drained the last dregs of coffee from it and hurled the cup at the wall. It smashed into tiny pieces that scattered far and wide over the flagstone floor, making Thomas jump. He'd never seen his son like this; in fact he'd never been around anyone whose emotion and anger was so raw and untamed.

Neither of them moved to pick up the pieces.

Marcus's body suddenly started bucking with sobs. He sat down heavily on one of the transparent kitchen chairs and lay his head on his arms. Thomas was rooted to the spot. He'd seen his fair share of histrionics from his wife and daughters over the years, but not from Marcus. Not solid, dependable Marcus. He slowly moved towards him and pulled a chair up close to his son's. He had no idea what to say or do to make him feel better, so just placed his hand gently on his son's back and let him cry.

CHAPTER 24

'I just have no idea how I'm going to explain this to people at the sailing club,' Judy said, knitting faster than Leila had ever seen her do before.

'That is a quandary, Mum,' Leila replied. They'd popped back to Leila's flat to give Tasha a bit of space. Actually, Tasha had more or less ordered Leila to take their mother away and keep her out of her hair. Judy had spent most of her time at Tasha's in tears with her head on the side, her bottom lip out, giving Tasha pitying looks and well-meaning but ill-timed advice. 'Don't worry, I'll take her back to mine for the rest of the afternoon and evening. She can even stay over if I can borrow your blow-up bed,' Leila had offered to a very grateful Tasha.

Judy continued, 'I can hardly say that my daughter-in-law wanted to have a baby with my son-in-law.'

'I don't suppose you can.' Leila knew that

she shouldn't find this amusing, but it was hard not to show a flicker of a smile at her mother's unique take on things.

'I mean, how does one even go about deciphering that?'

'I don't mean to be controversial Mum, but, do you have to say anything at all?'

'What do you mean?'

'Well, it's not really anyone else's business is it? And I'm sure Tasha and Marcus wouldn't really want you gossiping about them.'

'Gossiping? One can't gossip about one's own children Leila.' The needles were going at breakneck speed. 'If I ever get my hands on that woman, God help me.'

'Who, Lucy?'

'Don't even say her name Leila, it makes me feel sick just hearing it. When I think about how we've bent over backwards welcoming her into our family, putting up with all her demands over the wedding, and then she does this to us all.' Judy put the knitting down in her lap and shook her head miserably. 'All I wanted for each of you was a happy life, a happy marriage to someone that loves you. Now look at you all, two marriage break-ups on the same day, and you, with your lesbian nun thing. I don't know what we've done wrong.'

There was no use trying to set Judy straight on any of her mixed-up logic. And put like that, Leila could understand why Judy looked so despondent and despairing. It wasn't that clear-cut though, but Leila didn't fancy getting into that now with her mum. She wondered how her dad was getting on with Marcus. He'd texted a while before and said that he was going to stay the night to keep an eye on him, which didn't sound good. She should go up there tomorrow and see them both, but she'd have to find some sort of mother day-care option for Judy first — there was no way she could leave her to her own devices for the day, the world might implode.

Just then Leila heard a key turning in the lock and froze. *Nick.* She scrambled to her feet and ran out into the corridor, putting a finger to her lips before saying loudly for Judy's benefit in the next room, 'Oh hello Nick, did you forget some papers?' Leila motioned to the living room and mouthed 'My mother!'

He mimed back 'Oh God, sorry!'

Judy appeared in the doorway of the living room. 'You've got a nerve.'

'Mum, don't start, he's just here to get some papers for the Dubai project we're doing together. He sometimes works from here when I'm not home as it's quiet and the light's really good.' Leila didn't know why she added that in at the end. It was a basement flat that used to be a cellar, you needed all the lights on even on the sunniest day of the year. 'I mean, not the natural light, the ambient lights. The ones with bulbs, they're special bulbs that help with work and things.' Judy and Nick were just staring at her. 'So, that's why, he has a key. For the, um, light . . . When I'm not here.'

Nick started speaking, probably more to stop the agony of hearing his girlfriend dig herself into a hole than because he had something to say.

'Nice to see you Judy.'

'Wish I could say the same.'

'Mum!' Leila glared at Judy, then turned to Nick. 'Sorry Nick, it's still a bit tense around here.'

'Bit tense? Bit tense? Well that's a bit of an understatement. Nick, you should probably know that my son is currently on suicide watch because of what your sister has done.'

'Mum! Don't exaggerate.'

'Your father is staying up there to keep an eye on him Leila, of course that's what it means. While Tasha is now a single mother to three young children —'

'Mia's just turned sixteen.'

'Will you stop making excuses Leila, it's almost like you're on his side!' Judy pointed at Nick. 'We shouldn't even be speaking to him. I feel like I'm betraying my children by even being pleasant.'

'Don't worry Judy, you weren't being pleasant, so you've got nothing to worry about. Goodbye, and Leila, don't worry about what I came round for, I'll sort it some other time.' Nick then turned, strode down the corridor and slammed the front door behind him leaving the two women glaring at each other. Out of the corner of her eye Leila could see Nick's feet taking the outside steps two at a time. One of his laces was undone. She wanted to run after him and tell him to be careful, but she knew she couldn't.

Judy exhaled a big theatrical sigh, sat back down on the sofa, picked up her knitting and said, 'Well I hope that's the last we ever see of him.'

Chapter 25

'How's he doing?' Leila whispered as Thomas held her coat while she shrugged her arms out of it.

'Up and down. He's in the garden having a cigarette.'

'He doesn't smoke.'

'He does now. Don't tell Mum, she doesn't need to add lung cancer to her list of things to worry about. Coffee?'

Leila followed him into Marcus's pristine kitchen, where the remnants of the broken cup had been swiftly and subtly swept up by Thomas. He was wearing one of Marcus's shirts, the front few buttons straining open over his well-fed paunch. 'Speaking of Mum, how is she?' As much as they bickered, the last two nights were the first ones in forty years they'd spent apart.

'She's ok. She's taken Mia shopping with your credit card.' Tasha had called earlier that morning saying that she was a bit wor-

392

ried about Mia; she'd flatly refused to go to school, and since Leila had dropped her home after the hospital two days earlier she'd barely left her room. 'I thought shopping was safer than Mum just sitting in the flat or getting in Tasha's way,' Leila explained.

'And how is Tasha? She seemed to be coping remarkably well when I saw her before coming here.'

It was true. Tasha was remaining incredibly composed, possibly too composed, Leila thought. It was impossible to just shut the door on an eighteen-year relationship without a hint of sentimentality. Leila just hoped that Tasha wasn't being all bright and breezy for everyone else and then collapsing into a big snotty mess as soon as the kids were in bed and the last well-meaning visitor had departed. There was no way of knowing what Tasha was like when she was alone unless Leila started doing spot checks like a restaurant inspector looking for signs of slipped standards and unsightly spillages.

Marcus came in from the garden. His usual scent of expensive aftershave had been replaced by tobacco and unwashed laundry. He gave his sister a quick polite hug and reached across the worktop to retrieve a loaf from the bread bin. He took out two slices, turned them over in his hands to look for any traces of mould and put them in the toaster.

He hadn't bought any fresh food since Lucy's accident, and if he was being honest, he hadn't bought any before her accident either. Lucy was the one that organised the inventory of the cupboards and the fridges (one for drinks and one for food) with military precision. Everything was organic and pesticide-free. She could probably have named the farms that their meat and eggs came from, and he wouldn't have put it past her to know the exact co-ordinates of the vegetable patches and fruit trees the now decaying produce in their salad drawers started life in too.

The three of them were stood in a triangle of muteness, each leaning back against a work surface or a kitchen chair. The weather wasn't doing anything spectacular or worthy of note, and Leila had no idea what else to say. *How are you doing* seemed too obvious. She knew asking after Lucy would be a big no-no. She shouldn't have come. She wanted Marcus to know she cared, that she was thinking of him, but really, what did she think she could do to make it better? They were beyond the ages where a big knickerbocker glory with three spoons would put a smile on their faces. And he'd never been big on jokes, even if she had any in her repertoire.

'Now you're here Leila, you can help me,' Marcus said. That was good, thought Leila, I can be useful.

'Whatever you need.'

'You can pack up all of Lucy's things.' No, no, that wasn't the type of help she meant.

'Don't you think that's a little, hasty?' she replied. Hasty wasn't the only word she could have chosen; she had a ticker tape of hot-headed, impulsive, foolhardy, rash, reckless running along the front of her brain.

'It's got to be done sometime, it's not as though she's ever going to live here again is it?'

'I think Leila's right, for what it's worth,' Thomas added. 'You haven't even seen her since that first night at the hospital, I think maybe you should at least talk to her before deciding that your marriage is over.'

'Dad's right Marcus. Lucy's staying at Nick's at the moment, why don't you call her and just see how she is?'

'Because I don't care how she is. How's that for a reason? I. Don't. Care.'

'She's broken her arm as well as her leg, she's in a bad way.'

'I don't care.'

'And I think she really regrets everything that's happened.'

'You are wasting your breath Leila. And if you only came here to tell me that I should give her another chance then you also wasted your morning.'

He turned his back to them and started buttering his toast. His shoulders were hunched and tense and his movements were almost mechanical. He reached into the fridge for his marmite and faltered slightly when he saw Lucy's smoothie mix congealing in a cling-filmed jug, but then slammed the fridge door on it.

'Marcus, I don't want to make you angry, but it's only been four days. She only got out of hospital yesterday, and you were both really happy before this.' It wasn't a complete lie, they were sort of happy. As happy as two emotionally defunct people together could be.

'Are you going to help me or not?'

'Not.' Leila sighed. 'I'm sorry Marcus, but I don't think that you can just pack up all her stuff without even hearing her out. And if after you do that, you still want to pretend that she never existed, then fine, I'll come round and help you exorcise the place of her, but I really don't think that's what you should be doing right now.'

'I'll do it myself then,' he said huffily, not used to people telling him no.

'You're making a mistake.'

'What would you know Leila? How the hell can you stand there and tell me what to feel or what to do when you haven't had a proper relationship in your whole life? Have you ever even been in love and realised what it feels like to sign yourself over to one person only for them to squeeze the life out of you until you feel completely worthless and stupid and like they tied a massive boulder to your feet and chucked you in a river and you're gasping for breath but know that eventually, however hard you try, you're going to drown?'

It was the longest, most impassioned speech Marcus had ever made. Leila knew that he'd surprised himself with his openness as he suddenly looked really embarrassed and turned away again. His fingers gripped the edge of the work surface. 'Can you go now please? Both of you.'

'Marcus, I don't think that's a good idea,' Thomas said, taking a step towards his son.

'I think I know what's best for me at the moment, and having you two here telling me what I should be thinking and doing is not it. I'll call you later.'

They had no choice but to leave.

The journey back to central London in her dad's estate car was thankfully undertaken to the backdrop of a talk radio station so voices filled the car without either Leila or her father needing to open their mouths. As they got nearer the city, Thomas asked where they were going and Leila honestly had no idea. She couldn't indefinitely put her parents up on a blow-up bed in her living room. Tasha had made it very clear that she wanted to get on with her life without them tiptoeing around her. And now Marcus's wasn't an option either. She knew that her mum and dad wouldn't feel comfortable trekking back down to the west country leaving everything so unresolved, but in all honesty Leila couldn't see a quick fix to any of it.

'I feel that one of us should go and see Lucy,' Thomas said. They were at a standstill in the traffic. The radio host was inviting callers to share their menopause stories, so Thomas had instinctively turned it off, leaving the car in a silence that needed to be broken.

'I was thinking the same thing.'

'I doubt she knows that Marcus has called time on their marriage,' said Thomas.

'I don't believe he has though, I think it's just a knee-jerk reaction. It's what he thinks he needs to do in this type of situation, except I doubt this type of situation has ever happened before in the history of the world.'

'Will you do it?'

'What?'

'Talk to Lucy? I don't think it's good coming from her father-in-law, and there's no way I think your mother should be allowed within ten feet of her. Tasha's out of the equation too, obviously. So, it has to be you, really.'

Leila sighed. Seeing Lucy meant seeing Nick. Which was both wonderful and awful. They were stuck in this tug-of-war scenario where they'd replaced one set of reasons why they couldn't be together with another, even more compelling set.

'Why don't you get in touch with Nick? Her brother? He should be able to tell you the lie of the land? He seemed like quite a sensible chap when we met him at Christmas?'

Yes Leila, why don't you get in touch with Nick? That sounds like a splendid idea. Nothing could possibly go wrong with that plan.

Thomas had gone to meet Judy and Mia leaving Leila alone in the flat. It was unsettling. Judy's stuff had replaced Nick's on every surface. Her mother's reading glasses lay where he normally discarded his. An open book with a watercolour drawing of a cottage on a cliff on its cover rested on the side table, where a biography of a sports commentator had been the week before. A half-drunk cup of Earl Grey sat on the draining board where Nick's hastily drained morning espresso was usually left.

Nick answered on the second ring. 'I'm sorry about what I said to your mum,' he began.

'It's ok, she *was* being unpleasant.'

'But I shouldn't have said it. Hang on a second.'

Leila could hear him closing a door and then his footsteps. When he spoke again his voice was quieter. 'Me being like that makes things a bit more difficult for everyone to be happy for us though, doesn't it?'

'I think you saying that to her was not the thing that's going to make this difficult for us,' Leila said honestly. There was no point pretending that her family were going to be throwing them a party any time soon.

'Maybe not.'

'How is Lucy doing?'

'Not good. Like really not good. She just sits and stares into space the whole time. It doesn't help that she needs Mum to help her to the loo or to wash her, she can't support herself yet and she can't move her arm or shoulder properly. But it's more than that, she just doesn't seem to have any strength left in her at all.'

'I saw Marcus this morning.'

'And?'

'He's the same. He's started smoking.'

'Well that's good for me, means I won't be by myself in the garden at family parties.'

Leila gave a small laugh. 'Well I'm pleased to hear you still want to come to my family parties, but I'm not sure we'll be invited when it gets out about us.'

'I was thinking about that. I think we should just come clean now. There's been too many secrets and lies and I hate the fact that you're there, and I'm here and we're still sneaking about. We should be facing all this together.'

She smiled and cradled the phone closer to her ear. 'I'd love that. I've missed you so much this week, but we need to figure out how to do it. At the moment my family hates your sister, and by association, they hate you too.'

'But it wasn't all Lucy's fault though, surely they can see that?'

'What, you mean Alex and his wandering eye and inability to keep his trousers on?'

'That, but also the way that Marcus was to her.'

Leila could feel her heart beating a little faster. 'What do you mean?' she asked.

'You know, how boorish and cold he could be.'

'I would hardly describe him as boorish and cold.'

'But you weren't married to him, you don't know what he was like.'

'Neither do you.'

'But Lucy does, and from what she's said —'

'I thought you said she was just staring into space and not saying anything?'

'Well yes, she does most of the time, but then of course she talks a bit, and she has described her life as incredibly lonely. He works all the time —'

'For her extravagant home renovations and designer handbag habit,' Leila interrupted.

'And he shows no affection to her whatsoever. Never thanks her for all she does.'

'All their housekeeper does you mean,' Leila said petulantly.

'And then there's the fact that he's so closed to having any kind of personal conversation at all — he's so old fashioned and buttoned-up, he wouldn't even talk about his infertility. Lucy just felt so desperate.'

'He's not infertile,' Leila snapped. 'He didn't want a baby yet so has been trialling a new male contraceptive drug.' Her eyes widened as the last sentence flew out of her mouth. It wasn't her secret to tell, she shouldn't have said anything. She fervently hoped that it had got lost in the heat of the discussion, and he wouldn't pick up on it.

'He's been doing what?' Nick replied angrily. 'He's been deceiving her all this time? So she's been driving herself crazy thinking that the problem is her, doing all sorts of mad fertility stuff, when all this time he's been popping pills without her knowing?'

'He didn't know that she wanted a baby that much, if she had just told him that she had been having tests, then he would have told her, I'm sure of it. Anyway, it's hardly rational is it, all this cutting out food groups and walking through stones on a full moon? She's been totally unhinged!'

'So you knew? You knew that she'd been doing all that, and you also knew that Marcus had been making himself shoot blanks and you didn't say anything? You just let this go on? Jesus Leila, you're as much to blame as they are! My sister is sat in the next room with most of her body in a plaster cast because she was so desperate and feeling so unloved, and you knew? And you didn't try to stop it? I can't even talk to you right now, I'm so angry.'

It was one of those rows where you didn't know who should apologise first. Leila knew that by keeping Lucy and Marcus's secrets from Nick while she worked out what to do, she was *sort of* implicated in what had happened, but for him to say that it was her fault was totally over the top and not true. It wasn't as though she'd pulled a beanbag over to the sidelines and eaten a big tub of popcorn watching excitedly as things played out. She'd been genuinely going round in circles over how to intervene and make things better. Nick couldn't really believe that she didn't care, surely? Yes, it should totally be him who said sorry. He was so out of order.

She sat with the phone in her lap. She just knew that he was going to ring soon, or text. Bound to. She could feel it. Any minute now . . .

CHAPTER 26

It had been two hundred and sixty four hours since Nick had hung up on her. Two hundred and sixty four hours of refreshing her inbox, testing her internet connection and checking her mobile signal, and Leila was slowly coming to the realisation that maybe, just maybe, he wasn't going to get in touch.

Her eyes hurt. Not even the outside of her eyes, but the bit at the back where they joined her brain. That hurt. Over the last week she'd raced between her brother and sister, holding it together for her nieces and nephew, trying to placate her parents, and all the time this dull ache that nobody knew about, and nobody could see, was spreading behind the surface of her calm facade.

She tried to tune back in to what they were all saying. The Dartmouth roast dinner had been moved to Tasha's, on little

Talia's insistence who didn't understand why they hadn't had Yorkshire puddings for so long. Judy was frantically flapping a Sunday supplement in front of the smoking oven, 'You didn't tell me it was fan! This changes everything!' she cried. 'The parsnips and swede are ruined!'

After what they'd all lived through over the last two weeks, Leila thought that burnt root vegetables was a crisis easily borne.

Mia wandered into the kitchen. Leila hadn't seen her for a few days and couldn't help noticing her eyes dark and sunken into her young fragile face. Her bony body was cloaked in a shapeless black hoodie and black tracksuit bottoms. Her once bouncy and shiny hair was now greasy and haphazardly pulled back into a tight ponytail. 'Hey Mia,' Leila said, jumping down off her bar stool and pulling her niece into a reluctant hug. 'How's school? It's nearly exam time, isn't it?'

It couldn't have been worse timing for Mia. Her GCSEs started in less than a month and Tasha had confided earlier to Leila that she didn't think that Mia had been back to school since the accident. She still left home at the same time every day, wearing her uniform, and returned as normal just after four, yet the school had rung three times that week asking where she was, and Tasha had to admit that she had no idea.

She hated the thought of her teenage daughter just wandering around London all day, sitting in parks, or tube stations, or anywhere other than within the safety of her school or her home. Tasha had tried to talk to her, but Mia just ran upstairs and slammed the door in her face.

'It's as though she blames me, but I don't know whether it's for being so weak all these years, and letting him get away with it, or for finally chucking him out,' Tasha had confided in Leila. 'She just won't talk to me at all, and I don't know how to help her. She's going to ruin her chances at getting into sixth form college if she doesn't pass these exams, and there's no way she's going to pass like this.'

A few days earlier Alex had turned up in a taxi straight after being discharged from the hospital. A bandage was still wrapped around his head and on one side his hair was completely shaved, giving him the look of a crazed psychopath. He let himself in and was merrily pouring coffee beans into the grinder when Tasha walked into the kitchen and caught him. She'd quietly told him to leave, mindful of their two young children that she'd just picked up from school playing in the next room.

'Don't be silly Tash,' he'd said, 'I haven't done anything wrong! Coffee?'

'I don't want a coffee Alex, I want you to leave.'

'The stupid woman could have died had I not been there. I hardly think you should be angry just because I was trying to do the right thing.' Tasha had been incredulous that he was still keeping up the charade of being the hero of the hour when all the evidence proved that wasn't true. She asked him again to get out, this time hissing the words through her teeth. When he opened the cupboard to take out a cup she completely lost it and slammed the door on his hand, screaming at him to get the hell out of her house.

His voice remained eerily calm even as he stood and glared at her, asking with a sneer whose money had paid for 'her house', adding that if anyone should leave, it should be her and the kids. Tasha suddenly saw, to her horror, that Mia had been watching everything from the doorway. Without really thinking, Tasha silently walked over to Alex's small hospital bag, picked it up, opened the door and threw it down the front steps.

Apart from the time that she should have been at school, Mia had left her bedroom four times since then. Today was the fifth.

Mia shrugged in response to Leila's question. 'Three or four weeks I think.'

'What's first?'

Again, a discernible shoulder movement. 'Dunno. Haven't looked at the timetable.' At the far end of the kitchen island lay a stack of revision aids — a new pack of highlighters, some index cards, and some York crib notes for her literature and history exams, but all were unopened. 'What time's lunch?'

Judy snorted while picking the least black bits of parsnip out of the roasting tray.

'Enough time to go and wash your hands,' said Tasha. 'Can you oversee Talia and Oscar too?'

Just then the kitchen was plunged into darkness. An anguished yell from the family room next door confirmed that CBeebies was also not working.

'It's probably a tripped switch,' Thomas said. 'Where's your fuse box Tasha?'

'I don't know, ask Alex.'

There was a moment's pause where Tasha realised what she'd said, as did everyone else, resulting in a flurry of voices and activity to try to cover it up.

'I'll look in the cellar shall I?' Thomas boomed, at the same time as Leila scurried into the hallway to check the cupboard under the stairs and Judy made a show of opening all the kitchen cupboards, including the dishwasher that was concealed behind a unit door.

After a few minutes, the house erupted into life again, with TVs and radios blaring, and lights blazing. It was only after a power cut that you realise how loud and bright your room had been, Leila thought, not realising how prophetic that was.

Marcus had unsurprisingly turned down the invitation for Sunday lunch. Leila had called him every day, just to check in. Not that she thought that Judy was right and that he was busy fitting pipes to his exhaust ready to gas himself with, but she wanted to let him know that people cared about him. He'd never been a great talker, but the conversations couldn't have lasted more than three minutes each time.

'You ok?'

'Fine.'

'That's good.'

'You?'

'Yep.'

'Been out?'

'Nope.'

'Ok then. Do you need anything?'

'Aside from the obvious?'

'Ok then, well, bye.'

With each infuriating 'chat', if you could call them that, Leila was starting to see what Nick was getting at. There was no way that anyone deserved for their partner to plot to get pregnant with someone else, but if Marcus was always as closed-off and unsentimental with Lucy as he was with his family at the moment, then maybe Lucy wasn't quite the deranged harlot the rest of her family thought she was. That didn't mean that Leila was ready to concede defeat and pick up the phone to apologise to Nick though.

Lunch was a much more sombre affair than the normal good-natured riot. Aside from the fact that they were missing three of the normal guest list, there was an air of forced joviality that felt strained. Thomas made the same gravy gag that he always did — 'Where do you want it? Plate or lap?' — and Judy did her normal routine of pointing out everything on the table to everybody — 'Look, there's more meat, did you see the peas? Have you had some carrots?' — but even Oscar picked up on the atmosphere, asking why everyone seemed so gloomy. Leila looked over the table at Tasha as he said this, holding her breath for this to be the moment where her sister's mask of composure slipped a little, but it didn't.

'We're not gloomy Oscar, we're just hungry, doesn't this all look delicious? Shall we say thank you to Nanny for cooking it?'

Leila *was* sad though. Leila was pretty bloody miserable that this was meant to be the Sunday that she should have been bringing Nick down to meet everyone properly. He was supposed to be sat with them, laughing politely at her dad's awful jokes, gallantly accepting Judy's offer of thirds, while not moving his hand from Leila's leg under the table. Then after the meal would finish, they would have gone for a walk around Dartmouth, for her to point out all her old haunts.

They'd pass the pub she'd had her first drink in (while wearing a disguise so the landlord wouldn't call her dad), she'd have pulled him into the maze of cobbled streets that she'd walked thousands of times and they'd have sat on a bench on the river front watching the passenger ferries and Sunday sailors wind their way up and down the estuary as they talked about how his initiation into the family had gone.

She wondered what Nick was doing now. It was midafternoon on a sunny Sunday, so he'd probably be sitting with a beer in hand in a pub garden somewhere with his friends, or listening to jazz stretched out on a pile of cushions on his small terrace. Whatever he was doing, Leila felt an overwhelming and uncontrollable urge to be doing it with him.

This was the third *Antiques Roadshow* they'd watched in a row. According to the *Radio Times* that Stephanie had brought with her, there were another seven episodes still to go of the antiques marathon weekend on the obscure cable channel she'd managed to find on Nick's TV. In his hand was a chopstick that he'd been using to poke down Lucy's arm cast to relieve his sister's incessant itching. It was a sunny Sunday afternoon, so Leila was bound to be in her garden, pottering about planting some hanging baskets, no doubt with a glass of white wine somewhere nearby and some jazz on the stereo. Wasn't this the Dartmouth weekend? So if that went ahead she'd be sat on the hotel's terrace or wandering about the old town after having lunch. He was meant to be there today for the big reveal. The heaviness in his chest that had been a constant companion for the last week or so gave another lurch.

'Don't stop Nick, it's driving me crazy,'

413

Lucy moaned. 'You were miles away.'

'Yeah, sorry.'

'What are you thinking about?'

Nick shook his head. 'It's ok. Just, stuff.'

Lucy looked over at their mother, who had fallen asleep in her armchair and took the opportunity to probe a little more. 'You don't look ok,' she said quietly. 'You look . . . sad.'

And then he told her. He didn't even stick to the strict script that he and Leila had agreed on. He confided in his sister, telling her how Leila had captivated him at the wedding; how he laughed with her until his stomach hurt; how her smile, her flashing eyes, or even the way she stuck her tongue out a little at the side of her mouth when she was concentrating really hard on something, made him want to twirl her around and around until they both got dizzy and her feet left the floor.

Nick smiled his first proper smile since the accident as he recounted Leila's strength, and fierce loyalty, and how blown away he was at her creativity and sense of fun. His sister sat listening to him open-mouthed, with tears pricking her eyes.

'I've ruined everything,' she said eventually, when he paused for breath. 'I'm so sorry Nick, I've been so self-obsessed, so

414

single-minded and I didn't stop for a minute to think about anything other than the one goal I'd made for myself. I'm so, so sorry.'

Nick took her left hand. 'It wasn't all your fault, everyone involved in this sorry mess was too tied up with their own agendas. I don't blame you Luce, I really don't, but I think you could have saved yourself a whole lot of heartache — and broken bones — if you had just talked to Marcus in the first place.' Nick had decided not to tell her what Leila had blurted out about the drug trial. He'd been battling with the conundrum of whether that would make things better or worse. In the end he had made up his mind not to in case Marcus found out that Leila had betrayed his trust, and he didn't want to be the reason that Leila lost her brother's respect. He was realising that Leila hadn't deliberately kept secrets from him. He remembered her trying to hint at Lucy's state of mind the night before the accident, and trying to open up a discussion about them, but he'd shut it down and batted her concerns away. And she hadn't called in eleven days. Eleven days.

'But how would I have even brought that up?' Lucy asked.

'Having a family together is surely one of the things husbands and wives should talk

415

about, even before the wedding, isn't it?'

'Have you and Leila?'

'We'd love four kids. She wants quadruplets so the pregnancy and birth is done and dusted in one go, but you get the benefit of a big family. I pointed out that at five foot three, carrying four babies may well affect her centre of gravity, but she's adamant that's the way to go.' He ran his hand through his hair and sighed. 'But you know, that was then, who knows what will happen now.'

'I can totally see you together. You and Leila. I don't know why I hadn't thought of it before.'

'Really?'

'Really. You're both really laid back, and cool, in a way that Marcus and I aren't. I can imagine you both sitting in her little garden drinking beer and listening to jazz together.'

'Funny you should say that,' Nick smiled. 'So what would you and Marcus be doing on a Sunday afternoon then?'

Lucy looked a little wistful. 'I'm sorry,' Nick said. 'That was thoughtless, you don't need to say.'

'No, it's ok,' she said in a quiet voice. 'I like thinking of him. Um, on a non-Devon weekend, we'd probably be in the garden playing Scrabble.'

'Scrabble?' Nick raised his eyebrow.

Lucy gave a small laugh. 'Or Canasta. We used to joke that we were practising for when we moved to a retirement village in Florida, so that we'd be so good at old people's games we'd make a fortune hustling them. We'd planned to learn bridge next. We'd probably open a bottle of wine around five, and have some olives, and then we'd start to cook together.' Lucy's eyes had come alive as she was talking and turned her body towards her brother, as much as her leg cast would allow. 'He's a really amazing cook, and we had this funny thing where we would pretend that our kitchen window was a live audience and we'd talk about what we were doing to the food as we were doing it, so he'd say something like, "As you can see, diced carrot is best for this dish," and I'd then say, "Make sure not to slice your fingers though as it can be tricky," and we'd both laugh.'

Nick laughed along with her, he'd never had his sister, or Marcus, down as the goofy types that would find humour in mucking about, but he guessed they had brought that side out in each other.

'I miss him so much Nick. It hurts how much I miss him.'

Nick nodded. 'I know.'

'We need to get them back Nick. We need to make this right again.'

'I'm with you. But how the hell are we going to do that?'

'I could speak to Leila and you speak to Marcus?' Lucy suggested.

'Don't you think we should start off how we mean to go on, and *you* speak to Marcus and *I* speak to Leila?' Nick replied.

'You're probably right. But therein lies the problem; how is Marcus going to agree to meet me, and if Leila is as angry as you think she is about you being rude about her mum and her brother, then she's not going to say yes either, is she?'

Nick thought for a moment, different scenarios playing out in his head. 'Unless Leila *thinks* she's meeting you, and Marcus *thinks* he's meeting me?'

'Oooooo I like that, but then that's not honest either.'

'Good point.' Nick laid his head on the back of the sofa.

'He really likes you by the way. Marcus does. He told me he thinks you're a . . . what did he call you? "Jolly good bloke." That's high praise by the way,' Lucy said.

'So you'd think he'd be on side if Leila and I sorted things out?'

'I think he'd be really pleased.' She smiled weakly. 'Apart from you being related to me, but you can't help that.'

Somewhere in the back of Lucy's mind a germ of an idea started to form.

She'd had to wait for Nick to support her into her bed and her mum to wrestle her sleeping T-shirt on her before she could put part one of her plan into action. Thankfully their cousin had a printer in his room, with a stack of paper standing in the feeder at the back of it. Balancing on her good leg, she hopped over to his desk and took out a few sheets. Grabbing a biro from the pot next to his computer she hobbled back to bed. She hadn't really considered the fact that her heartfelt missive would look more like a toddler's scrawl as her right hand was bound up in heavy plaster of Paris. She could fire up the desktop and send Marcus an email tapped out with her index finger of her left hand but it would be very easy for him to just delete an email without even reading it. He was more likely to read it if he was holding an actual letter in his hands. Even if he opened it and didn't read it straight away, it would sit there on the kitchen table taunting him until he picked it up again.

God, where did she start?

She had to get up twice more to get more paper. Every time she thought she'd finished, she thought of something else she wanted to say. It didn't help that her handwriting was twice the size it normally was and with the absence of lines on the page her words veered dramatically diagonally the further down the page she got.

It was the first letter she'd written in years and despite her hand cramping up something chronic, it was like a massive lead weight had been lifted as she chronicled all the emotions, heartache, bad decisions, and clouded judgements of the last year. Her aim initially had been to tell him about Leila and Nick, to ask for his help in reuniting them, to beg him not to blame Nick for her own wrong turns, and to give his sister his blessing so she didn't feel so guilty. But as her mind loosened, she found herself writing things she'd barely allowed herself to think before.

There was something so therapeutic about writing your thoughts down. All the therapists they'd ever had at their events and workshops had urged all the women to keep diaries, to chart their feelings, to validate their emotions by putting pen to paper. What you did with them after that was up to you; whether you flushed them away or made a sacrificial pyre and struck a match to them, you'd gone through the process of articulating how you felt. So much of what she'd idly listened to over the last year was making sense to her now. Lucy realised she'd completely lost sight of everything other than her own aims — get married — get pregnant. That was it. She'd filled her time with stuff to do so that she never allowed herself any kind of perspective or stillness to realise what was happening.

As soon as she signed her name, she started on the second letter. Lucy's pen shook as she tried desperately to find the words that would describe how wretched she felt about what happened. A tear dropped onto the page smudging the words *Dear Tasha.*

CHAPTER 27

Four weeks later . . .

Liberation Red would be a much better name than *Drawing Room Red* thought Tasha, peeling off the tin lid and feeling a wave of pure joy engulf her. In her haste to cover the murky sludge grey walls of her study with a colour of her own choosing, she hadn't used the plastic sheeting and masking tape the man in the hardware store so urgently pressed upon her. This explained why two hours later everything from the rug to her computer screen had little flecks of red paint on it. Even the new cat (that Tasha had bought Mia in a shameless bid to cheer her up), who had nonchalantly wandered in and was weaving her way around the legs of the stepladder, had fallen victim to the scarlet meteor shower that rained off the roller. But Tasha didn't care. With every brush stroke, every stretch of the roller, she could feel her elation building.

Screw you Patricia-the-designer with your personality-less paint chart. Screw you Alex, making decisions on the decor of my study without even thinking that it might be nice to consult the occupant of it. Screw you Alex, for so many things.

Tasha had spent so long blindly repeating the mantra that you can't change other people's behaviour, you can only change how you feel about it, that without her even realising it, she'd been making excuses for Alex her entire adult life. She had made herself believe that she was fine about it, that she was cool.

She was not cool. He was not cool. It was not cool.

The divorce solicitor a friend of hers had recommended had been just the right combination of empathetic and ball-breaking. Tasha didn't want to see Alex spend the rest of his days in a rat-infested squat with rising damp and meth-dealers for neighbours; they'd shared seventeen years and had three children together. But equally she didn't want to lose her home in order for them both to live in anonymous flats in Zone 6. The solicitor had done some digging and found that Alex had investments that even Tasha hadn't known about, so instead of having to sell the house to split the assets, she and the kids could stay put. The first thing she did on hearing this news was buy the paint. The second was buy a small axe, which Marcus was now studiously holding in his hands.

'I don't think you need this Tasha,' he said, looking a little terrified.

'How else are we going to sort it?' Tasha replied.

'I think it's a bit extreme to be honest.'

Tasha took the axe out of her brother's hands, and again the weight of it surprised her. 'I just think this would be the most effective way.'

'Surely if you just loosen the hinges with a screwdriver the cupboard doors will come apart, I don't think you need to hack them to death.'

'Boo. I was looking forward to hacking something to death,' Tasha grinned underneath her floppy fringe. That was another change since Alex had left. Probably subconsciously always trying to keep up with whatever new and younger model he'd just left or was just moving on to, she'd always made sure she was always fanciable. In his eyes anyway. And he didn't like fringes, which, thinking about it, was a strange thing not to like. She could possibly understand someone always going for blondes, or brunettes, or being partial to an auburn-haired beauty, she could put that down to personal taste — but not liking someone for a fringe was incredibly shallow. Which she was coming to realise her soon to be ex-husband was.

Everything from the way he dressed, to the car he drove, to the holidays they went on, even the colour of their walls, was all for show. Every part of their lives had been an item on a checklist for the type of life Alex thought he should be living. Even the constant stream of younger lovers was an empty box ready to be ticked below 'Fresh olives in the fridge' and above 'Timeshare ski chalet in the Alps'.

'So did you just get me round here to help you unconceal your concealed storage or was there something else?' Marcus said, narrowing his eyes suspiciously at the choice of screwdrivers in the open toolbox on the new coffee table (the old glass table had been swiftly put in the garage ready for Alex to take to whatever gleaming penthouse he bought himself out of the divorce settlement).

Tasha paused. Marcus knew as well as she did that their dad was far more familiar with the contents of a toolbox than he was, as was probably any one of her friend's husbands, or friends themselves. There must be some other reason why she'd so fervently needed his help that afternoon.

'I just think it's important for everything to be out in the open,' Tasha said. 'Like these cupboards. Alex liked the fact that all our belongings, stuff we'd collected from our travels, things the kids have made us, all our books and bits and bobs were hidden from view. So everything looked neat and tidy on the surface and then the mess of our family was lurking out of sight. If you think about it, these cupboards are a metaphor for my life. That's why they have to go.'

'And am I to infer from that some subliminal message telling me to get over myself, to stop being so secretive about my feelings?'

'I'd hardly say it was subliminal,' Tasha smiled, handing her brother a screwdriver that she thought might be the right size.

Being involved in a task made talking easier. As they worked side by side loosening all the screws and helping each other support the weight of each door as the hinges were worked free, Tasha broached the subject of Lucy's letter. 'She said in my letter that she wrote to you too.'

'She did,' Marcus replied.

'And?'

'And I can totally see Leila and Nick as a couple.'

'I'm so glad you said that,' Tasha said. 'I can too. I don't know why I didn't before all this, but they're really well suited.'

'But now because of all this they don't feel like they can be together. Which is a bit stupid if you ask me. Have you got a slightly bigger screwdriver, this one keeps slipping out?'

'I don't think it's stupid, it's typical Leila isn't it, overthinking things and putting other people first. She's so worried about how we're going to react to being around the brother of the woman that seemingly caused all this that she's putting her own happiness last.'

'Seemingly?' Marcus raised one eyebrow.

'Yes. Seemingly. I don't know what Lucy put in her letter to you but the way she explained everything to me made perfect sense. I'm not saying that I would have done what she did, far from it, but I can see how she, with her own disjointed childhood and warped sense of what a marriage is, could have gone to any lengths to retain the status quo.'

'She'd never told me before, you know, about her upbringing. I knew her parents were divorced, but I didn't know why.' Marcus manoeuvred one of the doors off its hinges and leant it up against the fireplace, which incidentally was next on Tasha's DIY agenda. Patricia-the-designer, at Alex's insistence, had taken out the original wooden Victorian surround with pretty, painted tiles and replaced it with a minimalist white hole in the wall that oozed style but lacked any kind of character at all. 'She thinks that her dad left because her mum was too hectic, too messy and free-spirited. All of her intensity about being in control, getting everything right first time, and being so ordered came from her need to create an environment where nothing went wrong.'

'And the baby thing?' Tasha asked.

'The baby thing was part of that I guess. Not getting pregnant at the exact moment that she'd planned to was a new one for her, she'd always got exactly what she'd set out to do, and it made her crazy when she felt she was failing. Her words, not mine.'

'It was never about Alex by the way; she didn't deliberately set her sights on her own brother-in-law. He was just a walking sperm bank,' Tasha said, oddly detached from her words. Someone listening in to their conversation would have no idea that she was talking about her own husband.

'I know. That doesn't make it any easier

though. To know that she was willing to go to those lengths to trick me.'

'It wasn't to trick you though, was it? She must have explained in her letter that she was only considering it in order to protect you from finding out that you might be infertile.'

Marcus put the screwdriver down and reached into his jeans pocket. He took out a folded stack of paper and held it out to his sister. 'Her novel of a letter,' he offered in way of explanation.

'I don't need to read it Marcus, it's ok.'

'No, I'd like you to. I want to know what you think.' Tasha skimmed the first few paragraphs of the letter, in which Lucy described Leila and Nick's guilt at continuing their relationship when their siblings were in so much pain. She listed all the attributes of Nick's that were so aligned with Leila's, giving reason after reason why they would be perfect together if only they put themselves first. She asked for Marcus's help — just as she had asked Tasha in her letter — in getting them together again. Tasha turned the page and the tone changed.

My mum used to dance barefoot in the kitchen. Not graceful dancing either, she had swooping arms and legs flying in every direction. The music was always loud, always on, often different songs, different types of music in different rooms. It was impossible to say something to her without her following it up with, 'How did that make you feel? How do you feel inside here?' and she'd take my hand and place it over my heart. Dad could never say, 'I had a rubbish day at work,' because then she'd try and talk about it for hours, she'd ask him why he thought that was, how he could have done things differently, ask, what was he going to do now. He hated that. I hated that. The house was always filled with stuff from her many hobbies, mismatched sculptures she'd made on a new pottery wheel, crystals chiming from the windows, watercolours, oil paintings, posters, just stuff everywhere. It was overwhelming, chaotic. In the end it was too much for Dad and he left. He now lives in a white box, with an alphabetised filing system for his papers and blinds that come down when you press a remote control. His new wife leaves him alone to just 'be'. She doesn't bother him with stuff she can sort out herself, she doesn't feel the need to involve him in everything, she just presents him with solutions, not problems. And that's what I realise I do too. What I think I was trying to do that night in London. We've never had the type of relationship where we talk about our feelings, or the big stuff in life, and I realise now that we should have done. I know that I should have said, 'Marcus, I'd love us to have a baby of our own, but it doesn't seem to be happening for us, what shall we do?' and then we'd face it together, but I didn't. I came up with a solution. And I didn't realise until I came face to face with Alex in the hotel reception, how far off the mark this solution was. It wasn't a solution at all, it was madness. And I knew that I would rather be childless with you, than have a baby by deceiving you. I love you Marcus. You have every right to interpret my actions of the last few weeks as proof of the opposite being true, but I just want you to know that I will regret making you believe that for the rest of my life.

Tasha handed him the letter back. 'Wow.'

Marcus shrugged. 'Easy to write the words you know someone wants to hear.'

'Not really, she pretty much laid herself bare.'

He raised his eyebrow at his sister's choice of words and his pious expression made

Tasha laugh. 'Bad phrasing. Sorry. No laying bare of any kind. Which is also the point. She didn't actually do anything.'

Marcus grimaced. 'Seriously, you were the one person left who hadn't told me that, and now you've made it a full house.'

'But it is true. And I'm speaking as the wife of the person she was planning to do that with.'

'But you kicked Alex out over this, why am I supposed to be more compassionate?' Marcus had put down his tools and sat back on his heels looking up at his sister. Tasha knelt down next to him.

'I don't know how many affairs Alex had during our marriage, Marcus, but it was a lot. Twenty maybe, if I had to guess.' Marcus's eyes had grown wide, he'd had no idea that there were other women. 'I stopped making a big deal of it a long time ago as I stupidly believed that I could turn a blind eye, but then he started getting cocky and messing about closer to home.

At the start, I was too scared to lose this life, to be a single mother. I think he was faithful for a while after that. Then he wasn't. And again I did nothing. Then his Romeo radar spotted that Lucy was looking pretty vulnerable and swooped in. Even now I don't think that he's remorseful, or thinks that he's done anything wrong, and that's the difference. He absolutely would have followed through with Lucy's plan — but she didn't. And so I didn't kick him out over Lucy, I kicked him out because that was a step too far. I was livid that he couldn't stick to his usual pool of leggy receptionists and interns that no-one else knew, and that he hurt you, my little brother. This was my family he was messing with.'

'So all this time you've just played happy families while this was going on in the background?'

'I wasn't playing, that's the weird thing, I know it sounds strange but apart from the ones at the very start, and now Lucy, the other ones didn't bother me so much. I'd become sort of numb to it, as though it was just another part of the baggage that came with him. And when he was here, with me and the kids, he was perfect. Why upset the apple cart?'

'Well you think you know someone . . .'

'That's it exactly, none of us know what goes on in another person's marriage — I can sit here and tell you to give Lucy another chance because from what information I have, from my own seat in the stands, I think that's what you should do. But only you know what being married to her was like, and if you can work through this.'

Marcus sighed and sat back on the floor-boards. 'I haven't been entirely blameless you know.'

'*You've* had an affair?'

'No! God, no! I love Lucy.' Tasha was pleased to hear him say those words in the present tense. Marcus didn't seem to notice. 'I've been, um, taking, male contraceptive pills behind her back.'

'Are those even a thing?' Tasha asked incredulously.

'Not really. I've been trialling them. I guessed that Lucy would want a baby straight away but I wanted it to be just me and her for a while longer. I wanted us to keep playing Canasta in the garden on weekends, and making up our own TV cookery shows in the kitchen, pretending that the window is a live audience.'

'You're such a loser.'

Marcus smiled, and continued, 'I knew that if Lucy got pregnant and had a baby then that would be her entire focus and she'd put everything into it, and I'd feel, well, I'd feel sort of redundant.' He ran his hand through his hair, 'I do sound like such a loser don't I?'

'So you took the drugs without her knowing?'

'Yes, I overheard a young bloke at work talking about it, how it's great that he can just sleep around without halting the moment to get, you know, the things.'

'Condoms,' Tasha prompted.

'Yes, those things.' Marcus was flushed with embarrassment. Maybe Lucy did have a point, he thought; perhaps he wasn't open enough to have an adult conversation where words like 'sperm' and 'ovaries' were part of the vocabulary. 'And because we never talked about it, I had no idea that she was getting all these tests and whatnot done, because she thought *she* was the reason we hadn't conceived. I mean, we only got married ten months ago, so I thought by doing this I could give us some extra time. I feel gutted that me popping a little white pill every morning meant that she was putting herself through so much worry and all that poking and prodding. And what's worse, some research has just been released from the drug trial and in a couple of cases it has caused permanent infertility, so I have no idea if I've ruined any chance of ever conceiving. Which would be a massive dose of karma, wouldn't it?' he said sadly.

'Does she know?'

'No, I don't think so.'

'You have to tell her. It's not fair for her

to be shouldering as much guilt as she is. Even if you two never get back together, she can't carry around this amount of blame forever.'

Marcus leant his back backwards until he heard it click. 'I know.'

'So you will?'

'I think so . . . Thank you Tash. For listening.'

'You're welcome. So how are we going to tell Leila that we know about Nick and that we're happy for them?'

'See that's a tough one, she'll think that we're just saying it and don't really mean it. Let's come up with a plan.' Tasha's hands suddenly flew to her mouth. 'Oh God, what time is it?'

'Half four.'

'Oh shit! I was meant to pick Oscar and Talia up an hour ago! Can you stay here and let Mia in? I saw she left her key on the side this morning and she's normally back by now.'

'Sure, no problem. I'll do the cupboards the other side of the fireplace.'

'Thanks, bye, love you!' Tasha grabbed her bag and flew out of the door. Running to the kids' school that was just around the corner she saw she had four missed calls, three from the junior school and one from

Mia's school. It was her third week as a single mother and she seemed to be making a complete hash of it so far.

Talia and Oscar were sat in the school reception, two forlorn little figures clutching their lunch boxes to their chests and looking terrified. After a rather unnecessary telling off from the head teacher who had missed her Pilates class in order to stay behind and wait with them, Tasha smothered her children in hugs, kisses and apologies. 'Mummy's so sorry, Mummy loves you very much, Mummy's going to buy you whatever chocolate bar you like from the corner shop, even though it's only twenty minutes until dinner time, because truly Mummy is very sorry, and does love you so very much.'

During the very serious business of choosing the right sweet treat Tasha phoned Mia's school, which was usually open a bit later due to the amount of after school clubs they offered. When she gave her name she was put straight through to Mia's form tutor, who gave her her second bollocking of the day for Mia's absence, which means she'd missed her French Speaking and Listening GCSE exam. Shit. Tasha knew exams started soon, but didn't realise it was today, what the hell was Mia thinking? She garbled

437

an apology; the school knew their circumstances at home, which is why they hadn't got social services involved, but missing exams took truancy to a whole other level. One the school 'had to take extremely seriously.'

Tasha hurried the younger two down the road to give Mia a massive mouthful. It wasn't that she wasn't sympathetic, of course the events of the last month weren't nice or normal for a teenager to have to deal with, but knowingly screwing up your future for the sake of moping about wasn't going to solve anything.

'Where is she?' Tasha demanded the second the door opened. 'Where's Mia?' she shouted into each doorway. 'Mia?' she yelled up the stairs.

Marcus looked up from the corner of the living room. 'She's not back yet.'

'It's gone five, she's always back at four.'

'It's only an hour, maybe school went on a bit.'

'She wasn't at sodding school Marcus, I just spoke to them, she missed her first GCSE today. Fuck. Fuck. Where could she be?'

'Has she done this before?'

'Yes. A few times, that I know of.'

'Where does she go then?'

438

'I don't know, a park? A bus stop? God Marcus, she's sixteen, where would you go if you were a sixteen-year-old girl whose parents had just split up after your dad nearly died?'

'Calm down Tash. It's only been an hour, she'll turn up soon, hungry, demanding dinner. Just go and sort the little ones out, and if she's still not back by six we'll ring round some of her friends.'

Tasha sighed. 'You're right. I'm just so mad with her that she missed her exam. How bloody stupid can you get? I've told her so many times how important they are.'

'She's obviously not coping too well with things at the moment. Look, don't lose your temper as soon as she steps in the door. Let me go and put some pasta on for Oscar and Talia, and you go and do some meditation or deep breathing or whatever it is you teach, calm down a bit and then have a proper chat with her when she gets in. Going mental isn't going to help anything.'

As soon as the hour hand brushed six Tasha came bounding into the kitchen. 'It's been two hours now. I'm calling her friends.'

The three friends that Tasha had phone numbers for didn't know where she was, and Tasha didn't think they were lying. As she was making the calls her foot was tap,

tap, tapping against the breakfast bar leg, her teeth chewing at the inside of her mouth. Marcus silently took the younger two up for their baths, read them a story and tucked them into bed.

'Any news?' he said, re-entering the kitchen.

'None. I don't know anyone else to call. I need to go and look around, she might be near here somewhere.' She stopped, experiencing a horrible sense of deja vu. 'Oh God, what if she's had an accident? What if no-one knows who she is?'

'You need to call Alex. She might have gone to him.'

'No! No, I can't tell him that she's gone missing on my watch. He's already threatened to try and get custody, if he knows that she's gone missing, then I could lose her forever.'

Marcus put his arm around his sister's shoulders. 'I'll call him then. I'll say that I was looking after her and she disappeared. But we need to know if she's there with him.'

'You'd do that? You'd speak to him, even after all this?'

'For Mia, of course. What's his number?'

Mia wasn't there. And Marcus had barely got the question out before Alex said that he'd be right round.

'What about Leila? She loves Leila, she might be there?' Marcus suggested.

'Yes, but Leila would have called straight-away, she'd know how I'd worry.'

'Call her anyway,' Marcus ordered. 'If we're going to get a search party together we need as many people as possible.' The words 'search party' were horrific, conjuring all sorts of images that made them both shudder. 'I'm going to go and wander around the local parks. I've got my phone on me, call me if . . . when . . . there's any news.'

Just then a siren raced past her door and although this happened about ten times a day, it made them both freeze on the spot.

CHAPTER 28

To Alex's credit, when Marcus opened the front door to him, the only thing etched on his face was worry. The slanging match between him and Tasha that Mia had witnessed a few weeks before was clearly in no danger of being replayed. He appeared to be feeling exactly as Tasha did — anxious and desperate.

Tasha outlined the last time she'd seen Mia, which was earlier that morning as she left for school.

'Did she have a bag with her?' Alex asked.

'Um, yes, it was her school bag,' Tasha recalled. 'But it didn't seem fuller than usual, I don't think.' Tasha realised with a fresh wave of guilt that she hadn't paid that much attention. Oscar had just spilled his cereal all down his uniform, so she was trying to attack him with a wet sponge while Talia was refusing to get off the iPad that Tasha was trying to wrestle from her, so

Tasha couldn't honestly remember if she'd even replied when Mia had shouted 'Bye, then' and slammed the door behind her.

'That doesn't matter now,' Alex said briskly. 'We just need to find her. Have you called Leila to come and watch the kids while we go out and look?'

'Yes, she's on her way.'

'Ok, Marcus, I think it would be great if you could head to the park and walk up the High Street towards the tube, there's a few cafes up there that she might go to. Have you got a photo of her to show people?'

'Yes, I think there's one on my phone from Christmas.'

'Ok, great.' Alex continued, 'What about her friends?'

'I've called the few I know, but no-one knows anything,' said Tasha.

'Is there anyone else we should call? Have you called your folks?'

'No, I don't want to worry them, she's only been gone a couple of hours, and what can they do from there? Mum would just be fretting and jumping straight on the motorway, so no, I don't want them to know, yet.' Tasha had her sensible hat on, but in reality, all she wanted to do was phone her mum in tears and get her dad round with some sensible words of advice that made everything alright.

'Ok Marcus, let's go. We'll split up, you head up, and I'll go the opposite way down the High Street. Tasha, call us as soon as Leila arrives and then we can meet up. If anyone hears anything at all, then call.' Tasha followed them out into the entrance hall and held the door open for them to leave, first looking hopefully down the empty street, just in case.

Alex stopped in the doorway and turned to face his wife. 'It'll be ok.'

'Will it?' Tasha whispered, the words getting stuck in her throat.

Marcus gripped his mobile tightly in his hand as he circled the group of teenagers lying sprawled on the grass. He couldn't see Mia amongst them, but they were all wearing the same sort of baggy clothes she favoured, and had similar scowls and inappropriate-for-the-weather woollen beanies pulled down almost covering their eyes, so they might know her. He showed them a picture. They didn't.

He'd circled the park twice, and walked up to the tube station and back past the row of coffee shops serving their last cups of the day, past waiters wiping down tables and stacking up chairs and still there was no sign of her. He'd even ducked his head into the pub to check, although Mia had never given any indication of having tried alcohol let alone liking it enough to drink alone. He tried to remember the last time he'd actually had a conversation with Mia though. He'd tried, a couple of times, to ask about school, and at Christmas he'd said, 'One Direction, they're alright aren't they?' to which Mia had rolled her eyes and moved away to talk to Leila.

She was a good kid, but he just never knew what to say to her. To any child really. It was amazing how fast kids grew up. He'd blinked and she'd morphed from a cheeky toddler to a moody teen, who quite plainly thought that her uncle was a bit of a prat.

His phone started vibrating in his hand. It was Leila.

'Any sign?' she asked breathlessly.

'No, I've gone all round the area, but nothing. I asked a few kids her age, but they didn't know her. Where are you?'

'Just got to Tasha's. She's gone out in the car to look. I've got to stay here with the little two, but I feel like I want to get out there looking too, but there's no one else to look after them.'

'Isn't there a neighbour that can?'

'This isn't your little village Marcus, this

is central London.'

'It's a pity Mum and Dad don't live nearer.' An idea flashed into Marcus's mind. 'Look, don't say no before you've heard me out.'

'. . . Right . . .'

'What about Lucy?'

'Lucy? As in *your* Lucy?'

'I'm not sure she's *my* Lucy anymore,' Marcus said, a little sadly. 'But she's not that far away. I know it sounds odd, after what we've been through, but I'm sure that she and Nick would be happy to help out. I've got my car at Tasha's — why don't I call them, and see what they say and I can go and pick them up?' In his head it made perfect sense. Nick could help with the search and Lucy could stay at Tasha's and keep an ear out for the kids and ring round everyone at the same time. She couldn't actively join the search party as she was still in plaster, but babysitting was definitely not beyond her.

It wasn't a bad plan. Were it not for the fact that Lucy had probably played a starring role in the reason for Mia going AWOL, and Leila hadn't spoken to Nick since they indulged in a bitter volley of insults.

'Leila?' Marcus asked. 'You still there?'

'What makes you think they'd want to

help?' Leila said, still ignorant of the fact her siblings knew about her and Nick. 'Aren't our two families at war?'

'I'll explain later, but I think they'd be happy to help. Shall I call them?'

Leila still wasn't sure about this. 'But how will Tasha feel about having Lucy in her house?'

Marcus paused. The way Tasha was speaking that afternoon about him giving Lucy another chance made him think that she'd be alright about it. She certainly wasn't in the right frame of mind to be holding grudges, she was just concentrating on finding Mia, seeing the way she was with Alex proved that. 'I'll take full responsibility for it. I'll call them now.'

The only words spoken from Lucy's side were 'hello' and 'of course' and then she put the phone down, her hand shaking. It was the first phone call she had received in the last month, and it had thrown her into complete turmoil.

'Mia's gone missing,' Lucy explained to Nick who was looking curiously at her. 'That was Marcus, he wants us to help find her — they're all out searching, but need someone to stay home with the kids and man the phones. They want you to help too.

447

I said yes, I hope that's ok?'

'Oh God, of course, but how are we getting there? I don't fancy shoehorning you onto a tube.'

'Marcus has the car, he's on his way now.' As Lucy heard the words come out of her mouth, the realisation that she was about to see Marcus for the first time since the accident made her feel even more unsteady than she already was, and she sank back into her chair.

'Are you ok?' Nick asked worriedly.

'I'm fine, honestly, just a bit shocked, that's all. You'd better turn off the oven, the pie is going to burn. I'm just going to use your laptop a second to get some more numbers.'

Marcus drummed his fingers on the steering wheel. He knew he should be going straight in; his niece was missing and every minute counted. But his legs were frozen and he wasn't yet ready to step out of the car and start the next part of the evening.

Nick had one of those ultra trendy, converted warehouse apartments that didn't have any windows overlooking the street, so at least Marcus didn't need to contend with her looking out from behind twitching blinds or net curtains. He didn't know what state she was in, whether she was able to stand at a window, or whether she was confined to a chair. He knew her leg was pretty damaged, and one of her arms, but beyond the formal prognosis he didn't know how she was feeling physically. Emotionally, on the other hand . . . well, he had a pretty good idea about that after reading her letter.

It was all very well everyone telling him to take her back, to give her another chance, but would she even want that after he told her about how he'd been deceiving her for the duration of their marriage? The more he mulled it over in his mind, flipping the roles, assessing both sides, he realised that half the blame fell on his shoulders.

'How could you not have talked about this?' both his sisters had asked him incredulously, as though having kids was the most obvious thing in the world for a newly married couple to have spoken about, but it had honestly never come up. Apart from Lucy once referring to the front box room as a nursery — which he'd pretended to not hear — she'd never even mentioned it again. So, in his defence, how was he to know it had become so important to her?

But he should have known.

He saw the signs, he knew she was

stressed. He wasn't completely blinkered to her moods and anxiety. There were times when he was sure she'd been crying, her eyes a little swollen and her make-up obviously newly applied, but his automatic reaction was to back away from that sort of thing. He could have mentioned it, or asked her how she was feeling. Why didn't he?

He must have been the only man with two sisters that was completely inept at dealing with women. He'd spent most of his teenage life making himself scarce whenever one of his sisters had some sort of drama going on, nipping down to the shed he shared with his dad for a spot of respite and an injection of testosterone rather than sticking around and getting some insight into the female species for later in life. It had become second nature to change the subject, make a joke, disappear off for a while hoping everything would sort itself out in his absence, both back then as a kid, and with Lucy.

Mia. Mia needed them. He slowly got out of the car and walked to Nick's front door.

He wasn't prepared for the way Lucy now looked and gave an audible gasp. Marcus thought back to the Lucy that greeted him every day after work, her wide smile and immaculate make-up, her above-knee skirts or those sexy jeans of hers that skimmed her slim legs.

In front of him was a dramatically pared-back version of that woman. One that looked vulnerable, dejected, and defeated, but still smiling. Not a bright, confident smile like the ones from before, but one that just looked so relieved to be standing within five feet of him.

He coughed nervously, and said that they should be going. Nick passed him the small leather handbag that Marcus remembered buying Lucy last Christmas, very much not sticking to the hundred pound limit. He'd given her an engraved bangle on Christmas morning in front of everyone, and then on Christmas night, as they wearily climbed into bed, it was there, under the covers, with a ribbon on the handle.

'It's got her painkillers in,' Nick explained.

'Oh. Righto. Um, do you need me to, er, do anything?' Marcus asked, as Lucy put her arm around Nick's neck, hobbling down the front step.

'If you can put the passenger seat all the way back then I should be able to swing her leg in. It works in the taxi when we go for her hospital appointments.'

There was nothing barbed in Nick's statement, no hidden agenda; Marcus knew Nick wasn't that type of bloke. But it still stung that it should have been him looking after his wife, ferrying her to appointments, making sure that she navigated steps ok.

All three of them were exceedingly grateful that the fifteen-minute journey to Tasha's wasn't a minute longer, as the silence in the car was painful. Every time Marcus had to change gear, his arm unintentionally brushed Lucy's, which both of them flinched away from, while in the back seat, Nick was consumed with his own heartache, counting down the minutes until he saw Leila. God, he'd missed her.

The car pulled into Tasha's street, and Marcus didn't take his eyes off the road as he said quietly, 'I got your letter.'

'Oh,' Lucy replied, looking straight ahead too. 'That's good.'

As the front door creaked open, Leila ran into the hallway, hoping to see a remorseful Mia, or even a defiant, unrepentant Mia would be fine, but it was Marcus, Nick and Lucy. Both men were flanking Lucy, one supporting her unbroken arm, the other guiding her plastered side through the narrow doorway so she didn't knock it on the door frame. It was the first time since the accident that Leila had seen Lucy and she looked shocking. She must have lost a stone or two in weight, and her normally bouncy bob was pulled back with a headband. Her staple uniform of skinny designer jeans and crisp white shirt had been replaced with tracksuit bottoms, one leg cut off at mid-thigh to stretch over the plaster, which she'd teamed with a shapeless dark T-shirt. The complete look was not dissimilar to Mia's.

Nick looked up from watching which bit of floor his sister was putting each foot on and met Leila's stare of undisguised horror. He nodded, as if to say, 'I know.' And then gave Leila another look; one that she gratefully interpreted as, 'Hello you.'

'Let me help,' Leila said, stepping forward and taking over from Marcus, who plainly looked a little embarrassed at touching his wife's arm, even through an inch of plaster of Paris.

'I'm good, honestly, I'm walking about a lot more now. I just need a seat and then you guys all go, I'm fine,' Lucy protested. 'I printed off a list of the local youth centres and hospitals when we were waiting for Marcus to arrive, so I'll try them, and Leila, do you have the contact for Mia's form tutor?'

'I think I saw it stuck on the fridge, hang on.' Leila ran over to the fridge to retrieve it. 'But I think Tash already called them, she hasn't been in school today.'

'I want a form list so I can call all the parents in the class. Someone must know something. Right, I'm all set here. Go, go.' Lucy shooed them out and picked up her phone before the front door had even shut. It was heartening to see a glimpse of the old Lucy, the Lucy that knew instinctively how to handle crises and what to do.

'So what's best? Do we split up, or stay together?' Marcus said when they were all on the pavement.

Leila shrugged. 'I just spoke to Tasha, she wondered if Mia might have gone to mine, so she's headed there. Before I left I did put a note on my door telling Mia to call me when she saw the note, but Tasha wanted to check anyway.'

'Didn't Mia have a boyfriend?' Nick said suddenly. 'I remember you saying once.'

'Yes, but that was back in February, I don't think he's still around,' Leila replied.

'Let me run back in and tell Lucy that anyway,' Nick said. 'Maybe she can ask the kids in the class if they know who he is when she calls them.'

When Nick ran back up the stairs into the house, Marcus said, 'I really like him. He's

454

a good guy.'

It was a strange proclamation in the circumstances, Leila thought, but a welcome one nonetheless. And she couldn't help but agree with him. Seeing Nick again, so ready to help her family out, so genuinely anxious and willing and eager to be involved, made her stomach tighten into an even bigger knot.

'Yes, he's nice.'

'Your year of being single is up soon isn't it?' Marcus asked.

Leila prickled. 'A few weeks ago, why?'

Marcus shrugged. 'Just thinking that perhaps after we find Mia, you should maybe ask him out for a drink. You could do a lot worse.'

Marcus headed back to Mia's school. As it was the only other place in the area that Mia knew well he wondered if she might have snuck back in there somehow. The buildings cast long shadows on the rapidly darkening playground as the caretaker assured Marcus that no-one was left on the premises. Their big bank of black and white TVs in the security hut showing every lino-lined corridor and every stark square classroom was proof that she wasn't there.

All the shop shutters were now down on

the High Street, which made Leila and Nick's job easier, as they didn't need to peer past extravagantly dressed mannequins and elegant window displays to see if Mia was lurking beyond them. After-work drinkers had spilled out on to the pavements from the various wine bars and licensed cafes, and Leila weaved in and out of them asking if anyone had seen a skinny sixteen-year-old in black, showing them her photo on her phone. She didn't know for certain that's what Mia was wearing, but as Leila had seen her in no other colour since the accident, she had taken an educated guess. Everyone she showed gave the same response: a shake of the head and a sympathetic smile.

Nick had silently taken her hand as they ran along the streets, not needing to ask her permission, or double guess if it was ok. They both knew it was.

They ran down the stairs into the bowels of the tube station, pushing against the tide of latecomers travelling back from work. A figure wrapped in a blanket was huddled next to the ticket machine. Leila approached it breathlessly, only to recoil when an elderly man's head lifted up from his arms where he'd been sleeping and glared at her before spitting on the floor next to him.

London was no place for a young girl alone at night.

They explored all the nooks and crannies of the local tube station, speaking with the staff who said they could only check the CCTV footage at the request of the police.

That time was drawing nearer. They all knew it but hadn't voiced it.

As soon as that phone call was made, Mia would cease to be Mia, and would become Missing-Sixteen-Year-Old-Girl-in-Central-London.

It was now nine o'clock. She'd been missing for five hours. It was time.

The two police officers, one male, one female, were taking notes at the kitchen table with Tasha and Alex. They were asking questions, going through photographs. In front of them were four cups of undrunk coffee and a plate of biscuits. Tasha didn't know, staring at them now, placed neatly on a white plate with silver rim that was part of her 'best' dinner service, why she'd put biscuits out. It was a strange thing to do when your daughter was missing.

'Has anything upset Mia recently? Has she been acting differently?'

Alex shifted in his seat. 'I, um, I've moved out. She was really upset and angry. About a lot of things.'

In the living room, Marcus, Nick and Lucy had set up an impromptu call centre, all on different telephones, all reading from the same script. No-one had seen Mia at all. Some friends hadn't seen her in days, and no hospital had a Mia Banbury, or a Jane Doe, matching her description.

'Is anything missing?' Leila heard the policewoman ask from the room next door, working her way through the checklist of questions. 'Can you check her room and also your wallet as well to see if she took anything with her? It would give us an indication of whether she was planning on being away a while.'

Tasha picked up her purse from the break-fast bar and opened it. There were two crumpled five pound notes in there and a lot of folded receipts. 'I think I had two hundred pounds in here that I took out yesterday, but I'm not sure.'

A glance passed between the officers that silently questioned how someone could not know if they had two hundred pounds in cash on them or not. A quick scan of the kitchen taking in the fresh coffee grinder, the massive American fridge, the plate warmer, and they realised that perhaps there were people that didn't do nightly inventories of their spare change.

Leila followed her sister and the police-woman up the stairs, taking the steps two at a time. Tasha was opening all her cupboards and drawers. 'This is impossible,' she gasped. 'How can I look for things that aren't here!'

'Does she have an overnight bag that she uses for sleepovers?' The police officer suggested.

'Yes, that's on top of her wardrobe,' Tasha said, disappointed. 'But she did have her school bag with her, I'm sure of it.'

Leila crouched down on the floor to peer under the bed. 'What about her teddy, you know the one with the jumper she knitted at Brownies? She loved that, where's that?'

'Eddy the Teddy? She hasn't bothered with him for years,' said Tasha, opening and slamming drawers at the speed of knots.

'But if she's run away then she might have taken him with her, and he doesn't seem to be here,' Leila said, lifting the duvet cover to see if he was lurking under the covers.

'It's not here, Eddy's usually at the end of that shelf, there,' Tasha pointed.

'That's a good thing, Natasha,' the officer said. 'If she has taken her teddy with her, then it means that she has run away of her own volition, rather than . . .' She didn't need to complete the sentence, the two sisters knew how it ended.

'Is there anything else missing?'

'Some underwear. I put a stack of clean pants and socks in there last night and most are gone. And her jeans aren't here and she was wearing her school uniform when she left the house, so she must have them.' Putting the pieces together of what Mia took with her were helping to calm Tasha's breathing. She still didn't know where her daughter was, but knowing she had planned to go was strangely comforting.

'Mummy?' came a little voice from the doorway. Oscar's George Pig pyjamas were ruffled from sleep, and his tiny hand clutched the ear of his threadbare doggy. 'Why is it so sunny in here?' he said, shielding his eyes from the harsh overhead light.

Tasha crouched down next to him and stroked his head. 'We're just looking for something, Oscar darling, go back to bed.'

'Are you a "pleece"?' he said blinking. 'Where's Mia?'

'She's just out darling, nothing to worry about sweetheart.'

'But it's middle of the night. Why is she gone out? What about the baddies?'

Leila swooped in and gathered her nephew's warm little body up in her arms and blew on his tummy. 'Come on Mister Moo, back to bed.'

When Leila came back in to Mia's bedroom, Tasha was doubled up on the side of the bed. The sympathetic policewoman was sat next to her, stroking her back, waiting for Tasha's sobs to subside before she asked another question. This was the worst part of her job. She'd been on training courses for it, had role play simulations, had spoken to colleagues that had been through it, but nothing prepared you for the raw emotion of sitting with a mother with a missing child.

A loud shout from the living room punctuated the sound of Tasha's crying.

'She's safe! Mia's safe!'

Lucy was holding her mobile aloft in the air as everyone came bounding into the room. 'She's just arrived in Dartmouth! I know you didn't want to worry them Tasha, but I just called your mum on the off chance and she's there!' Lucy gulped as tears ran down her face. 'She's safe.'

The sudden climax of two hours' solidly begging someone to have an answer had caught up with her. It had caught up with everyone. Tasha fell to her knees, succumbing to waves of relief. Alex gripped the bookcase for support and took a deep, audible breath. Lucy's head rested on Marcus's shoulder and he held her hand, stroking the back of it. Nick and Leila hung off each other, exhausted as the anxiety and distress of the previous hours dissolved into the air.

The officers let themselves out, leaving behind six people who until six hours ago had never thought they would share a room again.

After they'd all shared a bottle of gratefully consumed wine, Alex cornered Marcus in the kitchen. Even before the events of the last few weeks, Marcus had never really liked Alex, always finding him a bit *too* smooth, a bit *too* charming. In Marcus's world of floppy hair and pullovers, his heavily groomed brother-in-law, with his year-round tan and flash suits with coloured silk linings, was an anomaly. Knowing now how many times Alex had cheated on Tasha, coupled with the fact that Alex had wanted to sleep with Marcus's wife, mild disdain had turned into abject hostility. There was no reason to pretend otherwise just because Mia had been found safe and sound.

'No hard feelings, Marcus, about the Lucy business,' Alex said. He even put his arm around Marcus's shoulder as he said the last few words.

Marcus shrugged Alex's arm off and

moved about a foot away. 'I disagree Alex,' he responded in a cool, measured tone. 'I have nothing *but* hard feelings towards you. Not for what you did to me, but how you groomed Lucy into even considering being with you, and for the years of deceiving my sister and my family.'

Alex laughed. 'You can't deceive someone that knows what's going on Marcus. Tasha was cool about it. She knows what I'm like.'

'You mean shallow? Superficial? Stupid?'

'Hardly stupid, Marcus, anyone would think you were jealous,' Alex sneered. 'After all, isn't it every man's dream when you get to our age to have a nubile twenty-something hanging off your every word, thinking that you're God's gift. You'd be lying if you said that given the opportunity you wouldn't do exactly the same.'

Marcus could feel his fist clenching by his side and it took all his self-restraint not to punch the slimy arrogance off Alex's face. 'That's where you're completely wrong Alex. I am nothing like you. What Lucy and I have is worth so much more than you would ever appreciate. You had it too, with Tasha, you were just too selfish to realise. You have lost one of the best women around, and for what? A string of identikit trophy girlfriends who mean nothing? I pity you.'

Alex threw his head back and gave a throaty laugh. 'You do not need to pity me, Marcus, believe me. After tonight, Tasha is going to ask me to move back in, and this whole —' he put his fingers up in the air to put the word 'episode' into quotation marks, 'will be completely forgotten and everything will go back to the way it was. I'd put money on it.'

Three seconds later Marcus would have knocked him out, but just as he felt his fist twitching, Tasha's voice cut through the pause from the doorway. 'You are delusional Alex. Tonight alters nothing. Get out. Get out of my house and I think it's best if we only communicate through our solicitors from now on.'

Alex smiled his smug, smarmy smile and took a couple of steps towards Tasha, his arms outstretched. 'Tash, TishTash, you don't mean that. Come on, Mia's fine now, everything's ok, let's not be hasty.'

Leila appeared by her sister's side. 'I don't think you heard Tasha correctly Alex. She wants you to leave.'

'Really? *She* wants me to leave? From my own house? I don't think so.'

Marcus moved to stand next to his sisters.

'I'm not a violent man Alex, but I would wager that Nick and I could probably eject you from here quite efficiently, should the need arise. So, if I were you, and I am very grateful I am not, I'd go. Pretty sharpish, if I'm honest.'

Alex didn't need telling twice. Scuttling past the three siblings with his head down, he almost ran out of the house. In his wake, Marcus wrapped his arms around his sisters and the three of them stayed huddled together, each of them consumed with their own uncertainties, their own dramas, yet for the first time realising that they didn't need to face the future alone.

CHAPTER 29

Seven months later . . .

'Do you want this?' Tasha asked, waving a citrus-coloured piece of plastic in the air.

'What is it?'

'It's an avocado cutter.'

'Why did you ever buy an avocado cutter?' Leila asked. 'Can you not cut them with a knife?'

'I'm not sure, hopefully it came free with something rather than me losing all grasp on reality and spending money on it. Do you want it?'

'No, it's ok, you can keep it,' Leila said graciously. 'I'll live.' Half her body was wedged into Tasha's corner kitchen cupboard that was proving to be a tardis of utensils and crockery that hadn't been touched for years. 'What about these?' she said, leaning out holding a velvet-lined box of six champagne flutes. 'Didn't you get these for your wedding?'

'Yes, along with the 37,000 other champagne flutes we got from everyone else.' Tasha unhooked the clasp and opened the box. 'I don't think we even ever opened these, they're lovely.' She suddenly thought, and held them out to her sister, 'Happy Christmas Leila.'

'Are you sure? These are lovely.'

'Knock yourself out, I'll take the other 37,000.'

They'd been going through cupboards, drawers and wardrobes for days. It was amazing, thought Tasha, how she and Alex had come to the marriage with one suitcase and in seventeen years had managed to accumulate enough crap to fill a five-bedroom house, an attic and a storage unit. Dividing these down the middle was a formidable task, that so far, thankfully, was not the angst-ridden experience she had been dreading.

'You have three blenders,' Leila announced.

'One's for frozen stuff, like berries and ice, and the others are for . . . other stuff. I'll take the ice one, that's the red one, Alex can have the others, put them in that pile there.'

'A man living by himself does not need two blenders, Tasha.'

'He'll need them to make the kids smooth-ies when they visit.'

'He'll take them out for food. He doesn't strike me as a smoothie-making man.'

'He's not. Right,' Tasha said, standing up and dusting off her jeans. 'I should go and supervise Alex's packers, I don't want them to take the things that I want.'

'I saw them wrapping up the hall mirror, don't you want that?'

'The one we got in Cambodia and shipped back?' Tasha asked. She'd loved that mirror since she spotted an old man carving it on a side street in Phnom Penh. But she also valued the delicate peace treaty she and Alex were working hard to maintain, and he'd called first dibs on it.

'And as much as I love the dresser in the dining room, there's no way that's going to fit in the new house, so do you want it, or shall I eBay it?' Tasha continued, trying to remain unsentimental about all the furniture and accessories they'd spent years collect-ing being unceremoniously plonked into four piles, His, Hers, Sell, Chuck. Every glass vase or little footstool had a memory attached to it, a place they'd visited, a gift they were given. Things like their books and gadgets had been easy to divide, but when it came to the items that had an invisible label tied around them detailing the story of how it became theirs, well, that was much, much harder.

'It looks quite big though, the new house? From the brochure you showed me?' Leila said.

'Well yes, there's plenty of room, but you know what these old cottages are like, the doors are quite narrow and the ceilings are lower, so I don't think all the big bits are going to fit in.'

'Well anything you really love and don't want to get rid of can be kept at Mum and Dad's can't it? They've got loads of room and they're only up the road.'

'True, true.' Tasha couldn't help smiling at Leila's last sentence. Her parents hadn't been 'up the road' from her for nearly three decades and she couldn't wait to move back down to Dartmouth.

Tasha had asked herself if it was a whim, this decision to move away from London so suddenly, but although it seemed like a spur-of-the-moment choice, it really wasn't. She had been feeling increasing pangs of guilt every month as they packed up the car after a night down in Dartmouth and watched the kids giving frantic tearful waves to their grandparents from their open windows. Their car emitting a cheerful 'toot

toot' as it sped down the driveway. Her parents' figures getting smaller and smaller in the rear view mirror.

When Mia ran away, and headed for Dartmouth, so sure that it was there that she would feel safe and happy, Tasha knew that the time was right. She hadn't known how Alex would take it. It was one thing to accept that your marriage was over, but it was completely another to face the fact that your children would be a four-hour drive away. She had perhaps assumed he had a higher level of emotional maturity than he did. 'Doesn't bother me, I'm seeing someone actually, so I'm not sure I'd be able to make every weekend anyway — it doesn't make that much difference where you are.'

She'd been expecting that for months, so it was no surprise to learn that he had a girlfriend. And although Leila had teased her about the possibility of meeting a strapping fisherman that might fill the void where Alex had once been, Tasha was very much looking forward to it just being her and the children for the foreseeable future. She wasn't about to make a formal proclamation of celibacy like her sister had done, but she'd lost so much of herself along the course of her marriage, skewing her priorities and putting up with things she had since realised would be a complete deal breaker with a new partner. *New partner.* No, she didn't want that at all.

Thomas had actually cried when she'd told him they were coming back. For years she'd thought of her dad as such a stoic character — he needed to be with so many hysterical women surrounding him — but there was no mistaking the tears that formed in his eyes when Tasha told him that she'd enrolled the kids into the same school that she, Leila and Marcus had gone to and that she'd bought a house about a hundred metres walk from their gates. On the other hand, Judy's shriek of excitement and exuberant display of jazz hands was entirely the reaction Tasha was expecting from her mum.

'You should go,' Tasha pointed at the clock. 'It's nearly four, and your Christmas party starts at seven and you look like you've had your head in a cupboard all day.'

'Er, that'll be because I have.'

'But you don't want to look like you have! Now go, I'll see you there in a bit.'

'Ooo, can I borrow this?' Leila asked, picking up the axe that leant against the pantry door.

'Sure, but whatever for?'

Leila smiled. 'Something pretty important.'

'There's no way you got seventy-five!' Lucy
lifted each tile up, checking what was underneath.

'Yes, you see, B is on a triple word score
and W is on a double letter, so I think that
means, ladies and gentlemen, we have a
winner. I had an S to add to the final B and
it would be a record-breaking score.'

'I'm not sure that word is allowed anyway,'
Lucy pouted. 'It's very rude.'

'It is very much allowed. In Scrabble and
in life. Should the mood take you.'

Lucy laughed and threw a small Malteser
across the table, which Marcus caught in
his open mouth. The day after Mia's disappearance, back in May, Marcus had gone
over to Nick's and sat with Lucy for a few
hours. He admitted everything, from the
drug trials to his discomfort at dealing with
emotional issues, accepting his part in the
drama of the last few weeks and months.
When he had finally finished speaking Marcus held his breath, waiting for the fire to
flare out of her nostrils. But the flames never
came. A few moments of agonised waiting
passed before she gave him a sad smile and
quietly asked if there was any chance they

could start again.

So they did.

Marcus had taken a sabbatical from work for two months. He'd told the other partners that it was to help Lucy get around, to care for her while she was still in plaster. That was only partly true. She was more than capable of hopping around on her good leg, and had discovered that her left hand wasn't quite the incompetent appendage she'd considered it to be before. So they both knew that him being around more had less to do with manual lifting and more to do with filling the cracks of their relationship with something that couldn't be easily worn away again. Together they had decided to wait another year before trying to start a family, to enjoy married life, and not to rush into the next chapter of their lives too quickly. Marcus had come off the medical experiment programme and Lucy had, a little reluctantly, because old habits do die hard, deleted the tracker app from her phone.

'So if we both agree that I've won the game, we should probably get a move on,' Marcus said, looking at his watch. 'Did Leila say her party started at seven? Do we need to stop somewhere to buy flowers or something?'

'No, I arranged for some to be delivered.'

'Of course you did,' Marcus said, leaning over his wife's head to kiss the top of it.

'You know what a fan I am of them, but I'm not sure they entirely go with your outfit,' Nick laughed.

Leila gave a little shimmy in her off the shoulder mini dress, flexing her left foot in the air at the same time. 'What do you mean? My flat, my rules.'

'Don't you mean "our flat"?' he said, slipping his arms around her from behind and ducking his head so his lips grazed her bare shoulder. 'And as much as I love them, and you, I'm not sure the ski socks are entirely necessary . . .'

'They might not be necessary, but they are ridiculously comfortable. Having these as part of my life was the main reason I asked you to move in.'

'I know.'

A knock on the front door echoed around the flat like a starter's pistol, throwing them both into frenzied action stations. Leila whipped off the socks, shoving them haphazardly into the first drawer she saw, Nick pulled his shirt off the ironing board and buttoned it up while Leila folded the board away and slammed it into the wardrobe.

'Hello, hello!' For the next half hour, the hallway was host to flurries of hugs and kisses, bottles — many bottles — being passed over, flowers, boxes, gift bags, and a steady stream of friends and family traipsing through their bedroom straight into the garden that was nice and toasty thanks to a large gas heater.

The weather gods had listened and it was one of those blissful winter evenings that had a clear sky, completely devoid of rain, wind or God forbid, snow. Leila and Nick had divided the labour that afternoon. He'd spent most of it in the kitchen with Jayne's husband Will, who had brought a crate full of ingredients over earlier on, and the two of them had stood amiably side by side constructing canapés for a couple of hours. Tiny Christmas dinners with turkey, cranberry and stuffing balanced on delicate blinis, small Yorkshire puddings were filled with roast beef and homemade horseradish cream, while the mini Yule logs and individual Christmas puddings hot from the oven were sitting on Nick's wire mesh in-tray that was doubling up as a cooling rack.

Leila whiled away the afternoon in her own utopia in the garden, hanging up mistletoe over the arches, trimming back some of the bushes, taking cuttings of the wildflowers that she was going to stand in old fashioned glass milk bottles on the tables and stringing fairy lights along the walls and weaving them through the trellises.

The effect was magical. Soft strains of jazzy festive tunes filtered through the speakers, but laughter and chatter were the main background noise for the party. Drinks were topped up, trays of food were circling, and there was nothing left for Nick and Leila to do but enjoy their housewarming/ Christmas party.

There was a moment when Leila looked around and felt a little chastened by how happy everyone seemed to be for them, completely ignorant of the fact that she and Nick had been deceiving them for so much of the last year. They'd decided not to be too specific about when they'd got together, but she did still feel bad that it overlapped so significantly with her supposed celibacy. Tonight, there was nothing but well wishes and genuine pleasure from everyone.

Leila smiled as she saw how attentive Marcus was being to Lucy over by the water feature, engrossed in what she was saying, while she, in turn, was stroking his back. Lucy had presented Leila the month before with a year-long strategy for the upcoming events, she'd designed a whole series targeting all women — single, married, divorced, widowed — a sort of kick-start-to-happiness-programme, and as Lucy had spoken about it, Leila could see her eyes flashing with excitement.

Now that Tasha was going to be based down in Dartmouth as well, she could be a lot more hands-on getting the hotel ready for the monthly retreats.

It was funny how none of this would have happened had she not chased Freddie to Jaipur two Christmases ago. She could see herself having sat at home waiting for him, while pretending not to when people asked. Then, when his work placement finished and he returned to London, she probably would have just picked up their fledgling relationship where it left off, completely ignorant of the company he'd been keeping in India.

How could one moment, one decision be the catalyst for your whole life changing? And how could that Christmas, sat by herself on the airport floor in India, be so different to the one a year ago where she and Nick locked themselves in the bathroom on Christmas morning, which was now so different to this Christmas, where they were celebrating officially moving in together.

She glanced over to where Tasha was speaking to Jayne and Will in the corner, their three heads huddled over Tasha's phone as she showed them her new house in Devon. Her sister had surprised her in the last six months, taking such a stand and kicking Alex out for good. Her strength and confidence just seemed to grow by the day.

Next to them was Tom, Nick's cousin, who was newly single and in complete raptures over whatever statuesque redhead Shelley was saying. Now that Leila looked more closely, he didn't appear to be paying too much attention to her mouth moving.

A cluster of Nick's friends that he'd introduced her to a few months before had just arrived, and were making huge holes in the platters of canapés. Nick was laughing with Amanda and her husband Paul in front of the open patio doors. After spending the first half of the year actively avoiding talking to his colleagues whenever he found himself queuing up in the canteen behind them, or standing next to each other at the photo-copier, it was such a relief for there to be no more secrets or sneaking about. It had been a bit awkward, Nick had confided in Leila, knowing that Amanda was one of his girl-friend's best friends, and yet she had no idea that he and Leila were together. 'We should have them over for dinner,' he'd said earlier in the day. They'd never had anyone 'over for dinner' before, and the words did a little dance around her head.

He momentarily looked away from the conversation, caught Leila's eye and smiled. So this is what it feels like, Leila thought, when everything goes according to plan.

The last of the guests had just left, and the patio doors were still propped open with the fairy lights casting a warm and whimsical glow over the courtyard and into the bedroom. They were lying together on a large beanbag that Nick had dragged out to the garden, both of them huddled under a blanket trying to spot stars.

'I know the perfect way to end this evening,' Nick murmured into Leila's ear.

'Do you now?' she replied softly.

'I do. Are you ready?' Nick asked.

'I'm ready,' Leila replied. He pulled her up and led her giggling into the bedroom.

'Goggles on.'

'Goggles on.'

'And one, two, THREE!' Nick swung the axe and one of the bunk's legs buckled, making the whole bed come crashing to the ground. They both jumped back, doubling over in exhilarated laughter.

'My go, my go!' Leila grabbed the axe, held it high above her head and brought it smashing down on another length of wood.

'She may be small, but she is mighty,' Nick announced in a comical booming voice.

Leila splintered another plank into two neat pieces, and stood back admiring her handiwork. She gave Nick a big smile. 'You'd better believe it.'

ACKNOWLEDGEMENTS

Huge heartfelt thanks to the fabulous team at Harper Impulse, my editor extraordinaire Charlotte Ledger, and Dushi Horti for your continued support, and all-round shiny brilliance. To my awesome agent Luigi Bonomi, and Alison, you deserve a standing ovation for your unwavering belief in me, I am supremely grateful to have you on my side.

Huge thank yous to my best friends Anya, Jasmine, Lisa, Netty, Katie, Rachel and Annabel for your support, anecdotes and much-needed cheerleading and pep talks. To my wonderful friends on the Donald Duck compound, who have been a constant source of wine-soaked inspiration for the funny parts in this book.

To my parents Tim and Carol, I'm under no illusion that Dad will ever finish one of my books, but your support and love mean the world. My sisters, Hannah Cooper and Davinia Harper, who taught me the meaning of true sisterhood, you are the reason I love writing about strong, feisty and funny women.

And to my beautiful tribe, Ed, Amélie, Rafe and Theo. This journey would not be half as sparkly without you on it with me. Ti amo.

ABOUT THE AUTHOR

Former magazine editor **Charlotte Butterfield** was born in Bristol in 1977. She studied English at Royal Holloway University and an MPhil in Gender and Women's Studies at Birmingham University before becoming a journalist and copywriter. She moved to Dubai in 2005, but now lives in Rome with her husband and three children.

Twitter: @charliejayneb
Facebook: @charlottebutterfieldauthor

The employees of Thorndike Press hope you have enjoyed this Large Print book. All our Thorndike, Wheeler, and Kennebec Large Print titles are designed for easy reading, and all our books are made to last. Other Thorndike Press Large Print books are available at your library, through selected bookstores, or directly from us.

For information about titles, please call:
(800) 223-1244

or visit our website at:
gale.com/thorndike

To share your comments, please write:
Publisher
Thorndike Press
10 Water St., Suite 310
Waterville, ME 04901